THE SECOND SHIP

The characters and events portrayed in this book are fictitious. Any similarity to real persons, living or dead, is coincidental and not intended by the author.

Printed in the United States of America.

Published by 47 North
P.O. Box 400818
Las Vegas, NV 89140

ISBN-13: 9781612184937
ISBN-10: 1612184936

THE SECOND SHIP

BOOK ONE OF THE RHO AGENDA

RICHARD PHILLIPS

47NORTH

PROLOGUE

Although it was impossible to judge direction cleanly from these depths, far below Groom Lake, Donald Stephenson knew the tunnel ran southwest. A railcar, pushed by an electric locomotive, had carried him along the set of tracks that marched down the center to its end. Many years ago, a much different type of cargo had ridden the same rails to the huge steel door he now faced. Twin slots in the base of the door fit snuggly over the rail tracks, which disappeared inside.

Don hiked his army-issue field jacket more tightly around his neck and moved to the right toward a smaller door meant for human access. He paused outside to swipe his badge through the card reader. The door slid open with a small whoosh as the air pressure equalized.

A sudden shiver caused him to glance back over his shoulder. The tunnel stretched long and empty behind him until it disappeared around a slight bend to the left. His only company was the faint hum of the incandescent lights bolted high above on the ceiling.

He shrugged to dispel the prickly feeling on his neck, like someone had just stepped on his grave. Christ, he was jumpy tonight.

Happy Thanksgiving, Don thought.

He was alone in the cavernous room, as was often the case this time of night, especially on major holidays. Although he couldn't understand it himself, he supposed the novelty of working with the thing had worn thin for the band of scientists who had probed, pushed, and tinkered with its exterior for the last several decades without making any progress in unraveling its inner mysteries.

It occupied a significant portion of the center of the room, enclosed within a latticework of aluminum scaffolding that provided walkways for the scientists and workers as well as mounting brackets for the electronic instruments that clung to the object's skin like barnacles on an ancient whaler.

Even now, all these years after that day in late March, 1948, near Aztec, New Mexico, when residents had found evidence of a UFO crash, only a few dozen people knew for certain that the residents were right. Ironically, the abundance of media attention that the Roswell Incident had stirred up the previous year simplified the cover-up of the Aztec situation. By the time a reporter arrived in the Farmington area to do a detailed follow-up, enough false and contradictory information had been planted to ensure the local account would be discredited.

Moving across the room toward the scaffolding, Don surveyed the ship. It was amazing in every way. The original research team, at first glance, had assumed some internal malfunction had caused the ship to crash, but that assumption had shortly given way to a more disconcerting conclusion.

First, the ship had attempted to conceal itself after the crash, putting up some sort of electro-optical interference pattern that made it difficult to see. The smooth cigar shape of the craft blurred in and out of sight until you got right up next to it. At least that much of the shipboard system was still working.

Second, and more disturbing, was the damage to the ship. Even though the hull had not been penetrated, some force had bubbled and warped it in multiple spots. Testing had concluded the damage hadn't been caused by the impact with the Earth.

Based on the evidence, the current theory was that the source of the damage had somehow caused the crash.

Over the years since it had been moved here, despite an endless procession of high-energy experiments, some of which should have heated spots on the ship's surface to the internal temperature of the sun, the ship's exterior had never been penetrated. Diamond drills, cutting torches, arc welders, lasers, and finally, high-energy particle beams had not had any effect on the strange material that composed the beast's hide. The surface remained cool to the touch, no matter how much or what type of energy the research team directed against it.

Though it wasn't written in any official reports, popular opinion among the scientists was that only technology equal to the craft's could duplicate the damage, implicating some sort of alien weapon. Don agreed with the speculation and thanked God that whoever had attacked the ship hadn't found the Earth interesting enough to linger after shooting it down.

The research team hadn't been able to scrape a chip of metal from the outside, much less get to the interior. So much for the "genius" of the men who ran the program. But now, Don had his chance. Luck always had a way of finding him, and these last two weeks he had been very lucky. He had been allowed to install an experiment of his own design against the outer shell of the alien spacecraft. Luck aside, he preferred to think his success was due to working his ass off these last three years, ever since he had attained his master's degree and been assigned to this deep black program. Fortunately, the grueling hours of research had not been wasted.

On the far side of the ship, Don had set up a doughnut-shaped torus, its electromagnets providing energy that accelerated electrons close to the speed of light. Nestled up against what the team thought was the door of the craft, a long metallic cone extended out of the torus, terminating in a set of tubes that would produce Cerenkov radiation.

What, exactly, had triggered the idea, Don could not recall. Something about the classified eyewitness reports struck him as wrong, something about a faint blue glow coming from the ship as it streaked through the New Mexico skies.

It sounded like a description of Cerenkov radiation. That beautiful blue light was produced when something traveling at close to the speed of light in a vacuum entered a substance with a slower speed of light, like air or water.

It made no sense for the ship to be glowing with Cerenkov radiation. Estimates of the speed described by the witnesses were no greater than Mach 2. If Cerenkov radiation was present, it must have come from some of the starship's control or power mechanisms. And if those systems gave off that radiation, perhaps they would give off some measurable response to the right combination of Cerenkov waves.

Don had no doubt that it was only because the research team had made no progress in all these years that he had been given permission to conduct his own experiments over this Thanksgiving holiday weekend. Those experiments had been running around the clock since last night.

As he seated himself at the keyboard, above which thousands of light-emitting diodes twinkled, his eye caught on a flashing error indicator. He leaned forward.

"What the hell?"

Several of his experimental instruments were giving bad readings or were off-line altogether. There was also an error reading from the instruments that controlled the alignment of the Cerenkov mirrors.

Don cursed softly as he examined the data on the long computer printout that dangled from the printer to form a pile on the floor. Scanning down the pages, he identified the time of the malfunction. 18:53.

"Damn it!"

The entire system had gone off-line shortly after he had left to go make himself some dinner. More than two precious hours lost, not counting how long it might take him to find the cause of the malfunction and fix it.

Having satisfied himself that the malfunction lay not in the computer controls but in the instrumentation itself, Don walked rapidly around the scaffolding toward the spot where the particle injection tube fed electrons to his apparatus, high up on the far side of the ship.

As he rounded the tail of the cigar-shaped craft, Don caught his foot on a cable and would have fallen if he had not managed to grab the scaffolding. Righting himself, he gazed upward to where his instruments hung. The cables and mountings were broken and twisted, the Cerenkov mirrors torn from their brackets and tossed to the cement floor below. But the state of his instruments barely registered in his mind.

He stared at the large ramp that had lowered from the side of the ship all the way to the floor, crushing the scaffolding beneath it. A faint glow issued from the opening.

Don locked his knees to prevent them from buckling as hyperventilation threatened to knock him unconscious. Gasping, clinging to the crumpled scaffolding, Don surveyed the instruments along the near wall, the ones that monitored air quality and radiation levels. All normal. He might die today, but it wouldn't be from something so mundane.

He knew he should pick up the red phone and call the duty officer back at the main base. That would begin the recall of all the scientists and military people currently working on the project. Anything less risked him being kicked off the project, possibly even having his security clearance revoked.

Sweat dripped down his forehead and stung his eyes as Don looked up the ramp toward the doorway. A thought occurred to him—a risky one.

Why should he make that call before at least walking up and taking a look inside? After all, wasn't it his work that had triggered the breakthrough?

If he walked over and placed that call, he had a pretty good idea that he would never get his chance to look inside the ship. No. The same morons who had been scratching their heads for decades would come out of the woodwork and lock the whole thing down, tight as a snail's ass. Only the most senior scientists and intelligence types would be permitted anywhere near the ship.

Don was not about to let that happen, at least not until he had taken a look for himself. His pulse pounding in his temples, he strode up the ramp, paused at the top to take a single deep breath, and then stepped across the threshold, disappearing inside.

A single oscilloscope in the instrument racks along the far side of the room registered a momentary electronic signal flux before settling back to normal measurements.

Five miles away, in a small room just off Hanger One, the duty officer, an air force major named Stuart Greeley, made another entry in his duty log.

21:15, 24 Nov 1987, Groom Lake, Area 51, Nevada. All quiet.

CHAPTER 1

The magenta glow of the Ark Cave bathed the rail-thin figure in a light so pure it seemed to drip from his dirty, blond dreadlocks.

Perry Symons had first heard the voice of the Lord in July of 1998 as his fish knife sliced into the throat of his beautiful Vanessa. So much blood, bubbling out across his arms and hands, hot and slick, making it difficult to maintain his hold on both her hair and the blade as she flopped beneath him.

Vanessa had been the sacrifice that brought him to the Lord's attention, the act that made him worthy. Perry had sacrificed the love of his life, his sweet Vanessa, so that God would recognize the new Gabriel, the one to lead His children through the coming apocalypse.

There in the back of his green Volkswagen van, as Vanessa's lifeblood wept into a five-gallon bucket, God had spoken in his mind.

"Await ye the sign of the end of days."

At Bottomless Lakes State Park, just outside Roswell, New Mexico, Perry had carried sweet Vanessa's plastic-wrapped body out to the rowboat and paddled far out onto the lake before dumping her chained form over the side. Although he had bled it well, the corpse bobbed briefly on the surface before tilting down into the salty depths, trailing tiny red bubbles behind it.

Another sign. Even after making the ultimate sacrifice, sweet Vanessa's corpse was reluctant to leave him, struggling to stay afloat even as the weight of the chains pulled it inevitably down into eternal blackness.

Perry had returned to his apartment on South Main Street, sold everything he owned, bought some survival gear, and moved to the remote Bandelier canyon country near Los Alamos, an ancient stretch of land, once home to the Pueblo Indians' cliff-dwelling ancestors.

Perry was convinced that year 2000 would produce the Lord's promised sign, but his wait for the resultant disasters proved to be in vain. When nothing happened in the year that followed Y2K, depression seized him. Perry came to doubt his own sanity. Had he sacrificed his soul mate for nothing? Losing himself in heroin, cocaine, and crystal meth, he wandered the canyon country aimlessly, tempted by the relief a suicidal jump would bring.

God had challenged his faith in a manner reminiscent of the trials of Job, remaking him into a bedraggled wretch that little resembled his prideful former self. Then, one day in the autumn of 2002, he met Screaming Eagle. And Screaming Eagle introduced him to the ancient ceremonies of the native peoples, and to the wondrous pathways visible only in the smoke of a sweat lodge.

It was in one of those peyote-induced dream states, as he stumbled out of the sweat lodge and along the high canyon walls, that he first came upon the concealed entrance of the Ark Cave. It was there that God had given him his sign.

The memories faded as he looked around the cavern he had come to know so well. God's Ark rested at the back of the cavern, having cut its way through the canyon's stone walls as it plunged from the skies all those years ago.

Striding under the smooth, curving edges of the vessel, he found the hole that Satan's weapon had punched through the ship's hull. He swung himself effortlessly up and inside, as he had done countless times in the past. Bypassing the first landing, he followed the smooth borehole, pulling himself upward onto the second deck.

There on the silky smooth metal desktop that extruded from the wall, silhouetted in the all-pervading magenta glow, lay the four halos. Although they looked like shiny metal, they were much too light and flexible, glittering with a rainbow of hues no earthly metal had ever produced. As always, his hands were drawn only to the fourth halo.

Perry picked it up, turning it slowly in his hands, lost in the memory of the first time he had slid that supple band over his temples.

Pain. Even now, the memory of the white fire in his head sent tendrils of agony along his limbs, so intense he expected sparks to fly from his fingertips, arcing outward to consume this world. Baptized in that river of pain, he had emerged, no longer Perry Symons, but as the fourth horseman, anointed with God's own speed and power, along with a cunning the likes of which no mere mortal possessed.

But it was not the pain, nor his newfound powers, that drove him to become a hermit. The visions filled his dreams. God's Ark had not come to earth alone. There had been another...Satan's Chariot. In his visions, he had seen the two vessels battle across the night sky, both crashing to earth in tremendous gouts of fire. Although both had been damaged in the conflict, both survived, hidden away—each seeking out its champions. Armageddon's disciples.

All these years, Perry had waited, patiently biding his time for the final sign, a signal that God's Ark would call the other horsemen, a signal that the remaining three halos would no longer lie dormant, that each would fulfill its unique purpose in the coming apocalypse. Now the Ark had determined that the time for summoning Perry's three counterparts was at hand.

As Perry let his halo slip into place and its divine visions filled his head, a thin smile split his lips. His long wait was nearly over.

CHAPTER 2

Heather McFarland had always been an early riser, but the dreams were leaving her wide awake long before dawn. She couldn't even remember what the dreams were about, only the dread they left in their wake.

This morning, the digital clock on the microwave read 4:43 a.m. when she came downstairs. Far too early, even for her. The nightmares had started shortly after summer break began, and after a week, she had stopped trying to fall back asleep again after they awakened her. The general sense of wrongness that lingered made that impossible. She hoped they would stop before school resumed next week.

She prepared her morning pot of herbal tea and carried it to the back deck, looking out to the east as the sun crested the mountainous horizon. There was something about the sunrise in the high country of New Mexico that was pure magic. Perhaps it was the way the air was so thin a mile and a half above sea level that the sun's rays sparkled and danced across the rock cliffs, tinting them the pink of a dew-covered rose. Or maybe it was the way the reds and yellows of sunrise splashed the eastern sky. The tang of the high pines hung in the morning air, which was cold at this hour even in early August.

White Rock had been her home all her life, the bedroom community for the Los Alamos National Laboratory, providing homes for her closest friends, although many of her school friends lived a few miles away in the Los Alamos city limits. Heather chuckled to herself. Los Alamos and White Rock were beautiful towns situated in the stunning surroundings of the high canyon country of northern New Mexico, but the term "city" was a little generous.

Despite the lingering worry from the dream that tickled at the back of her mind, Heather still could barely contain her excitement. Today, Jennifer and Mark were scheduled to return from their family summer vacation. While a cruise up the coast of Alaska sounded fun and she did not begrudge them those activities with their own family, she had missed the twins immensely these last three weeks.

They still had a few days to work on their rock climbing before school started and basketball stole all of Mark's time. He'd been heavily recruited as a sophomore to join the high school team this year. They'd just have to pry Jennifer from her books and convince her that living up the last bit of summer was more important than reading about the latest computer theory. Jen could probably be coaxed if they let her bring a book along for the trip.

By the time Heather was into her third cup of herbal tea, she was almost relaxed enough to consider a trip back to bed. Then, the sound of dishes rattling in the kitchen announced that her mother was up and breakfast would soon follow. The screen door opened and her father stepped out, a mug of steaming coffee in his hand.

"Good morning, sweetheart."

"Hi, Dad."

Gilbert McFarland was tall and slender, with brown eyes and a mouth upturned in a perpetual smile. His thick brown hair was hidden under the old floppy fishing hat he always wore, which sported an assortment of hand-tied flies and a button that proclaimed ONE FISH, TWO FISH, RED FISH, BLUE FISH...

"It looks like it's going to be another beautiful day."

"Yep, but you've missed the best part of the sunrise."

"Your mom and I saw it through our bedroom window."

"That hardly counts. Glass filters the view."

"Hmm. Not everyone is born to rise before the sun. You hungry?"

"I'm getting there."

"Good. Breakfast's almost ready."

Heather followed her dad back into the house. Her mother, Anna, moved through the kitchen and breakfast nook with an efficiency that made everything seem as if it positioned itself of its own accord.

"Well, you're looking a little tired this morning," her mother said, touching Heather's forehead. "Are you feeling OK?"

"I'm fine, Mom. I was just a little bit anxious to get up this morning."

Her mother smiled knowingly. "As if we don't all know the reason. I suppose I should set out a couple of extra places for breakfast."

Heather was about to say she wasn't sure what time the Smythes were returning when the doorbell rang. The Smythe twins had been eating breakfast, and any other meal they could get away with, at Heather's house for years. Mrs. Smythe's cooking was legendary for being inedible. She didn't even like eating her own cooking, so she hardly blamed Mark and Jennifer for taking advantage of the

McFarland hospitality. The favor was returned in the form of regular barbecues Mr. Smythe hosted at the Smythe abode.

Heather opened the door and then stepped back. "Wow. You guys look great. I didn't think you could get a tan in Alaska."

Mark grinned. "Don't kid yourself. I did some rock and glacier climbing. You'd love it there."

"Good atmosphere to catch up on some reading, too," said Jennifer as she gave Heather a quick hug.

Heather laughed. "You guys hungry?"

"Starved," Mark said. "Mom almost got up and made omelets this morning." The look of horror on his face made Heather laugh even harder.

Her mother met the twins with huge hugs, immediately ushering them to their chairs and passing around the pancake platter, which everyone set about doing their best to empty. By the time breakfast was over, the family had heard all about cruising Alaska, followed by Jennifer's excited summary of the biography she'd read about Madame Curie.

A horn honked outside and Heather's father rose, wiping his chin with a napkin. "Oops. My ride's here. Gotta run."

"Have fun at the lab today," said Heather.

"Always do."

While he had never gotten a doctorate, or even a master's degree, Heather's father was one of those indispensable people at the lab known as a tech. So was Mr. Smythe, who currently waited outside in their driveway. It was his week to drive the carpool.

Heather's dad had a knack for building any mechanical contraption to exact specifications, given the most cursory information. His real title was machinist, but he had turned the job into an art form. He loved the lab, which provided him access to an unequaled machine shop and the opportunity to make an assortment of oddities for the scientists.

While her father was master of all things mechanical, Fred Smythe was lord of electronics. Together, there was nothing they could not create or improve upon. It was only fitting that they were next-door neighbors.

As Heather's dad reached for the front doorknob, it burst open, and he was almost bowled over by Fred's blocky form as he raced into the living room. Before Heather's dad could react, Mr. Smythe grabbed the remote and brought the old television set to life.

"Gil, get your butt in here. You've got to see this!"

The CNN logo accompanied by "Breaking News" formed a banner along the bottom of the screen. The camera suddenly cut away from the news anchor to the president seated at his desk in the Oval Office, backdropped by the presidential seal and an American flag.

The president began speaking directly into the camera.

"My fellow Americans. It is with great pleasure and excitement that I come before you today with an announcement, an announcement for which you have unknowingly been kept waiting. Through multiple presidencies, several wars, the landing of men on the moon, up through today's troubled world situation, a matter of unfathomable scientific importance has been preciously guarded by this government.

"As will become clear in moments, this secrecy was required so the government could investigate the national security and public safety ramifications of this discovery. However, recent breakthroughs promise such huge benefits to mankind that I, in consultation with key congressional leaders, have decided to make them public."

The president paused momentarily, and Heather wondered if he had lost his place on the teleprompter. Then, taking a deep breath, he continued.

"In late March of 1948, just outside Aztec, New Mexico, the United States military discovered a crash site for a ship of unknown origin. That origin has since been conclusively determined to be from a star system other than our own. In short, it is a spaceship from another world, constructed using advanced technologies, many of which we still cannot fathom.

"For the past several years, a team of our top scientists has studied this ship under a program called the Rho Project. I will now turn this briefing over to the lead scientist on the Rho Project."

The McFarland household erupted into pandemonium, with excited shouts eventually drowned out by bellows for quiet from Misters McFarland and Smythe.

On the television, the president's image had been replaced by a speaker standing at a podium in a press conference room. The speaker was immediately recognizable to anyone from the Los Alamos area: Donald R. Stephenson, deputy director of the Los Alamos National Laboratory, in charge of special projects, many of which were unnamed. Apparently one of those projects was about to make a name for itself.

Looking at the man had always made Heather feel uncomfortable somehow, as if those sharp eyes were picking her out of the crowd, drilling through her. He was a wiry, slender man with a sharp face, a high forehead, and an intense mouth that looked as if it had never been forced to twist into a smile. His brown hair still showed no sign of graying or thinning, even though he was in his midfifties.

Timeless. That was how Heather thought of Dr. Stephenson. No age fitted him. It was like the way the funny Pat character on the old *Saturday Night Live* reruns was gender-ambiguous. You certainly couldn't tell by looking.

Dr. Donald Stephenson was widely regarded as the smartest man on the planet. He had gotten out of the army in his midtwenties and quickly attained doctorates in astrophysics, mathematics, and chemistry from MIT. Three Nobel Prizes before he was forty had been enough to propel him into his current high position at the laboratory. Heather had heard from her father that if the man were not so completely dislikable, he would no doubt have been named director instead of deputy director, not that he showed any interest in moving away from the projects he kept under his strict control.

Both her father and Mr. Smythe despised the man, although that was a sentiment so widely held among the scientists and technicians around the laboratory that it raised no eyebrows. To her it seemed that Donald Stephenson reveled in making others hate him.

Now, before a roomful of reporters, he spoke steadily as a sequence of slides flashed on the screen behind him, scenes filled with a cigar-shaped ship draped with instruments, workers moving along catwalks that clung to its surface, a ramp extending up into the interior. There were no shots of the interior of the spaceship.

Although Heather was too excited to follow the droning monologue, the gist of it was clear. Recent breakthroughs in deciphering some of the alien technology had yielded results so important and startling that they could not, in good conscience, be kept from the world, results that had ramifications on both energy production and on the health of the world's population.

In coming weeks, those results would be carefully released to a select group of the world's scientists for verification and to allow for external analysis of whether the breakthroughs were safe for rapid dissemination to the governments of the world.

The slide show ended. Dr. Stephenson's steel-gray eyes swept the room. "I will now take your questions."

Bedlam. It took a full five minutes to get the reporters settled down so individual questions could be heard. After that they came hot and fast.

"Why keep this from the American people all this time?"

"Will independent scientists have access to the starship?"

"Shouldn't this discovery be turned over to the United Nations?"

On and on went the questions, many of which were deferred to the political leadership to answer. It was immediately clear, however, that despite the US government's declared willingness to share technologies from the project, that openness did not include access to the starship itself.

As the news conference ended, a slow shudder crawled along Heather's back, up her bare neck, and into her hairline. For a split second, it seemed that she would recall the details of last night's dream. Then the feeling was gone, replaced by the lingering sense of dread with which she had awakened.

CHAPTER 3

Mesa. The Spanish word for "table." Why they had come to call their favorite ridgeline retreat The Mesa, Heather couldn't remember. The high finger of land that extended out between two deep canyons bore no resemblance to a table, or even the top of one.

In most respects, it was similar to hundreds of other places in this red rock region of the New Mexico highlands, a place where it appeared the land had split and cracked on three sides, falling away into steep canyons hundreds of feet deep, carved from the rock by the effects of water and wind over the millennia.

Their mountain bikes had carried them to this remote hideaway they'd visited on dozens of other weekends. But it was not rock climbing or hunting for mythical lost gold mines that brought them to The Mesa this first Saturday of the school year. It was the contents of the large box strapped to Mark's bike.

After Heather slid to a stop and dropped her kickstand, she pulled off her bike helmet and slung it over her handlebars, glad to feel the fresh air blowing through her hair. Mark already had the box unstrapped and was lovingly carrying it out beyond the trees into the clearing.

Here, the ridgetop was flat and treeless for a quarter mile before dropping away steeply into the canyon beyond. It reminded Heather of the fingernail on a giant hairy finger pointing southwest. Perhaps Cortés himself had used it as a guidepost back to Mexico.

"Here, give me a hand with this," said Mark, unwrapping the packaging that cradled his prized airplane.

It was a beautifully painted model of a Piper Cub aircraft, complete with engine and remote control. They had built other model aircraft before, but this was the most detailed kit to date. It had taken them most of the summer to build, and so far they had only flown it in the park near their house. This would be its true maiden voyage outside that protected training ground.

As Mark held the small funnel, Heather filled the fuel tank, careful not to spill any of the fuel on the ground.

Jennifer moved up beside them, fumbling with the control unit and a small handheld TV. It had been her idea to attach the tiny microcamera to the aircraft, a camera that broadcast a short-range color signal that could be picked up on a selectable frequency by the TV. True, the picture was not high resolution and required line of sight between the camera and the receiver, but it was still a fun addition to the project.

Heather had routed the signal through her cell phone. That way they could save a couple of minutes of the video on a memory card and replay it later. Their fathers had helped, too, with little hints here and there to get the teens past sticking points. But, for the most part, this was their own work.

Getting the thumbs-up from Jennifer, Mark turned toward Heather. "How's the wind speed?"

She held up the small anemometer, its four little half Ping-Pong ball cups whirling in the gentle breeze. "Steady at four knots. Looking good."

"OK then, here we go." Mark spun the small propeller, and the engine coughed to life on his second attempt.

Jennifer moved the throttle control, and the engine revved up and down as she played with it, the sound cutting through the quiet rim country like a bright flashlight in a cave. She moved the controls, getting the thumbs-up from Mark as he checked to see that the control surfaces on their aircraft responded correctly to the commands.

"How's the video feed?" Jennifer yelled above the whine of the engine.

Heather grinned. "Looks good, at least when Mark keeps his face out of it."

Mark shook his head. "Very funny. Are we ready?"

Jennifer held up five fingers, lowering them one at a time as she counted backward out loud. The engine gunned as Mark released the small plane, sending it shooting out and up. Jennifer brought it banking around in a circle above them, gradually getting a feel for the thing, before putting it through some climbs and dives.

After a couple of minutes, Mark moved up beside her. "My turn, Jen."

Jennifer arched an eyebrow at her brother but handed him the control box, keeping the long antennae out and away from his body.

She moved over by Heather. "How's the video?"

Heather shrugged. "Good, but the way you guys are looping the airplane around, it's just making me airsick."

"Let me try." Jennifer took the set from Heather. "Hey, Mark. How about flying it flat and level?"

Jennifer stared down at the screen. "Keep going straight for a bit. It just passed over the rim."

"Not too far now," Heather cautioned.

Suddenly the small plane jerked sideways and down.

"Crap," Mark said. "It's caught in a gust."

He struggled to regain control of the small plane, his thumbs working the twin joysticks on the control. For a moment, it seemed to work. Then, just as the red Piper Cub tried to climb back over the ridgetop, it spun wildly, plummeting out of sight.

"Damn it," Mark yelled, setting down the control and running toward the rim, Heather close on his heels.

Reaching the spot where their airplane disappeared, Mark and Heather halted. Luckily, at this point along the rim, the slope, though steep, wasn't a cliff face like it was farther to their right. On the bad side, the slope was covered in thick, thorny brush. Scanning it from the top of the ridge, they saw no sign of the spot where their pet project had impacted.

"Christ," Mark moaned. "We might never find it in that."

"We'll find it," said Heather, although her heart sank. "It won't be fun, though."

Jennifer arrived, clutching the video unit. "Hey, guys, take a look at this. I've got the last thirty seconds of the crash on playback."

Mark and Heather crowded behind Jennifer, peering over each shoulder as she pushed the play button on the cell phone. The video spun wildly, then steadied. Jennifer paused the playback.

"You see that spot?" she asked, pointing to a lone pine tree amid thick brush. "Do you see that tree down there?"

Mark walked back to the edge and scanned the slope below. "Yeah. I think I see it."

"OK. Now watch the end."

Stepping through the remaining few seconds of the video frame by frame, they watched as the view spun back and forth between sky and ground. The last several frames of video showed the plane falling into the brush, perhaps a hundred feet up the slope from the pine tree.

"What's that?" Heather asked, pointing at the dark screen.

Mark squinted down at the screen. "What? That's just darkness after the crash."

"No. There." Heather pointed to the pale red glow at the upper-left corner of the screen.

Jennifer adjusted her glasses, leaning closer to the small screen. "I don't know. The camera must have shorted out."

Mark stood. "I'll climb down and get it."

Glancing down the slope toward the thorn brush, Jennifer shook her head. "Not fun."

"You don't want to flip for who goes?" Heather asked.

Mark laughed. "Nice, but no. I crashed it."

"OK," said Heather. "Pay the price for machismo."

Mark climbed down the rocky crest and into the brush beyond, working his way along a narrow goat trail before plunging into the thorn brush below. The girls watched from above as he pushed forward, thrashing his way into the bushes.

As he neared the crash site, Mark gave a startled yell and pitched forward, disappearing from view. From their high vantage point, Jennifer and Heather had a clear view of the slope. Of Mark, however, there was no sign.

"Mark! Are you OK?"

As Jennifer continued to yell, Heather moved rapidly over the rocky edge, toward where she'd last seen Mark.

"Wait," Jennifer yelled, scrambling toward her with the video unit in hand. "Look at this."

"We don't have time to look at more of the recording."

"This is a live shot."

"What?"

"The camera's still sending. I didn't notice it because it was mostly dark. Look at this, though."

Heather's mouth dropped open. There in the darkness on the screen lay Mark's prone form, his skin dimly illuminated by a red glow.

CHAPTER 4

"Look, he's moving!" Jennifer pointed at the screen.

As they watched, Mark rolled to his side and then out of the view of the camera.

Heather turned back toward the canyon. "Come on. Let's get down there."

The two girls moved down the steep hillside as rapidly as they could. The thick brush clutched and tore at their jeans and shirts, scratching arms and legs, and kept their progress to a crawl.

"Mark. Can you hear us?" Heather yelled as they got closer to the spot where he had disappeared.

"I'm OK." Heather and Jennifer both gasped with relief at the sound of his voice. "I'm right here."

Jennifer peered over the rims of her glasses into the thick brush ahead. "Here, where? I don't see you."

"You won't believe what I've found. Careful, there's a drop-off in front of you. Go right, then loop back toward me."

Heather shook her head. "Mark, you aren't making any sense. I don't see you."

"Trust me. Go right about ten feet, then down the hill until I tell you."

Heather bit her lip. "What's with the mystery? Do you know how badly you scared us? We thought you fell off a cliff."

"Hurry up." Mark's reply didn't curb her annoyance.

Jennifer was already moving in response to her brother's directions, and Heather followed. Mark's voice brought them to a stop.

"OK, far enough. Now come toward my voice. Watch your step. Here, take my hand," Mark said.

Both girls screamed as a disembodied hand reached out toward them, followed by Mark's head. The rest of Mark's body materialized as he moved toward them, a huge grin on his face.

"Sorry. I tried to warn you."

"What the hell just happened?" Heather gasped.

"You've got to see this for yourselves. Oh, and don't worry about the optical illusion. It won't hurt you."

Mark turned and stepped back the way he had come, his body disappearing into space before them.

"Come on," he called back to them. "Take the plunge."

As Jennifer started to reply, Heather took a deep breath and stepped toward where Mark had vanished. Reaching out to move one of the thorn branches away from her face, her hand disappeared into nothingness, the branch having no more substance than the air she was breathing. Another startled cry escaped her lips as her entire body moved forward into darkness.

Mark's strong hand gripped her arm to steady her as her eyes struggled to adjust to the dim light. She was in a large cave entrance. Looking back in the direction from which she'd come, it was as if a mesh screen had been pulled down across the opening, leaving everything outside dimly seen, as if through a translucent film. Jennifer stood just beyond that screen, hesitating, unable to see what lay beyond no matter how hard or long she stared.

"Quit fooling around and come on in," said Mark. "It's not going to bite you."

Her mouth twisted. "Unlike you two, I prefer knowing what I'm getting into, especially when it appears to violate several known laws of physics."

"For Christ's sake. It's just some sort of hologram."

"And that doesn't set off any alarms in your brain?"

Heather turned to look back into the cave again, and a gasp escaped her lips. "Oh my God!"

A dim red glow illuminated the cavern, the sides of which appeared to have been carved by a massive impact. The texture of the stone looked like it had melted and flowed before solidifying again. It was roughly fifty feet wide and nearly as tall. However, it was not the melted rock that made her heart pound.

At the back of the cavern rested a huge, saucer-shaped object. There was no longer any doubt about the source of the hologram or the soft red glow.

"Jennifer, get your butt in here," Heather called without turning around.

There was no adequate description for the scene before her. The smooth and graceful lines of the ship were clearly visible in the magenta glow, a glow as beautiful as it was otherworldly. Heather was not sure what it was about the lighting that left no shadows. There appeared to be no single source for the light, almost as if the illumination radiated from the air itself.

"It's beautiful," she breathed.

"Isn't it?" Mark said. "When I fell through that opening, I just lay here for a couple of minutes trying to get my mind wrapped around it. I thought at first I was hallucinating."

He walked slowly toward the ship.

Heather turned back to the entrance of the cave and saw Jennifer standing just inside, unable to move, unable to speak. Heather moved over and put her arm around her friend's shoulders, a broad smile on her face.

"It's all right, Jen. You can breathe now."

"My God, Heather. You know what this means? We must have stumbled into the restricted area where they're storing the *Rho Ship*. We're in big, big trouble."

Mark's voice echoed in the cave. "No way. There's nobody around, no security, no instruments. And look. The ship shown on TV was cylindrical. This ship is more like a jelly doughnut. Or a giant bagel without the hole."

"Must everything be food related with you?" Heather laughed, although it sounded nervous instead of mirthful in the empty confines of the cave.

Mark had reached the closest edge of the spaceship, moving under the curved edge until he could run his hand over the surface. Heather followed him, anxious to feel the skin of the thing.

She touched it and jerked her hand back as if she had received an electric shock. She hadn't, but the feel was like nothing she could have expected.

The ship just felt…wrong somehow. It was almost as if she hadn't really touched anything, but that her hand suddenly wanted to go in another direction. It was like the repulsion she felt when she tried to touch the same poles of two magnets together. Slippery, or even frictionless, did not begin to describe the substance of the hull.

As if reading her mind, Mark took a small coin from his pocket and tossed it against the ship. The coin ricocheted soundlessly off the hull.

"I don't really think it's a good idea to go throwing things at it," Jennifer said, moving up closer. "It clearly still has a working power source and technologies we can't even begin to imagine. What if the owners are still around? Do you think we should be attracting their attention?"

Mark paused. "I doubt we'd still be alive if they were around. I explored this cave a bit before you guys got down here. It looks like the ship crashed right into the side of the ridge here, melting its way in as it hit. From what I can tell, the impact didn't even scratch the hull, but there's something you should see."

Signaling for them to follow, Mark led the way around the right side of the ship, staying under the outer edge of the hull where it curved up away from the ground. The three ducked down, squeezing between the cavern walls and the hull of the ship. After about ten feet, the space widened to where they could all stand once more.

Mark pointed upward. "Something sure did more than scratch it."

In the otherwise symmetrical hull, a perfectly cylindrical hole had been cut upward through the ship's interior, all the way out the topside. Punctures should show bending or melting effects on the surrounding materials. This hole showed none of these. It was like a cookie cutter had punched through dough, leaving behind clean, bright edges all the way through, level after level, all clearly visible in the magenta glow.

"It looks like they came out on the short end of an encounter with something."

Jennifer moved up beside them. “Three guesses for what did this.”

Heather’s eyes went wide. “The *Rho Ship*.”

Mark nodded. “That would be my guess. Here, give me a boost up.”

“Have you completely lost your mind?” Jennifer asked. “For all we know, we’ve already received a deadly dose of alien radiation.”

“Then it won’t matter if I get a little more. Come on, give me a leg up.”

“Now just wait, Mark. For just once in your life, think a minute before you charge in.”

Mark rolled his eyes. “OK. I’m listening.”

“This is too important to just go poking around by ourselves. We need to report this to someone so the government can investigate it. This is a scientific find of historic importance.”

“The government already has a ship.” Seeing Jennifer’s glare darken, Mark continued. “Do you know what they’ll do when we tell them about this one? They’ll take this ship and haul it off for study. That will mean that this is the closest we’ll ever get to looking inside something from another world. Are you really willing to give up that chance? How about you, Heather?”

Heather shook her head. “I want one good look inside before we give it up.”

Jennifer’s frown deepened, but she nodded reluctantly. “I guess a look won’t hurt anything.”

As Mark’s exultant whoop echoed through the cavern, Heather’s gaze drifted up to the hole five feet above her head. As badly as she wanted to peek inside, a small spider of worry skittered across her mind. Breathing a prayer that her worry was nothing, Heather linked hands with Jennifer, boosting Mark up so that he could grasp the edge of the hole. With a powerful heave, he pulled himself inside.

CHAPTER 5

After several seconds, Mark's head reappeared in the hole, looking down at them. "Heather, jump up and grab my hand so I can pull you up."

"What about me?" Jennifer asked.

"Don't worry," said Mark. "Once she's up here, Heather can hold my legs and I'll lean down to grab your hands."

With her rock climbing experience, Heather swung up into the opening with ease, and together they soon hauled Jennifer up as well.

They found themselves in a curved room, what must have been the entire lower deck of the ship. An odd assortment of translucent tanks and long tubes, filled with glowing, iridescent gasses, lined the walls.

The interior walls, floors, and ceilings of the craft were of a different material than the outer hull, something that felt more closely akin to plastic than metal. Here also the magenta ambient lighting left no shadows. The room was spacious in all dimensions except height, not quite six feet of space separating floor from ceiling so that Mark was forced to stoop slightly to keep from banging the top of his head.

Heather moved to the center of the room, where a circular shaft a dozen feet in diameter rose to the ceiling. An open doorway led inside. Mark moved up beside her as she peered in.

"An elevator?" Heather asked.

"Or a garbage disposal," said Jennifer, joining them.

Mark grinned. "Jen, you're a breath of fresh air."

"Just pointing out that we don't know a damn thing about this ship," she said, arching her left eyebrow.

Mark turned back toward the opening. "Who, besides me, wants to be first to find out?"

Heather's heart had not slowed since she had first seen the starship. Even free climbing the massive rock spire called The Needle had not pumped so much adrenaline into her bloodstream. But with the rush came a strand of dread that wormed its way into her brain.

Heather shrugged off the feeling. "It's a little late for caution. I'm game."

Jennifer shook her head. "I'll wait out here, thank you. If you guys get vaporized, then at least I can tell our folks how you met your fate."

Stepping into the shaft, Heather scanned the walls for a control panel. The walls were uniformly smooth and plain, the same material as the rest of the lower deck. Heather pressed her palm against the wall, then both palms, while Mark tapped and banged beside her. Nothing.

After several minutes of fruitlessly trying to make something happen, they stepped back out of the small, cylindrical room.

"Well, that was exciting," Mark muttered.

"It looks like we're going to have to keep hoisting ourselves up to the other decks through the same hole that got us into the ship," Heather said.

Mark led the way upward. This time the access was much easier. All they had to do was reach up and pull themselves through the hole, although Jennifer still required a helping hand to make it.

Whereas the deck below had covered the entire lower portion of the ship, the next level found them confined to a single small room with a closed door barring exit to the remainder of the deck. The room was a dozen feet across with a curving desktop extending out from the arc of the outer wall. Positioned at equal intervals along this desk were four stools mounted in a track, apparently intended to allow the occupants to slide back and forth along its length.

On the desk in front of each stool lay a partial loop of metal with marble-sized beads on each end. Mark plopped onto one of the stools and picked up one of the loops, twisting it slowly in his hands. Heather followed suit, finding the loop very light and flexible, more of the translucent substance like what they had seen forming the tubes on the deck below.

"Hmm. Could be a headset," Mark mumbled. "Here, let's try them on and see."

"Wait just a minute!" Jennifer said, her hand catching Mark's before he could proceed. "Looking doesn't mean punching every button or pulling every lever on this ship. Even if we keep this secret, we have to investigate in a way that doesn't destroy the ship, or worse, us."

Mark ignored her, sliding the band smoothly over his temples.

Stretching her own band gently, Heather slid it up over her head, exactly as she would her headphones. It settled naturally into place, elongating slightly so that the small balls on the ends slid into position directly over her temples. The slight pressure actually felt nice.

Heather smiled. "These actually feel pretty good—like a temple massage. Come on, Jen. Try on a set. They don't seem to do much else."

"They haven't exactly killed us yet." Mark grinned.

Jennifer reluctantly slid onto the stool next to Heather, then, after close examination, slid the band into place. Within a few seconds the tense look disappeared.

Jennifer smiled. "You're right. They do feel good. I could almost take a nap if I wouldn't fall off the stool doing it."

Mark leaned forward, letting his palms rest flat on the desktop in front of him, then straightened suddenly as a cry of surprise escaped his lips. Fire exploded in Heather's brain as every neuron in her skull triggered simultaneously. She struggled to remove the headband but found her limbs unresponsive. Every nerve in her body pulsed with an intense tingling as though all her limbs had fallen asleep and were now waking up with a vengeance.

She screamed, dimly aware that nearby her two friends screamed in accompaniment, the sounds barely registering in her overloaded brain. Although Heather had never dwelt on death, she had always assumed death would creep up on her suddenly when it came, taking her with it in a couple of ticks on the clock, perhaps preceded by a long fall off the rocks or the screech of car brakes.

Now death tore at her from the inside, and it was taking its sweet time.

When Heather was small, she had been badly shocked trying to get a bagel out of the toaster with a knife, but that had been an instantaneous trip into the land of nod. This endless eruption of every nerve ending in her brain held her here, unwilling to let her consciousness flee from the agony. For what seemed like an eternity there was only pain. Then, as if all her pain receptors had been seared out of existence, it faded, replaced by a flood of imagery, hallucinations that lacked the faintest connection with any reality she had ever known.

Three-dimensional symbols rolled past her as beings with large heads and skinny torsos darted about in all directions. They spoke at her. No, that wasn't right. They thought at her, sending out the strange symbols that encapsulated those thoughts, and when she questioned them, her questions rolled out toward them as much simpler symbols that encapsulated each question. She understood none of it.

Shift. Gone were the beings and their symbols. She found herself strapped into a craft darting between the planets of a star system, the walls of the craft completely transparent, as if she were sitting in a large soap bubble. A ringed planet darted by, its many moons careening away as her ship banked so hard it seemed the gravitational strain would destroy it.

Then she saw it, flitting across her field of view, far ahead. It expanded in a magnified view, surrounded by circles and cross-hairs as her ship attempted to establish a lock on the target.

The long, cigar-shaped craft she chased suddenly sent out a spear-like vortex that rippled through the space separating them, a narrow tube in which the view of the stars beyond twisted and bent.

Heather's ship torqued hard right and dropped, the ripple passing within a hundred meters of her. In response, a beam of solid red pulsed outward from her own ship, missing the cigar ship ahead, but pulverizing a small asteroid as they passed through a field thick with the spinning rocks.

Ahead, a blue planet with a single moon loomed large, the other ship racing toward it. Almost simultaneously, the weapon systems on the two ships fired again.

The red beam played across the other craft's cigar-like surface, bubbling and warping parts of its hull as the enemy's vortex beam punched through her own ship, sucking four small bodies out through the hole into the vacuum of space. All maneuvering control lost, Heather's ship plunged onward, and the surface of the blue planet rose up to meet her.

The imagery stopped. Heather stumbled from the stool, pulling the alien band from its place on her head. The room spun around her, only gradually stopping as she sank to her knees. Beside her, Mark leaned against the wall, his own headset held tightly in his fist. Struggling to his feet, he held out a hand to help her up.

Heather's eyes swept the room, panic threatening to rob her of her breath.

"Jennifer?"

Mark shook his head. "I already looked. She's gone."

CHAPTER 6

There were times when loneliness hung so heavy in the air that it stuck a lump in Nancy's throat, the tears at the corner of her eyes upwelling from tiny springs of misery. Tonight, here by herself in Rho Lab, long after everyone else had left, she knew all too well the source of her feelings.

She had been raised in a way that seemed straight out of a Norman Rockwell painting, the tenth child in a New England family of eleven children, all girls except for John, the baby of the family. All those wonderful growing-up years, her organized mother carefully delegated tasks to each of the kids in a way that had given them a wonderful camaraderie. Despite the family's old New England money, a rigorous work ethic was a requirement rather than an option.

Then it had been off to Princeton to study computer science, her bachelor's degree followed quickly by her doctorate at

Carnegie Mellon University. Working with Dr. Stephenson at the Los Alamos Laboratory had been a dream come true, a dream that had grown far more wondrous once she had first been shown the *Rho Ship*.

How things had deteriorated in the two years since that day. Now everything had come to a head in a way that was about to force her to betray the famous Dr. Stephenson.

With the information she had discovered on his personal laptop, there could be no doubt that he would not be deputy director of the Los Alamos National Laboratory much beyond tomorrow. Despite an authorization to access Dr. Stephenson's computer that came directly from Senator Connally, chairman of the Senate Intelligence Committee, she felt soiled.

What would her family think of her now?

She removed the USB memory stick, sticking it in her purse, then powered the laptop down, flipping the lid closed with a snap.

"Find anything of interest?"

Nancy jumped up with a gasp of surprise, sending the chair rolling across the floor like a runaway shopping cart in a supermarket parking lot. The lean form of Donald Stephenson stood staring at her through eyes that showed no hint of emotion. Nancy had seen eyes like those before. Shark's eyes.

Her hand fluttered to her breast. "Dr. Stephenson. You startled me."

"Did I? Imagine my own surprise when I return to my lab to retrieve an item I forgot, only to find you in my private office, browsing through files on my personal computer."

Nancy felt sick. The confrontation had been coming, but she had expected to do it tomorrow, during the relative comfort of the normal business day, not here in the semidarkness of the most secret facility at the Los Alamos National Laboratory, probably the most secret laboratory in the country.

"Dr. Stephenson, I am sorry that you had to find me like this. I have just completed an audit of this program for the Senate Intelligence Committee, the information on your laptop completing the information I required. I will be filing my report tomorrow."

"And may I assume that your report will not be favorable?"

The unflinching calm of the deputy director's face made Nancy more nervous with each passing moment. "I am afraid that you are correct. I would say that I am sorry, but my compassion for you died once I realized that there are large portions of the work you are doing here that are hidden from the other scientists, even from the US government. And from what I can tell, you have made considerable progress unraveling portions of the alien technology that have tremendous implications, although I do not claim to understand many of the derivations in your equations."

"Very impressive. Of course, that is why I selected you for the program. Still, you surprise me. I doubt that there are more than a handful of physicists and mathematicians in the world who can understand many of those equations, even fewer who could have hacked their way past the encryption on my laptop."

A thin smile crinkled the corners of Nancy's lips.

"You are not the only one who was first in your class. All that will become moot once my report is filed tomorrow."

Dr. Stephenson stepped closer, leaning down so his face was only inches from her own, but Nancy did not flinch.

"I was not ready for this, young lady."

He paused a moment before continuing.

"Do you know the significance of the Greek letter *rho*? I chose it from an inscription in Olympos, an ancient Lycian city. It is an alphabet oracle which, loosely translated, says, 'Your journey will proceed faster with a brief delay.' In other words, don't go off half-cocked, but don't wait until the other fellow shoots you either."

A mirthless grin spread across Dr. Stephenson's sharp features.

"You think your report is complete, but it is not. If you will follow me, young Dr. Anatole, I will show you something that may make you reevaluate."

Without waiting for a response, Dr. Stephenson turned and strode out of his private office in the laboratory. Curiosity aroused, Nancy followed him into the huge room where the *Rho Ship* rested, its cigar-shaped hull clamped between curved supports that held it elevated a full ten feet above the floor. Stephenson did not pause to look at the ship, instead continuing directly beneath it to where the ramp led upward to the doorway through its hull.

Nancy followed him into the narrow passageways that honeycombed the interior of the ship. She had been inside it often enough over the last year and a half that it should have seemed routine to walk through these alien rooms and hallways, but it didn't. There was nothing beautiful about the ship. Everything was gray, shaped for efficiency and utility, not aesthetics, functionality trumping beauty at every twist and turn.

Dr. Stephenson stopped before a wall that blocked access to the back third of the ship. In all the years the research team had studied this ship, nobody had gained access beyond this wall. At least, that was what everyone believed.

As the deputy director's hands pressed against it, fingers tracing out a complex set of patterns, the wall slid open.

Nancy gasped as Dr. Stephenson walked inside.

"Now, now, Doctor, don't delay," the deputy director's voice called out to her from within. "Do you want to make a complete and accurate report to the good senator or don't you?"

With a deep breath, Nancy stepped through the opening, her eyes sweeping the large room that stretched out before her. The aliens had made no attempt to group equipment in any way that made its functionality apparent, instead positioning everything so that the tubes and bundles of conduits that connected the various apparatuses optimized efficiency. Very narrow walkways led through, around, even over the various machines and instruments. Spreading her arms in wonderment, she turned back toward Dr. Stephenson.

His fist hit Nancy in the stomach so hard it sent all the air in her lungs whistling out through her teeth. She twisted into a fetal ball, her shoulder dislocating as she hit the floor. Try as she might, Nancy could not uncurl herself as she struggled to breathe. Dr. Stephenson strolled slowly around her prostrate form, moving in with a sudden kick to her injured stomach that rolled her three times across the alien floor.

Nancy vomited; the pain was so great, she prayed she would lose consciousness. She could no longer focus well enough to see Dr. Stephenson's face, although his feet were clear enough, pacing slowly back and forth before her. Once more he stopped, his foot seeming to swing toward her in slow motion, impacting her midsection harder than either of the two previous blows, sending her rolling into the wall.

The pain embraced her, squeezing so hard that her vision narrowed to a straw's-eye view, a view outlined in red. Into that narrow tunnel swam the deputy director's face peering down at her, his features lined with concern.

"My dear Dr. Anatole. Your breath is bringing a bloody froth to your lips. Now, I am not a trained physician, but that can't be good. One or more of your ribs must have punctured a lung."

As Nancy struggled to breathe, the sound of footsteps moved away from her, ringing loudly through the floor her ear rested upon. The steps stopped for several seconds, then returned, growing in volume until she thought her eardrums would explode.

Then his face was back, leaning down very close as he took her head in his hand, twisting it up to face the dull gray ceiling. His other hand moved slowly down toward her neck, a long hypodermic syringe clutched in a three-finger grip. And within that syringe a dull, gray, viscous liquid quivered with an energy all its own.

The needle pricked her neck, and Nancy surprised herself by finding the strength to scream, the sound echoing out of the ship into the darkness of the empty lab.

CHAPTER 7

Heather gagged, just managed to avoid hurling her breakfast onto the floor, and staggered to her feet, her brow wet with a cold, stinging sweat that dripped into her eyes. Mixed with the bile in her throat, the dread had returned.

Mark cupped his hands to his mouth and yelled. "Jennifer! Hey, Jen, can you hear me?"

Heather joined the yelling, fear clutching at her heart. Suddenly, the doorway leading out of the room snicked open. Framed against a multicolored backdrop, Jennifer smiled calmly at them, her alien headband still firmly in place, its coloring now a shifting rainbow pattern that made Heather a bit dizzy looking at it.

"Get that damned thing off your head. It nearly killed Mark and me."

"Calm down. It hurt, but it didn't try to kill us."

Mark shook his head. “It may not have tried, but it came damn close to doing it. I thought my head was going to explode.”

Jennifer stepped into the room, the doorway sliding closed behind her. “It scared me, too. But once the download started, I sort of got the hang of it.”

“Download? What the hell are you talking about?” Mark asked.

“Well, it just came to me. All that imagery and strange symbology. You saw that too, right? It seemed like a link to the central computer system, so I focused on visualizing questions. That caused me to get new imagery back, most of it incomprehensible. But I managed to open the door.”

Heather glanced down at the floor where her own headset lay. “Then why did it hurt so bad?”

Mark nodded. “I’ll tell you why. The damned thing puts off so many microwaves that it cooked part of our brains.”

“No. I don’t think so,” Jennifer said. “I think the aliens used the bands to communicate with the ship’s computers. Instead of keyboards and monitors, they put these on and their thoughts were tied in to the system. The computer ‘talked’ back with images, sounds, maybe even feelings.”

Heather nodded. “That makes sense. We haven’t seen anything resembling manual input devices to the onboard systems. No keyboards, joysticks, mice, nothing.”

Mark scowled. “What’s the point of a system that fries your brain in the process?”

“Maybe it didn’t hurt the aliens,” Heather said. “I’ll bet the connections to our brains are different than the aliens’. Maybe the computer had to explore its way around our heads to figure out how to link up.”

“And so it has. Now put your headsets back on and follow me. I want to show you something,” Jennifer said.

Heather hesitated. “I don’t really want to go through that again.”

Mark took a deep breath, then placed the band back on his head. After several seconds he looked over at Heather. "It's OK. No pain this time."

Heather stooped to pick up her own small band. Sliding it into place, Heather focused on the doorway, which cooperated by sliding open. "Interesting. One other thing before we proceed," Heather continued. "Did anyone else see imagery of the ship crashing?"

"Sure did," said Mark, as Jennifer nodded in agreement.

"Maybe the computer automatically gives a dump of the last entries in the ship's log whenever it detects a new user," Jennifer ventured.

"Hard to say," said Heather.

Mark headed toward the door. "Doesn't matter. Let's take a look around."

Heather would rather have taken a bit of time to analyze the amazing amount of information that had already presented itself before going further. Certainly the computer link theory cried out for investigation. Still, Jennifer had already been inside the next room and Mark was not about to be slowed down, so her theoretical musings would have to wait.

While not as spacious as the room below, this one bled beauty. It reminded Heather of the museum of modern art at the Smithsonian in Washington, DC. Abstract table shapes, as though blown from a glassblower's pipe, grew from the floor, still pulsing with the colors of the melting flame.

Several of the tall, slender shapes pulsed in rhythm with their own heartbeats, each alive with cascading colors.

Heather touched one of the structures rising from a single pedestal, the feel as soft and smooth as baby oil. As the pressure of her hand increased, the material molded itself to match the shape. No doubt if she lay atop the thing, it would cradle her body in complete comfort.

"What do you think? Medical lab?" she asked.

Jennifer paused in her examination of one of the delicately curved, lamp-like objects. "Some of these are definitely responding to our body readings, but who knows? I tried to focus a question about this thing, but all I get is a sequence of the strange symbols, some warbling sounds, and imagery of the light patterns shifting. I don't have enough information to make any sense out of it."

Mark walked over to a doorway into the wall opposite of that where they had entered. Standing before it, he concentrated for several moments. Nothing happened.

"Hmm. Hey, Heather. See if you can get this one to open."

Heather moved up beside him and pictured the doorway open. A sequence of three-dimensional symbols floated across her vision, so real that she actually reached out to touch one of the iridescent shapes, her hand passing through the space where it appeared without feeling anything. The door remained closed.

"That's odd."

Jennifer joined them, having no more success than either of them had enjoyed. "There must be some security code that allows access to this area."

Mark shrugged. "Or it's broken. Either way it doesn't look like we're getting in there today."

Heather's head shot up. Today. What time was it anyway? The question brought a cascade of symbolic imagery into her head until she reached up and pulled off the headset.

"Mark. What time do you have?"

Mark glanced down at his sports watch. "Two thirty-eight."

Heather began striding toward the exit. "Oh my God. I promised Mom I'd be home by three. I'm already late."

Jennifer and Mark both followed her, returning their headsets to where they had found them.

Together they made their way out of the ship, retrieved the small model plane, including the small piece broken off the right wing, and passed out through the holographic veil that hid the cave entrance. Then, blazing a trail back through the thorn brush, they made their way up the ridge to where they had left their bikes.

By the time they repacked their equipment and completed the ride back to their houses, four o'clock had come and gone. Agreeing among themselves not to divulge any of what they had discovered that day, at least until they had taken time to discuss all possible consequences, they parted.

Heather opened her garage, lifting her bike to the twin hooks hanging from the ceiling. Then, after a brief pause to collect her thoughts, she stepped through the door. She had reason to fret. Just inside the foyer stood her mother, arms crossed, eyebrows arched, awaiting an explanation better than she expected to receive.

"Mom, I'm so sorry. We were flying Mark's new model airplane out on the mesa when a wind gust crashed it into the canyon. By the time we found it I was already late. I rushed back as fast as I could."

Her mother's expression showed this explanation was about what she had anticipated, something less than satisfactory.

"Heather, I know how important time with your friends is, but family time is important, too. We agreed on three o'clock so we could meet your father for an afternoon matinee before dinner. Since he has to work tomorrow, he took off early to meet us. Do you think it's fair to make him wait like that?"

Heather's head dropped. "No, Mom. I'm sorry."

Her mother sighed, then draped an arm around Heather's shoulder, making her feel even worse. "I know you are. Let me call Dad and tell him you've shown up. Maybe we can make the five o'clock showing."

"Mom, before we go, have you got any aspirin?"

"Sure. What's the matter? Did you hurt yourself?" She raked her eyes over Heather's frame with sudden intensity.

"No, it's nothing like that. I just have a bit of a headache that I'd like to get rid of before the movie starts."

"You probably haven't been drinking enough water today. Grab a bottle from the refrigerator and meet me in the car. I have some aspirin in my purse."

Despite the water and the aspirin, Heather's headache intensified throughout the movie and dinner, although she was unwilling to mention it again lest she spoil what was left of her parents' day. After dinner, Heather stumbled to her room, crawling into her bed still fully clothed.

With pain hammering at her skull, she drifted off to a dreamland where alien species fought across the galaxy, world after world succumbing to harsh masters. And while her dreams identified no single alien race, each planetary war was preceded by a common event: the arrival of a lone cigar-shaped ship.

CHAPTER 8

Heather, who had not missed a sunrise in ages, morning person extraordinaire, squinted through eyes that felt like someone had painted them closed with nail polish during the night. 10:13 a.m. The glowing digital numerals on her alarm clock winked at her, replacing the thirteen with fourteen. She moaned, rolled over, then with an effort worthy of Supergirl, swung her legs off her bed and sat up.

Unlike some classmates, she had never raided her parents' wine rack, but she was now certain what a hangover might feel like. Even so, the sleep had helped, and although her head still throbbed, it felt better than last night. Right now, all she wanted was to stand under a nice, hot shower and let the pulsating massaging showerhead pummel her neck and head until the hot water exhausted itself.

Heather smacked her lips. Gag. If her breath smelled as foul as the inside of her mouth tasted, it was a case for the Centers for Disease Control. Looking down, she noticed she still wore yesterday's clothes. Her blouse looked as if she had wadded it into a ball and then steam ironed it that way. Jesus, she must have been out of it last night.

Heather changed into her warm bathrobe and shuffled down the hall to the bathroom. By the time she emerged, hair wrapped in a towel, she felt like a new person.

"For heaven's sake, the dead has arisen." Her father grinned at her from the end of the hallway.

"Morning, Dad," she said. "I guess all that hiking after Mark's plane yesterday must have done me in."

"I guess so. I was going to wake you for breakfast an hour ago, but your mother wouldn't let me."

Heather laughed. She could just picture her petite mother setting her little foot down on an issue like that, not that her father would do anything that would displease his wife if he could help it. From the way he touched her whenever he passed near her, it was readily apparent that he adored her. And she adored him right back. Heather only hoped that someday she found a relationship like her mom and dad's.

"Don't worry, Dad. I'll just grab a bowl of cereal when I get downstairs."

"Nothing doing. I have some batter set aside, and I just need to fire up the griddle for the bacon. It'll be ready in ten minutes."

"Sounds great."

By the time Heather dressed and made her way downstairs and into the kitchen, everything was ready, the smell of the bacon making her mouth water.

Her mother joined them at the breakfast table, though she just sipped coffee and shared in the conversation. Heather was relieved that they focused on why her dad was so busy at the lab this last week. Although he couldn't talk specifics due to government security, he was quite excited that the first of the Rho Project technologies would soon be released to the public.

This topic led inevitably to the growing problem of the demonstrators and curiosity seekers now crowding Los Alamos and White Rock. Fortunately, White Rock held much less appeal to these crowds than did Los Alamos.

Heather had grown accustomed to the secrecy surrounding the home of the nation's principal nuclear weapons design facility. It amazed her that people thought they could just use their computers to Google the place for a nice satellite view. In most places you could zoom in and take a close-up look at the houses. But not here, at least not at the highest zoom level. While you could see the countryside from a high-altitude view, zooming in on the Los Alamos area either showed very fuzzy imagery or pictures that were stamped with the message: "We are sorry, but we don't have imagery at this zoom level for this region. Try zooming out for a broader look."

The conspiracy fanatics were already going nuts trying to get information that went beyond the official government line, something that was leading to rampant speculation about imagined nefarious Rho Project schemes. Thinking back on yesterday, Heather wondered if some of that speculation might be on the mark.

Heather leaned back from the table. "Thanks for the great breakfast, Dad. I'm going to go next door for a while."

"Remember you have that history assignment due Monday," her mother called out. "Don't put it off too long."

"I won't, Mom."

Before she could reach up to knock on the Smythes' front door, Mark stepped out to greet her.

"Come on in. Dad took Mom down to Santa Fe for the day. We got out of it by using the homework excuse."

"The history report?"

"Exactly."

In contrast to the comfortable country style of the McFarland house, the Smythe living room was decorated in an eclectic collection of artifacts ranging from Tahitian war masks to towering fluorescent lights that looked something like spaceships on poles. The Nuevo Flea Market look, as Mrs. Smythe called it, was the result of her irresistible urge to experience every antique shop, flea market, and auction in the Southwest.

Heather plopped down onto the hacienda-style sofa next to Jennifer while Mark settled into his father's leather recliner. "Tell me you guys didn't have the same dreams I did last night," she said.

Mark and Jennifer glanced nervously at each other. "My guess is that we did. At least, Jen and I had almost the same one."

"You mean you saw ships similar to the *Rho Ship* landing on planet after planet and then all hell breaking loose?"

Jennifer raised her left eyebrow. "It was always a single cigar ship landing followed by scenes of massive destruction, wars raging everywhere. It must have been part of the data dump we got from our ship."

Unable to sit still, Heather rose from the couch and began pacing back and forth across the living room. "And how are you guys feeling?"

"Both of us had bad headaches last night, though they seem to be fading this morning," said Jennifer. "It's a good thing, too. I wouldn't want to think about starting that history report feeling like I did last night."

Mark shook his head. "Forget about the damn history assignment for now. We need to figure out what to do about the ship."

"I've been thinking about that," said Heather. "The sensible thing would be to tell our parents and the authorities about what we found."

"Are you nuts?" Mark jumped out of his chair. "Or am I the only one who remembers the images from the dreams and the ship? If we turn that ship over, it will probably go to the same division that has the *Rho Ship*. I have a strong feeling that wouldn't be good."

Jennifer nodded. "I agree. That would be a very dangerous thing to do, at least if we assume that our ship was trying to send out a warning about the *Rho Ship*."

Heather shrugged. "I only said it would be the sensible thing to do. We all seem to agree the *Rho Ship* is dangerous. But we might be wrong about that. Just because we picked up a bunch of troubling images doesn't make it a fact. Concealing our ship could be a huge mistake."

"OK, it's risky," said Mark. "But let's look at our options. If we report it, we'll never get to see the ship again. I don't like that idea, even if we're wrong about the other thing."

"I don't think we should report it either," said Jennifer. "What's the rush?"

Heather hesitated, looked into Mark's eyes and forced her rising disquiet back below the surface. "That's the same conclusion I talked myself into before I came over here. I just needed to hear what you guys had to say. If we're wrong, we can always report the ship later."

Mark grinned. "OK. We don't tell anyone else, especially our moms and dads. We'll also have to be careful that nobody follows us out to the ship."

Heather and Jennifer nodded. They wouldn't have time to return to the ship until next Saturday, anyway. In the meantime, they would have to be careful not to talk about it unless they were alone. No phone chats, e-mail, or texting.

As the morning slipped into afternoon and the afternoon waned toward evening, they huddled together, discussing in detail their experiences on the ship and what might happen if their fears about the *Rho Ship* were correct.

Unfortunately, all they could do was hope that the Rho Project research team had effective safeguards in place. Certainly, the security would be the US government's best. Based upon the secrecy the Rho Project had maintained for decades, they had things firmly under control.

Mark reached over and flipped on the light beside the recliner, setting one of the disk-shaped fluorescent lamps aglow.

"Well, if that quote in the paper from Senator Connally is any indication, the Senate Intelligence Committee has carefully reviewed the program and found no problem with the way things are run."

Jennifer turned to look at him. "What quote?"

"Oh, it's just something I saw on page four while flipping to the sports page."

Jennifer grabbed the paper off the coffee table, flipping it open to page four. "Which article?"

"Third column, twenty-third line down. The quote starts out, 'Today I am pleased to report that an internal audit of the program, conducted by Dr. Nancy Anatole, has revealed that all proper safeguards are in place to ensure that no potentially dangerous technologies will be released.' "

Jennifer's jaw dropped. "You quoted that word for word." Glancing back at the page, she said, "You got the column and line number right, too. How did you do that?"

Mark's brow creased in concentration. "Hmm. Interesting. I didn't notice it until just now, but I can see every page as if they were here in front of me. The image is in my mind."

A sudden thought crystallized in Heather's brain. "Jennifer, hand me that paper for a second."

Heather flipped through the pages, taking a quick glance at each one, even the advertisements. Then she handed it back to Jennifer.

"I want you to do what I just did, take a quick glance at each page. Don't read it, just flip through."

Jennifer did as instructed then set the paper aside, already in tune with the forthcoming experiment. "Page three, second column, fifth line down. What does it say?"

"Campus eatery touting benefits," said Heather. "Now your turn. Page thirty-six, classifieds. What is the last entry, lower right corner?"

"Comfortable three-bedroom, two bath, eighteen hundred-and-fifty-square-foot ranch home, two hundred and fifty thousand, owner financing available."

Mark pumped his fist in the air. "Yes. I can see it in my mind and read it later. You know what this means? Tests just got a hell of a lot easier."

"It may not last," Jennifer said. "This could be a short-term side effect of the download from the ship's computer."

Heather paused as she considered the implications. "I think it's more than that. Just like a phased-array radar can direct a beam by synchronizing radar emissions, it's possible for the neurons in our brains to function in a more synchronized way. I think the reason the headbands hurt us so badly was because the computer was scanning all our neural pathways and accessing them, even neural centers we don't normally use. I think that may have left those neural pathways synced, even after we de-linked from the ship's computer. One of the side effects seems to be a true photographic memory."

"All right!" Mark shouted.

Heather thought Mark was perhaps a little too happy, almost as if he didn't want to think about what it all meant.

A worried look settled on Jennifer's face. "You don't think it did anything to our DNA, do you?"

"Not likely. Not with how we linked with the ship. There weren't any bodily fluids exchanged."

"Now there's a moderately disgusting thought," Mark said.

Heather ignored the interruption. "As for other side effects, I don't have a clue. I guess we'll just have to wait and see."

Glancing at the gathering darkness outside the windows, Heather rose to go. "Since we can't tell anyone else about this, we're just going to have to protect each other, even more than normal."

"And hope we don't wake up with a third eye," Mark called after her as she stepped out the door.

Heather's laugh sounded hollow in her own ears. Mark's comment, light and funny as it was, bore the weight of Jacob Marley's ghostly chains.

CHAPTER 9

Los Alamos High School had endured disastrous starts by students before, but Heather doubted it had seen a worse start to junior year.

True, they had been a bit distracted, unable to resist whispering among themselves. And that forced several teachers to split them up, seating them as far apart as possible. Worse, it seemed that the teachers talked to each other over lunch, forming a cabal that zeroed in on Heather and the twins like homeland security.

Then Mark failed his first science test in record fashion, having ignored Jennifer's admonitions that he study.

"Why?" Mark had said, tapping his head. "I scanned the book. Got every page, right up here."

It had only been during the test that he realized that having the textbook scanned into his brain was no substitute for reading it. Although he'd been able to read through its pages during the test, he ran out of time with only a third of the problems finished.

Game over. Grounded for a week. As a result, the three had to postpone their planned trip out to the ship on Saturday.

And now this. The three of them sitting in Principal Zumwalt's office as Ms. Gorsky leaned her large form against the principal's desk, banging a chubby finger on their test papers so vigorously that the vibrations threatened to send the pencil jar over the edge.

Ms. Gorsky's beady eyes swept angrily back over Heather and the twins.

"Cheats! That is what they are, and I, for one, want you to make an example of them. To start out the first test of the year in my class by cheating indicates a lack of character all too common in their generation. If it had only been the two girls, I may not have caught it, but when I noticed that Marcus had also quoted a paragraph from the history text exactly the same as the girls did, there could be no doubt. They were copying."

The principal, a big man with kindly features who embraced his thinning hair by shaving his head, leaned forward, motioning for Ms. Gorsky to move out of his line of sight to the juniors.

"Marcus. Is that true?"

Mark's face flushed a bright red. "No, sir, it is not."

"Then how do you explain the exact quote on one of the essay questions, a quote which appears to be several sentences long?"

Mark cleared his throat. "We studied together. I got grounded for doing poorly on my science test last week. I spent a lot of time with Jennifer and Heather studying to do well on this test. We memorized a good portion of the text."

"Ridiculous." Ms. Gorsky stomped her foot to emphasize the point, an act that reminded Heather of the dancing elephant on the GE commercial. "The wording is exactly the same. Nobody memorizes the text. They copied from each other."

"Sir," Heather said, "even if we wanted to copy, it's just not possible. Ms. Gorsky has us sitting across the room from each other. There's no way that Mark could see either one of our papers, or vice versa."

"Is that correct, Ms. Gorsky?" Principal Zumwalt asked.

The rotund history teacher scowled at her students before turning back toward the principal. "Yes, but that only means they came up with some sort of signaling scheme to pull it off."

Principal Zumwalt interlocked his fingers under his chin. "So, you're saying they tapped out the paragraph in Morse code?"

Where Mark's face had been bright red, Ms. Gorsky's turned purple. "Yes. Maybe not that way, but they passed the information somehow."

"But you didn't actually hear any tapping or see them passing a note or anything of the kind?"

"No, I didn't. But I didn't have to. Look at the paragraphs I circled with my red marker. If they all memorized that so well that they can quote it word for word, then I am an idiot." Ms. Gorsky glared at the principal, as if daring him to accuse her of being wrong.

Principal Zumwalt paused for several seconds, then turned toward Mark. "Young man, would you mind telling me the quote you used from your text in response to question number three?"

A look of hope dawned on Mark's face. " 'Whereas Longstreet was consumed with a growing dread at the thought of an attack up that long gradual slope, an attack which reminded him of the slaughter his own men had inflicted upon the forces of the north at Fredericksburg, Pickett was overcome with enthusiasm. Feeling that his unit had been unfairly kept from achieving their share of the glory in the previous two days of battle, General Pickett demanded that he be allowed to lead the charge on the morning hence, a charge that would eternally bear his name.' "

As Mark spoke, Principal Zumwalt's eyes followed along the paragraph circled in red. Raising an eyebrow, he turned back to Ms. Gorsky.

"Well, Harriet, unless you have some additional evidence, I have to conclude that these young people did, in fact, memorize that section of text from the book. Although it is unusual that they all used the same quote, this appears to be a case of a zealous study group, not a case of cheating."

Ms. Gorsky's mouth opened and then shut with an audible snap. Grabbing the papers from the principal's desk, she stormed from the office, glaring down at the three companions as she opened the door. "Don't believe for a second that I won't have my eye on you, all of you. You don't fool me. Watch yourselves."

With that, the large woman swept from the office, not bothering to close the door behind her.

The principal waved his hand at them. "You are all free to go."

Heather grabbed her backpack, leading the others out into the empty hallway and then through the broad double doors onto the entrance walkway, her head still spinning from the encounter. This wasn't really the way she had wanted to make a name for herself as a junior in high school.

"Great. We missed our bus," Mark exclaimed, throwing his hands into the air. "Can this week get any better?"

"I'll call Mom to come and pick us up," Heather said. "I'm not really looking forward to explaining why."

Jennifer sat down on the step. "No kidding."

Heather made the call, then flipped her cell phone closed before stowing it back in her bag. "She's on her way."

"You think Mom and Dad will buy what we told Principal Zumwalt?" Mark asked.

"It's the truth," said Jennifer.

"Yeah, but they know me," said Mark.

Heather patted his back. "They also know how much we've all been studying together since you got grounded. They'll believe us."

"Well, I'll tell you one thing. If we keep screwing up like this, it is only a matter of time until someone finds out about our ship."

Jennifer sighed. "We're just going to have to act more normally."

"Yeah," said Mark. "If anyone can remember what that's like. Oh, speaking of acting normal, has anyone else noticed any coordination issues?"

"Like what?" asked Heather.

Mark took three coins from his pocket, placing them on the back of his right hand. As he wiggled his fingers, the coins began rolling end over end between his knuckles like a magician might do. As they watched, he flipped one over the other, hopping them up and down so that the coins spun between each other on the backs of his fingers.

"Like this."

Jennifer gasped. "When did you learn to do that?"

"I was messing around in study hall today."

"Well, stop it before someone sees you! Christ, you're creeping me out."

Mark flipped the coins in the air, snagging them in his fist and putting them back in his pocket. "I figured it must be more of that neural enhancement we got."

Heather nodded. "Odd that I haven't picked up the same benefit. What about you, Jen?"

"Are you kidding me? I tripped over my front step this morning and almost fell in the rose bushes. If Mark hadn't caught me, I'd still be picking out thorns."

Heather pursed her lips. "Hmm. All of us had our memory enhanced, but either some of the effects kick in more slowly for us or perhaps it's some individually dependent behavior. After all, our minds are all unique. That might account for it."

"That would make some sense," said Jennifer. "Learning to use some skills may take a while."

"Or maybe we are each more naturally adapted to certain things," said Heather. "I guess only time will tell."

The conversation came to a close as Heather's mom pulled up in her red station wagon, the Grunge Buggy, as Heather called it. Heather slid into the backseat beside the twins. The good news about the ride home was that Heather's mom bought their story. The bad news was they were going to have to repeat it for each parent, something that could lead to questions where uncomfortable half-truths would be the best they could give.

As they rounded a bend, her mother screamed and slammed on the brakes, throwing them hard against their shoulder harnesses as the sedan fishtailed. The car slid to a stop barely two feet from a pedestrian who stood calmly in the center of Pajarito Road, the main road between Los Alamos and White Rock.

The man was tall and thin, his greasy blond hair hanging down below his shoulders, his eyes so deeply set that the shadowed sockets looked empty. Clutched in his right hand, a crudely lettered sign screamed at the world.

BEG HIS FORGIVENESS. THE END OF ALL THINGS IS AT HAND!

As the strange man moved closer, Mrs. McFarland activated the door locks with an audible thunk. The man grinned, his mouth a horror of stained, misaligned teeth. As he reached for the door, Heather's mom hit the gas, accelerating past him down the highway toward home.

Glancing back, Heather saw the ragged man standing in the center of the road still staring after them, the mad grin fixed upon his face as if it had been painted there. The feeling that he was still there grinning at her persisted long after he had disappeared around the bend.

CHAPTER 10

Since 1970, when President Nixon had presented the White House with an oval mahogany conference table, its massive surface had filled the cabinet room in the West Wing. This table had been the platform for countless meetings of the highest-ranking executives of the United States government.

Vice President George Gordon leaned back in his leather chair, trying to maintain his trademark calm, businesslike exterior. Directly across the table from him, President Harris leaned forward in his taller chair, elbows on the mahogany of the table, the corners of his mouth tugged downward by a slowly emerging scowl. The secretary of defense also leaned forward, looking ready to blow a gasket that would send steam spurting from every bodily orifice.

"Mr. President. As you recall, I counseled against the announcement of the *Rho Ship*'s existence, advice that recent events have shown to be very sound. But what is done, is done. We can't undo that. We can, however, retract your promise to publicly release the *Rho Ship*'s technologies. We can still stop this madness."

Peering over cupped fists, Vice President Gordon stared at the president. Many people who did not know the man regarded President Harris as something of a stubborn dunce, a self-absorbed man, ill suited to the mantle of leadership placed upon him. But over his long political career, the president had left a broad trail of political corpses—those who had underestimated his intellect and his ability to make a decision and see it through.

Someone once described the president as the one the family would send out to shoot Old Yeller. Gordon could no longer look at the man without that caricature springing to mind. President Harris was a man of conscience who, right or wrong, fulfilled his perceived duty, then left his staff to sort out how to spin the situation for political advantage.

The president's bulldog gaze now affixed itself to his defense secretary. "Bob, we have already discussed this. If you don't have anything new to add, then you are done."

"I do have something. The secretary of energy proposes we release the cold fusion technology, that we provide a detailed publication describing the steps that make the process efficient and repeatable. While I understand the importance of the technology, must I remind everyone of the more than handful of incidents where scientists overseas have been kidnapped or killed for reasons that seem related to this technology? I say it looks more like someone already wants the competing methodology kept private."

Porter Boles, the secretary of energy, interrupted. "Hogwash. Nobody else is close on cold fusion. There are a few guys out there tinkering with aquariums in labs, producing a little more heat than what is put in. Using current techniques, the nuclear interaction probabilities are too small for significant nuclear fusion."

When no one said anything Porter Boles continued. "What we have at the Rho Division at Los Alamos is completely unique, a procedure that enables commercially viable cold fusion production. It has the potential to get us off of fossil fuels within five years."

The secretary of defense rose to his feet.

"And that doesn't scare the shit out of you? You may be right. This may truly be a wonderful thing for our country. But I say we can afford to take our sweet time analyzing all ramifications before jumping into bed with this thing.

"What are the weaponization possibilities? Will oil futures collapse, causing mass shortages before the other energy can come online? And what about our big OPEC buddies? Are they just going to sit idly by waiting for their world to be replaced, or panic and lash out? This little Kyoto-friendly project of yours could spiral into a world war."

The lines in the president's forehead deepened. "Sit down, Robert. These are tired subjects. The energy and defense departments have had access to the *Rho Ship* for decades. I will not keep this thing bottled up to appease the parochial fears of the defense department, the net effect of which would limit mankind's advancement."

But Robert Caine did not sit down. Instead he leaned forward, scribbling a single sentence on a yellow pad before him. Gordon had a good idea what it was. Indeed, he'd watched the secretary push closer and closer to this with each passing week.

Pushing the pad over in front of the president, he said, "Mr. President, I cannot, in good conscience, continue serving an administration that would share critical national technologies with the world at large. You believe your job, as president, is to make the world a better place. I believe your sole responsibility is securing the future of the American people. Please consider this my formal resignation." With that, Robert Caine turned and strode from the room.

Absolute silence settled over those assembled in the cabinet room as all eyes watched the president. After several seconds, he turned toward his chief of staff.

"Andy, I want that list of potential replacements for sec. def. on my desk by six. Get the vetting process rolling. Get the press secretary briefed right away because there is going to be a firestorm she will need to handle very shortly."

"Yes, Mr. President." The chief stood and departed through the doorway into the office of the president's secretary.

Turning back toward the energy secretary, President Harris removed his reading glasses. "Porter, the ball is in your court. Get that publication finalized if it isn't already. I'll make the announcement from the Oval Office in the morning. Gentlemen, get ready. Tomorrow we will let the world know that a brand new future, independent of fossil fuels, is at hand."

All members of the cabinet stood as the president of the United States left the room, and then they filed out behind him. Vice President George Gordon waited several moments, carefully returning his Montblanc pen to his daily planner. He looked around the empty room where once again history had been made, a thin, tight smile on his lips as he rubbed the soft leather on the back of his chair.

CHAPTER 11

Even though Heather didn't usually follow the news that closely, it was hard to avoid for the next few days—and the more the news media went into a feeding frenzy, the more she worried about their discovery of the second ship. First there had been the shocking resignation of the secretary of defense, followed almost immediately by the president's announcement that the first of the alien technologies to be publicly released was cold fusion.

Then the scientific papers on the production of controllable cold fusion were published, sending every scientific laboratory in the world scrambling to independently reproduce the results. Confirmation had come flooding in, numerous universities announcing the results almost simultaneously, while major companies scrambled to commercialize the applications.

As if that weren't enough, the stock market stumbled into another Black Monday decline with two days of record sell-off.

That then reversed when several energy companies appeared able to adapt parts of their infrastructure to support some of the anticipated automobile technologies.

Outcries from oil-producing countries were largely ignored by industrialized countries, including emerging economies like China and India. Clearly the perceived benefits of the release were winning widespread support around the globe.

But even within the United States, opposition arose. A large contingent of congressmen from both parties, along with commentators from assorted think tanks, complained the information was released too quickly, without fully scrutinizing national security implications. Still, these voices were drowned out by the enthusiasm of the world's academic communities.

Finally, it got so overwhelming, Heather switched off the news one evening and pulled her blankets up under her chin, peering out the dark window beside her bed. The wind was up, and a thin branch of a pine tapped softly against the pane. The image of the ragged homeless man with the sign from the week before slipped across her mind. A call to the sheriff had brought a visit by two deputies, but there had been no further sign of the man. From Heather's perspective, that was a good thing.

Sleep claimed her, pulling her into troubled dreams in which she needed desperately to do something unattainable, something that, try as she might, she could not recall. From far away her mother called to her, a note of desperation in her voice.

"Heather. Are you hearing me? I need you."

Heather's eyes popped open. "Heather! I need you up and ready or we'll be late for the picnic. Get a move on." Her mother's face appeared at her door. "Are you hearing me? I've been calling for five minutes."

Clearing her throat, Heather sat up. "I hear you, Mom. Give me just a minute."

"OK, but make it snappy. The Smythes have to be there early to set up the grill and we're carpooling. You know how the deputy director likes to make the rounds at these events, just to show the non-Nobel laureates that he really cares. You've got twenty-five minutes." She glanced at her watch. "Make that twenty-four."

"All right, Mom. I don't really think a countdown will help."

Heather stumbled groggily to the shower, letting the hot water and steam bring her back to life. What was up with her sleep pattern? Ever since they had found the ship, she couldn't seem to get enough sleep. And the stress of her unremembered dreams was sapping her energy.

Despite hurrying, by the time Heather reached the bottom of the stairs the horn on the Smythemobile blared impatiently. Locking the front door behind her, Heather slid into the van's backseat beside Jennifer and Mark.

Mark grinned at her knowingly.

"You ready to flip some burgers and dogs?"

"Hmph."

With the arrival of the Smythemobile at the Los Alamos City Park, their parents put the teens to work setting up the grill, hauling bags of charcoal, and performing other picnic preparation tasks. All around them, the smells of the giant potluck circuit wafted over. Despite their urge to wander among the offerings, their mandate was clear. They would hold down their assigned positions at the grill or at the condiment table until the lunch crowd died out.

The crowd continued to fill the park, and soon the sky at the eastern end was filled with an assortment of competing kites. Scores of kids and adults held everything from basic diamonds with knotted cloth tails to massive multibox contraptions, carefully controlled by professionally engineered handles on twin cables. A minor scuffle broke out between parents as one of the fancier kites became entangled with a looping Black Hawk Kite.

As lunch wound down and the friends prepared to abandon their grill duties, the deputy director, Dr. Donald Stephenson himself, stopped by, purportedly to sample the finest hamburgers at the festivities.

Shoving past his security detail, Dr. Stephenson stepped up to the grill, open-faced bun already decked out with tomato, onion, and lettuce; he paused, his hawklike gaze sweeping the adjacent table. "Any more mustard?"

Jennifer moved toward the condiment box tucked behind the table. "I'm sorry, sir. Let me get it for you."

As she stepped forward and bent down to grab the bottle, she tripped, plunging face-first toward the hot grill.

Mark moved so quickly to help his sister that the startled deputy director had no time to get out of his way, a glancing blow sending the startled scientist staggering away. Grabbing his falling sister's waist, Mark's powerful arms tossed her over the top of the grill, sending her tumbling to the grass on the far side.

Hearing the crash, Heather turned with the long hot dog fork still in her hand, the twin tines burying themselves in the flesh of the spinning Dr. Stephenson's upper arm. The deputy director doubled over, cursing as he staggered away. Heather froze, watching the blood drip from the tongs of the fork in her hand, as two large members of the dark-clad security detail grabbed her from each side.

Stunned, unable to move, Heather could only watch as Mr. Smythe was the first to reach the deputy director's side, Dr. Stephenson's bodyguard close behind.

"Sir, are you all right? Here, let me take a look at that."

With a violent thrust of his hand, Dr. Stephenson shoved the startled technician away as the bodyguard came between them.

"I'm fine. I don't need your assistance. Thank heavens those tongs missed me. See? Not even scratched." He pulled up the short sleeve of his shirt to reveal an undamaged arm.

Moving quickly back toward the grill, Dr. Stephenson angrily snatched the fork from Heather's nerveless fingers.

"If you kids can't safely operate this station, then you shouldn't be near it. Get away from it now," he bellowed. "Try something your small brains can handle. And stay away from me."

Without waiting for a response, the deputy director, accompanied by his bodyguards, stormed off, the hot dog fork still clutched tightly in his hand, as the Smythes and McFarlands gaped after him.

"Dad, I'm so sorry," Heather sobbed.

Her father moved over and hugged her. "It's all right. You didn't hurt the mean old bastard. The fork missed him."

"It wasn't your fault, anyway," Jennifer said, her face burning a bright red. "What a jerk."

Mr. Smythe nodded. "Too bad you missed him."

Heather wiped at her eyes with the back of her hand, giving her best effort at a grin. "It's OK. I didn't mean to lose it like that."

Mrs. Smythe patted her arm. "Anyone would have, dear. Come on, gang, the burger and hot dog station is now closed. Let's go check out some of the other food."

As they worked their way around the food circuit, Mark walked between Jennifer and Heather, his arms circling their shoulders.

"When we get a chance, we need to talk," Mark whispered. "No matter what the good doctor said, I saw that fork go knuckle deep in his arm. I saw the blood. I can play it back in my mind. I don't know how he did it, but he was sure as hell hurt. And he made damned sure he got that fork away from you before he stormed off. Three guesses as to how long it took him to wipe it clean."

Heather stopped, shock prickling her scalp. She, too, had seen the prongs stab him. Even worse, she had felt the resistance as they had penetrated the skin and muscle.

As their parents moved on toward the homemade brownie station, the three companions stood close together, gazing off to where the deputy director had disappeared. And as they looked, a sudden chill settled over them.

CHAPTER 12

Heather smiled, hardly able to contain her excitement. Today they'd finally get back out to their starship. In a way the charge of cheating on the test had been good—it had scared them, made them more cautious.

Now they were going to have to name their discovery. Referring to it as "our starship" didn't seem either appropriate or palatable to her. The *Rho Ship* was already taken. The *Los Alamos Ship*? The *White Rock Saucer*? If they left it up to Mark, it would be the *Bandelier Bagel* or the *Taos Taco* or some other god-awful name. Oh well, it would come to her.

By the time Heather had dressed in jeans, tennis shoes, and an old pullover sweatshirt and lifted her bike from its hooks in the garage, the Smythe twins were waiting in the driveway. The hour-and-a-half ride out of White Rock and then along the rough mountain bike trail to The Mesa left her exhilarated, the excitement rising as they got closer to the spot where they would hide their bikes and proceed on foot.

After the picnic escapade, the three friends had decided that telling anyone else about their ship would be foolhardy. It would probably lead to the ship being turned over to the loving mercies of Dr. Donald "Miracle Healer" Stephenson. Considering what they had seen using the headsets and Stephenson's decadeslong hold on the Rho research, that seemed like something to avoid at all costs.

Caution seemed warranted. She didn't really want to think about the implications of his ability to heal so quickly. It was too much to process at once, the second spaceship and that strange moment at the picnic, even though she knew it might all be related.

With a shroud of concern draping them, they proceeded carefully, checking over their shoulders as they rode through the backcountry. At the edge of The Mesa, they stopped to watch and listen. With the pungent scent of pine strong in the clear mountain air, the silence of the wilderness was undisturbed. Even the soughing of the wind that normally swept the high canyon country was missing.

After securing their bikes in thick brush, high on the slope, Heather, Mark, and Jennifer worked their way to where the hologram hid the cave entrance. Just outside of the cave, they paused, taking time to experiment with the illusion. Heather stepped forward until it looked like half her body was gone.

Mark laughed. "It's a good thing that's more comfortable than it looks."

She ducked inside, followed by Mark and Jennifer. Although the sun should have been visible from the entrance, no direct light passed into the cave. They could see out, but only dimly, and they had to allow a couple of minutes for their eyes to adjust to the familiar magenta glow.

With little time to waste, they moved quickly across the cavern and climbed up into the ship. Reaching the small room on the second level, each of the three took a deep breath. Then, once again, they placed the flexible bands on their heads.

This time Heather paid close attention, wanting to see if she had imagined the band changing shape when she put it on. She hadn't. As the marvelously light material settled into place, it adjusted itself to the shape of her head, lengthening so that the bead on each end settled over her temple.

The sensation of mild vibration felt wonderful, like a gentle, professional massage. Relaxation rippled through Heather's body until she could feel the cool air and her cotton clothes against her skin.

This time there was no automatic dump of imagery, just the heightened awareness and relaxation. It was as if the computers of the ship recognized her. Heather glanced over at Mark and Jennifer.

Mark nodded at her. "I could get used to this."

Jennifer grinned. "Sorry, Bro. Relaxation time's over. Let's stick to the plan. Maybe we can get some answers out of the computer."

Without further urging, Mark led the way up, scrambling through the hole onto the third deck, then reaching down to lift the two girls.

Bypassing what appeared to be a deck filled with sleeping quarters and a recreation area, they continued upward.

The top deck of the ship was a single large room. Four pedestal-mounted couches seemed to sprout from the floor near its center. Heather found it difficult to judge distance in the room, a side effect of the curvature that made it hard to tell where floor stopped and wall began, an effect magnified by the lighting.

Jennifer spread her arms wide, spinning in a slow circle. "Command deck?"

As if in response to Jennifer's question, the room vanished, leaving Heather and her friends hurtling through the vastness of empty space.

Vertigo assailed Heather as she struggled to breathe, her heart hammering in her chest.

"Wow! This is so cool!" Mark's voice caused her to glance to her left.

There, standing beside her, were Mark and Jennifer, the former grinning broadly while the latter cupped her hand over her mouth as if to conserve oxygen.

Standing! They were standing. So was she, for that matter, but on what? Below her feet, an endless void of stars and galaxies dropped away.

And how were they breathing?

Mark strolled toward four dim shapes floating in the vastness nearby, plopping down atop the nearest of them, sending it spinning in a circle.

Suddenly, understanding dawned on Heather. It was one of the chairs they had just seen. They were still on the ship's command deck, but somehow Jennifer had activated the view screen. The whole deck was one massive view screen with resolution so good that you couldn't tell what you were seeing wasn't real.

Fighting back a wave of nausea, Heather followed Mark, seating herself in the chair to his left while Jennifer sank into another.

Mark held his hands up like he was on a roller coaster ride. "Awesome."

It was only then that Heather realized she was clutching the moldable material of the chair so tightly she had formed imprints of her fingers. With great effort, she forced herself to relax.

"Jen? You all right?" Heather asked.

"I'm getting there," Jennifer replied. "I started breathing again, so that's good."

Mark laughed out loud. "You girls are a riot. We could charge big bucks for this."

Jennifer scowled. "Yeah. Right before they throw us in prison for not reporting this thing."

Heather gazed out, stunned by the beauty of the scene. It appeared to be a recording of space the ship had passed through. The crew probably sat in these very chairs when they needed to observe what was happening outside. Or maybe the entire deck served some other function, as a massive movie theater or computer monitor.

"I wonder."

Without bothering to explain what she was wondering about, Heather suddenly reached up and removed her headset. Although she had no doubt that the others were still seeing vast reaches of interstellar space, to her the room looked exactly as it had originally appeared.

"Very interesting."

CHAPTER 13

For more than two hours they roamed the ship, headsets on and off, taking those first halting steps that babies take to reach their mothers' outstretched arms. And though their access to the central computer remained limited, it felt great to make at least some headway.

As Heather had speculated, the visualizations were triggered, not by the room, but through the headsets, which broadcast imagery and other sensations directly into their brains. Being on the upper deck was not necessary, but the room's design enhanced the experience. The more cluttered the room, the more those distractions intruded upon the imagery.

Also, the chairs on the command deck, or more accurately, individual couches, cushioned the body in such a way that she could not even tell she was sitting in them. It felt almost like she floated weightlessly. This made it easier to focus on the sights, sounds, and feelings the computer delivered.

Most interesting to Heather was that each person had his or her own individual view. While Mark might be experiencing the ship cruising into Earth's solar system, Jennifer might see herself surrounded by strange instruments and symbology, while Heather experienced something completely different.

Getting the computer to respond was still somewhat frustrating. If she managed to create a clear question in her head, then the ship would respond with a combination of imagery, sensations, and symbology. But that only happened if the ship's computer understood what she wanted.

Heather pictured the starship's arrival and the computer responded, correcting her initial thoughts as the events played out all around her. The plunge through the atmosphere in pursuit of the *Rho Ship*, followed by the ground rushing up and smashing into her face, left her gasping for breath, even after playing it back five or six times. It was like floating in a clear soap bubble with scenery flashing by all around you, a somewhat disconcerting feeling when that imagery involved a crash.

As the afternoon waned, Heather confronted more and more roadblocks as she sought to refine her ability to extract information from the computer. The computer presented information when prompted, but most of what she saw took the form of incomprehensible, three-dimensional symbols. She could not decipher the meaning, whether it was the alien language or, more likely, their version of mathematics.

That made sense. Many of the questions she had been asking would have mathematically based answers. Asking something like "What caused the crash?" probably caused the computer to spew out the equations describing the damage.

Although she had grown up in the Los Alamos school system, surrounded by the kids of the world's top scientists, and despite her exceptional record in all her honors math courses, interstellar math had not yet been covered.

Leaning back in the couch, she let her mind relax. *Think, Heather. Think.* She visualized a grid containing the origin of a coordinate system. A perpendicular set of lines labeled "x axis" and "y axis" appeared to float before her.

She drew a single point located right three ticks and up four ticks from the origin on the grid, then followed up with another point, connecting the two with a line. It was there, floating perfectly in the air before her.

Right, she thought. She added another dimension to the grid to form a cube, and into this cube she drew spheres, ellipsoids, cubes, and pyramids.

It was easy. The equations came faster and faster, as if she had fumbled around and found a switch in the dark. A part of her mind turned on, big time.

Adding a fourth dimension was easy. She took her three-dimensional grid cube, shrank it to the size of a pinhead, then formed a line of these cubes. Five dimensions formed from a plane of the 3D grid cubes. Six: a cube made of cubes. Seven dimensions: a line made of the new cube of cubes. On and on the mental sequence spun from her mind. Easy. Oh so easy.

She no longer had to think about the equations that represented the shapes. Merely visualizing the shape brought the corresponding equations to her mind. She didn't have to solve them; she just knew them. It was beautiful beyond her wildest imaginings.

A familiar, small hand shook Heather's shoulder. She sat up, slipping off her headset.

"If we don't leave now, we won't make it home before dark," Jennifer urged.

Heather glanced at her watch. "Wow. Good thing you noticed. I was completely lost in the moment."

"I have some very interesting stuff to tell you guys, but tomorrow," said Jennifer.

Mark shrugged. "Sounds good. My brain is fried."

Heather led the way out. Once again they deposited the headsets where they had found them. Somehow, it just felt like where they belonged.

Pedaling hard to beat the sinking sun, the three teens were silent until they halted outside their houses. Heather waved at her friends as she activated the garage door, sending it rumbling noisily upward on its track. By the time her bike was hanging from its proper hooks, her father had poked his head into the garage, an inquisitive look in his eyes.

"You sure are huffing and puffing. Did you guys race home or something?"

Heather followed her dad into the house. "Not really. We had to hustle to make it back by dark."

"Good girl. Your mom and I were starting to worry. We don't like the idea of you kids out after dark, even if you are worldly juniors."

At some point during dinner, Heather realized just how physically and mentally tired she was. Thank God they had no weekend homework. Now, as she leaned back from her empty plate and the smell of the apple cinnamon tea wafted up to tickle her nostrils, a warm glow spread through her body.

Her mother leaned back in her chair. "What's that smile about?"

"Oh, I was just thinking how nice it is to be a part of a comfortable family. No matter what, I can come home and know that underneath everything, all is well."

Her father laughed. "That's a good thing, although at your age you hardly have the fate of the world resting on your shoulders."

Heather sipped her tea, but the warmth it held just a moment earlier had somehow slipped away.

CHAPTER 14

Heather rolled out of bed, knocking her alarm clock to the floor, its green 1:33 a.m. display shining after her as she ran for the bathroom.

God, just let me die.

She hugged the sides of the commode, hurling her stomach's contents into its porcelain interior with such force it splattered her face. If not for the ongoing bout of vomiting, she would have screamed. As it was, she shook so violently she could hardly stay upright over the toilet bowl.

Her mother's concerned voice preceded a knocking on the bathroom door. "Sweetheart, are you all right?"

"Fine, Mom. I'm just fine." That was what she intended to say, but the words never made it to her lips, as another bout of violent nausea overwhelmed her. The room swam before her: the toilet, the sink, the shower curtain, the tile floor, the ceiling, and then her mother's terrified face looking down at her. And swimming next to it all, an endless stream of numbers and equations.

Then, as her mother cradled her head in her lap, yelling for Gil, Heather's world went black.

"Give me that back, you wascally wabbit."

The sounds that greeted her return to consciousness could not have been more reassuring. Surely Elmer Fudd could not have made it to heaven or hell, so perhaps she was still alive.

The bed didn't feel right. When she tried to move, she found a needle embedded in her left forearm, secured by white tape. Without opening her eyes, she knew that the needle was attached to the end of a long rubber IV tube, into which fluid dripped from a bag dangling from a mobile steel rack.

Moving her right hand across her body, she confirmed that her assumption was correct. She took a deep breath through her nose. Hospital smells.

Heather kept her eyes firmly closed, unwilling to face the possibility that upon opening them she would see, not only the physical things that occupied the room, but also the accompanying equations. The thought of going through her life with that dual view terrified her. Better to be blind than that. Better to be dead.

Savant. The thought came unbidden into her brain. Three months ago the whole family had watched a PBS special on a British man, a high-functioning autistic savant. He had the uncanny ability to answer all sorts of mathematical questions without doing any calculations, at least not in any way most people thought of calculations.

While his abilities were incredible, they left him so distracted and impaired that he had great difficulty performing the day-to-day tasks that give normality to life. Heather did not want to live like that.

From the way someone had stuffed her mouth with cotton and pasted her lips together, she guessed it had been a good while since any liquid had made it over those lips. With effort, she managed to work up enough saliva to wet them with her tongue. God, she was thirsty.

Screwing up her courage, Heather slowly opened her eyes. At first she thought that the equations and numbers were gone. Then, as she thought about it, they materialized again, a set of three-dimensional symbols that swam through her brain, near whatever object she focused on. Heather squeezed her eyes shut tight, trying to calm her hammering heart.

Afraid that the rising panic would overwhelm her, Heather fought it with a tide of anger. Why was she just giving up without a fight? Several years ago, her parents had encouraged her to take the Myers-Briggs personality type test, and the results had been most enlightening. She was a rare bird, an INTP personality, a type that loved theory, problem solving, and scientific work. INTPs were normally risk takers, blissfully uncaring of what others thought of their chances for success.

Whatever the reason for her fear, she wasn't going to allow herself to curl up into a fetal ball and surrender. It was a problem. Problems had solutions. Simple as that.

Clearly this was connected to her breakthrough on the ship. It could be that her initial connection had activated the neural pathways that made such thinking possible and that on her last trip she had merely discovered the trick to turn it on. If so, then it should be possible to turn it off.

She opened her eyes, holding her dread firmly in check and setting her mind to experimentation. As she looked at the bedside lamp, she could clearly visualize the equation describing its three-dimensional shape. She changed her focus, thinking about the lamp's volume, and the symbols in her head morphed to create the equation for volume. Even that small change left her feeling empowered.

Once more, she changed her thoughts—this time to surface area—and again the equations changed. In her mind, she imagined the lamp rotating, and a set of rotation matrices cascaded through her brain.

Encouraged, she again focused upon the lamp. She let herself relax and unquestioningly accepted its physical existence and appearance. The symbols faded. Then, as she was about to congratulate herself, they reappeared.

The effect was very similar to subvocalization, she thought. Like when a person looks at a chair and thinks the sound "chair." Or when a person reads the symbols c-h-a-i-r, but sees a picture of a chair and hears the sound of the word "chair" in her mind. Heather could look at something and know the equation for it in much the same way.

Apparently, quieting her inquisitive mind was going to take some effort and a good bit of practice. But she had managed to do so, even if it had been for just a short time, which relieved her immensely.

Her thoughts were interrupted by the arrival of her mom and dad.

"Heather. Oh, thank God you're awake. Your father and I have been worried sick." Her mother moved to sit on the side of her bed, wiping tears from her cheeks with the back of her hand.

"Good to see you back in the land of the living," her father said, his own eyes glistening with moisture.

"How long have I been here?" Heather asked, her raspy voice reminding her of how thirsty she was. "Dad, could you get me some water?"

Her dad was out the door before she finished asking.

"You've been unconscious for three days," said her mother. "We rushed you here when you passed out. The IV is to rehydrate you. So far they still have no idea what made you sick. At first we thought it was food poisoning, but the tests ruled that out. The doctors' best guess is some sort of allergic reaction, but it's just a guess."

Three whole days?

Heather groaned. And they'd been making such good progress with the ship.

At that moment, her father reappeared with two tiny, cone-shaped water cups in his hands.

He shrugged, causing some of the cold water to spill on Heather's hand as she reached for a cup. "Sorry. It was the best I could do on short notice. I did ask the nurse to get you a tall glass of water, though. She was quite upset that she didn't already have a jug in here."

Heather downed both cupfuls of water, equations coming and going as she lost and regained her concentration. Smiling, she crushed the small cones of paper in one hand and handed them back to her father. "Thanks, Dad. That was so good."

"You're welcome. Glad to see you looking so much better—awake, for one thing. Mark and Jennifer stopped by several times, along with Fred and Linda. They wanted to stay, but we sent them home saying we'd send word once your condition changed."

At that moment the doctor walked in. Heather's mother moved aside as he leaned across the bed. Pulling a small pen-light from his pocket, the doctor promptly began doing his best to blind Heather by holding her eyelids open and shining the bright light in first one eye and then the other.

"Good morning, young lady. I'm Dr. Johanson," he said, pulling out his stethoscope. "You gave us quite a scare."

Heather gasped as Dr. Johanson applied the stethoscope to her chest. Did he store it in the freezer between uses?

"Nice, deep breath. Now, give me another. OK, again. Very good." The doctor grinned and straightened up, revealing a handsome face complete with blue eyes and a shock of unruly blond hair. He looked not a day older than twenty-five, though Heather figured he had to be at least in his thirties.

If she had to have a doctor, Heather thought, it could be worse.

Dr. Johanson pulled the clipboard from the end of her bed and scribbled something down.

"I was going to schedule a CAT scan and an electroencephalogram today, but it looks like that's no longer necessary. I'll have the nurse swing by and get your vitals, and we'll keep you around for another night. Barring something unusual, you'll be home tomorrow."

Heather pushed herself up into a seated position as her mom stacked pillows behind her. "Can't I get out of here tonight? That gives you all day to watch me."

Dr. Johanson smiled. "I don't think one extra night here will hurt you. I like playing things safe."

Her mother patted her hand. "Don't worry, dear. I'll stay with you until they kick me out."

"And I'll pass word to the Smythes," her father said. "After school, I'm sure Mark and Jennifer will camp out here."

After a meal of the hospital's finest cuisine, something vaguely resembling a veal cutlet, Heather slept again.

The remainder of the day passed slowly. In those rare moments when her mother was not beside the bed chatting with her, Heather practiced controlling her visualizations. She found relaxing her mind to be a very tiring activity. Apparently, in its natural state, her mind was full of mathematical questions, which were now being automatically answered. She would have to work to make the natural tendency stop.

Luckily, by the time Mark and Jennifer swept into the room to deliver big hugs, Heather felt like she had better control. The vertigo effect was gone. Unfortunately, with parents and doctors constantly walking in and out of the room, any discussion of the starship was out of the question.

At last, as the twins turned to depart, Mark called over his shoulder, "We'll see you at school tomorrow, right?"

"I'm planning on it," Heather replied.

"Well, plan again," her mother said. "You're staying home for a couple of days. At least until I am satisfied you are fully recovered."

"Mom!"

"That's final."

"Don't worry," Jennifer said. "We'll stop in every chance we get."

"Thanks."

With a wave, the twins disappeared out the door.

As Heather's parents prepared to leave for the night, the gorgeous Dr. Johanson stopped by and removed her IV. Then, after her mom and dad had kissed her good-bye, for the first time in a long while, Heather fell into a comfortable, deep, dreamless sleep.

CHAPTER 15

Carlton "Priest" Williams was having a bad day. The last several weeks had been filled with bad days, which by his definition meant he was bored out of his skull almost the entire time. If it hadn't been for his periodic excursions, he would have been stir-crazy long before now.

That damned Stephenson was driving him crazy. "Lay low. Stay calm. I'll call you when I need you." Stephenson's political agenda might be important to the Rho Project, but this lying low was driving Priest nuts.

Priest stretched his left hand in front of him, spreading his fingers wide on the table, palm down. In a smooth, quick motion, his right hand grabbed the SAF survival knife from its sheath, raised it high, and then brought it violently down. The blade penetrated the back of his hand, pinning it to the table so that the muscles in the hand spasmed involuntarily, the fingers twitching taut before he could force them to relax.

Pain exploded in Priest's head. So exquisite, so wonderful. Not only had the blade penetrated skin and tendon, it seemed to have broken at least one small bone on its way through his hand. The blood, which should have been spurting from the wound, bubbled out around the edge of the blade, the wound closing as he watched.

A sudden yank pulled the knife from both table and hand, momentarily leaving the wide puncture wound gaping in all its ragged glory. As he watched, blood congealed into the hole, tissue and bone knitting and binding, scar tissue expanding to close the wound, then destroying itself as it was replaced by flawless, fresh skin. The whole process took less than a minute, leaving his hand in exactly the same condition as it had been before his masochistic, sharp-trauma infliction.

You had to give the Doc credit. Whatever that gray stuff was that he had pushed through the IV tube into Priest's arm, it was liquid gold. Priest didn't care if it was alien blood, or even alien shit. All he knew was it gave him what he wanted.

But Priest was done with this be a good boy and "lay low" bullshit. It was time for fun. What the Doc didn't know wouldn't hurt him, and Priest was damned sure good enough to ensure that Stephenson would never know. Army Ranger. Green Beret. Airborne. Jungle Expert. Pathfinder.

Priest had been through all the qualifications and served in multiple combat operations during his army time before he'd been selected for Delta Force. The five years in Delta had been the best, especially the work in the backwaters along the Pakistan-Afghanistan border. If it hadn't been for the damned politicians and their squeamishness about the rough stuff, he would still be there.

Bunch of candy-ass pussies. Torture? If he got a chance to work on one of those clowns on the Senate Intelligence Committee, Priest would teach them what torture was all about.

The drive from Los Alamos to the outskirts of Taos took him less than two hours. Slow, to be sure, but Priest was in a slow mood. He wanted to savor the anticipation he felt. Besides, even at this pace he would be in place before five, long before the sun put in an appearance.

Just outside of town, he turned off onto a dirt road that became a park service access road, mainly used by hunters and fire crews. It took him another thirty minutes to get the four-wheel drive Dodge Ram up to the spot he had selected on his previous reconnaissance visits. He parked deep in rough woods with overhead cover that would make it impossible to see the truck from the air. Not that there was much air traffic around anyway, but Priest believed in being thorough.

Stepping out of the truck into the chill predawn air, Priest pulled on a charcoal gray sweat suit over his running shorts and T-shirt. It was nice to be able to combine his traditional morning jog with pleasure for a change.

Priest finished a set of stretching routines and then moved around to the bed of the truck. Opening the tailgate, he ran his hand along the lower right side of the bed. Finding the hidden catch, he pulled, lifting a section of the bed up and away. The false bottom hid a storage space just big enough to hold a couple of bodies snugly, if not comfortably.

Reaching into the compartment, Priest grabbed a small cloth pouch about the size of a cigarette box and stuffed it into the pocket of his sweats. Then, after one last bout of stretching, he moved rapidly along a narrow trail, barely visible by the light of the crescent moon.

It was only about half a mile to the hide position Priest had selected. In the past, someone had used this spot as a deer stand. Several expended seven-millimeter rifle shells provided ample indication that the shooter had not been particularly good at his craft.

But nobody had hunted here for several years, the expansion of subdivisions out into this canyon having pushed the hunters farther into the backcountry. What the spot did provide, though, was a perfectly concealed view of the golf cart path that wound up and along the hillside below, passing near the expensive new homes spread along the canyon.

Here the lots were at least five acres in size, and the views from the homes were magnificent. The cart path wound along the back side of a section of these homes, doubling as a jogging path, and led down to the clubhouse and then out onto the golf course.

Perfect. Priest had discovered this spot as part of his surveillance of his target. Not an assigned target. This was special. He had first seen her by chance as he filled his truck with gas at one of the quick-stop gas stations. From the moment he had seen her, he had known she would be his.

She was exquisite. Everything about her screamed upper-class elegance, from her blue BMW convertible to her long Burberry coat and shoulder-length blonde hair. California Dreaming. She took his breath away.

Following her back to her house had been easy, the way the BMW stood out making it child's play for him to stay way back in traffic, safely free from her notice. Once he had seen the house into which she'd pulled the blue Bimmer, he had moved on. He had her.

Since that day he'd made a number of trips up to the area, carefully scouting the surroundings, spending hour upon hour just watching the house from these hills, noting her habits and those of her husband.

The husband was a slight, balding man who left the house just before six each morning, his black Mercedes cruising down the winding road at an aggressive clip. Priest had seen his type often enough before. A man who got his trophy wife with his big house, fancy cars, and fat wallet.

As for Ms. California, she always started her day with a jog, except on days when the snow made it impossible to run along the cart path. Always the same routine. Exit the house as the sky lightened in the east, a brisk jog down the mile and a half to the clubhouse, once around the parking lot, and then back home.

Other joggers also used the trail, but the runners tended to be widely separated, hidden from each other for long stretches as the trail wound in and out of the woods.

Priest didn't have to wait long. Just like clockwork, the black Mercedes pulled out and sped away, followed less than an hour later by the golden girl in her white jogging suit.

Priest scanned the cart path. There were two other joggers on the trail, both men, well ahead of his girl. As he watched, the men expanded their lead, passing directly below Priest's hiding spot and disappearing around a bend in the trail before the girl was within a quarter mile of his position.

Counting to thirty, Priest stepped out onto the cart path and began jogging slowly back toward where the golden girl would be rounding the corner at any moment. As she came into view, he jogged heavily, his breathing coming in loud, ragged gasps. Glancing up at her, he lifted his hand in a runner's wave, meaning, "I'm too damned tired to say hi."

She ignored him, at least until his fist rocketed out to strike her square in the stomach, driving all the air from her lungs in one loud whoosh. She doubled over, her body curling toward the fetal position as she fell, but she never hit the ground. Priest swept her body up in his powerful arm, spinning her so that she faced away from him, his other hand pulling the cloth pouch from his pocket and crushing the small glass ampoule within it in a single motion.

As the pouch pressed against her nose and mouth, all struggling ceased. Priest tossed her limp form over his shoulder and turned off the path, disappearing into the woods above the trail, only the lingering hint of chloroform leaving any indication he had ever been there.

The trip up the steep hillside and through the woods to the truck elevated his breathing only slightly. Ms. California was light, and Priest was in prime condition. It took him only seconds to lay her on the truck bed and then to bind and gag her with duct tape. While she might wake up on the long ride back to his cabin, the tight, well-padded confines of the false bottom would not allow her to make any significant noise.

Priest grinned as he slid into the driver's seat, his heart thumping in anticipation. In less than two hours he would carry his new girl across the threshold and into his special cellar. And then he would show her why he was called Priest.

CHAPTER 16

Connie Stempson had already forgotten the feel of the sun. Being a child of California, the sun's warmth on her skin, the smell of the ocean, and the taste of salt on her lips were as important as breathing. To Connie, graced with an abundance of both beauty and money, time had never had much meaning. Strangely, alone here in the dark, she had developed an unerring sense of time. Before long now a key would rattle in the lock, then the merciful darkness would fade to light.

As if someone had tugged open an old crypt, the sound she was expecting struck her ears as her captor, the man who called himself Priest, stepped into the room. She caught a brief glimpse of the small space beyond and of the ladder that led up to an open trapdoor. Connie shook off the small hope that someone would see that open trapdoor and come for her. Over these last few days it had all become clear: if heroes really existed, none of them were riding to her rescue.

Priest moved around the room silently, except for the click of his Zippo lighter as he lit the thirteen red candles. Always the same ritual. Always the same order.

Connie remembered that, as a child, she'd thought candles were beautiful. Even now she loved them. Each one he lit pushed back the darkness. All except for number thirteen. That one meant her time was up.

As he finished the lighting ritual, Priest turned toward her, his black satin robe open at the chest in a manner intended to be sexy. It was time.

Her training was only in its second week, but Connie prayed that, this time, she would be good enough. The time of apprenticeship was almost used up, and soon, failure to please him would no longer be tolerated.

She sat on the foot of the bed. Except for the sink and toilet, it was the only piece of furniture in her cell. Slowly she unfastened her nylon stockings from the lace garters he had bought her. Priest watched as she pulled them off over her small feet and then slowly began unfastening her black teddy.

Connie tried to imagine Priest as someone else. If she could maintain that thought, she could get through this horror one more time. A worm of loathing slid through her mind despite her best effort to suppress it. Her eyes moved to Priest's face.

Shit. He had noticed. *Shit. Shit.*

But instead of his usual violence, Priest only smiled. "Your training time's almost up. I brought you a little something to help you focus." He delicately laid a small, decorative gift bag on the bed beside her. "Go on. Open it."

Connie stared at the sack. It was the cheap kind you could buy in any drugstore. This one was blue, decorated with pictures of small, multicolored merry-go-round horses. She didn't want to look inside, but a growing fascination pulled her hand toward it, overcoming the dread that filled her heart.

Connie's hand reached the handles, but she didn't pull it toward her. Instead she rolled up onto her knees, leaning as far away from the thing as possible while still being able to touch it. Unable to bring herself to reach inside the opening, Connie lifted it at arm's length, carefully dumping the contents onto the sheet.

Screaming, she struggled backward off the bed, her pistoning legs propelling her across the floor until the corner of the cell stopped her. For several seconds she continued to kick out, trying to push herself farther away from the thing that had fallen onto the sheets. But there was no getting away from what she'd seen.

Strung onto an eighteen-inch silver necklace, small, decaying fingers pressed tightly against one another, the fingernail of each lovingly painted with a fresh coat of red nail polish. She had recognized the shade and smell immediately. Summer Fling. The sick son of a bitch had painted those dead fingernails with her nail polish.

Priest grinned. Then, in a reversal of his entry ritual, he snuffed out the candles and closed the door behind him, once again leaving her alone in the dark.

CHAPTER 17

Heather's return to school, two days after she'd left the hospital, started auspiciously enough. The morning was bright and clear, and she felt much, much better. Numerous friends and acquaintances stopped her in the hall to ask about how she was feeling and to tell her how happy they were to see her again. Even the teachers went out of their way to tell her they were glad to see her back—except for Ms. Gorsky, whom Heather doubted knew the concept of happiness.

Heather's ability to maintain a relaxed state of mind that eliminated the mathematic equations from her head was improving in fits and starts. She had almost messed up and blurted out "one thousand one hundred twenty-three" when her dad spilled salt on the breakfast table while trying to fill the shaker. She had just known that there were 1,123 individual grains and another 465 that had spilled off onto the floor. It was weird, but as easy as people could glance at a group of oranges and think "3," she could glance at a pile of salt and think "1,123."

When she had started rubbing her temples, her mother had asked if she had a headache and suggested that perhaps she should stay home another day or two. Heather managed to mollify her mother with a quick grin and an explanation that she was just dreading having to tell everyone at school that she had passed out for no apparent reason. Worse, it kept dawning on her that she'd been away from the ship for over a week now.

During lunch break, Heather and the twins made their way outside to the football field to sit in the bleachers so they could be alone. By the time Heather finished explaining the developments on the ship and its ongoing impact on her life, Jennifer was wide-eyed.

Mark just grinned. "I'm just glad you're OK. Besides, the rain girl stuff may turn out to be useful."

Jennifer glared at her brother. "Is that all you can say? Can't you see this is causing Heather problems? God! Are you even related to me?"

Heather laughed. "It's OK." A serious look settled back over her face. "Are either of you having any issues with thinking?"

Mark shook his head. "Nope. Same as ever, except the memory thing."

"Don't let him kid you," said Jennifer. "His reflexes, balance, and coordination have improved drastically. And based on his recent grades in Spanish class, his foreign language aptitude is off the charts."

"And you?" Heather asked.

"I really haven't noticed much."

Mark snorted. "Right. Data here has scanned every book in the school library into her memory. But then her memory was getting cluttered, so she came up with a Dewey decimal scheme to mentally organize the books."

Heather's mouth dropped open.

"But here's the kicker. She even rescanned every book she'd already memorized. I swear, I laughed my ass off watching her do it, too. She just sat there, eyes closed, for hours. You'd have thought she was Gandhi."

Jennifer's face turned beet red. "Mark! That's not fair. I have to be able to find the information when I need it."

Heather nodded. "Don't let him get your goat. I think your solution is brilliant."

Jennifer turned back toward Heather, excitement shining in her eyes. "I figured something else out, too. Even though we have these perfect memories, we can't understand data we have no background for. We still have to learn the material in order to utilize it. We just learn things way faster than normal. But it's more than that.

"What happened to you these last few days just confirms what I was already thinking," she continued. "The ship affects us differently depending upon our natural strengths. That's why Mark's physical and language skills are surging. It's why you're the math goddess and I'm a data machine.

"There's one other thing," Jennifer said. "We can't afford to show off our new skills."

"She wants us to throw tests," Mark explained.

"Not throw them. Just avoid acing them all. We need to keep our scores close to our traditional grade point averages."

"Which I don't think is fair," Mark said. "You two are straight-A students, but I get Bs and Cs."

Heather laughed. "Come on, let's head back. Classes are starting. I like Jen's plan. Just stay inconspicuous."

"That might be OK for you two, but I want to make some noise in high school," Mark said.

Before Jennifer could deliver a harsh retort, Mark headed off, leaving Heather and Jennifer staring after him.

"It's all right," said Heather. "He'll be OK."

Jennifer shrugged. "I hope so. I really, really hope so."

CHAPTER 18

Inconspicuous.

Mark Smythe moved down the hallway of Los Alamos High School with unnatural grace, slightly shifting his weight so that the stream of students flowed past without touching him, a feat that would have been regarded as phenomenal had anyone else been aware of it.

He wasn't stupid—he wouldn't blow their cover—but he wasn't about to hide his talents either. He didn't have a problem with continuing to get imperfect grades, but at least one should jump to an A. The rest could remain Bs.

Jennifer was not going to like the rest of what he had planned for the year. Not one little bit.

Hopefully, Heather would be cool with it, but if not, then the girls would just have to get over it together. Maybe he should have told Jennifer that he had already asked Dad for permission to go out for the basketball team, and Dad had enthusiastically signed the permission slip.

"You know, at six feet, you're going to have to work a lot harder than the bigger guys," his dad had said. "Also, your schoolwork better not suffer. You sure you're willing to make that commitment?"

Mark grinned. Oh, he would practice all right, and keeping up with schoolwork wasn't going to be a problem anymore.

The gymnasium was empty when Mark walked in, something that wasn't surprising since tryouts weren't going to start until next week.

Mark grabbed a basketball from the rack against the wall and began dribbling it out onto the court, feeling the ball's responsiveness to the movements of his hands. Like most of his friends, Mark had played sports since grade school. Basketball had been his favorite of the team sports. He had been good, but not the best. That was about to change.

The ball felt different. Mark could feel every dimple in the ball's skin, the lines where the sections joined, how the rotation changed as it struck the gym floor and returned to his hand.

Left hand, right hand. Back and forth he worked the ball, adding different English to the spin, causing the ball to weave about crazily, but always bouncing to the spot he anticipated. Between his legs. Behind his back. Between his legs as he walked. Between his legs as he ran. He moved around the court—whirling, spinning—and always the ball bounced flawlessly from one hand to the other.

Mark moved back to the free throw line at one end of the court, bounced the ball twice, and then shot. The ball passed through the basket so smoothly that the strings at the bottom of the net made a gentle popping sound. Retrieving the basketball, Mark shot again and again. Ten in a row. Twenty. Fifty.

He began moving around the court and launching jump shots. The first of these missed, although he immediately knew why. He had surprised himself with the height of his jump, his new muscle efficiency propelling him far higher than ever before.

The next shot didn't miss. Neither did the one after that. Left hand, right hand: it made absolutely no difference.

He spun the ball up onto the middle finger of his left hand and then caught it and launched a shot, which landed the ball back in the rack right beside its fellows. He made his way out through the double gymnasium doors, giving one a flat-handed smack as he left. A broad smile spread across his face.

Inconspicuous.

CHAPTER 19

Heather had never studied so hard in her life. Considering she was ahead in all her schoolwork and had no tests coming up, her study load was nothing short of miraculous. But compared to the work Jennifer was doing, Heather felt like a slacker.

Sometimes life drives you to do entirely new things, things you never believed you could do. Heather remembered when she had first started skiing, midway through fifth grade. That was when she had met Bobby Jones. It had been forever since she had thought of him, but in fifth grade she thought Bobby Jones hung the moon.

He and his family had arrived from Steamboat Springs, Colorado. Bobby had asked her to go skiing with him, and although she protested that she didn't know how, he promised to teach her. Allow her to humiliate herself was more like it.

To be fair, he had spent the morning with her on the bunny slopes of Pajarito Mountain, the wonderful little ski area originally built by the lab employees. As thrilled as she was with learning the gliding wedge, the snowplow, the pizza slice, or whatever you want to call the uncomfortable beginner ski position, she probably would have terminated her ski career that day if not for Bobby's patient instruction. By noon, though, that patience had worn thin, and Bobby suggested that the she continue her practice solo.

Having fulfilled his duty, Bobby Jones spent the rest of the day swooshing down the black-diamond slopes with Kristin Beale, a sixth-grade girl whose long, blonde hair would never know a ski cap, not even if her ears froze off and fell into the snow. Kristin had been born on the ski slopes, and it showed, which allowed the vacuity of her speech to go unnoticed.

Her humiliation complete, Heather had worked on her skiing that year with passion that bordered on obsession. But by the time Heather had mastered the sport, her interest in the lovely Mr. Jones had evaporated. However, the motivation that had driven her—that, she could feel like it was yesterday.

So now that the otherworldly combination of high personal interest and event-driven need had superimposed themselves, Heather's study drive was fearsome.

Mark worried her, though. The seductive influence of his enhanced physical prowess only heightened his natural competitive drive. And basketball gave him the perfect outlet. Jennifer was furious at her twin and had hardly spoken to him in the last few weeks, convinced that his irresponsibility threatened them all.

When Jennifer first learned that Mark had tried out for and made the Varsity A basketball team, she had confronted him.

"Mark, are you crazy?"

"No, I'm good."

"I don't care that you're good. Our new gifts are too important to use for petty personal aggrandizement. I think we received them for a higher purpose."

"Higher purpose? You've been reading way too many comic books. I don't have a gift. I have talent the ship just released. And I'm not about to sit around and hide it. I plan on living my life."

Jennifer clenched her teeth. "Mark. Think for a change. What's it worth to become a big basketball star? Is it worth attracting all that attention? Is it worth the risk of getting our ship discovered?"

"Yes, it is. Let me tell you something, Jen. Life is risky. We might get hit by a bus tomorrow. Someone might wonder why you're leafing through every book you can get your hands on. Heather might slip up and let the cat in the savant hat out of the bag. The only really safe place is in a cozy straightjacket in a nice rubber room. If you want that, then go for it. Not me, though."

"Jumping off a cliff isn't being a risk taker. It's being an idiot."

Heather had stood there watching the confrontation, although she might as well have been invisible for all the attention her two friends paid her. It had concluded with Mark storming off as Jennifer yelled after him, "Don't be an idiot!"

Not that Mark would have liked helping with what they were working on, anyway. She and Jennifer were on a mad quest to learn, each focused on her own areas of special interest. Heather worked her way through book after book of advanced mathematics and physics while Jennifer focused on computer science and data mining, that obtuse art of storing and categorizing data so that a search engine can find it. In addition, Jennifer had once again redone her data-tagging scheme, which forced her to rescan all of the books she had already memorized.

What drove them was growing uneasiness with the work that was being done on cold fusion around the world. But they had to admit that they had discovered nothing that might indicate cold fusion technology presented any real threat to the planet. Quite the opposite.

Heather had downloaded and read every available publication on the alien cold fusion technology. No matter how many times she reworked the equations, the technology still looked good. And the peer reviews by physicists and mathematicians around the world had been very positive.

So why was she so scared?

Outside, the wind howled so hard it shook the glass in her bedroom window. Fine pellets of sleet tapped the glass like cold, drumming fingers. Heather wrapped her thick robe more tightly around her shoulders, stretched, and then rose from the chair to peer out.

The storm was getting worse. The first of the high-country blizzards for the year was getting ready to descend upon northern New Mexico. According to the local weatherman, they could expect between twelve and eighteen inches by morning, which would close all the roads in and out of town. That meant no school.

Heather smiled as she watched the sleet give way to large, thick flakes, now falling so heavily she could barely see the streetlight through the swirling whiteness. School might be closed tomorrow, but she would bet her left arm the ski area would be open.

With a sigh of regret, she moved back to her desk. She would not be skiing tomorrow or anytime soon. There was just too much to do.

A loud tap on her window caused her to look up. After several seconds, she shook her head and returned her attention to her studies. Another tap, this one much louder than the first, brought her to her feet.

Frozen in place, her pulse pounding in her ears, Heather stared at the dark window. Snow that had caked the lower-left corner of the pane had been partially scraped away. A white piece of paper fluttered wildly in the cleared space, secured by a thick wad of chewing gum.

Fascinated, Heather walked back to the window and opened it just enough to retrieve the scrap of paper. Her eyes focused on the typeset words that filled the partial page.

As when the melting fire burneth, the fire causeth the waters to boil,

to make thy name known to thine adversaries, that the nations may tremble

at thy presence!

—Isaiah 64:2

As though she were in a dream, Heather's gaze was drawn to the ground ten feet below her window. There in the swirling snow at the base of the streetlight, a solitary figure stood, ice caking his bearded, skeletal face, his eyes lost in dark sockets.

And as the sound of her scream split the stillness of the house, the figure below grinned up at her.

CHAPTER 20

By the time the police arrived, the man was long gone. Heather's parents had neither seen nor heard anything out of the ordinary. If it had not been for the note and the chewing gum, Heather doubted the two officers would have believed her account.

After taking statements, the officers took the gum and put it in a plastic bag. One of them examined the note.

"Looks like our man tore this out of a cheap Bible. The type you find in drawers at two-star hotels."

Either the cop had some highly developed deductive reasoning or he had way more personal experience than Heather cared to think about. Just as she was about to settle firmly on the latter conclusion, the officer paused in his study.

"Isaiah 64:2. Six letters, the number six, then two numbers that add to six. Mark of the beast, isn't it?"

Heather's father raised an eyebrow. "Superstitious nonsense."

"Oh, I agree with you, Mr. McFarland. I don't put a bit of stock in it. The question is, though, what about our man out there? Does he? Anyway, we'll let the boys back at the lab take a look at it."

With a nod, the officers departed.

"Their 'lab' is going to 'look at it,' " her father huffed. "Unless I miss my guess, that stuff is going into a shoe box on a shelf."

"It's all right, Dad," said Heather. "I shouldn't have overreacted in the first place. I can't believe I screamed."

The memory of that scream violated every aspect of her rock climbing, risk taker self-image.

Her mother shook her head. "Baloney. Any time a man climbs up to a young lady's second-floor window and starts sticking threatening-sounding notes to it with chewing gum, it calls for a bit of overreaction."

Her father's eyes tightened. "If he shows up again, he's likely to come down with a case of forty-five-caliber lead poisoning."

"Dad, please. I'm sure he's just some unhappy homeless person who needs help."

"Uh-huh. Well, I hope he finds it before he threatens my family again." With that, Heather's father turned and left the room.

Heather turned to her mother. "Dad wouldn't really shoot him, would he?"

"Don't get paranoid, now, but pay attention, won't you? At least until this guy is caught."

That didn't answer her question, but Heather nodded, anyway. "I will, Mom. Don't worry."

Sleep seemed an unlikely possibility as Heather crawled back into her bed and pulled the down comforter up under her chin. But before she knew it, she found herself rising to greet the new day. Once again she had beaten the sun.

She glanced over at the pile of books that awaited her and then at the snow piled on the outside of her windowsill. Something about snow, especially when it was falling heavily and piling high enough to call off school, made Heather feel like goofing off. All that study, and she still hadn't figured out a reference in the ship's imagery that would give them a key to understanding the tiny component they were studying.

They had tried to organize a good, specific query to the onboard computer system by coming up with a question about data transfer. Jennifer had gotten the idea, and Heather thought it a good one, that if they could get the ship to show them how it stored and transferred data, it would be a very basic starting point in understanding the underlying alien technology. But no matter how they phrased or visualized the question, the answering imagery was the same.

It looked like a simple pair of transistors or electronic microswitches. The problem was there were no wires or connections of any type between the switches the ship described, merely some symbols and mathematical equations that Heather did not understand.

It was frustrating because she thought they could probably build the switches themselves, given a good microscope, a computer, some small RadioShack stepper motors to control the instruments accurately, and an appropriate semiconductor material. But since it wouldn't form a circuit, why bother? What was the point of a pair of tiny electronic switches that weren't connected to each other?

The really annoying part was that they had gotten this far a couple of weeks ago. Despite Heather pushing herself through as many advanced mathematics books as she could read, she was no closer to understanding the mysterious equations than she had been when she first saw them.

"Oh well," she said to herself, sliding into her big, furry slippers and wrapping her flannel robe around her body. "It looks like a good cartoons and hot chocolate day."

The morning slipped away in wonderful wastefulness, aided along its path to Lounge Lizardsville by a breakfast of homemade biscuits and honey, followed by a pot of hot cocoa set on a coaster beside the couch. The television was tuned to the Cartoon Network as huge, puffy snowflakes drifted down outside the windows. By ten, Heather still had not dressed and had no intention of doing so anytime soon.

At the moment, an epic battle of wits raged between Wile E. Coyote and Road Runner. Having just plummeted to the bottom of the canyon—where he kicked up a small mushroom cloud of dust—the coyote had come up with a bold new plan.

Heather had always related to the hapless fellow. After all, his plans were truly ingenious, sometimes awe-inspiringly so. Still, no matter how brilliant a scheme he put together, the stupid bird would somehow violate several laws of nature and leave the coyote to suffer the consequences.

Curled into a tight ball on the couch, sipping happily at a fresh cocoa refill—"Thanks, Mom"—Heather watched as the coyote finished painting a perfect picture of a black tunnel through a rock wall. The wall, which lay along the bird's projected path, completely blocked the road so that when the bird came running down it, he would speed directly into the trap, pre-tenderizing himself in preparation for becoming roadrunner stew.

It was really impossible to get too much of this stuff. Sure enough, as she and the coyote watched in anticipation, the roadrunner screeched down the road directly up to the cliff. Then—once again thumbing his pointy nose at the pile of physics books that lay upstairs on Heather's desk—the bird passed harmlessly through the fake tunnel, continuing out the other side.

And, as could be expected, the coyote raced after the roadrunner, only to splat against the black paint on the near side of the rock wall. He stumbled around afterward in a dazed fashion until he fell off the cliff, generating another small mushroom cloud at the bottom.

Fire exploded in Heather's brain as everything clicked into place. Of course. The wall had two sides.

She jumped up and raced for the telephone. Hearing a familiar hello on the far end, she barely managed to keep her excited voice low enough that her mother did not hear.

"Jen! You won't believe it. I can barely believe it myself, and all because of a cartoon. Never let anyone tell you cartoons are mindless."

"I've got no idea what you're talking about."

Heather paused and took a deep, gulping breath. "I figured it out. I know what the microswitches do. I know how they work. I think we can make them."

CHAPTER 21

Abdul Aziz was not a religious man, although he often wished he was. How many years had it been since he had heeded the call to prayer, since he had even set foot inside a mosque? Allah would not look kindly upon his laziness in such matters, but perhaps his service for all of his Muslim brethren would rate some measure of reward in the afterlife. Egyptian born, Syrian trained, experience hardened in a way that few could have survived, Abdul could hardly believe the good fortune that had crowned him this day.

Direct action. Seldom in the world of international espionage were governments willing to take direct action to achieve their purposes. It was messy. It often left a trail. No, mostly they preferred to work slowly over a number of years to infiltrate and acquire the information they desired.

The now-defunct Soviet Union had been the master of this tactic, although the newly capitalistic Chinese Communists were giving the former Soviets a run for their money. Even his own government was reluctant to take direct action far from its own borders, although that reluctance certainly did not extend to his country's immediate neighbors.

But this Rho Project declaration by the United States government presented such a grave potential threat to the entire Muslim world that there was no time for anything less than direct action. The potential threat was abundant justification that any and all means be used to attain knowledge of what the United States had learned over the last several dozen years—information the United States still refused to share freely with the world.

Abdul Aziz was that means, and now he had what he had come for, although even his masters would be shocked at the import of the information. Perhaps Allah would make a place for him after all, despite his shortcomings.

He smiled to himself. Never had he crossed a border more easily than the border between the United States and Mexico. The desert was his home, and this desert might as well have been an oasis when compared to the great Arabian Desert in which he had lived a goodly portion of his life.

And once across that border, he had not paused longer than it took to highjack a car and dump its former owners beneath six inches of dirt somewhere in the desert between El Paso, Texas, and Alamogordo, New Mexico.

Now, as he glanced around at the wet mess in what had been a comfortable living room in a quiet Los Alamos residential neighborhood, Abdul shook his head. Getting back across that border was not going to be so easy. *Inshallah*, God willing, it would happen. At this point, whether he lived or died made little difference. No one would stop him before he returned to his hotel room and broadcast the e-mail message that would change the world.

Unlike some of his associates, Abdul did not enjoy killing. He was merely indifferent to it. The reason he was so much better at it than most was because he had no more emotional response to carving up a child than to preparing a steak for dinner. Even less, since the steak at least made him hungry. All those who had lusted after the kill had not lasted nearly as long as Abdul had because their lust forced them into mistakes that he never made. At least until today.

But this was no mistake of emotion. It was one required by his mission. Tonight there would be no time for cleanup, so he had not bothered to avoid the mess.

Stepping over the dead bodyguard, Abdul glanced at the armchair that held the body of Dr. Sheldon Brownstein, formerly the number three physicist working on the Rho Project. Beside him, bound and gagged with duct tape, were the bloody bodies of his wife and two children, a boy and a girl, ten and eight years old, respectively. Tomorrow these bodies would be found and all hell would break loose, but tonight, Abdul Aziz had what he needed. He would deal with tomorrow when it arrived.

Abdul nodded at Dr. Brownstein with grudging respect. The man had been strong, unwilling to break until after Abdul had finished with his wife and started in on the children. But finally the information had come, flowing out of the man's lips so rapidly that Abdul had to tell him to slow down, to ensure the digital recording was intelligible.

Switching on the television, Abdul swept the room one last time with his eyes, not that he thought he had missed anything. He merely wanted to remember this, the place where he had changed the history of the world. Perhaps one day even the Americans would thank him for what he had done. A thin smile spread across Abdul's hawk-like features. He would not hold his breath for that day.

Exiting through the kitchen door, the same one he had entered two hours earlier, Abdul moved into the backyard, then down onto the steep canyon slope that dropped off directly behind the house. His car was parked over a mile away, in the parking lot of an all-night grocery store, and he would not chance walking along streets to get back to it. It was full of gas for his run to the border, but that run would have to wait until he had returned to his hotel and sent the message.

A small sound brought Abdul to a sudden stop. It was impossible to move on the steep, shale-covered slope without making some noise, but the noise he had heard had not come from him. The light from the quarter moon created more shadows than illumination, but to Abdul's trained eyes it might as well have been daylight. In the shadows on the slope ahead, another shadow awaited him. In the shadow's hand, moonlight glinted from the blade of a knife.

Abdul glanced up the hill. He was much too near to the houses to risk the sound and attention a gunshot would produce, unless he absolutely had to. Apparently the shadow's thoughts were similar.

Aware he had been spotted, Abdul's adversary stepped out from his hiding place, moving at a steady walk toward Abdul. American Special Operations Forces agents, whether they were Army Rangers, Green Berets, SEALs, or Marine Recon, had a unique look and smell about them. Then there was Delta Force; most of the group had served in multiple types of special operations roles—cross-dressers, as Abdul thought of them.

Over his years of encounters with them, throughout the Middle East and Africa, Abdul had developed the ability to immediately spot which breed of the beast he was dealing with. Lean bodies, hungry eyes, the stink of reckless self-confidence, tattoos over large portions of the younger ones' bodies.

They came home from their wars around the world, quickly became bored with civilian life, and went back to what they knew best, becoming mercenaries or, as they preferred to be called, security consultants.

This one had the ex-Delta stench about him. That was good. It meant there would be no backup coming.

The two men lunged at each other simultaneously. Abdul spun aside from the underhand thrust of the merc, his own curved knife barely missing his opponent's throat. Abdul reversed the arc of the blade, sweeping in low, a move that was blocked with a left forearm.

The merc was good, no doubt about that, but not nearly good enough. Abdul drove his body forward so the other man's knife grazed his side but missed vital organs. With a rapid twisting motion of his wrist, Abdul dislodged his knife from the merc's block, bringing it up flat, the tip sliding smoothly in through the man's solar plexus.

Immediately, the merc grabbed Abdul's knife hand in a grip of iron strength, but it was too late. The entire length of the blade had penetrated the man's chest and lung. Still, Abdul had to marvel at his strength of will. Ever so slowly, the merc forced the blade from his body as his other hand pressed forward, locked in Abdul's grip.

As the knife jerked free of the merc's chest, a small stream of arterial blood spurted into Abdul's face. There was no second spurt of blood. A sense of puzzlement, even concern, robbed Abdul of breath. He should be drenched in the slick, warm wetness of the merc's blood, but he wasn't. Instead, a slow, knowing grin spread across his opponent's face as the fellow's grip continued to strengthen, driving the merc's knife closer and closer to Abdul's throat.

Apart from a great sense of sorrow as the knife smoothly parted the skin of his neck, Abdul had only one more thought: *Now, that is the correct amount of blood.*

CHAPTER 22

The national news media was rife with speculation about the sensational quintuple murder in Los Alamos, which brought things uncomfortably close as far as Heather was concerned. Fingerprints found in the house had quickly been identified as belonging to the international terrorist known as Abdul Aziz, and although a stolen car with the same prints was discovered nearby, no trace of Aziz himself had yet been found, despite a wide net of roadblocks and FBI raids.

Since the murdered man was part of the inner circle of physicists reputed to be working with Dr. Stephenson on the *Rho Ship*, a host of theories were being generated about what information might have been forced out of him before he died. Dr. Stephenson made the rounds of several Sunday-morning talk shows in an attempt to provide reassurance that nothing of great national significance could have been revealed. Project information was far too compartmentalized for that. No single person on the project had unfettered access to all the information.

"Except for you," a reporter had pointed out.

Dr. Stephenson had merely smiled that cold, thin smile of his and moved on to the next question, his response exactly what Heather had expected.

Amid congressional outcry, government security for the lab and its personnel was increased yet again, with special security contingents now being assigned to protect top figures on the Rho Project in much the same way that the Secret Service provided security for the president and his family.

With all of this excitement, Heather and Jennifer had finally gotten Mark's interest focused back on something other than basketball, although that game remained near the top of his priority list.

Over a year ago, Heather had read an article on quantum twins. Quantum theory predicted and experimentation had shown it possible to produce a pair of particles that shared the same quantum state. If something was done to one of the particles that changed its state, the state of the other particle changed at exactly the same time.

This was true no matter how much distance separated the pair, something that at first glance appeared to violate the special theory of relativity's prohibition on any information traveling faster than the speed of light. But the twin particles were bound together as if by magic.

What excited Heather the most was that the alien equations suggested a way to create a pair of semiconductor switches, each doped with a quantum twin that controlled the open and closed state of the switch. Apply a current that closed one, and its twin would close, no matter if it was located across the room or across the galaxy.

As Heather finished explaining the workings of the quantum twin microswitches, Mark's eyes lit up.

"The switches communicate with no transmissions?"

Heather nodded. "None whatsoever."

"That means we could send untraceable communications," Mark said.

Jennifer leaned forward. "More than that. We could send and receive any kind of digital data—video, audio, computer data, anything."

"And," said Heather, "if we put one of the twins in a device, all we have to do is hook up the other twin the same way and we get a clean remote copy."

Mark rose to his feet. "We're going to need some decent electronic tools to build them."

"I think we should ask Dad," said Jennifer. "You know how he's always trying to get us interested in the stuff he does."

"That's a great idea," Mark responded.

Heather rubbed her lower lip. "I think I can talk Dad into chipping in a little cash."

Convincing their fathers to outfit them with a set of good electronic instruments turned out to be the easiest part of the task. Both dads were ecstatic that their kids had finally gotten interested in electronics projects. They even scrounged up a used oscilloscope and red laser, the types commonly found in college labs.

All that week, working around homework sessions and basketball practice, the smell of solder hung heavy in their workshop, which was set up in a corner of the Smythe garage. By Thursday night, the laser modifications were complete, and while it would never burn a hole through metal, the end product was a laser capable of producing variable frequency light in a very tight beam, something that was crucial for the doping process that made the alien microswitches work.

Given time, Heather felt confident they could eventually improve the process to the point where mass production would be possible. For now, though, they just needed a single working quantum twin microswitch pair.

Exhausted but happy, Heather said good-bye to her two friends and made her way back to her house. It was funny. There were boatloads of news media reports and, no doubt, scads of foreign agents scurrying around the area, trying to dig up something on the *Rho Ship*. But here, right under their noses, was a small lab getting ready to produce its own alien technology components. And the whole thing was being done by some high school kids out of a garage in White Rock.

Heather's dad greeted her as she entered the kitchen.

"You look happy. What are you smiling about?"

"Oh, nothing, Dad. Just high school stuff. You know."

Giving her a hug, he nodded. "I can only imagine. It's getting late, though, and you do have school tomorrow. Not to mention, we're all going to Mark's first game tomorrow night. I hear he's pretty good."

"He'll have to be for good old LAHS to have any chance. Last year was embarrassing. I felt sorry for our cheerleaders."

Her father grinned. "We can always hope."

"Where's Mom?"

"Oh, she's taking a bath before bed. I'm headed up to join her."

"OK, Dad. That sounds really good, think I'll try it myself."

By the time Heather finished her bath and tucked herself under her covers, her eyelids were so heavy she could barely keep them open. The dreams began almost before her head hit the pillow.

She was in their workshop in the corner of the Smythe garage. Mark was there. So was Jennifer.

Heather found herself staring at the oscilloscope readout, the display filling her head with equations as Mark manipulated the laser. His fingers moved the controls, delicately positioning the beam with a dexterity that he alone could manage, using the microscope to confirm his pointing accuracy.

Suddenly the images in Heather's head changed, the equations governing the quantum manipulation decaying toward a singularity.

The laser was not generating the quantum twins. Instead a microscopic black hole appeared, a tear in the space-time fabric of the material being manipulated.

Spotting the danger, Mark's hand moved with unnatural speed to turn off the power switch on the back of the laser, but the subatomic blackness continued to grow. And as it grew, it consumed the nearest atoms. In an accelerating spiral, the event horizon expanded until the garage itself shrieked with the force emanating from the microscopic aberration.

As Heather looked up to see the horror in Jennifer's and Mark's faces, she realized the truth. The end of all things lay there, growing beneath that microscope, and there was absolutely nothing they could do to stop it.

CHAPTER 23

High atop Pajarito Plateau, the noise inside the Los Alamos High School gymnasium was deafening. Word had spread throughout the community of the Hilltoppers' new junior point guard, so the game was standing room only. And as Heather watched, Jennifer by her side, Marcus Aurelius Smythe had not disappointed.

The game against the high school's 4A Division II rival, Taos, was enough to ensure a capacity crowd on the first game of the season, but never had the gymnasium seen a crowd like this one. The fire marshal had to start denying entrance to a horde of latecomers. Luckily for the home team, most of the late arrivals were from Taos, so there were few tears shed by local residents. Outside, though, police had their hands full with angry Taos High alumni and fans.

Those inside were being treated to a basketball handling magic show the likes of which northern New Mexico had never seen. The young point guard wove his way between his opponents, spinning, whirling, and dribbling between his legs and behind his back in a manner that left the opposing players stumbling over themselves, often falling to the floor in a confused tangle. Although Heather thought she knew how good Mark had become, she found herself mesmerized by his performance. And, based upon the fan response, she wasn't alone.

By the time the starters were pulled from the game, midway through the fourth quarter, Mark had amassed twenty assists and scored thirty-two points, many of these on free throws as the other team had resorted to fouling him to try to get the ball from his hands. Throughout the stands people reverently whispered the names of Hall of Fame point guards, as if their spirits inhabited the building.

The game ended with the Los Alamos Hilltoppers doling out a devastating loss to Taos, 113 to 72. As the buzzer sounded, the crowd rushed out of the stands down onto the court, everyone in a frenzy to pat the back of the young star. The confusion made it impossible for the teams to make their way from the court back to their locker rooms and resulted in injury to two elderly women who were knocked to the ground in the crush.

Only after the police inside the gymnasium were reinforced by those who had been stationed on the outside was order restored and the crowd escorted out of the arena. In the cold air of the late November night, Heather stood beside Jennifer staring back toward the gym.

Jennifer's voice barely rose above the excited murmur of the parking lot crowd. "Oh my God. My crazy brother has really done it. We're as good as dead."

Heather laughed, threading her arm through Jennifer's as they waited for their families to join them. "Well, he's certainly done something here tonight, but I doubt he's killed us."

"You watch. His fans are going to swamp us. We'll probably have the press hanging around, too. I don't even want to think about what else might happen."

Heather shrugged. One thing she had to admire about Mark Smythe: he never did anything halfway. He wanted to make his imprint on high school, and he appeared to be well on his way to accomplishing that.

"No use worrying about something that hasn't happened yet. We'll deal with what comes."

By Sunday, the buzz about the hot young guard from Los Alamos had reached a new level due to the team's domination of their second opponent in two nights, thanks to Mark's outstanding play. As Jennifer had predicted, a band of interested onlookers and newfound friends suddenly attached themselves to Mark, making it difficult for him to get any time to himself.

Heather tried calling several times but could not get through on the phone line. Finally she walked next door to find Jennifer with her nose buried in a book while Mark was closeted in his room doing homework.

Jennifer smiled at Heather, although the smile appeared forced. "Sometimes I hate being so right."

Heather sat down on the couch beside her. "I've been calling you for thirty minutes."

Jennifer pointed to the phone line that lay curled up uselessly on the floor, the plug a foot away from its wall jack. "We had to unplug it to get some peace. Everyone in town wants to talk to Mark, and quite a few people from out of town. We even had kids we don't know dropping by to see if he could hang out. If this keeps up, I'm going to move in with you."

"Let's hope the novelty wears off soon."

About that time, Mark walked into the room wearing his charcoal gray sweat suit and tennis shoes. He looked exhausted.

"What's the matter?" Heather asked. "You look awful."

"Thanks. Good to see you too, Heather. Actually, I didn't get much sleep last night. The team bus had a flat on the way back from Espanola. It was three a.m. when I got in. Then some assholes started calling me at seven o'clock this morning." A scowl spread across his features as he glanced toward Jennifer. "And you know who kept walking in and handing me the phone."

This time Jennifer's smile was real. "If you want to be the big superstar, you have to pay the price. Besides, I'm not your personal answering service."

"And I've got this big honors Spanish paper due tomorrow, which I only started today. So, yes. You might say I'm a bit worn out."

"I'm sorry about that," said Heather. "I want to razz you too, but you look so pathetic. I can't do it."

"That's OK. Jen's been making up for it. She might as well tattoo 'I told you so' on her forehead."

Jennifer inclined her head. "Imagine when the student body sees their new basketball hero in the hallway tomorrow. Thank God we don't go to school on a cruise ship. The thing would roll over when everyone rushed to your side of the boat."

The image of the school tilting up on one end and going down like the *Titanic* while Mark yelled, "I'm king of the world!" started Heather laughing so hard that tears began rolling down her cheeks.

The twins stared at her until the chortling contagion spread, first to Mark, then to Jennifer, leaving them all gasping for breath and clutching at their sides. Just when it seemed that they had gotten their mirth under control, one of the three would give out a snort and the whole thing would start up again.

Mr. Smythe walked into the living room, took a long look at the three of them laughing uncontrollably on the couch, then shook his head and walked back into the kitchen. Heather knew that look. Understanding high school students was a task that required mental energies well beyond what he was prepared to expend on a Sunday afternoon.

CHAPTER 24

Happy as Heather had been to see the snow arrive, she was even happier with the sudden warming that melted it away. Fresh snow was fun and could sometimes get you an extra day off. Old snow made you feel as gray and dirty as it was. Luckily, New Mexico's state symbol wasn't the sun for nothing.

Work in the Smythe garage continued unabated, although most often now it was just her and Jennifer. She was thrilled with the progress they had made on the project.

First, they had successfully produced an acceptable pair of quantum twin microswitches, something that would have certainly been worthy of a Nobel Prize if they were at liberty to reveal what they had accomplished.

They had used these in two circuit boards, which converted the signals back and forth between analog and digital. They then added a programmable interface that allowed them to send or receive signals on either end, amplifying the output so that it could be routed through a computer system.

Next they repaired and modified their damaged model airplane, adding a larger fuel tank and a set of solar panels on the tops of the wings and fuselage. A cell phone app allowed them to program a flight route and provided for control of the onboard camera and microphone.

Lastly they added one of the quantum twin circuits to the receiver-transmitter on the aircraft. The plane could still receive control signals from the ground in the traditional radio way. But it could also be switched to receive commands through the quantum twins—or QTs, as they had started calling them. It could even send video and audio output through the QT circuitry.

They had just successfully sent a combined video and audio signal from the small plane to the ground station and had recorded the output on Jennifer's laptop. Admittedly, it was only a picture of the pegboard mounted to the garage wall, along with the sound of their own whooping and clapping as they watched the signal come in, but it was a successful test.

Heather had hoped to have the aircraft ready for its first flight before Sunday, and they had achieved this with a day to spare. Heather had to admit that Jennifer was now a computer sorceress.

"It's getting late. I guess we're at a point where we can wrap things up until Sunday afternoon," said Heather.

Jennifer looked down at the display on her laptop. "You go on. I want to put in a couple of changes to the payload controls before I go to bed."

"Mark is going to be around to help us with our first flight test on Sunday, right?"

"He says he is. They're due back from their tournament in Santa Fe late Saturday night. He'll have to figure out how to unglue the cheerleaders who have been stuck to him. Oh—have you seen the way Colleen Johnson has been draped all over him?"

Heather laughed. "It's a little hard not to notice. I swear, she has the best pair of boobs money can buy. Mark doesn't seem to mind."

"Mind it? I'd say he's left cloud nine and moved on to cloud ten. Anyway, he promised he'd ditch her for our test on Sunday. As soon as you get back from church, we're out of here."

Heather grabbed her jacket and headed for the door. "I'm going with my mom and dad to Albuquerque tomorrow. So I'll see you on Sunday."

The weather continued to improve throughout the weekend, resulting in a lovely day of shopping, dinner, and a movie on Saturday and an even better Sunday morning. By the time church was out, Heather was hearing birds that she thought had long since departed for Acapulco or Cancun. Since she, Mark, and Jennifer would be riding their bikes into Los Alamos for the flight test, a nice day would make the ten-mile ride a pleasure.

By the time Heather had pulled her bike from the garage, she found Jennifer and Mark already waiting for her, the airplane packed on Mark's bike rack. Mark seemed as genuinely excited by the opportunity to try out their project as the girls were.

Pedaling hard, they reached the Western Area Park in record time. Heather had always liked this little park situated near Sullivan Field, but that was not why they had picked it for today's flight. Although it was a bit risky, they had decided to see if the new fuel tank would give them range to get the plane close to the part of the lab where the Rho Project was located.

If it did, they might be able to zoom in a little on some of the buildings in the distance to get a feel for the layout. There were a bunch of signs around the restricted areas of the laboratory warning civilians to stay off and that deadly force was authorized, but it shouldn't hurt to peek over the fence from a model airplane, as long as they didn't cross that boundary.

In the past this would have been out of the question. The radio control unit would not have had enough range to keep communication with the aircraft as it traveled toward the lab. That was no longer going to be a problem since their communication range was now infinite. Gas was their only limiting factor.

"We ready for launch?" Mark asked. Seeing the thumbs-up from Jennifer, he spun the propeller, bringing the small engine roaring to life.

As he released it, the airplane climbed quickly into the sky. Jennifer made some entries in her cell phone, uplinking a flight plan that sent the aircraft turning to the southeast. In just a few moments it passed out of sight over the tall pine trees and buildings.

"How's our data?" Heather asked.

Jennifer fiddled with her computer for several seconds before responding. "Everything looks normal, and I'm showing no loss in signal strength. Of course, you wouldn't expect any with the QTs, but it's nice to see it working."

Mark moved over to look at the video display. "The camera image is great. Damn, we're good."

Heather found Mark's comment slightly irritating since he had done precious little work on the thing.

As the plane got farther away, they could determine its position by looking at the TV picture. It would have been nice to have added a GPS device to the airplane too, but it just couldn't handle more weight.

"That's it, turn it south, about a hundred and seventy on the bearing," Mark said. "There, that's perfect. Keep it going that way just a couple more minutes."

Heather leaned forward to look over Mark's shoulder. "Watch out. We're coming up on the outer fence. Don't cross that."

Mark shook his head. "Hold it steady just a little longer. I want to get a little clearer view of that L-shaped building in the distance."

Jennifer looked up at Heather. "Heather, tell me when to turn. Mark would have me flying right over it."

Heather stared at the screen. They should have already turned back, but now she could see what Mark wanted to look at. They were almost in position to look down over the top of the northern wing of the long building.

All at once the camera image spun wildly on the screen.

"What's happening?" Mark asked.

Jennifer's fingers played across her cell phone. "I can't control it. It's going down."

The image on the screen went dark.

Mark jumped to his feet. "Crap. We crashed it onto the restricted site. Get this stuff packed up. Let's get out of here before someone comes looking for who was flying it!"

In seconds they had everything back on the bikes and were spinning their wheels back toward White Rock. No one spoke, but a sick feeling had taken hold in Heather's stomach. Not only had they flown over an area that they weren't supposed to, but they had somehow managed to crash the airplane there. If it was traced back to them, there was no telling what kind of trouble they might be in.

As they reached the Smythe driveway, Mark leaped off his bike cursing. "Damn it. This could get me thrown off the basketball team."

Jennifer's eyes were wet with tears. "You idiot! I said keep away from the restricted area. What were you thinking?"

"You were flying the damned thing."

"But I couldn't see where it was," Jennifer moaned. "I was counting on you guys to tell me when to turn it back."

Heather took a deep breath. It wouldn't do for her to start crying, too. "Maybe they won't find the plane," she said. "Even if they do, they probably won't trace it back to us."

Mark shook his head, looking deflated. "I wouldn't bet my ass on that."

"Anyway," Heather continued, "we can't let our folks see us upset."

Mark bowed his head. "Jen, I'm sorry I yelled at you. It was my fault."

Jennifer looked up at her brother and gave a weak attempt at a smile. "I'll be all right. I think I'll go in and wash up before dinner, though. I've had about all the excitement I can handle for today."

Heather shrugged. "We'll just have to hope for the best."

Turning to push her bike back to her garage, Heather felt the weight of the world descend, and the probability equations that danced in her head did nothing to make her feel better.

CHAPTER 25

The wind swept beneath the seals of doors and sills of windows, sounding a low moan that rose and fell along the eves of the houses.

As Heather rode the school bus in silence, the moan leached into her soul, a portent of what awaited her. But she refused to yield to depression, stubbornly clinging to the tiny seed of hope that everything would yet be OK.

By early afternoon that hope had grown, sprouting small leafy shoots that reached longingly upward, seeking the sun. Then Principal Zumwalt walked into their English class, requesting that Mark, Jennifer, and Heather accompany him back to his office, and she felt the seedling get ripped out by its roots.

To Heather's ears, their footsteps in the empty hallway sounded like dancers' tap shoes on a stage. Both Mark and Jennifer looked like fugitives from one of those old vampire movies. The blood had been drained from their faces as thoroughly as if they had just finished an embrace with an undead Transylvanian count.

Heather felt sick. She wanted to curl up in her bed, pull the covers over her head, and never come out again.

Principal Zumwalt led them into the waiting area outside his office and asked them to sit. Then he disappeared inside, closing the door behind him so that the voices drifting out to where they waited were unintelligible. Several times the principal's voice rose in anger before subsiding.

After several minutes, a man in a dark suit stepped out of the principal's office and stopped in front of them. Heather had never seen him before, and as his cold, gray eyes lingered on each of them, she decided that she did not care to see him again.

His thin smile added no warmth to his face.

"My name is Special Agent Nixon. I need to ask each of you a few questions, so I will be calling you into the principal's office one at a time. Your principal has insisted that he remain in the room to witness the questioning, and I have agreed."

Once again the cold smile warped his lips.

"As I finish with each one of you, please return to your classroom. Do not pause to discuss anything with the others on your way out."

Agent Nixon pointed at Mark. "Son, you're first."

Mark stood and followed the man back through the door. Thirty minutes later, Jennifer replaced Mark. By the time Jennifer emerged, puffy eyes indicating that she had not successfully kept her emotions in check, Heather was a basket case.

As she entered, she spotted Principal Zumwalt standing against the left wall, arms crossed as he glanced up at her. Agent Nixon motioned toward the low chair that had been positioned directly in front of the principal's desk.

Heather sat down. Not only was the chair low, it was a soft leather that threatened to swallow her, leaving her with the unfortunate illusion that she had sunk so far into the seat that only her nose and eyes stuck out.

As Agent Nixon moved behind the desk and took a seat in Principal Zumwalt's chair, Heather thought she detected a slight scowl on the latter's face.

The agent leaned forward, elbows on the desk. "Now, Heather, I want you to describe to me in your own words the sequence of events that led to you and your friends crashing a model airplane outfitted with video and listening devices onto a highly restricted and sensitive area of the Los Alamos National Laboratory."

Heather had once read that in an interview you should try matching the body posture of the person conducting the interview. However, there was just no way to lean forward in the soft leather armchair that had her butt closer to touching the ground than her feet were.

For fifteen minutes she described how they had been excited to do a project where they modified a model airplane to add video and audio transmission capabilities, plus an onboard computer that enabled them to uplink simple flight plans. She made no mention of quantum switches, instead wrapping up with a description of how they had launched the plane, uplinked a flight plan, and then lost control of it as it flew out of the range of their radio control device.

"So you knew it was flying toward the laboratory?"

"Yes, sir. We launched it from the Western Area Park in Los Alamos and it was flying southeast. We must have lost line of sight while we tried to uplink a return plan, so our uplink didn't make it, or something else went wrong. Once it was out of radio range, there was nothing we could do. We knew it was bound to go down, but had no idea it would make it all the way to the lab."

"And you didn't try to find out where it crashed?" The agent clenched his hands below his chin.

"We rode down the street a long way, but it had gone out toward the canyon. We didn't know how far it traveled, so it seemed like searching for a needle in a haystack. We were upset, but it didn't look like we had any choice but to give up and hope someone would find it and report it."

Agent Nixon smiled. "But you weren't worried enough to tell your parents that you had lost your airplane? When I polygraphed your father and Mr. Smythe this morning, neither one of them seemed to know a thing."

Heather gulped. This was a nightmare. Their fathers had been pulled out of work at the lab and administered a polygraph test because of this? She knew they were periodically required to undergo lifestyle polygraph tests because of the classified nature of their work. But being tested because of something their children had done was unbelievable.

"I don't know. We were upset and embarrassed that we had modified the plane and had it crash on the first outing. They gave us the money for the whole project and it was gone." She shrugged. "I guess we just wanted to wait a couple of days to see if someone found it before we had to confess."

"Is that so?"

"Yes, sir."

"Young lady, are you aware of the penalties for lying to a federal officer in the conduct of an official investigation?"

"No, sir."

Principal Zumwalt stepped forward. "I have had enough of this fishing expedition, Agent Nixon. I have stood by as you questioned each of these students and have listened as all of them have told you essentially the same story. Now you have moved from legitimate questions to what I regard as intimidation and harassment. I will remind you that these children are juniors in high school, that I am their principal, and that at no time did I hear you read them their Miranda rights. So unless you are now going to do so and place my student under arrest, this interview is finished."

The smile returned to Agent Nixon's lips, but not to his eyes.

"Very well, Principal Zumwalt. I have the information I came for. Ms. McFarland, you are free to go."

Heather struggled to her feet and walked from the room. Her hands shook as she opened the door and, glancing back, Heather thought she detected a smug look of satisfaction on the agent's face.

A sudden heat flushed her face. Heather felt disoriented, at a loss to figure out where she should be going. The big round hall clock indicated that it was two fifteen. That meant study hall, but before she went anywhere near anyone she knew, Heather felt the need to wash her face and spend a few moments trying to recover. They'd been rash; they'd jeopardized the secret of the second spaceship. What had they been thinking?

The rest of the day was a haze that failed to dissolve even when she, Mark, and Jennifer stepped off the school bus and made the short walk home. The shock of what had happened was so deep that they barely spoke to each other. What was there to say?

As she stepped off the sidewalk and into her driveway, Heather's feet slipped on an icy spot, setting her down hard on her rear end, scattering her books across the asphalt. Mark and Jennifer rushed over as she gathered herself, blinking back hot tears.

"It's OK, I'm all right," Heather said, her voice sounding hoarse to her ears.

As Mark retrieved her scattered books and papers, Jennifer hugged her friend tightly, tears leaking from her own eyes.

Mark gently handed her books back to her. "It's going to be OK. We have each other, and we'll get through this." It was a good thing Mark wasn't being his usual oblivious self, because otherwise, she would have punched him.

Heather sniffed and nodded, then turned and walked to her front door.

Dinner that evening was uncomfortable; it had been a while since Heather had felt so awkward with her parents. Once again, she was forced to tell the same tale she had told Agent Nixon, along with a description of what had happened at school. Her father did not reprimand her for failing to tell him about what had happened in the park, or for allowing him to be blindsided by the resulting investigation, but she could feel his disapproval in the tone of his voice and the weight of his gaze.

Heather considered herself to be a generally upbeat person, but by the time she went to bed she had been locked in depression for more than twenty-four hours. In fact, her black mood was sinking deeper. Not only had they violated the law, she had been forced to lie to a federal agent. Worse yet, she had lied to her own mother and father.

Instead of doing her homework and taking a bath, Heather just slid into her pajamas and crawled into bed. But sleep was a long time in coming.

For the next two days the three friends heard nothing about the progress of the investigation. School came. School went. Stress sat so heavy on their shoulders that Heather and the Smythe twins acquired a visible slump. It was odd—finding the spaceship, seeing Dr. Stephenson recover from that wound so quickly, none of that had affected them like this. The accumulation of pressure had finally cracked the veneer of Heather's self-confidence, allowing depression to seep through the hairline fractures.

Shortly after Heather's dad returned from work on Thursday afternoon, they received a call summoning the entire McFarland family next door to the Smythe house. As Heather stepped outside, she immediately saw the reason her dad had responded so quickly to the call.

Standing in the Smythe driveway, along with all of the Smythes, was Dr. Helmut Krause, director of the Los Alamos National Laboratory. Beside him stood Dr. Donald Stephenson.

As they moved up beside the Smythes, Dr. Krause nodded a welcome.

"As you know, I'm not a fan of seeing my laboratory in turmoil. I'm sure this investigation has been stressful for your families, but anything impacting the Rho Division is so important that the questioning and corresponding pressure is trebled. That's why I came here personally to let you know the results."

Heather's mouth felt so dry that she thought her tongue might permanently adhere to the roof of her mouth. Appalled to find herself staring at Dr. Stephenson's arm where the fork had stabbed him, she shifted her gaze to Dr. Krause's face.

"As should be obvious, the two of you, Fred and Gil, passed your polygraphs. As for your children, while they may have acted irresponsibly, we know that the range of the transmitter on their model airplane could not have reached the lab from the park. Nor could they have received any video or audio feed from that distance. Therefore we have concluded this was an accident."

The director looked directly at Heather, then Jennifer, and finally Mark, smiling warmly. "I was once a young person myself, as hard as that may be to believe. You three have been quite the topic of discussion at the lab. Our scientists who looked at the airplane you built really liked the innovative modifications you added. Of course, on future projects you need to program a reliable return home plan, in case your data link is lost."

Then, turning to Mark, Director Krause said, "I hear you are quite a basketball player, young man. I don't usually make the high school games, but I think I will try to come tomorrow night."

Mark grinned. "I'm sure our entire school would be honored to have you there, sir."

Director Krause nodded and shook hands with Gil and Fred. "I hope this puts your minds at ease. You have a good bunch of kids."

Both men thanked the director, who got into his car and drove off with a wave.

Suddenly everyone became very aware that Dr. Stephenson was still standing in the driveway. As the director's car disappeared around the bend, the deputy director stepped forward.

"Be assured, if the decision were mine, neither of you men would ever work at a national laboratory again. It doesn't matter one whit that you didn't know what your kids were up to. You are responsible for their actions. No excuses. No exceptions.

"While your children may not have intended to spy on the lab, I'll bet they were up to no good. Luckily, they are also no good at what they were up to, as evidenced by their incompetent construction and operation of their aircraft."

Dr. Stephenson turned on his heel and walked back to his car, a classic model Jaguar convertible. As he opened the door, he turned toward them once more.

"Consider yourselves on probation. I'll be personally checking the quality of your work to ensure it is better than the quality of your child rearing."

He slammed the door, and the Jaguar departed with a squeal of tires.

Heather had never heard her mother cuss, but the stream of language that erupted from the petite woman's lips was both creative and vile. When she stopped, there was a moment of awed silence.

Then, Mr. Smythe began to laugh, and the laughter soon spread to everyone in the driveway.

"Well, Anna, I don't think anyone could have said that better."

With a massive sigh of relief, they decided on a celebratory barbecue to be hosted by the Smythes that evening. While the dads fired up the grill, the moms worked on the appetizers and salad.

In the meantime, Heather, Jennifer, and Mark moved to their workshop in the Smythe garage. As soon as the door closed behind them, the three shared a round of high fives.

Jennifer melodramatically wiped her brow. "Thank God that's over. From here on, no more wild schemes."

Heather laughed. "You said it."

"Hey, guys. You need to see this." Mark's excited voice caused them to spin around. "I never bothered to look at our receiver units since the plane went down—but guess what? We're still getting a feed from the QTs. There's a faint audio signal, and we even have video coming in from the camera."

"Wait a second," Heather said. "I thought the camera was destroyed in the crash."

"It went black. Maybe the lens was in the mud. Now, wherever it is, it must be getting some light to power the solar cells."

Heather was stunned. "You know what this means? Our stuff is still out there and working. We might want to start a recording."

Jennifer's jaw dropped. "Didn't we almost get our heads handed to us? And didn't we just agree not to stick out our necks again?"

Mark shook his head. "This is different. Our airplane is already out there somewhere. The QT doesn't send detectable signals. There's no risk."

Heather paused a moment to consider, then nodded. "He's right. It won't hurt to investigate a bit more."

Jennifer sat down hard on the bench, rubbing her temples with both hands. "Mystifying. OK, stop. Don't say another thing. I think I'm going to be sick."

Mark grabbed his sister by the hand, pulling her to her feet. "Come on, Jen. Let's go grab some dinner. Once you have some good food in your stomach and get a good night's sleep, you'll start seeing things our way."

As Heather followed the twins, Jennifer replied, "That's exactly what scares the crap out of me."

CHAPTER 26

The smell of mahogany and Old English furniture polish hung thick in the air. Ventilation had never been installed in Dr. Stephenson's private office, just off the huge laboratory that housed the *Rho Ship*. He didn't need it. He didn't want it. The thick, old smell matched the dark, ceiling-to-floor mahogany of the bookcases. It matched the oversized mahogany desk, the mahogany captain's chair that had once seated Sir Francis Drake.

People were uncomfortable in Dr. Stephenson's presence under the best of conditions, but here, in the heart of his lair, their discomfort became a physical thing. He hadn't designed the room with that intention, merely selected furnishings and decor that felt right to him. The stifling effect it had on others he regarded as an unexpected and pleasurable side benefit.

The nerve of the man standing before his desk annoyed him to no end. Fred Smythe seemed completely oblivious to the oppressive atmosphere in the room and to Dr. Stephenson's own overbearing personality. He just stood there patiently awaiting a response.

"No, Mr. Smythe, I will not return the airplane that your kids and the McFarland child made. It became classified the second it penetrated restricted airspace. I will not waste anyone's time clearing its onboard memory just so your young hooligans can have it back."

The deputy director moved over to retrieve the airplane from a closet in the far wall. It had a broken left wing but showed no other signs of damage.

"You know what I am going to do? I am going to put this right here on my memento shelf so that whenever I am tempted to relax my demanding nature, I can glance to my left and remind myself that security threats spring from everywhere, especially from the seemingly innocent. Now get out of my office and get back to work."

With a curt nod of his head, Fred Smythe walked out of the deputy director's office, closing the door behind him.

Donald Stephenson leaned back in his chair and smiled. That felt really good. All in all, things were going very well.

Disposal of Abdul Aziz's body had been completed in a manner that left no possibility that it would be found. It was too bad his agent hadn't been able to intercept the man before he had gained entrance to the Brownstein house. Once Aziz was already inside, it was too risky to attempt a rescue.

So he had opted, instead, to have his man wait until Aziz finished his work. After that, once the assassin was killed, everyone who might have overheard classified information would be dead. After listening to the Aziz digital recording, Stephenson was confident he had made the correct choice.

With that situation cleaned up, there was nothing to delay the release of cold fusion technology around the world. It was all so easy. Especially since, less than a hundred feet from where he now sat, on the short side of the L-shaped building, the second alien technology was well into its final round of prerelease testing. And thanks to a couple of unofficial volunteers, that testing had now extended beyond the laboratory confines.

As Donald Stephenson leaned all the way back in his chair, his fingers interlaced behind his head, the thinnest of smiles creased his lips.

CHAPTER 27

Heather didn't know whether it was because of the announced presence of the director of the Los Alamos National Laboratory or just because Mark had a pent-up reservoir of energy from the stress of the week, but his performance on the Hilltoppers' home court that Friday night was record shattering. By the time Roswell Goddard High School found themselves facing the LAHS second team, Mark had left the game to a standing ovation, having scored sixty-two of the team's ninety-three points.

The national sporting newswires were suddenly abuzz with the story, thanks to an AP reporter, in town covering the *Rho Ship*, who happened to attend the game. The keys of his BlackBerry almost caught fire as he relayed a game rundown to his best friend and famed ESPN sports reporter Bobby Harold.

The story was also picked up by the *National Inquisitor*, a tabloid best known for its two-headed-baby stories. The lead story in their special Saturday edition screamed, "Alien Child of Rho Project Worker Scores 62."

When Jennifer looked at Mark's face staring up at her from the copy Heather bought at the grocery store, her eyes nearly popped from her head.

"Oh. This is just great."

Heather leaned against the workbench in the Smythes' garage. "Where is your alien brother, anyway?"

Jennifer shook her head. "His new cheerleader girlfriend picked him up an hour ago."

Heather frowned. "Colleen 'All Cars' Johnson?"

"That's the one. What does 'All Cars' mean?"

"That she's never found a backseat she didn't like." Heather's frown deepened. "What does Mark see in that girl? She's older than him and gives blondes a bad name."

"You have a way of answering your own questions." Jennifer crumpled the news rag in her hands and tossed it at the trash can next to the garage door. It missed.

Heather didn't know what it was that made her so angry when she thought of Mark out with Colleen. After all, he was free to make his own decisions. But someone so shallow? She was stunned.

"Well, don't worry about Mark," Jennifer said as she walked to the trash can and stuffed the wadded paper in. "The way the press is camping him now, there's no way he can go anywhere near the ship. We'll pack up the receiver equipment and take it out there ourselves."

They had decided it was too risky to keep the equipment in the Smythe garage any longer. Instead, they opted to take a laptop and the QT receiver unit and set them up on the ship. Power was a bit of a problem that they would have to resolve, but they had a plan for that.

They had a variety of photovoltaic cells that would turn light into power, which they could then use to keep the batteries charged. Both Heather and Jennifer were confident they could have the ship focus light on the solar collectors in a way that would give them a sufficient power stream to keep everything running. It would just take a little work to configure it all. With that in mind, they packed a complete set of tools.

It was almost noon by the time they loaded everything onto their bikes and made their way out to the starship, which they had named the *Second Ship*. The trip out had taken them twice as long as normal since they stopped several times to be sure they weren't followed.

Once through the holographic field, Heather climbed up into the ship first, leaning down to retrieve the packages as Jennifer handed them up to her. Jennifer struggled climbing up but, with Heather's help, finally managed. Then, pausing only to slip the headsets into place, Heather and Jennifer climbed up to the command deck.

For two hours they worked, laying out all of the receiver equipment, the laptop, and their tools and then hooking in the solar panel battery charging system. They were very happy with the way the ship responded to their request for enhanced lighting directed to the panel. A bright beam focused itself directly on the spot where they had laid out the solar array.

Another wonderful discovery presented itself completely by accident.

As Jennifer and Heather worked on the wiring from the solar collectors to the battery charging circuitry, Jennifer said, "I don't know about you, but I wish we had more pleasant surroundings to work on this stuff."

"I know what you mean. It would be nice to be on the beach in Bora-Bora right now."

The rose-colored light surrounding them dissolved away, replaced with the cobalt waters of the reef-sheltered island, gently lapping at the shore.

"Incredible," said Jennifer, standing and looking around.

Behind them, a high volcanic peak wreathed in clouds rose majestically into the sky. Heather could feel the soft breeze, smell the sea air, taste the salt on her tongue. It was so real that Heather knelt down to run her fingers through the sand, an act that almost resulted in her breaking a nail on the smooth floor of the command deck.

"How did it know what Bora-Bora looks like?" Jennifer asked.

"It must have gotten it from my mind," said Heather. "We stopped there on our Tahiti cruise last year. It's my favorite Tahitian island. If you've seen the old musical *South Pacific*, then you've seen it."

The illusion was so beautiful, the girls took a while to return to work.

When they finally finished and powered the system up, they received an unpleasant surprise. The QT receiver was not picking up a signal.

Jennifer turned to look at Heather. "What's going on? Do you think they destroyed the airplane?"

Heather paused to think. "I don't know, but I doubt it. More likely it's somewhere dark, so there's no power to the system. When the light comes back on, it'll start sending again."

"You mean *if* the light gets turned on. What if it's in a box?"

"Well, we can't worry about that. Let's go ahead and set the output to be captured to disk if the computer detects an incoming signal. We'll just leave it and come back tomorrow after church. Then we'll see if we have anything."

Jennifer moved to the keyboard and began programming in the instructions. As familiar as Heather was with how good

Jennifer had gotten, she still found herself amazed at just how fast her friend was on the computer.

After just a few minutes, Jennifer stood up. "OK, that's done. I guess all we can do now is wait."

It felt odd to leave all of their equipment set up on the floor of the command deck, but it made climbing the steep canyon slope back to their bikes much easier. It also made for a pleasant ride back to White Rock. As they approached the turn in to their houses, Meadow Lane held a surprise that killed Heather's good mood.

A small crowd had gathered in front of the Smythe house, clad in an assortment of outlandish garb and carrying signs such as SEND OUT THE ALIEN and BASKETBALL IS FOR EARTHLINGS.

Braking hard enough to leave skid marks, Jennifer barely managed to miss a woman who danced out into the street whirling a long scarf. It reminded Heather of one of those Olympic ribbon gymnastic routines.

"Hey, watch it! What do you think you're doing?" Jennifer demanded.

The woman stopped whirling, a vapid smile on her lips. "A welcoming dance, of course. The young alien must know that some of us welcome his presence here on our planet. Not everyone on Earth is a bigot."

Seeing Jennifer's raised eyebrow, Heather leaned over.

"Forget it. Let's get inside."

Two policemen were on the scene and managed to keep the group off of the Smythe front lawn and out of their driveway. One of them was kind enough to escort Jennifer through to her garage. Heather waved at Jennifer and then ducked into her own garage. Fortunately, the crowd remained oblivious to her presence.

By the time her mother had dinner ready, a larger contingent of police had arrived with a van and, having made several arrests for unlawful assembly and trespassing, managed to clear the area.

Heather's father peered out through the curtains on the front window before joining Heather and her mother at the table.

"Finally. I was wondering when the authorities would get that under control."

Her mother shook her head. "All it takes to stir up the nutcases is a story in the *Inquisitor*. Poor Mark. They almost attacked him and his girlfriend when they came home this afternoon. She seems like such a sweet girl."

Both her parents looked over at Heather as she almost choked on her spaghetti.

"Are you all right, babe?" her father asked.

Heather grabbed her water glass, taking a big gulp before responding. "Fine, Dad. I just swallowed wrong."

Relaxing, her parents returned to their discussion. By the time dinner was over and she made her way up to bed, Heather had gotten her fill of what a lovely family the Johnsons were and how proud they were of Colleen. After all, she was a two-time All-State Cheerleader and a shoo-in for her third selection in a row. And wasn't she just the cutest in that pretty little outfit she had been wearing this afternoon? And didn't Mark seem to be enjoying her company? And wasn't it about time he found a nice girlfriend?

On and on the conversation had revolved around the lovely Miss Johnson until Heather excused herself from the table, professing exhaustion. It was that or have her head explode.

Of course, the church service Sunday morning featured a sermon entitled "Love Thy Neighbor," all about how many people poison their minds with unkind thoughts toward others. By the end of the hour, Heather was thoroughly ashamed of herself and angry that she felt ashamed. Thank God she had not mentioned to her mom or dad her nickname for Colleen.

"Why the glum look?" her dad asked as they got into the car.

Heather forced a smile. "Was I looking glum? I must have been thinking about homework."

Great. Now she was lying to her parents again. God must be having a tough time keeping track of the sins she was racking up this week.

As they pulled up at their house and got out of the car, Heather found Jennifer waiting for her on the front porch. She noticed the Smythes' front lawn was protestor-free and looked back at Jennifer in question.

"Mark drove off with Colleen, and the crowd left," Jennifer said. "We didn't even have to call the police this morning."

"Then let's get going before some new ones show up."

"Exactly what I was going to suggest."

Jennifer's mom had packed them a picnic lunch of peanut butter sandwiches and diet sodas. Since a peanut butter sandwich was one of the few food items Linda Smythe could adequately prepare, Heather looked forward to it.

By the time Heather and Jennifer reached the *Second Ship*, they were both starving. Donning the headsets, they ate their lunches gazing out toward snowcapped Mount McKinley, its peak rising majestically in the distance, courtesy of the amazing graphical capabilities of the ship's computer system.

Leaning back on her elbows and taking a sip of her soda, Heather sighed. "You know something? I could get used to this."

Jennifer grinned. "Me too. Nothing like a little atmosphere to jazz up a picnic."

Packing up their trash, Heather moved over to examine the receiver unit. Her pulse quickened. "Hey, Jen. We've got something."

Jennifer moved to pick up the computer, setting it across her lap as she settled into one of the command couches. A rush of soft clicking sounds accompanied her slender fingers dancing across the keyboard. As Heather leaned in to look at the display, Jennifer activated the playback.

The scene before them was partially blocked, but the rest of the screen showed what looked like a Victorian sitting room.

A slender woman in a lab coat stood before the desk, dark hair tied in a tight bun. Her eyes were wide. Scared.

"Dr. Anatole, once again you disappoint me."

Heather and Jennifer both gasped as they recognized Dr. Stephenson's voice.

The woman's voice shook. "I am so sorry. You know how hard I am trying to please you with my work. But when I see things that I regard as dangerous, I feel it is my duty to bring them to your attention."

Dr. Stephenson paced into view, circling behind the woman, who looked frozen in place.

"And your judgment in this matter is somehow supposed to be comparable to mine?"

"No, Dr. Stephenson. Please. I did not mean to imply any such thing."

He leaned in close to her ear but did not lower the volume of his voice. "Then how do you assume that I would not have accounted for all possible mishaps and consequences in my plans? After all, it is my design, and unlike others on this project, I make no mistakes."

"Doctor, we all make mistakes. Even someone as brilliant as you are must have others double-check their work to avoid the possibility of error—especially with something as potentially dangerous as this second alien technology. The consequences of any miscalculation before it is approved for release could be devastating."

Dr. Stephenson moved to sit in the chair, facing slightly away from the camera. His hand moved out of view of the lens.

Both Heather and Jennifer jumped as Dr. Anatole screamed. Terror washed over the doctor's face as she collapsed to the floor and continued to scream. The girls stared, transfixed, as Dr. Anatole struggled to crawl across the floor but failed as her body convulsed and her hands began to claw at her own skin.

Suddenly, the screaming stopped, leaving the doctor curled on the floor, small whimpers escaping from her lips. Dr. Stephenson moved over beside the prostrate woman, kneeling down to gently stroke her forehead.

"If there is one thing I don't tolerate, it is anyone questioning my competency. If I say a technology is ready for release, it is ready for release. I don't learn about technologies. I master them. For example, I know that in a few minutes you will feel better. You will have no memory of this little lesson I have administered except for a conviction that your concerns about the new project are completely unfounded."

Dr. Stephenson ceased petting her head and moved back to his desk. "Now let us continue with your instruction."

Dr. Nancy Anatole's face contorted until it seemed the skin would split to reveal the bone beneath it. Unable to bear the screaming any longer, Jennifer switched off the playback.

Heather was stunned. Sick to her stomach. Sick to her soul.

"Oh my God." Jennifer's hands trembled as she closed the laptop. "Heather, what was he doing to her?"

Heather leaned on the back of the couch, her legs unsteady. "I don't know. He wasn't even touching her."

"We have to help her."

"I wish we could," said Heather, her thoughts spinning. "But she may not be the only one who needs our help. Did you hear what they were saying? It sounds like Stephenson is getting ready to release another of the alien technologies. We haven't even figured out what's wrong with cold fusion yet. Dr. Anatole sounded scared of this second one in a way she wasn't of the first."

Jennifer shuddered. "How can we stop it? No one is going to believe a couple of high school kids."

A lump rose in Heather's throat. "I think we have to consider showing the video to the authorities."

Jennifer shook her head. "But that would lead to questions we couldn't answer. They would want to know how we got it. They would find out about the ship."

Heather stared into her friend's eyes. "I know. I'm sorry. But I don't see any other way."

Over Jennifer's shoulder, lightning arced among the dark clouds that clutched Mt. McKinley's peak. Unable even to cry, Heather stared out at the hauntingly beautiful scene, drinking it in, one last time.

CHAPTER 28

The predawn wind was cold. Damned cold. Its cutting bite brought tears to Mark's eyes and then froze the wetness on his lashes as he stepped out his front door and jogged to the passenger side of Colleen Johnson's red Jeep Cherokee.

It irked him that he didn't have his own car. As he slipped inside, he was met halfway into his seat with a kiss that would have steamed his glasses if he had worn any. One thing he had to admit: as uncool as it was to need to have his senior girlfriend drive him everywhere, she sure had a way of taking the sting out of it.

After last night, he could use a little of that kind of attention to take his mind off other worries. It had taken him nearly two hours to talk Jennifer and Heather out of the idea of giving the recording to the authorities, an action that would certainly result in the three of them spending several years in federal prison. Only his argument that their dads might also be implicated changed the girls' minds.

The US government did not take kindly to someone making unauthorized recordings of highly classified material. Their intentions wouldn't matter.

"Whacha thinking about?" Colleen asked as she sped along Pajarito Road toward school.

Mark smiled, putting his hand onto her knee. "Nothing, really. Just trying to get my head together this morning. Why are we off so early? School's going to be locked up."

"I have a surprise for you." She glanced over at him and winked. "Bill, the custodian, said he'd leave the side door open for me. Anyway, I think you'll find it exciting."

Mark grinned. While people talked about Colleen's "bad girl" image, she was really just fun. She was far and away more exciting than any girl Mark had ever dated. She had also surprised him by not being as wild as people said she was. Oh, she was willing to make out in public places for the thrill of it, and the way she kissed and moved her hands and body across him made him feel like a young bull that wanted to paw dirt and snort twin blasts of steam from his nose.

But when it came right down to it, Colleen always pulled back from going all the way, something Mark had no experience with but was more than willing to try. Colleen was more of a serious tease than a truly naughty girl, but man, could she ever torture him with the teasing. It reminded him of something he had once heard a famous comic say: "Man, if this is torture, chain me to the wall."

So, if Colleen had a surprise for him, Mark was willing to play along.

They weren't the first car at the school, but you could never really beat the custodian in, no matter what time you showed up. Colleen drove past the entrance to the school parking lot, bringing the jeep to a stop in the side lot. As he slammed the door, she grabbed his hand and led him surreptitiously around the side of the building, glanced around quickly, and then ducked in a side entrance.

"Ooh. Feeling pretty frisky this morning, eh?" Mark crooned.

Her laughing blue eyes crinkled at the edges as she whispered back, "You have no idea. Now come on."

Turning a corner, Colleen led the way into the dark gymnasium. She pulled a small keychain light from her purse and then moved on across the court, pulling him into the boys' locker room. As Mark grinned and reached for her, she pulled back.

"No, you have to wait a second. This is a surprise. Now turn around and close your eyes. Promise me you won't open them until I tell you."

Mark laughed softly. "OK, OK. I promise. Just don't take too long."

"Just make sure they are closed tightly. I don't want you spoiling everything after I've gone to all this effort to make it happen."

"Don't worry about me. I wouldn't dream of messing up your surprise."

Mark stood there facing the lockers, although he couldn't have seen very much even if he had his eyes open, with as little light as the keychain flashlight provided.

A slight noise behind him brought goose bumps of anticipation to his arms and neck. What could the little vixen be up to? His imagination supplied a variety of intriguing answers to that question as he waited.

The large canvas ball bag came down over his head, arms, and waist so fast and with such force that by the time he realized that it wasn't Colleen grappling him, he found he could barely move, much less fight back. Several sets of strong arms tackled him to the floor as he struggled against the canvas, but it might as well have been a straightjacket. He felt a knee on his back and another on his neck as yet another person pulled some sort of strap tight around the outside of the bag, binding his arms tight against his side.

"What the hell? Get off me, you assholes," Mark yelled, although the sound came out muffled.

"Dream on, punk."

Mark recognized the voice. It was Doug Brindal, senior star quarterback of the Hilltoppers' football team, ex-boyfriend of one Colleen Johnson. A trail of little dots started to connect as a light dawned in his mind.

He felt his body lifted by four sets of hands, no doubt some of Doug's good buds who had volunteered to lend a hand. His head banged hard against a corner as they carried him along, and he heard the doorway back into the gym swing open. Something screeched, and he was thrown down hard on a metal rack. From the hard, curved lumps and narrow rods he felt pressed against his chest, it could only be one of the wheeled basketball racks.

He yelled again, but this time a chorus of laughter was all that greeted him. "There's nobody here to hear you but us, Smythe. No teachers or coaches to save your sorry ass from getting a lesson you've had coming all year."

"You tell him, Doug!" Mark recognized this new voice as belonging to another senior member of the football team, Bob Fedun, a hulking 230-pound defensive tackle. "Every basketball wimp needs a lesson, and you seem to think you're somewhere above your true station in life."

Mark focused, channeling all his enhanced neural pathways, coordinating his muscles into one concerted effort. The bag bulged, accompanied by the sound of canvas thread popping at the seams, but the straps that had been looped around the outside held.

"Hey, watch it," Doug yelled. "This cheap bag is starting to rip. You guys hold him tight while I give this strap a couple more wraps around his body. That's it. Now slide him back this way. I want him hunched over the end of this thing like he was humping this line of basketballs. That's right."

Unable to get any leverage, Mark felt himself being tied firmly. His feet were pulled apart and tied just above the wheels, while his upper body was bent forward along the line of the rack and strapped down tight against it, his arms pinned to his torso.

Doug's panting voice came close to his ear. "OK. Give me that knife."

With a loud ripping sound, the top of the canvas bag was torn away from around his head.

"You son of a bitch," Mark spat out. "If you don't let me loose, I'm going to—"

A vicious pull on his hair jerked his head up so that he could see the knife blade inches from his throat. "You're going to what? Kick our butts? I don't think so, Smythe."

The others laughed loudly.

"Tape his mouth," Doug said. A long strip of duct tape accomplished the task.

The gang worked rapidly. Pulling his pants down around his ankles, they pulled out a large permanent marker and carefully lettered the words *FOOTBALL RULES*, one word on each butt cheek.

Doug pulled Mark's head up by the hair one more time, grinning into his face. "I believe you know my girlfriend."

Colleen bent down, her beautiful, full lips just inches from his own.

"Did you really think I would dump Doug for you, just because you can play a little basketball? Don't get me wrong. You're cute, but get serious.

"Doug's father was number one in his class at Cal Tech. He got his PhD in chemistry by the time he was twenty-three. He started his own company and made his first million before he was twenty-five. Now he runs a division at the lab just because he likes it.

"Your father, on the other hand, doesn't even have a master's degree. He's just a technician. Do you really think I would slum over to your side of the tracks?"

Her laughter was musical.

Doug let go of Mark's hair. "OK, enough of this. It's showtime."

The wheels of the rack squealed as it was pushed rapidly across the gym. A door banged shut as they left him alone in the dark locker room.

Mark continued to struggle against his bonds but to no avail. There were too many straps and too much tape to allow him to break free, and the duct-tape gag made it difficult to breathe, much less yell loudly enough to be heard.

After what seemed like an eternity, but which must have been only an hour, distant sounds in the hallway alerted Mark to the arrival of the first wave of students. There was no mistaking the unique crescendo of squealing laughter, yells, and banging lockers of a school hallway in full-throated cry.

Almost as soon as the sound began, the door banged open and his tormentors were back, wheeling the cart out into the gym and toward the hallway door.

Doug gave the command. "Ready. Go."

With a shove, the gang of four opened the gym door just enough, pushing the cart, Mark's butt first, out into the hallway. In the sudden suffocating silence that followed, and before the gym door could swing closed behind the cart, Mark heard their footsteps racing back through the gym toward the far exit.

"Oh my God!" someone yelled.

The hallway of Los Alamos High suddenly exploded into a chorus of laughter that rattled the wall lockers in accompaniment. There, amid the commotion, too stunned to move, Jennifer and Heather stared at the words printed on the naked posterior of Marcus Aurelius Smythe.

CHAPTER 29

As Jennifer's hands played her keyboard like a concert pianist at work on a grand piano, it occurred to Heather that her friend must have also picked up some neural enhancement that refined her finger dexterity, despite protestations to the contrary.

Heather glanced over to where Mark had pulled up a chair next to Jennifer's computer desk. He had laughed off the embarrassing incident at the school, refusing to tell anyone who the perpetrators were, but she knew him. Inside he was seething.

If the boys who had roughed him up knew anything about him, they would not sleep for the rest of the school year. Mark was a bulldog. Once he got motivated, he didn't let up until he emerged victorious.

"Jen says you've started working out," Heather said.

Mark glanced over at her. "Yep. Dad wasn't using his old free weights, so I got him to give them to me. A little extra muscle mass on this body wouldn't hurt."

"Just don't go getting so muscle-bound that you look like one of those magazine guys."

Mark laughed. "Nope. I just want toning and strength."

"And those books on aikido you bought?" Jennifer asked.

"That's just for flexibility."

Heather nodded. "Uh-huh. And just how much time are you spending trying to stay flexible?"

"No more than two hours a night."

"Every night?"

"Yes. Why?"

"Sounds like you're going to be one flexible dude."

"Well, it relaxes me after a hard day of school, basketball practice, and homework."

Heather looked at Mark closely. He seemed relaxed. Obviously, he had a plan in the works and was comfortable that it was progressing on schedule. She changed the subject.

"I've got an idea how we may be able to tip off the authorities about Stephenson."

Jennifer spun her chair to face Heather. "All right. I guess I'm ready to hear this."

"I'm all ears," said Mark, leaning forward in his own chair. "Uh, by the way, would you stop? I'm getting whiplash."

Heather stopped pacing. "Sorry," she said, and sat down on the corner of Jennifer's bed. "We can send an e-mail message to the National Security Agency."

Jennifer's jaw dropped open. "Have you completely lost your mind? They would trace an e-mail in a heartbeat, right back to our three little teenaged butts."

Mark nodded. "I hope that isn't the whole plan. I'd get plenty of workout time in the prison weight room."

Heather scowled. "Of course that isn't the whole plan. Do you honestly think I would spend a whole week coming up with that?"

"Just making sure the numbers in your head haven't stopped adding up."

Heather ignored the jibe. "We've got to get a message to someone in the government with the ability to look into highly classified stuff. And from what I've found out, the NSA is the king of the secret world. They have computers tracking every e-mail and phone call on the planet."

Jennifer nodded. "Yes. And that makes it safe for us to e-mail them, how?"

"Look, I didn't say it was going to be easy. What we'll have to do is send the e-mail from an untraceable source." Heather paused, looking directly at Jennifer. "We'll have to hack our way into some remote system on the Internet, then drop a virus. The virus will send the e-mail after it has covered its tracks."

"Oh great," said Jennifer. "There are just a few problems with that scheme. First, it's highly illegal."

"Well, I think we burned that bridge a long time ago," Mark injected.

"And," Jennifer continued, "the government, along with major corporations, has gotten pretty darned good at tracking people putting viruses on the Internet. As a matter of fact, they catch almost all of them."

"We're just going to have to be better than those people," said Heather with a shrug.

"And," Jennifer continued, "last but not least, e-mail isn't secure. When that message gets sent, every major government is going to know what it says, even if it's addressed to the NSA. And you can bet Dr. Stephenson will find out."

"I've been thinking hard about that. Let's talk about the e-mail security first," Heather said. "Anyway, the virus is going to have to sense when it has hopped around the net enough to send the e-mail. The e-mail needs to include an encrypted computer address containing where the real message is stored. The first one to break the encryption on that message will be the first one to find the computer where the real message is."

"What if the NSA doesn't break the code first?" asked Jennifer.

"They're supposed to be the best in the world at that. We'll just need to hope that the US government isn't wasting all that money. They will also have one more slight advantage. Anyone else will have had to pick up the e-mail from spying on the net and identify it for analysis. That should put the others a little behind, since the NSA will directly receive the e-mail clue."

Jennifer shook her head. "The NSA is supposed to have more PhD mathematicians than anyone else and the best code-cracking super computers. How can our encryption stand up to that?"

Heather grinned. "That's the beauty of it. I've been reading up on encryption theory. The best schemes are mathematically based. That's why all those mathematicians work at the NSA."

"I feel much better now," said Jennifer, making Mark chuckle.

"Don't you see? Even though the encryption methods I could research were not the classified ones, they were produced by some pretty darn good mathematicians. And I can see the solutions, automatically, easily. I don't even have to think about it."

"Now you're freaking me out," said Mark.

Heather smiled. "And I can do far better."

A sudden light dawned in Jennifer's face. "So you come up with an encryption that is difficult, but not impossible to break. Then we encrypt the e-mail message and count on the NSA to crack it first. What about the back trace they're going to put on our virus?"

Heather shrugged. "We'll launch the virus from some public place. You're going to have to come up with a way of countering their trace."

"I don't know. The guys hunting us will be the best in the business."

"Yeah," said Mark. "They're going to be on our asses like pigs on shit."

Jennifer frowned. "Lovely image."

"We'll need to be able to see how the back trace is coming," Heather said.

Jennifer rubbed her chin. "I guess I could have the virus leave a little agent program on each infected computer before it jumps to the next. That little guy's job would just be to report on his health by posting a code to some public chat site we could monitor."

Heather's eyes widened. "What a great idea. I could design an algorithm to generate a unique code for each agent. All it would need to contain would be a unique ID, a time stamp, and the address of the computer it was on."

Mark rubbed his hands together. "Now we're getting somewhere. Jen just has to monitor those codes to see when they drop off the net."

Jennifer nodded. "But the antivirus companies are going to try to kill off our virus."

"That won't be a big problem," said Heather. "We don't need it to last forever, just long enough to send the clue e-mail."

"Yes," said Jennifer, "but as that antivirus starts wiping out our little agents, it will make it hard to tell whether or not they are dying from the trace or just from the antivirus."

"Actually I think that will help us," Heather said. "I'll be able to spot the difference in the patterns."

Mark stood up. "Problem solved, then. Sounds like you two have some work to do."

"Not yet, buddy boy," said Heather. "A couple of last details. Our laptops and cell phones are going to have incriminating data on them. I'll come up with another encryption algorithm that I think will be unbreakable, and then I need Jen to add that to our virus program."

A confused look settled on Jennifer's face. "Add it to our virus? How does that have anything to do with protecting the data on our systems?"

A sly smile settled on Heather's lips. "Look. It won't work to just have a program on our machines that encrypts any data we don't want others to know about. If someone looks on our computers and finds a bunch of data with a supersophisticated encryption scheme, they'll just want to know where we got the encryption. Game over."

"OK?"

"We let the virus encrypt some data on every machine with the unbreakable code. On our machines it will encrypt important stuff. On everyone else's computer, it'll just encrypt random garbage."

Jennifer clapped her hands. "Then if anyone snoops around, it just looks like we got an infection like everyone else."

"Yes. We'll just need to make sure we get our computers infected from the Internet after we launch our virus."

Jennifer closed her eyes. After several seconds she opened them. "I think it'll work."

Mark walked over and patted each of them on the back. "That's it, then. You two hop right on it and report in to me with your progress."

"Not quite," said Heather with a smile. "I need you to do something for us."

Mark shook his head. "Why doesn't that shock me?"

Heather continued. "With your enhanced language skills, do you think you could learn some Russian?"

Mark perked up, looking intrigued. "Russian? That's a rather odd choice, isn't it? What have you got up your sleeve?"

"I haven't got it all worked out yet. Can you just do it?"

Mark grinned. "Sounds mysterious. I'll give it a shot."

"Good," said Heather. "Jen, I'll try to have the algorithms ready for you tomorrow."

Jennifer nodded. "In the meantime, I'll make sure I know everything I can about computer worms and viruses. I want to feel comfortable before I write a single line of code."

Mark paused at the door and glanced back at his sister.

"Jen, don't wait until you're comfortable. By that time the sun will be a red giant. We need something by the time Christmas vacation is over."

The eraser she threw bounced harmlessly off the door as Mark ducked out of the room.

CHAPTER 30

The next three weeks passed in a flurry of activity, with one day blending into the next. The Los Alamos Hilltoppers basketball team continued their winning ways, although Mark's scoring settled down to an average of closer to twenty-five points a game. By the time Christmas break came and went, Mark's workout program was beginning to bring about a noticeable change in his physique. His arms and shoulders had thickened, and his waist had narrowed. Heather had seen him without his shirt after one of his workout sessions, and his stomach looked like it belonged to a comic book superhero. Apparently his neural augmentation made him incredibly efficient at training his muscles, and they had responded with a vengeance to his indomitable will. It wasn't that he looked like a weight lifter, far from it. He just looked extremely buff.

On a national level, the hubbub about the murders and cold fusion died to a low roar, viewers getting bored by the lack of new facts or evidence. Despite a feeling that she should maintain her vigilance, it made Heather relax a little bit, her fear of the second spaceship being discovered slipping farther and farther from her mind.

January first arrived with little fanfare. Heather had stayed up late the night before to watch the annual dropping of the New Year's ball in New York City, but she had been the only late bird in her family. Not that she was a party animal herself; she had just had a hard time sleeping, and the televised party coverage had provided a welcome distraction. Now she was tired but anxious to get on with what they had to do.

Today was the day. Virus Day. They had actually been ready to launch the virus for several days now but just couldn't bring themselves to do it over Christmas. So the dawn of the New Year would see the first salvo in a war that began decades earlier in the skies above Aztec, a war between good and evil. At least, that was how Heather thought of it.

Mark, Jennifer, and Heather parked their bikes in a rack some distance from their objective. They had selected a public pay phone in the same Los Alamos shopping center where press reports said Abdul Aziz's car had been found abandoned all those weeks ago.

Thanks to the ancient, acoustically coupled modem Jennifer had scrounged up, they could access the Internet from Jennifer's cell phone without using a traceable wireless connection. As Mark and Heather watched from a distance, Jennifer made her way to the pay phone. She leaned into it in a way that looked like she could be deep in a private discussion with a boyfriend.

It only took her a few minutes to access the Internet and upload the virus. As soon as Jennifer hung up the handset, pocketing her cell phone, Heather and Mark moved from their lookout to meet her by the bikes. While crossing the parking lot, Heather had a moment of déjà vu, feeling as if she were a refugee from some 1950s cold war spy movie. The feeling passed as they got on their bicycles. There was just something about the picture of a band of international espionage agents making their getaway on bicycles that didn't fit the way she felt.

Heather looked down at her hands. She had not been able to stop them from shaking since Jennifer had walked up to the phone booth. Now, as Heather pedaled hard to keep up with Mark and Jennifer as they sped away from the parking lot, she hoped with all her heart that their plan would work. If not, well, she didn't care to think about it.

From the corner of her eye she glimpsed a tall, thin man with long, stringy, blond hair standing near the corner of the shopping center, but when she turned her head to look, there was no one there. Easy, Heather, she told herself. Don't get paranoid now. She upped the pace of her pedaling, moving past Mark into the lead as they raced for home.

In the bike's mirror, she saw a gaunt, ragged man step out into the open, his expression as blank as the mannequin in the nearby store window. But by the time she skidded to a stop and turned to look back, the man was gone.

As she struggled to determine whether the mirror vision had been real or imagined, Mark's concerned voice interrupted her.

"Something wrong?"

With one more glance back, Heather shook her head. "I thought I heard something, but it was just the wind."

Then, before he or Jennifer could follow up on this line of questioning, Heather stepped down hard on the pedal, laying a short streak of rear tire rubber on the pavement as she accelerated away from the twins.

"Race you home!"

Her yell sounded playful, but it rang hollow. As hard as it was for her to believe, she'd just lied to Mark. And she didn't even know why.

CHAPTER 31

Deep within the bowels of the massive black glass structure affectionately known as Crypto City, Jonathan Riles leaned back in his executive chair, surveying the others assembled around the small conference table. He was a stocky man, ex-navy football star, Rhodes scholar, number one in his class at the Naval Academy, vice admiral. His friendly face served as an unlikely platform for intense, icy gray eyes. As he looked around at his team, he smiled. They were the National Security Agency's best of the best.

"So, Dave," Riles said, "tell me what you've got."

David Kurtz sat immediately to Riles's left, looking every bit the part of the wild-haired, absentminded professor. If there was one thing that Kurtz was not, though, it was absentminded.

Kurtz reached for a wireless remote control, clicking a button that brought the flat-screen video monitor to life. The far wall showed a map of the United States covered in clusters of red dots.

"As everyone in this room is aware, what the public is calling the New Year's Day Virus appeared on a large number of systems on New Year's Day. But since many companies were closed for the holidays, the true extent of the infection wasn't known until January third.

"Another reason for the slowness of the response was the apparently benign nature of the infection. The virus just hops from computer to computer, leaving behind a small agent program on each infected system."

Kurtz aimed a red laser pointer at the flat-screen monitor on the far wall. "This was the estimated extent of infection sites in the US as of the last report, about thirty minutes ago."

The slide changed to a map of the world. "Here is a map showing the estimated extent of the worldwide infection."

Riles leaned forward. "Hell, Dave, that thing looks like it has spread everywhere but North Korea. At least *their* computer systems seem well protected."

Laughter rippled around the table. A satellite view of Asia at night showed lights everywhere except for a dark outline of North Korea. The country was so backward it didn't even have a developed electricity delivery system so, of course, it had no notable computer network.

A serious look returned to Riles's face. "So what are all these agent programs doing?"

"We aren't quite sure yet," Kurtz said. "One thing they are doing is encrypting data on each computer."

"What kind of data?" Riles asked.

"From what we can tell, nothing significant. It looks like it picks a few temporary files on each computer and encrypts them. The files it picks don't really cause any damage because they are temporary."

"Why is it encrypting trash?"

Kurtz shrugged. "Sounds harmless, doesn't it? The problem is the encryption algorithm."

"Yes?"

"We haven't been able to break it."

"What?" Kurtz now had Riles's full attention.

"The little agent programs are encrypting the data in a way that we haven't even begun to scratch. Once we saw we had a problem breaking the code, I put our best systems and people on it. That was two days ago. No progress."

For several seconds Riles sat speechless as a babble of voices from around the table echoed in the room.

"OK. Everyone hold it down!" Riles said, and then stared at Kurtz. "I didn't think that was possible."

"Anything's possible. It is just not probable."

"Why would anyone go to the trouble to come up with an unbreakable code and then use it to encrypt garbage everywhere?"

"Our people think it's a calling card. Someone put it out there to say, I am very, very good. Come find me."

"Damned right we are going to find them. Then we are either going to throw their asses in prison or hire them."

"Which brings us to the reason I asked you to assemble the core team for this briefing," Kurtz said. "The virus did something new two hours ago. It sent the NSA an e-mail."

Kurtz pressed another button on the remote and the text of a short e-mail message appeared on the screen.

NSA. You are supposed to be the best. Let's hope you are. The clock is ticking…

Jonathan Riles moved along the side of the table toward the video screen. "What is that garbage down at the end of the message?"

Kurtz waved the laser pointer so that it drew a little circle around a bunch of strange-looking characters that formed the end of the message. “That, gentlemen, is another encrypted message. It looks like they want us to break this one, although it is taking us some time. You can bet your ass that every other spy agency in the world is trying their best to beat us to it right now.”

A light dawned in Riles’s eyes. “It’s an address.”

Kurtz nodded. “Very likely. The real message probably exists on only one computer out there somewhere, and this code tells us how to find it.”

“Then let’s make damned sure that we are the first ones to get there. How long until we crack it?”

“I would say we will have the answer within the hour,” said Kurtz.

Riles turned to the others sitting around the table. It wasn’t the NSA’s job to meddle directly in special operations. But thanks to a presidential finding, the special directive signed by the president of the United States himself after 9/11, Jonathan had acquired the services of a very special “cleanup team.”

The actual wording of the directive had been vague enough that Riles had been able to use it to gather a team of his choosing without the president being aware of any of the details. It was always important to let the old man maintain legitimate deniability when things bordered this closely upon unconstitutional action.

“Jack.”

A lean man, whose curly brown hair framed a face that looked like it had been freshly chiseled from Potomac granite, leaned forward.

“Yes, sir?”

"Get your team ready. As soon as our people crack that code, I want that system physically removed from wherever it is. Don't take any chances on this one."

"How about a warrant?"

"I'll get the special request started, but if it is late getting here, don't wait. I want that system, whatever it takes. If we have to get dirty, we'll clean up later. Now get going."

Jack Gregory stood up and strode from the room, followed closely by Janet Price and Harold Stevens, two more of the finest special field operatives in the world. As the door closed behind them, Riles had the sudden impression that the room felt a lot less…deadly.

CHAPTER 32

The brown UPS uniform fit Jack as if it had been made for him. As he walked from the truck toward the house, he adjusted the box he was carrying so it hid the small aerosol can in his right hand. He had expected the address to be close to Fort Meade, and indeed, once the code was broken, it led to a computer inside a house in Glen Burnie, Maryland, just a few miles from the NSA headquarters.

It certainly looked like someone was doing everything they could to make sure the NSA was the first on the scene. But doing something like using an address near the NSA headquarters indicated a lack of sophistication, maybe even naïveté, that would have the organization's profilers going nuts. If you wanted to put the message in a bigger nest of foreign spies than were located close to the Puzzle Palace, you would have to put it inside the UN.

Jack rang the bell, and a woman opened it with a smile. "Hi. I wasn't expecting a—"

The knockout gas hit her full in the face, the surprised intake of air that followed finishing the job as her legs lost their rigidity. Jack continued his momentum, catching the woman's slumping body as he stepped across the threshold. Immediately behind him, Janet Price, also in UPS attire, walked calmly up to the house carrying another package.

The two of them moved with quiet efficiency as Jack laid the unconscious woman on the couch next to the phone and then moved on, rapidly glancing in each room as he passed. Behind him he could hear Janet pick up the phone and dial familiar tones: 9-1-1.

"Hello, police? Help me. Please hurry. Someone is trying to get into my house. Aaaah." She coughed weakly then dropped the telephone handset beside the woman's body on the sofa.

Spotting the computer, Jack pulled the power cord from the back and rapidly disconnected all the other cables from the system. Then, leaving behind the monitor and all the peripheral equipment, he opened the UPS box and placed the computer inside.

As he moved out of the small office back into the living room, he saw Janet coming down the stairs giving him the thumbs-up signal. There were no other computers in the house. They had what they were after.

Picking up the two boxes with which they had entered, Jack and Janet walked out the front door, closed it behind them, stepped into the truck, and drove off. The police would be there shortly, and that was a good thing, not that Jack was worried about the unconscious woman. People rarely died from a single whiff of the gas. But there was going to be unexpected company at that address before long, and those late arrivals needed to see the police already on the scene or much worse violence was likely to occur.

Rounding a corner, Jack pulled the UPS truck into a parking lot where he and Janet left it, carried the box around the side of the building, and slipped into the backseat of a gold Honda Accord.

"Home, James," Jack said.

Harold Stevens smiled as he pulled out into traffic.

CHAPTER 33

"Heather! Have you got the news channel on?" Jennifer's voice on the phone sounded more anguished than excited.

"What's happened? Just tell me."

But Jennifer wouldn't. "Turn on CNN now. Hurry up."

Heather carried the wireless telephone with her into the living room and picked up the remote control from the coffee table with her left hand, almost knocking over the small pot of poinsettias in the process. The aging television hummed to life, the picture gradually fading in over the course of several seconds.

"Are you seeing this?" Jennifer breathed into the phone.

"Hold on a sec."

"Well hurry or you're going to miss it."

"I'm doing the best I can. My TV's coming on now."

The announcer was standing in front of what looked like a typical New England–style home in a quiet suburb. The police had established a large cordon around the house and a car that had crashed into a nearby streetlight pole. The car window was bloody, and the camera zoomed in to show several bullet holes in the windshield of the black Ford Explorer.

Heather turned up the volume.

"And so the peace and quiet of this little neighborhood in Glen Burnie, Maryland, was shattered earlier today as the home owner was repeatedly victimized in a strange set of circumstances that has left two men dead and three police officers severely wounded.

"Mrs. Mary Okanian says she was accosted by a man dressed as a UPS delivery man, knocked unconscious, and then robbed. Although she doesn't remember how, she apparently got in a short nine-one-one call before succumbing to her assailant.

"Then, in a bizarre twist, as police arrived on the scene, another car pulled up, then tried racing away. When police attempted to stop that car, the men inside opened fire on the officers, wounding three of them before being shot and killed themselves.

"Although police are unwilling to comment on the ongoing investigation, an anonymous source in the department tells CNN that the woman was likely a victim of a turf war between rival organized crime syndicates. When asked what was stolen from the house during the first assault, police declined to comment."

Heather had a sick feeling in her stomach; her chest felt tight. She flipped off the television. "God! That's the address we selected to drop the final message. I'll be right over."

Jennifer met Heather at the front door of her house, obviously distraught.

"Is Mark home yet?" Heather asked as she followed Jennifer up to her bedroom.

"No. He's not back from basketball practice. Mom and Dad aren't here either. They had bridge club tonight."

Jennifer closed the door behind Heather as she entered her room. "Heather. Those men that got killed. You don't think they were the NSA people, do you?"

Heather shook her head. "No way. Our government agents don't get into shoot-outs with our own police. The NSA must have already been there."

"But that poor woman. Someone assaulted her and then people were killed. We got those people killed and those policemen shot." Tears streamed down Jennifer's cheeks as she sat down hard on her bed, sending a large, overstuffed floral pillow tumbling across the floor.

"No, we didn't," said Heather, trying to convince herself of the truth of the statement. "Those men were bad people, and they caused the situation, not us."

"But we were the instigators," Jennifer sobbed. "I'm the one who had the virus pick that machine. I caused all of this."

Heather sat down beside Jennifer on the bed, hugging her friend tightly, fighting the sinking feeling that continued to assault her.

"Hey, Jen, you in your room?" Mark's voice echoed down the hallway.

"Just a sec," Jennifer replied, wiping her eyes with the back of her hand.

Mark stuck his head in the door. "What's up?"

"Did you hear what I said?" Jennifer said angrily. "I said to give me a second."

Mark started to pull back. Then, seeing her face, he came into the room. "What is it? What's the matter?"

Heather repeated the news story they had just heard.

"You're kidding," Mark said, slumping into Jennifer's chair.

"I wish I was. We caused this." It was true, no matter how she wanted it not to be. She kept going over the probability in her mind and it always came back to them.

"Damn it!" Mark leaned back in the chair, his hands clasped behind his head.

Heather heard him take a deep breath and hold it for a full two seconds before slowly exhaling.

"Jen, I know you're upset, but you have to focus. If we don't get it together, the NSA is going to trace this right back to us."

Feeling her anger boil up, Heather's eyes locked with Mark's. "Do you hear yourself? Because of us, people are dead!"

"Yeah and I'm sorry about it. But if we let that freeze us up, they won't be the only ones."

Jennifer wiped her eyes, then placed a damp hand on Heather's arm. "I'll be all right. Just give me a few minutes."

As Heather hugged her friend, Mark rose from the chair and walked over to place a hand on his sister's shoulder. "I'm sorry I'm such an ass. Just scared shitless, I guess."

Looking up into Mark's tight face, Heather felt her anger melt away.

"We all are."

Jennifer extracted herself, rose from the bed, and moved to her computer.

"I'm pretty sure I can finish the antivirus by morning," she said, looking at Mark. "How's your Russian?"

"I've been reading everything I can get to on the web with no problem. Unless it's local slang, I can handle it."

Heather got to her feet. "I'm going to get my laptop. We probably won't have more than forty-eight hours to get Jen's targeted antivirus uploaded before the NSA traces the first one back to Los Alamos.

"In the meantime, we both have the monitor program on our cell phones and laptops so we can watch the progress of the trace on them. By the way, how's it looking?"

Jennifer's fingers blurred across her laptop keyboard. "Fine. Some antiviruses have started nibbling away at the agents, but they're regenerating. I'd say we have the antivirus companies guessing."

"Great. I'll be right back."

By the time Heather retrieved her laptop and made her way back to Jennifer's room, trouble had surfaced.

"I lied to you," Jennifer said without glancing up from the keyboard. "Someone has a trace on us. I started seeing indications right after you left."

Heather glanced over Jennifer's shoulder at the readout on the computer screen, a cascade of equations flashing through her mind.

"Crap. We don't have forty-eight hours. At this rate they'll track down the source by this time tomorrow night."

Mark leaned over Jennifer's other shoulder. "Looks like tomorrow morning it is."

Jennifer switched back to her compiler but did not respond, her mind already locked away in a world of bits and bytes. Heather glanced once more at her friend's face, features tight with concentration and worry, then turned to carry her own laptop to Mark's room. The pounding of her heart echoed the pounding worry in her head. For the sake of her friends, for the sake of their families, for the sake of their very lives, she hoped she chose better this time.

By midnight, Heather and Mark found a computer location Jennifer could use as a false source to lead the trace back to. Since the best thing they could do to help Jennifer was to leave her undisturbed, Heather went home and, after letting her parents know she was back from the long homework session, went to bed.

Although she was exhausted, Heather found that sleep evaded her. About the best she could manage was a fitful doze. Her death-filled dreams were so disturbing that she awoke feeling more tired than when she had gone to bed.

At breakfast her mother fretted over the dark circles under Heather's eyes. "I don't think these late-night cram sessions are effective. If you three can't get an early start on homework, then your grades and your health will suffer."

"Mom, I know that. We'll try to get on top of things earlier next time. Believe me, I think we learned our lesson."

Her father chuckled as he sipped his coffee. "I seem to recall making that same statement myself. At least a couple hundred times."

Heather rose from the table, kissed her mom and dad, and then headed for the door, grabbing her backpack on the way.

"See you after school," she yelled as the door slammed behind her.

If she looked bad, Jennifer looked terrible. "I see you didn't sleep either," Heather said as she walked up to the twins.

"Sure I did," said Mark, who indeed looked disgustingly bright-eyed and cheery.

Jennifer rolled her eyes. "No, I didn't. I just got finished a half hour ago. I barely had time to shower and grab a bagel on my way out the door. I got the virus copied to my cell phone, but the thing is completely untested."

"You can test it after school," said Heather.

At that moment the bright yellow school bus arrived amid a squeal of brakes. Only after they were on board and the doors snicked closed behind them did Heather realize how cold the wind outside had been. She had been so distracted that she had forgotten to put her headband over her ears. Now, the heat inside the bus started her ears tingling so violently it felt like a horde of biting insects had descended on them, intent on gnawing the appendages from the sides of her head.

An itch was also building inside her nostrils. One thing she could always count on. Having acquired a critical mass of young passengers, the odors within the school bus became capable of reaching inside her nostrils and tugging on her nose hairs until her eyes watered.

From a loving mother's carefully packed roast beef sandwich, complete with horseradish, to the partially burned gasoline fumes, to the young men, generously splashed with TAG Body Spray, this morning's odiferous warriors were engaged in an all-out charge into Heather's sinuses.

While some people howled out a hurricane-force sneeze and were done, Heather's came out as tiny little "chi" sounds that seemed to go on forever. Although she tried desperately to hold it back, when the sneezes started, they kept coming until everyone around her was laughing.

Fortunately the bus pulled to a halt in front of the high school before Heather had to endure a second attack. By the time she, Mark, and Jennifer had made their way to Ms. Gorsky's first-period history class, Heather's sinuses actually felt clear again.

As she pulled out her history book, Heather's cell phone spilled out, hitting the floor hard enough that Heather grabbed for it in a panic, turning it over in her hands to see if it had broken. She pressed the tiny "on" switch, holding her breath as she waited to see if it would respond.

If it was broken, she wouldn't get another for the rest of the year. Five hundred dollars was a lot of money, and this cell phone had been a highly anticipated birthday present from her dad.

To her relief, the screen came to life, responding normally as she cycled through the program screens. Just as she was about to switch it off, Heather stopped, a sudden constriction clamping her chest. The cell phone had made a wireless connection to the school's Wi-Fi network and the trace-tracking program finished updating.

As Heather scanned the data, it was clear that the NSA had drastically accelerated their progress since the last time Heather had checked. Entire branches of their network of agent programs had ceased reporting. The new trace rate arced through her head like an exploding transformer.

Heather signaled to Jennifer across the room, catching her eye and pointing to the cell phone.

"Two hours!" Heather mouthed the words with increasing desperation, holding up two fingers, pointing to the cell phone and then making a slashing motion across her own throat.

Jennifer looked confused, but then pulled out her own cell phone. After several seconds, a look of horror crept onto her face.

Thank God, Heather thought as Jennifer began typing on her own cell phone. At least Jennifer could send the launch command that would go across the network and uplink the Counter Trace Virus. Once that was complete, she could activate it. It hadn't been tested, but it would have to do. They were out of time.

"You two!" Ms. Gorsky's voice brayed like a kicked mule. "Heather McFarland and Jennifer Smythe. Bring those devices to my desk. Now! You know cell phones are not allowed in the classroom.

"Come on. Switch them off and drop them right up here on my desk, young ladies. Then you can just waddle your little fannies down to Principal Zumwalt's waiting room until I get a chance to get down there."

Heather felt as if she had been slapped across the face. A glance at Jennifer's terrified eyes gave her all the answer she needed. Jennifer wasn't done.

Ms. Gorsky smacked her hand down on her desk. "I didn't say for you to come up here when you got around to it. I said now."

Heather and Jennifer scrambled to respond. Ms. Gorsky's meaty hand reached out and snatched the cell phone from Heather and then from Jennifer before either had a chance to lay them on her desk. She dropped them unceremoniously into a lime green bag bulging with homework papers.

"Now move it."

As they made their way out into the hallway and the door closed behind them, Jennifer mumbled something that Heather couldn't quite make out. Before she could ask Jennifer what she had said, though, Jennifer repeated it, then repeated it again, then again, all the way to the office. A single, three-word phrase.

"We are dead."

CHAPTER 34

Heather kept reviewing their situation in her head, looking for a solution. Mrs. O'Reilly's desk sat at a right angle to the entrance to Principal Zumwalt's office, facing directly out toward the door that opened into the hallway. Most days, as students waited for their respective turns to see the principal, they stared directly across at the spot where Mrs. O'Reilly pecked at the keys of her keyboard, occasionally peering out at them over the narrow rims of her spectacles, her wispy red hair making her head look like it was on fire.

For the moment, that spot was vacant, as was the office of the principal. The space was deathly silent except for their breathing, which, in stark contrast, seemed preternaturally loud, like the huffing of a dinosaur sniffing around for some hidden animal to eat. Unfortunately, it seemed Jennifer and Heather were the animals about to be eaten.

Heather had a clear mental image of a digital display counting rapidly down toward zero. How had the NSA made such a big jump in tracking down the source? There must have been something that she had overlooked, some hidden pattern in the virus that the supercomputers at Ft. Meade had spotted, enabling them to accelerate the trace.

That was the problem with not being a computer expert herself. She could only make accurate estimates of things she thoroughly understood. While Jennifer understood the computer world very well, Heather must have missed something in what her friend had described to her about the network configuration of the Internet.

She glanced over at Jennifer, who sat beside her with her head in her hands. There must be something they could do besides give up. *Think, Heather. Think.*

The mental countdown in her mind stood at one hour, thirty-two minutes, fourteen seconds, and counting, accounting for the nonlinear acceleration she had observed in the trace data.

"Jen, you hanging in there?" Heather asked, although her own desperation had her near hyperventilation.

Jennifer looked up at her numbly. "Heather, I was so close. I had started uplinking the virus when Ms. Gorsky caught us. I barely had time to throw the cell phone into screen saver lock before she grabbed it from me."

Heather's heart sank even further. "So you didn't get it uplinked?"

Jennifer shrugged hopelessly. "I don't know. I left the uplink going when I locked the screen saver. If she didn't turn it off, then the uplink would go ahead and finish, but that doesn't do us any good. I have to get on the Internet to activate it."

Their chances of activating the Counter Trace Virus, or CTV, in the remaining amount of time did not look good. They needed to activate it as soon as possible to give the virus a chance to work its magic before the NSA got so close that there would be no masking the trail.

If they could just get the CTV going, it would act like antivirus software, but with one huge advantage. It knew the original virus pattern and could hop around rapidly eliminating all traces of the agents, even slightly modifying information in the appropriate Internet routing tables.

Actually, it would leave behind a subtle trace, designed to lead the NSA to a false source, on selected routers.

One hour, twenty-nine minutes, forty-six seconds.

Heather glanced around desperately. Suddenly the nucleus of a plan formed in her brain. Standing up, she walked to the doorway and peered out into the hall. Except for an occasional passerby, it was empty. There was no sign of Mrs. O'Reilly, Principal Zumwalt, or Ms. Gorsky.

Glancing from the open doorway to the computer on Mrs. O'Reilly's desk, Heather shook her head. There were just too many people passing in front of the office to make it possible for Jennifer to hack her way into the secretary's computer. Closing the door wasn't an option. That door was never closed during school hours.

Heather glanced at the door beside Mrs. O'Reilly's desk, the door into Principal Zumwalt's office. It stood open awaiting his return. As Jennifer watched, wide-eyed, Heather walked over to the office and peered inside. There on the corner of the principal's massive oak desk sat his computer keyboard and monitor, the screen saver showing an aquarium of colorful swimming fish, which seemed to peer out at her suspiciously.

With a deep breath, Heather walked back to check the hallway door once more. It was all clear, at least for the moment.

"Jen, can you hack into the principal's computer?"

"Are you insane?" Jennifer looked as if she were debating making a run for it.

"Probably. But we're out of time. Can you do it?"

Jennifer shook her head. "If I had enough time, but they could return at any second."

"I'll watch the door to the hall. You get in there and try. I'll signal if someone comes."

Jennifer's hands began to shake.

Heather placed a hand on Jennifer's shoulder. "Jen, I can't do it. I need you. Mark needs you."

At the mention of her brother's name, Jennifer's back straightened and the muscles in her jaw clenched.

"OK. I'll try."

Seeing her gentle friend push her glasses higher on her nose and boldly stride into the office of the principal almost brought tears to Heather's eyes. But she didn't have time to cry now. With one more glance toward Jennifer, Heather moved to the hallway door and peeked out.

The minutes dragged by. Each time someone rounded the corner or came out a doorway and walked toward the office, Heather held her breath, moving back to her seat until they had passed.

A sudden exclamation from the principal's office caused her to glance inside.

"I'm in," Jennifer exclaimed. "I just need a couple more minutes to access the CTV and activate it."

"Thank God," Heather gasped, then, realizing that she was no longer watching the hall, moved back over to that doorway.

Just a little luck now, she thought. *Just give us a little luck.* Those thoughts splattered against the pavement of her mind as Ms. Gorsky rounded the corner of the hall fifty feet away, shaking a plump finger pointedly at Principal Zumwalt, who walked beside her.

Out of time. Heather lunged forward, racing down the hallway, crashing directly into Ms. Gorsky, then ricocheting off to stumble sprawled out on the floor.

"What in the name of all that is holy?" Ms. Gorsky gasped, having almost fallen herself. A look of stunned surprise quickly changed to one of fury as she rushed toward where Heather lay grasping her ankle.

As the large teacher reached her hand toward Heather, Principal Zumwalt stopped her.

"What?" Ms. Gorsky almost screamed.

Principal Zumwalt turned his stern face toward her, his stare silencing the outburst, although Ms. Gorsky's face looked like an oil well that was about to blow.

As he turned back toward Heather, his eyes locked her own, robbing her of her voice.

"What is the meaning of this, Ms. McFarland?"

Heather gulped. "Ow. I'm sorry, Principal Zumwalt. I was running for the bathroom. I held it so long I didn't think I could make it."

The desperation in her face was more real than either Principal Zumwalt or Ms. Gorsky could imagine, even though the reason behind it hardly matched her excuse. Heather let go of her bladder, a wet spot spreading rapidly across the floor beneath her.

She began to sob, something that took no effort whatsoever. "I'm so sorry. And I think I hurt my ankle, too. I'm so sorry."

For once, both Principal Zumwalt and Ms. Gorsky were rendered momentarily speechless.

Principal Zumwalt was the first to recover. "Ms. Gorsky, go get the school nurse. Quickly now."

As Ms. Gorsky sped off back down the hallway, the principal leaned down.

"Heather, look at me a second. Can you move your ankle?"

Heather wiggled it. "Ow. It hurts, but I don't think it's broken. I'm so sorry about peeing on your floor." She began sobbing again.

The principal smiled down at her tenderly. "It happens to all of us at some time or other. I can see why you were running. Can you stand up now if I help you?"

Heather stood, gingerly testing her right ankle before putting weight on it. Her jeans were soaked from crotch to knees, and now she had pee on her tennis shoes. With a hand on Principal Zumwalt's shoulder, she took a couple of hopping steps away from the puddle, her face a bright beet red.

Just then Ms. Gorsky arrived with Mrs. Harold. The nurse took one look at the scene and then bent to examine Heather's ankle. After several seconds of moving it around, drawing small gasps of fake pain from Heather, she stood once again.

"It's Heather, isn't it?" she asked.

"Yes, ma'am," said Heather.

"Well, Heather, it's definitely not broken. I think you may have a slight sprain, though. Here. Take my arm and I'll help you down to my office so I can wrap that ankle. We'll retrieve your gym clothes while we run your wet things through the washer and dryer."

"Thank you so much," Heather said.

As Heather glanced back, she saw Jennifer peer briefly out of the waiting room, giving her a quick thumbs-up before disappearing back inside.

As Heather limped down the hall, the custodian walked past her pushing a mop bucket. As he reached the spot of the accident, the school bell rang, immediately filling the halls with young humanity.

"Stay clear of the pee spot on the floor! Stay clear of the pee!"

The custodian's bellow, accompanied by the stares as students began to notice her soaked pants, brought a new shade of red to Heather's cheeks before she could duck inside the nurse's office.

As Mrs. Harold began wrapping the ACE bandage around her foot, Heather moaned again. And this time the moan was for real. She knew she should feel lucky that Jennifer had been successful. But somehow, sitting there in soaking-wet pants, stinking of pee, her level of appreciation for her good luck failed to reach the appropriate level.

CHAPTER 35

"So, Dave, what have you got for me?" Riles looked over Kurtz's right shoulder at the banks of computer monitors.

David Kurtz turned toward his boss and shrugged. "A whole lot of nothing as far as I can tell."

"What do you mean? I thought the search was narrowing in on something."

Kurtz nodded vigorously enough that if the floor had not been a static-free raised platform, Riles would have expected to see bolts of electricity arcing between the wild strands of his hair.

"Oh, we narrowed in all right. Right to a computer in the Russian Ministry of Transportation. This one is physically located in Terminal Two of the Sheremetyevo International Airport."

"Moscow?"

"You've got it, sir."

"One of the secure systems?" asked Riles.

"No—at least, not in any sophisticated sense of the word. This is just one of the standard tourist information terminals."

"That could make it a little tough to lay our hands on."

"More like impossible. The system was just taken off-line by Russian customs authorities. They received an anonymous tip that it was being used by foreign agents as an encrypted message server."

"Were we able to trace the tip? Where did it originate?"

"Actually, we saw it get generated. You're not going to like the answer to your question, though."

"Look, I can't dislike it any more than I'm disliking how long you're taking to get to the point, Dr. Kurtz."

"The e-mail tip was generated from that same airport computer."

"And the tip was in Russian?"

"Flawless Russian, according to the boys downstairs," said Kurtz.

"I don't believe this."

Kurtz grinned. "I didn't either. No one is that good or that lucky. That's why I started a complete analysis of the New Year's Day Virus pattern from early-stage infection until the trace program was completed. When that analysis run finished, we spotted a very interesting anomaly in the data. Everything was consistent until about an hour before we identified the source computer in the Moscow terminal. Then it changed."

Riles's gaze narrowed. "How so?"

"The agent programs left behind by the virus got cleaned from the net, leaving almost no traces. We barely managed to identify the trail back to Moscow. It looked like a really effective antivirus program swept the net."

"Did you recheck the routing tables on all the Internet routers?"

"That's how we found Moscow."

Riles paused, rubbing his chin. "The tip was in flawless Russian you say? Maybe too good, as in textbook? I think someone is playing a little game with us.

"I want you to go back several hours before the trace completed. Figure out the key routers in the network pattern you were following and compare the most recent routing tables with those saved off from the previous night."

Kurtz nodded. "I'll get right on it. We are going to need some subpoenas to get those records, unless you want Gregory's team involved again."

"No, go through normal channels this time. Since we've hit a dead end, we have plenty of time to backtrack. Besides, I have other plans for Jack."

Jonathan Riles turned and strode out of David Kurtz's lab softly whistling the theme song to *Titanic*.

CHAPTER 36

It was Saturday morning and Heather had made tea. At first she barely registered the scratching at the kitchen window, so softly did it intrude into her consciousness. When she did look up, there was nothing there, just a large section where the condensation had left a cloud on the pane. Only as she started to turn away did she see it, crude letters in the condensation where a finger had traced them on the outside of the glass.

"I know what you are."

Heather set down her tea and walked across to the windowsill. On closer inspection, it was a thin layer of frost, not steam or condensation, that had been scratched away.

She shifted her gaze to the tree line at the back edge of their yard. There, standing in the snow beneath the pines, stood the Rag Man, his long, greasy, blond hair and the mouthful of bad teeth in his grinning face immediately recognizable. His eyes, though. Where were his eyes?

For a brief moment Heather considered calling her dad, but her fury wouldn't let the man escape yet again. Grabbing a long butcher knife from the block on the countertop, Heather opened the sliding glass door and stepped out into the predawn darkness, the garden dimly illuminated by the light from their back porch. As she stepped out, the Rag Man slid back into the trees.

Heather lunged after him, almost slipping on the ice coating the deck's lower step, but she managed to right herself as she plunged into the snow-covered grass beyond. She reached the tree where she had last seen him, whirling to make sure he did not jump out of the darkness behind her.

There in the snow beneath the tree, a clear set of footprints led into the woods just beyond her backyard. Heather sucked in a deep breath, then moved, head bent to keep the trail in sight as she made her way forward. In seconds the trees behind her masked her house from view, bringing down a deeper darkness that would have been absolute, except for the light of the three-quarter moon that filtered through the branches high above.

Those tracks in the snow pulled her onward, her hand clutched so tightly around the handle of the big knife that it seemed the skin would peel away from her knuckles at any moment. She felt like screaming after the Rag Man: Who are you? What do you want from me? Stay the hell away from my family!

"I know what you are."

The voice behind her was so close she could feel the hot breath puff against the back of her neck, could smell the rot in those decaying teeth. Suddenly all the anger and strength leached out of her body, replaced by an icy terror that left her frozen in place, unable to move. Unable even to turn her face to look into those vacant eye sockets.

"I know what you are becoming."

Heather tried to scream but somehow could not manage to get the sound out of her throat. Only when she heard the soft thud of something heavy hitting the snow at her feet did she realize she'd dropped the butcher knife.

"Becoming…"

The feel of the hand on her shoulder was more than she could bear, rousing her to twist and lurch away.

"…going to becoming?"

The weight of the blanket dragged her down, and she lifted her head, struggling toward the light.

"Heather, wake up. Are you going to be coming down to breakfast?"

Heather sat straight up in bed and found herself staring into her father's face.

"Wow. That must have been some dream you were having. It's after eight o'clock."

Heather suddenly remembered that she could breathe. The shock of transition from the vivid dream to wakefulness left her dazed.

"Heather?"

"Sorry, Dad," Heather said, wiping at her face with both hands. "I must have really been out. What was it you were asking me?"

He laughed. "Maybe I should let you go back to sleep. The Smythes are going to be here in forty-five minutes for brunch."

"Oh. Thanks. I definitely want to shower and get cleaned up first."

"OK. We'll see you in a few minutes, then."

As the door closed, Heather sank back into bed, amazed that her father hadn't heard the pounding in her head. She had never been subject to migraines, but this one was a real skull cracker of a headache. If she hadn't just told her dad that she was going to come down for breakfast, she would have taken a couple of aspirin and crawled back into bed. Recalling the dream, Heather decided she didn't really want to sleep again, anyway.

By the time she had drained the hot water heater and stepped out into the steam-filled bathroom, Heather was feeling a little better. The headache was still there, but the rest of her seemed to be ready to greet the land of the wakeful. She glanced up at the mirror, half expecting to see finger-printed words in the condensation. No words. Thank the Lord.

Heather was several minutes late getting downstairs, but she had still somehow managed to beat the Smythes. That surprised her, considering the Smythe family's notorious punctuality.

"Hi, sleepyhead," her mother said as she pulled a pan of hot biscuits from the oven and applied butter.

"Hi, Mom."

Her father looked up from his paper. "Glad to see you looking perkier. I don't think I've ever seen you that deep into the land of nod."

"It's their exhausting study schedule this week," said her mother as she set a large red-and-yellow plate in the middle of the table, biscuits piled high atop it. "It's too much, coming right out of the holidays. I've a good mind to complain to the principal."

"Mom, please don't," said Heather quickly.

Her mother snorted. "It was just a thought."

Just then the door opened, and the Smythes poured in to happy greetings all around.

"Sorry we're late," Fred Smythe began. "We had a tough time getting these two kids roused this morning. You would have thought they were dead."

Heather's head popped up. Sure enough, both Mark and Jennifer looked like they needed to go directly back to bed.

As the parents chattered in the background, Mark leaned over to whisper in Heather's ear. "It's the weirdest thing. Both Jen and I had exactly the same dream last night."

A cold shiver crept up Heather's spine. "The same dream?"

Jennifer nodded. "Exactly the same. It was all about you chasing a weird man into the woods with a knife."

Mark leaned closer. "Yeah. Really creepy."

A loud clatter caused everyone to look around at Heather, who stood by the table staring down at the butcher knife she had just dropped on the kitchen floor.

CHAPTER 37

Jack Gregory stepped down from the small private jet, carrying his two black bags. Glancing back, he saw the lithe, muscular form of Janet Price exit the aircraft carrying a slightly larger, soft leather duffel.

Without waiting for Harold Stevens, Jack made his way over to the Executive Aviation office, the late-afternoon Albuquerque sun providing plenty of light but little heat on this cold January day. By the time he had retrieved the keys to the two cars that awaited their arrival and had made arrangements for the refueling and the parking of the jet, Harold Stevens had joined Janet in the waiting area.

Jack tossed him a set of keys and then stepped outside to find his own car, a bloodred Audi Quattro. Popping open the spacious trunk, he lifted his and Janet's bags inside. As he opened the driver's-side door and slid into the leather seat, Janet distracted him by gliding into the passenger seat, her legs as shapely and defined as a professional dancer's, the little black skirt not quite reaching her knees.

His glance swept up her body, catching her laughing eyes with his own.

"Same old Jack, I see."

"Just scoping out my surroundings." Jack grinned, slammed the door, and brought the engine roaring to life. "We're supposed to be married, you know."

"Then you may want to tone down the heat in that gaze of yours. That's more of a mistress look you have going on."

"They never said we had to play an old married couple, now did they?"

As he pulled out onto Interstate 25 headed north, Jack glanced back to see Harold following some distance back, the big, white Ford F250 pickup clearly visible.

"How's Bubba doing back there?" Janet asked.

"It looks like he's enjoying his ride."

"He'd like it more if he could get back out on some of these ranch roads. He's probably having flashbacks to his childhood days out in Arizona. What's the name of that little town he came from?"

"Show Low. It sits up in the high country above the Mogollon Rim. Pretty place."

"Thanks, but I'll stick to New York and leave the backcountry to you hillbillies."

Janet smiled at the thought. Jack Gregory looked about as much like a country boy as James Bond, comfortable in either a tuxedo or jeans and a brown leather bomber jacket, equally elegant in either. No. The man was silk and leather, a shot of James Bond with a spritz of Carlos the Jackal blended into one lethal martini, never shaken or stirred.

"What did you find out from the Old Man?" Janet asked.

"They still don't know where the virus originated, although they're pretty sure it wasn't Moscow."

"So the router tables had been modified?"

"Sometime between the night shift and the end of the trace. Kurtz's people checked against the nightly backups and several of them didn't match, although the differences were quite subtle."

"How was it done?"

"That's the tricky part. You know those little agent programs that Kurtz thought were just doing a little encryption of random data?"

"Right," Janet said.

"It turns out that they were posting a periodic health and status code up onto several public websites. Someone snooping those codes could tell when the agents quit reporting and get a map of how our trace was coming. They apparently launched a cleanup virus as we closed in."

"But can't our people find out who was checking the codes on the websites?"

Jack laughed. "That's the funniest part yet. They picked out a selection of movie star fan sites. You know. The ones with pictures and juicy gossip. Anyway, the little agent programs were changing little bits here and there in the images, so small it wasn't noticeable to the viewers."

"Buried in the hits."

"You've got it. Those sites get millions of daily hits. Determining who was downloading the pictures for the data instead of for their viewing pleasure is impossible."

"So why are we headed to Los Alamos?"

"Two reasons. Kurtz decoded the message from the computer we heisted. It makes some pretty wild claims about Dr. Donald Stephenson and the Rho Project."

"So Riles wants us to snoop into the Rho Project? He must be desperate. You go to prison for spying on a deep black operation when you don't have need to know. Did the president approve this operation?"

"We work for Riles. It's his ass on the line."

"What's the second reason?"

"The decoded message was loaded with inside information from the Rho Project."

"So we have a mole in the project leaking out damaging information on his boss?"

"A very brilliant mole. Probably a mathematician, based upon the incredible encryption algorithms used. It's not an intelligence operative, that's for sure. They made too many mistakes in the way they tried to hide the trail in Moscow. This is an amateur playing at the spy game."

Janet nodded. "So we take out the amateur, find out what he knows, and then decide how deeply to dig into the *Rho Ship*."

"We'll work both sides at once. I want you to focus on finding our mole. Harold and I will take a little look into the Rho Project and see what turns up."

A smile of anticipation lifted the corners of Janet Price's beautiful mouth. "I've never liked rodents. Snuffing this one should be entertaining."

"Get the information first."

A needle-thin ice pick glittered in Janet's hand as she grabbed her hair and gave it a couple of quick twists before shoving the pointed weapon through it, firmly securing her long brown locks in a tight bun atop her head.

"Of course."

A large green sign slid toward them along the right side of the highway.

Santa Fe, six miles.

Good. Best to get a hotel room for the night. No use letting deadly little Janet's sudden hunger go to waste.

CHAPTER 38

Heather, feet propped on the oak coffee table, watched Mark pace. With Mr. and Mrs. Smythe at an appointment, the privacy offered by the Smythe living room was a welcome change.

"I hate to state the obvious," Mark said, "but three people having exactly the same dream isn't normal."

"What was all that business about knowing what you're becoming?" asked Mark.

"Sometimes dreams don't make any sense," said Heather.

"That wasn't the feeling I got from this one."

"Well," said Jennifer, "let's hope it was just a freak event."

"Anyway," Mark continued, "no matter what the dream means, we're all becoming something more than we were. I didn't want to show you guys this, but I think it's time. Follow me."

Heather and Jennifer glanced nervously at each other but followed him up the stairs and into his room. It had been rearranged since the last time Heather had visited. The bed and dresser were pushed all the way against one wall to accommodate a weight bench.

The bench took up most of the room. An Olympic weight bar loaded with 250 pounds of weight rested across hooks at the top of the bench. Another stack of weights lay on the floor nearby.

"Wow," said Heather. "You're benching two hundred and fifty pounds?"

Mark's eyes narrowed. "That's just for show."

Mark moved over to the bar, adding two additional fifty-pound plates to each end and then lay down on the bench beneath the elevated bar. Without hesitation, he lifted the bar, pumping it steadily up and down. The weight caused the ends of the bar to droop slightly.

Heather felt her pulse quicken. "Oh my God! That's four hundred and fifty pounds."

"Four ninety-five, counting the bar," Mark said, continuing to evenly knock out repetitions. After several more seconds, he stopped, setting the bar back in its rest with a thump that shook the floor. "I could lift more, but these are all the weights we own."

Jennifer finally found her voice. "But how is that possible? What's your max lift?"

"That's just it," said Mark. "I don't know. I guess the neural tune-up enables near-perfect synchronization of my muscles, making them easier to train and way more efficient. Either that or we're wrong about our DNA not being affected."

Thoughts raced through Heather's head so rapidly that her headache began to worsen. "You could hurt someone, even accidentally."

Mark sat up. "I've been thinking about that. I don't think so. My reflexes are just too good. So long as I control my temper, no problem."

Heather's right eyebrow lifted. "So long as you control your temper?"

"We need to get back out to the ship," said Jennifer. "We have to know what's happening to us."

"I don't get how that'll help," said Heather.

"Don't you see? The medical lab. I think I can figure out how to use that equipment, at least at a rudimentary level, so that we can get some physical readouts and measurements. Maybe there will be some clue indicating the extent of the changes going on in our brains and bodies."

"Worth a try," said Mark. "We can, at least, check on the QT device to see if we have any more recordings of Stephenson."

Heather moved toward the door. "Well, if we're going, it better be soon. It's almost noon. I'll tell mom we're going biking. Then I'll meet you out front."

Stepping outside into the cold gray light that filtered through the clouds, conditions hardly seemed favorable for a bike ride. Nevertheless, anticipation propelled her onward. As Heather opened her front door, she saw her mother sitting on the couch, her entire attention fixed on the television, a rare scene for the ever-busy Anna McFarland.

Glancing up, Heather's mother beckoned Heather with her hand. "Sweetie, come watch. This is important."

By the time she had sat with her mom for five minutes, Heather had a lump in her throat from the steady stream of breaking news. A new power facility had been brought online at the Palo Verde nuclear power plant in Arizona, the first commercial usage of the Rho Project cold fusion technology.

This first venture was being housed in a building at the Palo Verde facility. The reaction had been initiated without problem, and the power being produced already surpassed that of the rest of the plant.

Scientists and industry leaders from around the world were praising the project as the first truly "green" commercial energy project that had the potential to satisfy most of the world's energy needs.

In related stories, rioting had broken out in Riyadh, Saudi Arabia, as well as in the Saudi cities of Mecca, Medina, and Dhahran. The royal family had been deposed in a violent religious coup, many of them killed. The king himself had barely escaped with the help of US Special Forces. All US military facilities in the kingdom were on a full state of alert with fighting reported outside the US airbase near Riyadh.

A statement from the Iranian government praising the overthrow of the Saudi royal family called for the immediate withdrawal of all US forces from the Middle East. The statement also condemned the new cold fusion technology as the "hot spawn of the devil," an evil assault on Allah's people around the world, and threatened an immediate cutoff of oil to all countries pursuing the technology.

An emergency meeting of OPEC ministers in Qatar was scheduled for Monday, to discuss a unified response to these events.

In the meantime, the United States armed forces around the world had been placed on a state of high alert. The president had just issued a stern warning that the US government and its allies would neither permit nor tolerate an attack on its deployed forces or on the oil facilities in Saudi Arabia, Iraq, or Kuwait.

Despite her pounding heart, Heather maintained an exterior calm. "Wow. That sounds really bad."

"Bad? Heather, this is terrible. I don't mean cold fusion—that sounds great. But it sure is causing some very dangerous events around the world."

"Well, I'm sure the government will handle it." Heather rose from the couch. "Mom, if we're done watching the news, do you mind if I go biking with Mark and Jen?"

Her mother raised her eyebrows, but smiled. "I guess it's all right. But be home before dark."

"Thanks." Heather kissed her mother and headed toward the garage, grabbing her heavy coat off the peg by the door as she passed.

"What took you so long?" Mark asked as Heather wheeled her bike out of her garage. "Jen and I were about to come break you out."

Heather took a deep breath, then swung her leg over her bike. As she stepped down hard on the pedal, spinning her rear tire, she breathed two words.

"It's started."

CHAPTER 39

Although Heather constantly checked her surroundings as she rode, she didn't stop on the way out to the *Second Ship*. Time was short if they were going to make it back by dark, and they had a lot to do. Besides, for the time being, no crowds dogged Mark's footsteps—possibly because of the embarrassing hallway incident, or maybe due to his intentionally reduced scoring in recent basketball games. Whatever the reason, Heather was thankful for the respite.

Only slight variations in grayness allowed her to see texture in the clouds that draped the sky, the air as still as death itself. While no wind was blowing, the speed of the bike whipped the cold air past her cheeks with enough force to make them tingle and to turn her feet into small blocks of ice inside her sneakers. Heather regretted having been so distracted that she had forgotten to change into some warmer shoes.

By the time they dropped off the bikes and finished their descent into the steep canyon, Heather's circulation had returned to her lower extremities. Still, it felt good to climb up into the ship with its controlled temperature. As she slipped on the headset, feeling the wonderful, relaxing pulses it generated, Heather realized just how much she had missed this place. Jennifer barely hesitated, a pleasant smile lighting her features as she led the way into the medical lab.

The doors snicked closed behind them as they entered the room. Heather relaxed her own mind, letting herself pick up the same computer imagery that Jennifer was calling up. The visuals changed rapidly as Jennifer focused first on one oddly shaped couch and then another, color patterns shifting and pulsing, great columns of symbols and figures cascading across her vision.

Jennifer settled quickly on one particular apparatus: a table that rose from a single pedestal that looked like it had been pulled from the floor while it was still molten and allowed to solidify into its smooth, oblong shape.

Jennifer sat on the edge of the table and then lay down. Immediately the table changed, flowing up and around her body in long tendrils that moved to gently encase her, the thousands of small tips looking like acupuncture needles, although they did not appear to penetrate Jennifer's skin.

If Jennifer had not appeared so relaxed and at ease, Heather was sure panic would have overwhelmed her. A quick glance at Mark's tight face indicated he was considerably less comfortable with what was happening than was his twin sister.

A perfect bubble appeared in the air above Jennifer's body, as big as a large beach ball, colors shifting and pulsing along its surface, symbols and numbers scrolling around the top. Inside the bubble, three-dimensional graphical displays rose and fell in a familiar rhythm.

Pulse. Suddenly Heather began to recognize what she was seeing. One of the displays corresponded to the measurement of Jennifer's pulse while another showed a clear picture of her vascular system, every small vein showing its blood flow in a small, rotating hologram of her body, the heart pulsing with a steady and powerful beat.

In another section of the beach ball's interior, a clear hologram of Jennifer's brain activity drew Heather's attention. The image of the brain looked like a lumpy clear jellyfish, its insides lit with a lightning storm of electrical pulses. As Heather concentrated, she found she could view it from any angle, zooming in and out at will.

As fascinated as she was, something troubled her. They had assumed that because of each of their natural preferences, the neural activity in different parts of each of their brains would be enhanced more than others, but Jennifer's brain looked like the whole thing was on fire. There was no indication of a preferentially influenced area.

"Jen? Can you make it let you up?"

Heather gasped as Jennifer rolled her head to look at Heather, something that should have impaled her on the sharp tendrils fastened to her face and head. Instead, the tentacles moved with her, perfectly maintaining their needlepoint touches but doing no damage to her delicate skin.

Jennifer swung to a seated position and hopped down from the table, the tentacles melting back into the tabletop as she moved.

"That felt marvelous," said Jennifer, stretching her arms high overhead.

"My turn," said Mark, hopping onto the tabletop without waiting for a response from Heather.

Once again, as Mark lay back, the table flowed like a living creature, thousands upon thousands of clear, little pinpoint tentacles crawling over his body. Mark looked like a refugee from a horror movie as each pinpoint found the spot it was looking for. Dozens of the things even attached directly to his eyeballs, while others ran inside his nostrils and ears. Heather had not noticed this with Jennifer, but playing back the previous scene in her mind, she realized that Jennifer had been attached in exactly the same way.

The points had even penetrated Jennifer's clothing, so fine and thin that they had left no mark.

Once more Heather focused on the hologram display of the brain activity. Mark's brain showed the same raging electrical activity that Jennifer's had, all centers active at the same level—no favorites, no laggards. Something was wildly wrong with her theory on how they were being affected. By what she was seeing, they should all be displaying the same types of enhancements instead of specialized effects.

"This is magnificent," Mark said. "It's perfect biofeedback."

His speech and the accompanying grin produced a reaction that looked completely alien as the hundreds of needles attached to his face moved, forming a wave in the sea of clear tentacles.

"Watch this." Mark breathed in deeply and then exhaled slowly, repeating the technique again and again.

As Heather watched, the display of his vascular system changed, the heartbeat slowing steadily. The count in her brain shifted, forty beats per minute, thirty-three, twenty-nine, twenty-four, eighteen, fifteen, thirteen.

"Mark, stop it!"

Jennifer's panicked voice brought a slow smile to his lips as the count began to rise steadily to a normal resting heart rate.

He suddenly sat up and leaped off the table, the tentacles melting away as if they had no more substance than air.

Heather did not know how long she had not been breathing, but by the size of the gulping breath she now took, she guessed that it had been a considerable time.

"Mark Smythe!" she exclaimed angrily. "If you pull something like that again without telling us first, I'm going to kill you myself."

"Sorry about that," Mark said, although his grin did not seem sorry at all. "It was just some of the meditations I've been practicing in my aikido. I got the idea that, with this kind of biofeedback, I could take it a lot farther than before. It felt wonderful."

Jennifer continued to scowl at her brother. "Well, it looked like you were dying. You scared me to death."

Mark shrugged, turning toward Heather. "You want to give it a try?"

Heather was already up on the table. It felt like lying down on some sort of warm, soft gel. The tentacles flowed to embrace her, and at the spot where each tiny tip touched her skin, a warm glow spread outward in waves. It should have left goose bumps, it felt so wonderful.

My God, she thought. *I'm never getting up. I just want to lie here and feel this good forever.*

After a couple of minutes, she began refocusing on the displays above her. The sensation was odd. Despite the tentacles attached to her face and eyes, she could clearly see the bubble and its displays in her head. Just like Mark and Jennifer, Heather saw that her entire brain was lit up in an ongoing storm of electrical activity. While this wasn't like any medical equipment on Earth, Heather had no doubt that none of them wanted to be hooked up to an electroencephalogram. Not if they didn't want to freak out the entire hospital.

Heather stepped off the table feeling more rested and relaxed than ever before.

Mark glanced at his watch. "Much as I would love to stay and play around with this stuff, we have to get a move on. We barely have enough time to check the QT recording."

The review of the recordings proved disappointing. While the QT device had captured some small snippets of activity, for the most part the devices on the model airplane had remained off. The lights in the room were not turned on often enough to keep the battery charged. This meant that all that had been recorded was a few minutes here and there of Dr. Stephenson typing at his computer.

As Jennifer and Mark reviewed the recording, mumbling in disgust at the lack of any useful data, Heather sat in one of the command couches exploring her headset connection with the central computer. She began working on something that fascinated her: physics.

Heather decided to start with the basic assumptions that girded all of modern physics, to see if she could communicate ideas that would generate understandable responses. Everything in humans' modern understanding of the functioning of the universe eventually came back to the notion that energy is neither created nor destroyed, only changed from one form to another. Almost immediately, the imagery she was seeing changed to a set of distant stars, accompanied by a very deep sense of wrongness.

The scene focused on a single star and then swept away from it, the color of the starlight shifting to red as she got farther away. This repeated itself with star after star, from multiple directions, over and over, faster and faster.

Every star shifted red the farther the observer was from the star. OK. Nothing new there. The redshift was a well-known phenomenon and was explained by the theory that all stars were moving away from a central big bang, the first stars flung out the hardest and fastest. Of course, this caused the light coming from them to have a bigger Doppler effect, like the changing sound of a train's horn as it approaches and then passes a stationary listener.

Again, she felt the wrongness. A new sequence began, showing a single star, her perspective stepping away from it in all directions, and always yielding about the same redshift. Now that made no sense.

Another rapid shift in data, then another, then another. Heather gasped in shock, stunned to her very core. Energy was not conserved.

The bulk of the redshift was not caused by the Doppler effect. It was caused by a tiny fraction of the energy of the light waves leaking between the quantum grains of space-time into subspace. The farther light waves traveled outward from the source, the more energy leaked off into subspace, causing the wavelengths to shift toward the red end of the spectrum.

Ideas were spinning so fast in Heather's head that she barely noticed Mark prodding her with his finger.

"Heather. We have to go. We'll barely get home by dark, even if we pedal like hell."

Reluctantly, Heather followed the Smythe twins back to the lower level and out of the cave. Her mind was still reeling with the incredible implications of her discovery as they spun their tires onto the dirt trail leading back toward home.

A rush of cold air swept down from the high peaks above, stirring the branches of the thick brush lining the top of the canyon. Suddenly, Heather felt *watched*, in a way she didn't like, a way familiar from her dreams. When a quick scan of her surroundings yielded nothing out of the ordinary, she pushed the feeling aside. Now was no time to let her overactive imagination get the best of her.

CHAPTER 40

Vice President George Gordon crawled out of bed quietly, pausing to stare down at his wife's naked body sprawled across the bed. The slight smile that lifted the corners of Harriet's sleeping lips showed a deep satisfaction that, until just a few weeks ago, he had never expected to see again.

He glanced at the clock: 3:02 a.m. He felt new, strong, young. He felt more alive now than he had since his early twenties.

Passing out of the bedroom and into the bathroom, he stared across the sink at his reflection in the mirror. How good it felt to see that old vigor back in his eyes, to feel the muscles beneath his skin. It was like being back at the Naval Academy once more, getting psyched up for the Army-Navy game that weekend. He could almost hear his fellow midshipmen raising their voices, cheering their team on toward the coming victory.

Looking back now on the last several weeks, George Gordon thanked his lucky stars. Better yet, his intuition. Something had pulled him to Los Alamos to check on Dr. Stephenson's progress. Something had made him pressure the deputy director into showing him more. And Dr. Stephenson had responded.

Once he had learned about the second alien technology, the old Gordon recklessness had taken over, leading him to insist that Stephenson inject him with the gray fluid. In hindsight, it had been madness, a madness borne of desperation at his deteriorating heart, at the loss of the vitality that made him who he was. Thank God for that madness.

Reaching into the medicine cabinet, Vice President Gordon retrieved a pair of tweezers. Setting them on the vanity, he moved across to the cabinet atop which a small picture frame stood, a recent image of him and his wife at the inaugural ball. Moving the picture onto the vanity and retrieving the tweezers, he began carefully plucking hairs from his high forehead, removing the new growth to match his preexisting receding hairline. It would never do to let the press discover such an obvious difference in his body, at least not yet.

Throwing on his robe, George grabbed his cell phone and moved out into the hallway, heading for his office. As he dialed, a thin smile twitched his lips. One of the pleasures of power was the ability to wake your chief of staff in the middle of the night, just because you felt like it.

The phone rang three times before Gordon's chief of staff picked up, his voice still thick with sleep when he answered. "Hello? Carl Palmer."

"Carl, this is George."

On the other end of the line, the vice president's chief of staff cleared his throat. "Yes? What can I do for you, Mr. Vice President?"

George Gordon's grin widened. Now he knew that the man was struggling to wakefulness, having used the formal salutation that he normally dispensed with in dealings with his boss.

"Carl, I need you to look up something for me real quick. When am I scheduled for my next physical examination over at Walter Reed?"

"Just a second, I'll check." The phone clattered as Carl set down his receiver. A minute later, he returned. "I have you down for an appointment on February fourteenth."

"Valentine's Day? Those doctors over there are getting a little funny with their heart jokes, don't you think?"

"It could be a coincidence."

"Uh-huh. Carl, you don't believe that for a second, and neither do I. Anyway, it doesn't matter. I want you to cancel it. With all that's going on in the world right now, I don't want to be out of the loop, even for a day."

"Sir, do you really think that's wise?" A note of concern sounded in Palmer's voice.

"Carl, I feel fine. Once things settle down, they can prod me to their hearts' content. For right now, though, make the call."

"OK. I'll do it this morning. Anything else, sir?"

"No. I think I've bothered you enough for one night. Go back to sleep, Carl."

"I'll see what I can do. Good night, sir."

"Good night, Carl."

As he clicked off his phone, the vice president leaned back in his chair, hearing the creak of soft leather as he settled all the way into it. You just couldn't beat the feel of Italian leather.

CHAPTER 41

The sunlight streaming through the dirty attic window spotlighted a small cloud of dust specks that floated above the secure SATCOM link. That link to the NSA provided fax, voice, and data, all digitally encrypted. The attic provided a discrete office, exactly the type Jack wanted, complete with pull-down steps from the second-floor hallway below. It was why he had chosen to rent this house.

"Janet, what have you got for me?"

"Just what you've been looking for, Jacky boy." Janet Price walked across the small attic space and dropped a small stack of papers on Jack's desk. "Hot off the fax. The profile of our mole is on top since I knew you were hot for it," she continued. "Next are the security clearance background investigations of every person assigned to the Rho Project."

Jack leafed through the stack.

"Hmm. Heavy-duty mathematician. Real shocker there. Excellent computer programmer but inexperienced with top-level security systems. Good language skills but nonnative Russian speaker. Blah, blah, blah…" Jack tossed the top couple of pages in the shredder pile. "Exactly what we already thought. Why do they pay those folks?"

Jack continued through the rest of the background reports on Rho Project personnel. Now this was more like it. After several minutes, he looked across the small room to where Janet sat patiently awaiting his response.

"So let's run through what we know and what we suspect. We know this person is a math wizard and really, really good with computers. We suspect they haven't had much secure network experience. That last one rules out a Special Forces or spy type."

"Unless they're trying to look amateurish."

"No. That doesn't feel right. This person's no spy."

"So he or she is a scientist."

"Yes. Number one or two in his class, Cal Tech type, doctorate by twenty-five, flat-out genius."

"That describes about half the people on the project. Hell, Jack, a third of the physicists and mathematicians in Los Alamos fit that profile."

"That's OK. We can narrow it down. It has to be someone on the project, but we can eliminate the technicians. They don't have the math background."

Janet crossed her legs, leaning farther back in the chair. "So that's our in."

"You've got it. We don't want to go after anyone who could be our man. He'd get suspicious. We want to start with someone on the project who we know can't be the mole, but who has access."

Jack shuffled the papers, finally pulling two sets.

"This one is perfect. A technician with a reputation for being able to build anything. Everyone uses him to build specialized equipment."

Janet reached over to take the papers from Jack's outstretched hand. "Gilbert McFarland? Looks boring enough. Maybe we'll get lucky."

"We did that last night." Jack winked at her.

"Play your cards right and it might not be a one-time occurrence." Janet's wicked smile seemed to heat the room.

Jack shook off the thought. That would have to wait. "Did you notice that the McFarlands are regular churchgoers?"

"Lutherans. Sounds like we're going to get a little religion, Mr. Johnson."

"We could use it, Mrs. Johnson. By the way, how'd it go down at the school today?"

"No problems. I met with Principal Zumwalt. I told him we had just moved here and that I wanted to apply for a teaching job next year. He seemed impressed with my application and certifications and said I'd start getting substitute calls right away. It's cold and flu season."

"Good. We want you hopping around the classrooms. And anything let slip in front of a high school kid is guaranteed to slip further. Besides, we only need to spot little oddities."

"How about you, Jack? How'd your day go?"

"As expected. I made the rounds of all the local government offices. Introduced myself as Jack Johnson, field agent for the Environmental Protection Agency."

Janet's throaty laugh once again elevated his blood pressure. "That must've made you quite popular."

"I don't need to be popular. Just expected to be out snooping around the area."

"Did you get in touch with Harry?"

"Just talked to him over lunch."

"How's the telephone line repair business?"

"He seems to have found a home over at the phone company. He gets the fun outdoor work."

"Too bad we're staying away from him. I'd take him a hot chocolate and some soup. Poor boy."

Jack stood and walked over to the hatch leading down from the attic. "I've got to run a couple of quick errands. In the meantime, pull up everything you can on Mr. McFarland. Before church comes around this Sunday, I want to know everything about his inner circle: wife, kids, everyone."

As he climbed down the stairs, Jack could already hear the click of Janet's fingertips on the computer keyboard. The McFarlands were about to acquire some special new friends.

CHAPTER 42

If there was one thing Heather didn't feel like doing today, it was going to Ms. Gorsky's history class. After the incident in the hallway, Heather's level of self-consciousness around the woman was epic. While their smart phones had been returned the next day, Ms. Gorsky still stared at Heather at times during class, the barest hint of a malevolent grin distorting her jowls.

As Heather neared the classroom, Mark intercepted her in the hallway.

"Did you hear the news?"

"What news?" Heather asked, angling through the mass of students toward the doorway to the classroom.

"Ms. Gorsky's out sick. The flu bug got her."

"What a shame. Who's the sub?"

"Don't know. Don't care. I figure it's a day of freedom no matter who it is."

"You've got that right," Heather said, sliding between two girls blocking the doorway.

As she pulled out her book, notebook, and pencil and slid into her seat, a sudden hush fell upon the room. Heather half expected to look up and see the pope himself—white gown, pointy hat, and all.

The woman bore no resemblance whatsoever to the pope, although all the boys in the room appeared to have suddenly found religion.

"Hello, class. I am Mrs. Johnson," said the dark-haired woman in the dark skirt and blouse. She peered over dark glasses positioned well forward on her perfect nose. As Mrs. Johnson stood in the doorway, Heather wasn't sure why all the dark adjectives were suddenly popping into her mind. After all, the skirt was navy blue, not black, and the blouse was a red, tending toward scarlet, that bled down into navy blue lace that perfectly matched the skirt. Her hair, pulled back into a tight bun, would have looked prudish on most women, but on Mrs. Johnson it merely looked aggressive.

As the substitute made her way across the front of the room toward the teacher's desk, Heather had a brief déjà vu moment. Mrs. Johnson moved like one of the dancers in the musical *Cats*. And the way the boys followed the woman's movements reminded Heather of an audience at the US Open tennis tournament. If this kept up for the entire class, all the guys would have whiplash.

Glancing across the classroom, Heather spotted Jennifer staring around in wide-eyed wonderment. She had also noticed that the herd of normally babbling males in the room had become as enthralled as kittens watching a dangling strand of yarn. It suddenly struck Heather: another sexy female named Johnson. Christ. What was it about that name?

"Please close your books and take out a single blank piece of paper and a pencil. Ms. Gorsky has left instructions for a pop quiz."

A low groan arose from the group as the spell broke.

As the lengthy quiz progressed, Mrs. Johnson moved among the desks, glancing down at each student's work, once again causing the male members of the classroom to lose all semblance of concentration. Heather had no doubt the quiz would set some sort of record in gender-gap performance. From what she observed out of the corner of her eye, it would be a miracle if any of the guys scored above 50 percent.

By the end of the class, Heather's impression of Mrs. Johnson had improved significantly. Heather had to hand it to her: the woman was a consummate professional. Mrs. Johnson collected the test papers and moved through the scheduled work with such comfort, self-confidence, and skill that Heather wished Ms. Gorsky could be out permanently.

Well, come to think of it, she had wished for that long before Mrs. Johnson's arrival. Her reflections were interrupted by the sound of the bell and the subsequent jumble of movement and noise that accompanied the hourly student migration pattern.

As Heather opened her locker, Mark stepped up beside her.

"Have you got an oxygen tank in there? I think I need some."

"You and about fifteen other guys."

Suddenly Mark straightened, a more serious look settling on his chiseled features as Mrs. Johnson walked past.

"What are you looking at, basketball puke?" Doug Brindal's grinning face came nose to nose with Mark's. "Haven't you already learned not to chase after women out of your league?"

The snarl that twitched at the corner of Mark's lips barely registered in Heather's brain before he moved, lightning fast. Mark grabbed a fistful of Doug's shirt, just below the throat, and slammed him back hard into the locker. Doug dangled in Mark's grip, his feet barely touching the floor.

Heather lunged forward, grabbing Mark's arm, trying to pull it free, but the corded muscles felt like rolled steel.

"Mark! Stop it. Please!" Heather begged as several students swung their gazes toward the commotion.

Mark glanced down at her, sanity leaching rapidly back into his face as he loosened his grasp on Doug.

The senior stepped forward, giving Mark a hard shove in the chest that somehow failed to move him. Pushing his way through the onlookers, Doug yelled back, "You'd better watch your back, Smythe. I will be."

Without a moment's hesitation, Heather pulled Mark into the crowd and down the hall toward their next class. As Jennifer joined them, Heather leaned over to her friend and whispered, "Someone please call the testosterone police."

CHAPTER 43

The rat lay on its side. Its pink left foreleg twitched periodically, as if by doing so it might be able to roll its diseased body over and give some relief to the pressure the rat's weight applied to the weeping sores on its underside. Not that the action would have made much difference, even if the animal's strength had permitted it. The sores had already ravaged every part of its dying body.

It blinked a beady eye covered so thickly in cloudy cataract tissue that it could not have seen him. Still, Dr. Ernesto Rodriguez could not shake the feeling that the rat stared up at him accusingly.

Dr. Rodriguez—Ernie, as his friends called him—walked along the line of cages, each housing a rat in a different stage of disease. The diseases ran the gamut of genetic illness. Animals used for contagious experimentation were kept separately in a biohazard area.

At the end of the row, Ernie stopped before the next-to-last cage, bending low to stare at the readouts from the instruments attached to the little brown fellow. As opposed to its dying brother, this little guy was the epitome of health. Heart, lungs, circulatory system, and brain function—in every category the lucky fellow exceeded the norm.

Ernie reached a finger through the cage, gently stroking the tame animal's soft side with his fingertip. Noticing that his glasses had fogged, he withdrew his hand, dabbed at his eyes, and then wiped the lenses on his shirt.

As usual, Ernie had stayed at the lab until everyone else in this wing had called it a night. It was almost time for him to go home, although the thought ripped at his heart. He should be there now, helping Angela care for their son. Most women would have broken under the strain long ago. But not Angela.

For two years now, their son, Raul, had struggled valiantly against the cancer eating at his brain, maintaining a sunny attitude despite his deteriorating strength. Raul should be in his third year of high school; instead, he had to be rolled from side to side during the day to try and keep the bedsores under control.

They had tried everything: chemo, radiation, cryosurgery, self-administered homeopathic cures, everything. Now all that was left to them was self-administered hospice care to ease his final days. Angela had rejected the hospice workers who had offered to assist her with the burden, insisting that she would care for her son.

She had moved a rollout bed into Raul's room and now slept next to his bed, just in case he needed something during the night. Sometimes, during the sleepless nights, Ernie would tiptoe down to Raul's doorway and listen to his wife's prayers to the *Madre*, to the *santos*, and to *Jesus Christo* himself to grant her just one miracle. Just one.

Ernie wiped his eyes once more and returned his glasses back to their accustomed position on his nose. He stared at the rat as it scurried about its cage sniffing for food, now completely accustomed to the wireless electrodes attached to its skin.

One week. Ernie could not get the thought out of his head. It had been only one week since he had applied the test serum to this rat. One week since this healthy rat had lain in a cage next to the dying rat, its condition even worse than its unfortunate sibling.

Human trials were scheduled to begin next month. He didn't have a month. Angela didn't have a month. And Raul damned sure didn't have a month, either.

Having made up his mind, Dr. Rodriguez walked over to the intercom and pressed one of the buttons. After several seconds, a familiar voice answered.

"Stephenson here."

"Dr. Stephenson, this is Dr. Rodriguez from Omega Lab. May I speak with you? It is very urgent."

After a brief hesitation, the deputy director's voice continued. "I'm in my office, Ernie. Come on down."

Ernie logged himself out and switched off the lights, enabling the security system before locking the lab behind him. Then, exiting the Omega Wing, he made his way rapidly across the huge room that housed the *Rho Ship*.

Coming to a stop just outside the door into Deputy Director Stephenson's private office, Ernie paused to wipe his glasses yet again. Then, with a deep breath, Ernesto Rodriguez straightened his shoulders and stepped through the doorway, one thought screaming in his mind.

For Raul.

CHAPTER 44

At breakfast, Heather was unusually quiet, despite the presence of the entire Smythe family, the twins bantering in their usual, boisterous fashion. The headaches were back, worse than before. If they lasted longer, Heather might have mentioned it to her friends. But this was a brief, stabbing pain. It was probably only stress. After all, it wasn't as if the three of them hadn't been under some pressure lately.

"What's up with Heather? I need to pull her aside and get to the bottom of it, if only Mark will leave us alone for a bit."

Heather looked over at Jennifer. "What was that?"

Jennifer glanced up questioningly, her mouth full of honey-buttered biscuit. She swallowed hard. "What? I didn't say anything."

Heather rubbed her temples. "Sorry. I must be hearing things."

Her mother set down her coffee cup. “Is something wrong, honey? Are you feeling all right?”

Heather smiled. “I’m fine, Mom. Just a little headache this morning. I’m sure it’ll pass as soon as I get out and start moving around.”

“I’ll get you some ibuprofen.” She rose and moved toward the stairs to her bedroom.

“Mom, eat your breakfast. I’ll be fine.”

Heather might as well not have spoken for all the effect it had on her mother’s progress. She returned shortly with the medicine. Heather took the small, burnt-orange tablets, popped them in her mouth, and washed them down with a swig of orange juice.

“Thanks.”

“You’re welcome.” Her mother beamed over her coffee cup. “No use suffering through a headache.”

“Great game last night, Mark,” said Heather’s father. “It’s been a while since you got into a scoring groove like that. Not that you haven’t been outstanding all year, but it’s been a while since you scored forty points.”

Heather watched Mark’s grin spread across his handsome face, shocked by the intense attraction that coursed through her veins. Christ, the headache must be making her delirious.

“I guess I was just feeling it last night. We all have to get hot sometime.”

Mr. Smythe leaned forward, slapping his son’s shoulder. “I keep telling him to shoot more. No need to overdo the passing when you’ve got the best shot in the state.”

“Dad, I shoot when I’m open. If someone has a better shot, I pass the ball. That’s the only way I know how to play. It’s a team sport, you know.”

Mr. Smythe grinned. "You know we have to give you advice. It's the only way we old cats get to be involved in the game. Sort of like yelling at the refs."

Heather's father laughed. "Good analogy, Fred. It's pretty much our civic duty."

"Speaking of civic duty, that was a nice young couple sitting on the other side of you at the game."

"Oh, yes, the Johnsons. We met them at the church bingo night on Wednesday. Jack and Janet."

A warm smile lit Heather's mother's face. "The nicest young people. Reverend Harvey introduced us. Jack's an EPA man, and Janet is a teacher. She's subbing at the school and applying for a full-time position for next fall. Both of them volunteer at the hospital. I hope you don't mind, but I invited them to dinner tomorrow night so they could meet everyone."

Heather choked on her juice. Mark gave her a look that said he understood.

"That sounds wonderful," Mrs. Smythe said. "In all the commotion of the game, I barely got a glimpse of them over Fred and Gil. Especially the way our guys kept jumping up and yelling."

"It's a game, Linda," said Mr. Smythe. "You're supposed to cheer."

"I understand that, dear. My point is that the environment wasn't conducive to introductions."

"Good, then," said Heather's mom. "How about meeting here at four o'clock? That way we can visit for a while before the roast is ready."

By the time the breakfast chatter ended and the plans for Sunday afternoon were finalized, it was well past nine. Mark, Jennifer, and Heather pulled out their bikes and headed for the *Second Ship*, taking their time this morning. The day was the first warm day in weeks, the sun so bright it seemed almost as if there were no atmosphere present to filter its rays.

The ibuprofen had worked. Heather's headache was now a thing of the past. Being outside in the sunshine, feeling the warm breeze brush her cheek as she pedaled, made her feel as if she had suddenly awakened from hibernation. The tang of pine-scented air, the songs of birds in the trees, and the beauty of the mountain country lifted her soul.

At one of their stops along the way, a group of squirrels scampered through the leafless branches of a large cottonwood tree. The little animals looked like they were playing a huge game of "follow the leader" as they raced around and around the large branches, then up and out onto mere twigs, leaping out to grab neighboring twigs, then scurrying back to thicker limbs.

For several minutes the friends watched the squirrels at play, probably some sort of mating ritual. Obviously she wasn't the only one feeling a hint of spring in the air, Heather thought.

When Heather, Jennifer, and Mark arrived at the top of the canyon, above where the *Second Ship* lay hidden, they paused under a group of pines, spreading out the picnic lunch they had brought with them. Best to eat now, even if they weren't hungry. They had a lot of work to do.

Unfortunately, by the time they finished lunch and made their way down to the cave, Heather's headache was back, her head throbbing so badly she wished she hadn't eaten the sandwich. Doing her best to ignore the pain and nausea, she boarded the ship and slid her headset into place.

No sooner had the lightweight band slipped over her temples than she became aware of a new sensation. Instead of the gentle massaging action that usually followed sliding the headset into place, a gentle thrumming filled her head. It felt—no, it *sounded* like it was coming from the medical lab. In her mind she could see the table of the tentacles, pulsing red, shifting to orange.

A strong compulsion to go to the medical lab engulfed her, almost as if the table called to her. Heather found herself moving in response to the call before she was aware of having decided to do so.

Without waiting for Mark or Jennifer, she moved to the hole leading up to the next deck and jumped up, landing crouched on the floor above. It was a bit surprising to be able to jump like that instead of pulling herself up and kicking a leg over the edge as she had been forced to do in the past, but the compulsion left no time for reflection on the oddity. Without pausing, Heather moved through the doorway, which slid open to admit her. She could hear faint cries behind her, someone calling out her name. Then the door swished shut, blocking all external sound.

Heather moved to the table, hopped up onto its edge, and lay back, feeling its tentacular embrace enfold her body. So wonderful.

The tentacles on her head were doing something new this time, crawling across the surface of her face and forehead as though seeking new connections. Searching, in the way a mother seeks a lost child in a crowd. Rapidly. Urgently.

The tiny tentacles moved from nerve ending to nerve ending, spreading the lovely warmth along her central nervous system, gradually easing the pain in her head. And as a smoky haze glazed her eyes, the lights in the room slowly faded away. Just like the old Pink Floyd song, she...had become...comfortably numb.

CHAPTER 45

Heather sat up, the wondrously supple tentacles melting away from her body as she moved. She felt something. What was it? Somehow different.

For one thing, for the first time in days she felt not even a hint of the headache, which had been coming and going but always leaving just a fragment of itself in her head. It was as if a loose connection in an electrical circuit, one that had been spitting sparks, had been correctly spliced and wrapped with electrical tape.

Looking around the medical lab, Heather suddenly noticed that the door had remained closed. Mark and Jennifer must be frantic on the opposite side. As she visualized the door opening, it complied. Mark and Jennifer both raced into the room before it could close again.

Mark looked as if he were ready to kill something. "Heather, are you all right?"

Jennifer raced over and threw her arms around Heather's shoulders, a flood of tears streaming down her face. Heather hugged her back.

"It's OK. I'm fine now."

"What the hell happened?" Mark yelled. "We were just about ready to go get help."

Heather paused, looking at Jennifer's accusing face as she pulled away. "I'm not sure. I think the ship detected something wrong with me and decided to fix it. I hadn't told you, but I have been having the headaches again. This morning was especially bad. Anyway, when I put on the headset, I felt compelled to come directly here, so I guess that's what I did."

"You didn't just come up here," Jennifer said. "You jumped up the six feet to the second deck like you were Batgirl or something. Mark followed, but the doors had already closed and wouldn't open for us. It's been half an hour since you disappeared."

"We banged on the door, yelled, tried visualizing the thing opening, but nothing worked," said Mark. "You really scared the crap out of us."

Heather touched him on the arm softly. "I'm sorry. I must have been in some sort of trance. Anyway, I think the table fixed whatever was wrong with me." Heather paused. "You say I jumped up instead of climbed up?"

Mark nodded. "You just leaped straight up in the air and landed on your feet on the next deck. I had to concentrate to manage the same thing myself."

"Well, there is a big difference in weight."

"Don't give me that. It's a matter of weight ratio to muscle mass. Your muscles were performing like mine or there's no way you could've done it."

Heather shrugged. "There's something else I didn't tell you guys. This morning at breakfast, I think I heard Jen's thoughts in my head."

Jennifer turned pale. "All of them? You were in my head?"

Heather shook her head. "No. It wasn't like that. You were thinking about telling me something, and I picked up on that. It was just the one time, but I thought it might be a good idea for all of us to keep each other in the loop on what is happening to us during the change."

Mark tilted his head. "Did you just say, 'during the change'? What change?"

Heather paused. "Did I? A Freudian slip. I didn't mean to say that."

"Aren't Freudian slips supposed to be based upon a real thought?" Jennifer asked.

"Forget I said anything about Freud. It doesn't mean anything."

"You got away from explaining the world record girls' high jump," said Mark.

"I was getting to that. It just confirms an idea that's been growing in my mind for a few days now. Do you remember when we first got onto the medical table? It showed our brains with about the same level of activity. There weren't any real differences between us."

Mark's lips tightened. "Yes. What of it?"

"I think we all have almost exactly the same abilities."

Jennifer shook her head. "But that's just not true. I'm not coordinated and strong like Mark, and I don't see numbers in my head like you do. But I'm better at data manipulation than either of you."

Heather paused, struggling to put her thoughts into an explanation that made sense. "We all have a picture of ourselves in our heads. You know, a self-image. I think I'm good at certain things, Mark thinks he's good at other things, and you think you're good at others. Our brain enhancements interpret those self-images as goals. Our brains are taking those goals and implementing them, including our self-imposed limitations."

Jennifer crossed her arms. "So you think if I imagine I'm strong, I can jump up here like you did?"

"I doubt it. Our self-images are probably difficult to retrain. I'm only saying that we may have considerably more untapped potential than we realize. But even if we change our self-imagery, I'm still going to have things I prefer. And I'll still practice those things more than either of you would."

Jennifer finally smiled. "Makes sense."

Suddenly remembering what she'd set out to do, Heather changed the subject. "That reminds me, I want to get up to the command deck and search for more data on subspace. If I'm right about what I saw last time, subspace vibrations should leak back into our space and vice versa."

Mark raised an eyebrow. "And other than boring me out of my mind, this is important, why?"

Jennifer frowned. "I think I see where Heather is going with this."

"Think of the different spaces like tuning forks a little distance apart. If I hit one with a small hammer, the others pick up the same vibration, the same tone, only more weakly. Using a variation of that principle, I think we may be able to make a subspace receiver."

"Two questions," Mark said. "Number one: Why bother? We already have the QT circuit. Number two: Wouldn't we also need to build a subspace transmitter?"

Heather let a hint of frustration seep into her voice. “Look. We’ve been scrambling to do anything that can get someone like the NSA to help us. And every time we do, we come closer to getting ourselves caught than to bringing heat on the Rho Project. It’s time to step up our game. With the quantum twins, we have to physically plant one of them somewhere to be able to send and receive from that other location. But with this, we should be able to tune our subspace receiver to focus on a mapped location in real space. It’s completely hands-off. With this technology, we can hack the planet.”

“So we could aim it to listen to anything, so long as we know the location?” Jennifer asked.

“I think so. The problem is that everything rings the subspace tuning fork. So we would be listening to white noise or static. But that brings us to the next answer. We don’t need a subspace transmitter because everything transmits into subspace.”

“So how do we get around the white noise problem?”

“That’s why I want to spend more time on the command deck. I think we can introduce a carrier signal that we can detect in the noise.”

Jennifer started moving toward the door. “We can embed a data signal on it.”

“Right. With that, we could remotely tap any line, so long as we knew its exact subspace coordinates.”

“Then what are we waiting for?” Jennifer said as she led the way out of the medical lab. “Like you said, time to hack the planet.”

As Heather followed Jennifer out of the room, she felt her anticipation throttle up to maximum.

CHAPTER 46

Making the rounds of the Sunday morning talk shows was never pleasant, and this morning it was downright annoying. For one thing, the host usually selected congressmen or senators wholly intent on making complete asses of themselves. This was especially true of the guest on Vice President Gordon's left on this last of his scheduled appearances. Senator Wilkins from Wisconsin not only strove to be an ass, he was wildly successful at it.

Charles Paul, the host of *Sunday This Week*, knew that the end of his hour was approaching, and since he had Senator Wilkins on a roll, he tossed out more raw meat.

"So, Senator, you are saying that even though the bulk of the scientific community around the world has embraced the environmental benefits of cold fusion technology, it is not as green as it seems?"

"Actually, I have a number of concerns about this alien technology and the alien race that is behind it. Who's to say that they sent this robot ship to earth with benign intentions? The little the government has revealed about this *Rho Ship* doesn't include a thing about its creators, only a sample of their technology. Not only is cold fusion not environmentally friendly, this technology threatens all the gains made by the environmental movement over the last thirty years."

"How so?"

"Look, just producing energy cleanly doesn't clean up the environment. Energy is the fuel of consumption, and rampant consumption is what drives the train of environmental destruction. This promise of clean, cheap energy is the siren sitting on a rocky shoal, calling us all toward an ecological shipwreck. It says, produce more. Consume more. No need to fret or worry about conservation.

"And all that stuff we are consuming is made from plastics derived from petroleum, or steel, which requires coal, or through the use of harmful chemicals. And that is without even mentioning the rape of the Earth's resources."

Charles Paul turned to the vice president. "Mr. Vice President, your response?"

Vice President Gordon smiled. "I think that the worthy senator's words speak volumes about his party's true agenda. When he says consumption is the root of all evil, he means capitalism is the root of all evil. He and his allies would have us adopt a model of European socialism. Beyond that, they want the government to be able to tell the American people what kind of cars they can buy, how much of each item they can consume.

"And by his argument, if consumption is 'bad,' that must mean lack of consumption is good. But if nobody consumes, nobody buys. If nobody buys, nobody makes. If nobody makes, nobody works. His party's policies, if followed to their ultimate conclusion, would have everyone walking or riding an animal to work, but only if that work produced things that nobody could consume and that were not made of anything."

"That is ridiculous!" Senator Wilkins fumed.

"For once, Senator, I agree with you."

"The fact that you and the president are in the hip pockets of the big multinational corporations makes everything coming from your mouth a product, bought and paid for by the richest of the rich."

"Senator, I believe last year you were claiming that the president and I were both owned by big oil. Isn't it odd that we are embracing a technology that will take the world off of fossil fuels?"

"You are merely helping those same corporations shift to new technologies."

"And that is bad, how?"

Charles Paul interrupted. "Gentlemen, I am afraid we are out of time. I want to thank you both for coming here to discuss this important topic. To my audience, I say, have a good Sunday, and I will see you next week."

The vice president reached across the table and shook the host's and then the senator's hand, enjoying the fake smile on the latter's face. Then, accompanied by his Secret Service team, Vice President Gordon exited the building, got in the backseat of his limousine, and leaned back for the ride to the West Wing of the White House.

Another Sunday and another set of guest appearances down. The truth of the matter was that he and the president had a winning hand on the topic of cold fusion, and they intended to press that advantage home. True, it was not regarded by everyone as a beneficial thing. Even groups within the Republican Party were suspicious that it came from Rho Project alien technology.

Several Christian religious groups had come out in opposition equivalent to the fatwas being issued by radical Islamist groups. However, their loss of support was more than compensated for by the large numbers of Democrats and Independents that had come on board in support of the policy. Considering the rate of worldwide adoption of cold fusion technology, there would be no putting that genie back in the bottle.

The Middle East was a problem, but even that could be dealt with. OPEC was in disarray, several of the member states calling for an all-out ban on oil exports, but those voices could not overcome the group's addiction to cash flow. Fact was, even though new cold fusion power plants were coming online around the world at record pace, it would be several years before a portable power unit usable in automobiles was in mass production and affordable.

In the meantime, the second technology from the Rho Project was secretly getting ready to move to human testing next month. Vice President Gordon had no doubt about the outcome of that testing. He just needed to be a little patient. Let the world get accustomed to how great the first alien technology was before introducing the next.

Gordon clasped his hands behind his head as he looked out the window. He never tired of the sight of the White House from the backseat of the vice presidential limousine. Of course, it was only a matter of time before the "vice" came off the name.

Vice President Gordon smiled. He could afford to be patient.

CHAPTER 47

The Johnsons arrived at the McFarland house at 3:30 p.m. and immediately received a traditional country greeting: they were put to work. Nothing about that surprised Heather. In the extended McFarland family, the process of preparing the meal for a party was as much a part of the gathering as the dinner itself, maybe more so. Whether it was the church picnic or a Sunday-afternoon gathering like this one, the hostess delegated jobs in a way that would make an army first sergeant proud.

At the moment, Jack Johnson was helping Fred Smythe expand the dining room table and add the removable center leaves. Janet Johnson was in the kitchen, tossing salad and laughing at something Linda Smythe had just said. As for Heather, Mark, and Jennifer, they scurried around gathering the table settings while Heather's father carved the roast.

Heather cast fleeting glances at Jack; she noticed Jennifer doing the same. As striking as Janet appeared, Jack lit the room like a supernova. He was brown haired, lean, and muscular, a little over six feet in height, and dressed with a casual elegance that would have made Hannibal Lecter proud. Although his chiseled features were handsome, it was the confident ease with which he moved and interacted with those around him that set him apart. Heather was amazed. Where were all these cat people coming from?

Heather noticed that Mark seemed intent on checking if the ladies in the kitchen needed anything else carried out to the table. And although his actions mildly annoyed her, Heather didn't require her enhanced imagination to guess why he was going the extra mile.

Dinner passed very pleasantly, the Johnsons chatting with the Smythes and McFarlands as comfortably as old friends. Heather couldn't recall her dad and Mr. Smythe ever telling so many tales about their exploits. The pleasant laughter of the Johnsons just seemed to pull the tales from them.

Toward the end of the meal, the talk turned to the Johnsons. Interestingly enough, they had been college sweethearts from eastern Maryland, where they had met in a ballroom dancing club. Having seen the way Jack and Janet moved, Heather imagined that the sight of these two doing the tango would probably generate enough heat to send the other couples scurrying to rent rooms.

After dinner, as the Johnsons received a walking tour of the McFarland and Smythe houses, Mark, Jennifer, and Heather retreated to Heather's room.

As she closed the door behind them, Heather said, "It's OK to stop drooling now, Mark."

"Me? What about you two? I haven't seen that much mooning around in my life."

Jennifer held up her hands. "Enough already. So the Johnsons are hot. It's not as if we haven't seen really hot people before."

Heather and Mark simultaneously raised an eyebrow.

"I'll grant you they're hotter than most."

Mark plopped down on the end of Heather's bed. "So what have you come up with?"

The question pushed the Johnsons to the back of her mind. "I finished reviewing all the data we got on our last trip out to the ship. As much as I hate to admit it, it turns out Mark is right. We do need to build both a subspace receiver and a subspace transmitter."

"I keep telling you to listen when I speak," Mark said.

"It's not that we need it to receive a signal. But we're going to want to put data on remote network lines, not just receive. For that we'll need a focused subspace wave packet that will induce a signal in normal space. You can almost think of it as Faraday's induction principle applied across a subspace to normal space interface."

"I hadn't thought of that," said Jennifer.

Mark frowned. "How about boiling that down to the Cliff's Notes version."

Heather sighed. "It gives us an untraceable wiretap, almost as if we had a QT device installed on the far side. There are two problems, though. The transmitter is going to require a significant power source, capable of generating high-energy photons like hard X-rays or gamma rays."

"Why?" asked Jennifer.

"It has to ring subspace hard enough to cross the subspace to normal space induction threshold. We need high energy for that kind of signal amplitude. I'm afraid that energy is going to have to come from the hard photons."

"Well, then, we're screwed," said Mark. "Unless, of course, you know someone willing to sell us some plutonium."

"Actually, I've been thinking about that, too," said Heather.

"How did I know that you were going to say that?"

"Cold fusion generates those energetic photons. I think we can build a cold fusion tank the size of an aquarium."

Mark groaned. "And what, may I ask, is this likely to cost us?"

Heather didn't like what she was about to say any more than Mark wanted to hear it. "I read that a physicist at Cal Tech built one in his basement for around ten thousand."

Jennifer's eyes widened. "Ten thousand dollars! Where are we going to come up with that kind of cash?"

"Relax. His apparatus was almost as big as my bedroom. Ours shouldn't cost more than two thousand."

"And that helps, how?"

"I have over a thousand dollars in my checking account. I'm sure each of you has a few hundred saved up."

Mark gasped. "You want us to personally fund this crazy scheme? I worked hard for that money. I'm saving up for a used car. No way I'm going into senior year without a car."

Jennifer shook her head. "I don't know, Heather. I only have seven hundred and thirty-seven dollars and twenty-two cents in my account."

"Look, I know it's not a pleasant idea. Do you think I want to spend all my savings on this little science project? I don't. But I don't think we have any choice. Right now we're flying blind. We hope our little venture into cyberspace got the NSA people checking out the Rho Project, but we don't know."

"Why don't we just hack into the net again like last time?" Mark asked.

"I don't want to risk it," said Jennifer. "They almost caught us last time. My guess is that they would be on us quick."

"Jen is right," Heather said. "And we need to be able to hack into any remote network untraceably, even secure ones. The subspace receiver could even pick up signals on fiber-optic networks since light leaks energy into subspace the same as any other source."

"OK. I'm just not big on getting cooked by gamma rays."

Despite the fact that she worried about the same thing, Heather forced herself to continue.

"If we were dealing with high levels of the fusion reaction, that might be a problem. We'll only be producing and using low levels of gamma and X-ray flux. That means we'll need to have some lead shielding around the tank, but not a lot. The main byproduct of the reaction will be hot water."

Jennifer's stare looked doubtful. "Maybe so, but I think it would be a good idea to set up a little generator that uses the heat to generate electricity and feeds it back into the power for the house. That way if anyone checks out our setup, it just looks like a normal cold fusion experiment."

"Makes sense," said Mark, reluctantly. "But we can't be running back and forth to the ship all the time. That means we need to build this thing in our old workshop in the garage. With something like this, you can bet our dads will want to review our plans to ensure it's safe."

Heather paused, rubbing her chin. "I know I can sell Dad on the idea if we pitch it right. And I think I know how to do that. This could be our entry into the National Science Competition for next year."

"Our subspace receiver is going to be in a science contest?" Jennifer asked.

"Not the subspace receiver, just the cold fusion apparatus. The project would be to build a household cold fusion power supply. The gamma probe can be hidden in a small detector that we use to keep track of internal radiation and reaction levels. That way the subspace transmitter and receiver can be hooked to the power supply through an external connection and controlled from a laptop."

"There's no way we'll be able to hide this project from Dad," said Mark. "And he'll know how much it's costing us."

"That just means our sales pitch has to be good. If they believe we're serious about this contest, I think they'll be supportive."

Mark looked morose. "I can't believe I'm even considering giving up my car savings for a science contest."

A new thought occurred to Heather. "Look at it as an investment. Sometimes companies give nice grants to the winners of this contest or even buy the winning technology."

Mrs. McFarland's voice interrupted their planning session. "Heather, Mark, Jennifer! Come on downstairs."

As Heather and the Smythe twins reached the bottom of the stairs, they could see that the Johnsons had retrieved their coats and were saying their good-byes. Seeing the three friends, Jack walked over and shook each of their hands.

"Janet already had the pleasure of having you in her class at school, but I wanted you all to know that I enjoyed meeting you." Jack's face grew serious as he turned toward Heather, his dark eyes flashing in the lamplight. "Your parents told us about the creep stalking you."

"Stalking may be a bit of an overstatement," said Heather nervously.

"Maybe so, young lady. He's probably just a deranged homeless man. All the same, you should be watchful. I don't like the idea of someone leaving threatening notes on your window."

Heather nodded, oddly flattered that Jack had taken enough interest to warn her. "I'll be careful. Thank you."

The dark look passed from Jack's face as if it had never been there, and once again he and Janet were smiling and saying their farewells. Then they swept from the house, like Mary Poppins floating off on her umbrella, with an otherworldly grace that left the room feeling empty.

"A vigorous young couple," said Heather's father as the Johnsons drove away.

"With anyone else I would say that was an odd choice of words," said Mr. Smythe. "But somehow, I have to agree with you."

"Well, I think they're nice." Heather's mom's voice held a slight note of disapproval.

Heather's father raised his eyebrows. "I didn't say they weren't."

Mrs. Smythe laughed. "Well, I guess it's perfectly reasonable that someone can be both nice and vigorous. Anyway, let me gather my tribe and head them home. Thanks for the lovely evening."

After a round of hugs, the Smythes grabbed their coats and made their way out the door. Heather kissed her parents good night then headed upstairs for bath and bed.

She wasn't quite sure why Jack Johnson's comment about the Rag Man had disconcerted her so. For a brief instant, Jack's pupils had reflected a red glint in the dim lamplight, leaving Heather feeling as if the grim reaper himself had swept through the room.

Heather shook off the recollection. Once again, her overactive imagination was getting the best of her.

CHAPTER 48

While January had started with a bang, it left with little more than a whimper. The weather, their classes, and even the impact of the cold fusion science project on their bank account, all turned out to be much less threatening than Mark, Heather, and Jennifer had foreseen. A lazy mildness, reminiscent of an Indian summer, settled over the entire high plateau region, coloring all the teens' activities.

Although the fact that the government hadn't discovered their starship or their involvement in the New Year's Day Virus was comforting, worry about the ongoing Rho Project and increasing world tension weighed on Heather's mood.

Progress on the cold fusion apparatus was slower than expected. Acquisition of materials and the welding, soldering, and gluing of all the components were slowed by the additional requirements imposed by the national science fair. Every plan, measurement, and activity had to be carefully recorded according to the scientific method. The only things the three friends did not record were the special modifications that would allow them to hook in the subspace transmitter.

Heather was thrilled with the outcome of their sales pitch to their dads. Not only had both dads agreed, they were so thrilled they volunteered to fund half the cost.

Heather worked out several modifications to the cold fusion theory that allowed them to design a much smaller and cheaper version of the tank. As she solved each piece of the physics and mathematical puzzle, Jennifer created simulation programs that let them test the design. That finished, Heather and Mark began building it, quickly acquiring a degree of skill with the machine tools that even impressed Heather's dad. Still, there was plenty of work yet to be done.

All of this would have gone much faster if not for the distraction of having to go to school. For Heather, the week had started no different from most: endless boring assignments, talking between classes with her other school friends, and the challenge of ignoring the annoying Ms. Gorsky.

All that had changed with the arrival of a new boy in her class. Heather found herself attracted to him as soon as she looked into his deep, brown eyes. He was only slightly shorter than Mark, his skin an attractive olive brown that glowed like his personality. And from what she could tell, he liked her right back.

Raul Rodriguez was a cancer survivor, someone who had gone to the ragged edge of the life-and-death boundary, maybe even dipped a toe in on the other side. As Raul told it, largely due to the power of his mother's prayers, a miracle had happened. God, in all his mercy, had healed Raul of the cancer that had riddled his body, bringing a new happiness to his family and strengthening his mother's faith in the Lord.

Raul's doctors had worked to save him through a combination of chemotherapy and radiation before giving up and handing him over to hospice care so he could be comfortable for his last days. After his miraculous recovery, those same doctors had asked Raul's father for permission to study Raul, in the hope that they could determine the cause of his recovery.

Ernesto Rodriguez had firmly refused, saying that God had healed his son and that was all they needed to know. Heather understood the residual anger Raul's dad must feel toward the medical community that had failed him, but she still felt that the denial was shortsighted, possibly hurting others who might be helped by understanding Raul's condition.

Now, having met Raul, she was delighted his light still shone on this world. They had gone out twice already, if you counted a trip to McDonald's for a Big Mac and fries a date. And now he had asked her to the dance on Thursday night. It was going to be a last-millennium, retro sock hop at the school gymnasium, complete with the girls dressing in skirts and bobby socks while the boys wore jeans, collared shirts, and slicked their hair back with copious amounts of hair gel.

Just thinking about going with Raul to the dance distracted Heather horribly. Already this morning she had been scolded twice by Ms. Gorsky for daydreaming in class. Mark noticed her infatuation, and his snide comments as the class ended added to her annoyance. As he walked by singing "There's a new kid in town," Heather elbowed him hard.

"Mark, I'm really not in the mood for your needling."

"Needling? Me?" The look of wounded innocence on Mark's face didn't improve her mood.

"I'm serious."

Just then Raul walked up to her. "Am I interrupting something?"

Heather smiled. "No. Mark was just leaving."

"Sure was. I'm sure the reason why will come to me shortly." Before he could catch another elbow, Mark moved off into the crowd.

Raul did not seem to notice the quip. "So, Heather, are you doing anything over lunch?"

"Well, let's see. I was planning on eating."

Raul grinned. "You know that isn't what I meant. I wanted to ask you to have lunch with me. My folks are going to swing by and will treat at the café."

"That sounds like fun. I like getting treated, especially when it avoids the school cafeteria."

"Great. It's a date then."

"You've got it."

As Raul turned away, he yelled over his shoulder, "Oh—meet us out on the front steps at noon."

"I'll be there," said Heather.

As she turned back toward her next class, she bumped into Mark, who had his hands cupped over his mouth.

"I'll be there. I'll be there," he pretended to yell after Raul.

Although his words were only loud enough for her to hear, Heather felt sudden anger redden her face. She stormed past him, sweeping into the classroom like an ancient pterodactyl swooping down on its prey.

By the time noon approached, Heather had recovered her composure, determined not to let Mark's teasing get under her skin. Still, she carefully avoided running into him as she made her way down the hall and out onto the front steps of the school. Raul was already there, along with his parents.

"Hi, Heather," Raul said, stepping forward to take her hand. "This is my mom and dad."

Mr. Rodriguez was a slender man who looked every bit the scientist that Raul had described, the dark frames on his glasses making the skin on his face appear a lighter shade than Raul's. Mrs. Rodriguez was a motherly looking woman wearing a floral-patterned dress and leather pumps. Her dark eyes shone with an intensity Heather found disconcerting.

"I'm very pleased to meet you, Mr. and Mrs. Rodriguez."

There was a brief moment of uncomfortable silence before Mr. Rodriguez extended his hand. "Very nice to meet you, Heather."

Mrs. Rodriguez only nodded. "Well, shall we go?"

Heather wasn't sure why she had the feeling she was less than welcome on this outing, but seeing Raul's smile eased her discomfort.

As they followed Mr. and Mrs. Rodriguez toward the aging green Suburban, Raul leaned in and whispered, "Please be patient. My parents were so protective while I was sick, they're having trouble adjusting."

Heather nodded and smiled. She could only imagine the trauma the little family had been through as Raul's cancer had advanced. If that didn't leave significant emotional scarring, then she didn't know what would.

The café the Rodriguez family had picked out turned out to be McDonald's, something that almost made Heather laugh out loud. She could not imagine her mother referring to Mickey D's as a café, although, to be fair, it did serve burgers and sodas, pancakes and coffee, and many other things that fell within the realm of typical café fare. Still, it just didn't seem right to utilize any word of French or even European origin to describe a fast-food joint.

As they settled down in a booth to eat, an awkward silence descended. For once, even Raul seemed reluctant to break the spell, which weighed more heavily upon Heather with each passing minute. Finally, in a desperate attempt to generate some pleasant conversation, her mouth opened of its own accord.

"So, Mrs. Rodriguez. It was so wonderful to hear the story of Raul's recovery. I found it tremendously inspiring."

Mrs. Rodriguez turned a stern gaze on Heather. "Really? It is not inspiring. Raul is a miracle from God."

Heather gulped. Determined to keep Mrs. Rodriguez talking, in the hope that she could break through that icy reserve, she continued. "Yes, it is a miracle. And I think it's inspiring because his example can give others hope that they can recover in the same miraculous way."

"Raul did not receive a miracle. He is one. His recovery is not something that others can accomplish through Earthly means. God saw fit to bring Raul to us, immersing him in a second baptism of pain and suffering so that we could observe his recovery. So that we might see how this world's healing is impotent and know that all true power lies in Him."

Heather was confused by the intensity of the sudden verbal onslaught. For one thing, the odd manner in which Mrs. Rodriguez spoke almost made it sound as if she were confusing the terms *God* and *Raul*.

Heather struggled to recover. "I really didn't mean to argue with you. I can't even imagine the pain that you have endured. And I understand why you wouldn't want to let any doctors study his recovery. At least until you're ready."

Mr. Rodriguez banged his fist down on the table with enough force to cause other customers to stare. "Until we are ready? How dare you question us. We will not let anyone poke and prod our son anymore. They had their chance and proved their impotence. We will do nothing to aid them in their quest for self-importance."

Mrs. Rodriguez leaned forward, her eyes blazing with a zealous light that scared Heather. "It is so easy to be an unbeliever, to walk the path laid at your feet by Satan. But I always knew that God had a plan for my son. Soon everyone will be given a choice—to walk with glory or to burn in the depths of hellfire. Be thankful that He is giving you the chance to become worthy. I, for one, cannot see it within you. Be thankful that His mercy is beyond mine."

If Heather's hair could have curled on her head, it would have, as surely as if she had undergone a two-hour perm at the closest beauty salon. She was beyond speechless. She was stupefied.

She glanced at Raul, who stared at her as he lifted a golden french fry to his lips, twelve small grains of salt clinging to its greased, 61.6345-millimeter-long form. Heather felt like some insect, pressed between glass slides, as a giant peered down at her, twisting knobs to adjust the focus of his microscope so that he could determine exactly what made her tick.

When Heather got nervous, she lost focus, and whenever she lost concentration, numbers and equations swirled through her mind in a maddening storm. For 11.857 seconds, nobody said anything.

Miraculously, Raul put down his golden french fry, uneaten, and dispelled the silence with a musical laugh. "Mom. Look at me for a second."

The woman's harsh gaze turned toward Raul, and as her eyes met his, a mystical transformation occurred. Her look went beyond love to one of adoration, maybe even worship.

"Mom, I invited Heather because I like her, and I wanted you and Dad to get a chance to meet her. Did you hear what I said? I like her. And I expect you to like her too."

If he had slapped his mother's face, her expression could not have been more pained.

"Raul, I am so sorry. I don't know what came over me. You know I would never question your judgment or think to stand in the way of your desires. Please forgive me."

To Heather's horror, the woman began to cry, burying her face in her hands, sobs shaking her body. By this time, the people at the nearby tables had not only quit looking at them, most had found a good excuse to move to another part of the restaurant.

Raul rose and walked around the table to his mother, taking her face between his own palms. A look of beatific peace came over the young man's face.

"Mom, I know you meant only the best. You have protected me for so long that it is hard to stop doing it. But I don't need protection now. You know that, don't you?"

Mrs. Rodriguez nodded.

"Good. I am not angry with you. I just want you to be nice to Heather and to like her as I do. Can you do that for me?"

Mrs. Rodriguez nodded more vigorously, achieving a rate of 3.13256 head oscillations per second.

When Raul released her face, Mrs. Rodriguez turned to face Heather, and if it had not been for the wet trails of tears down her face, Heather would have thought she was a different woman, so bright and cheery was the smile warming her features.

"Dear, I am sorry that I gave you such a grilling. I let my overzealous protective instincts cloud my judgment."

Heather struggled to breathe. "I completely understand. No apology necessary."

Not only did Heather not understand, she felt almost as if she had once more fallen down that rabbit hole after Alice. A quick glance at Mr. Rodriguez put her farther down that hole. He did not look apologetic, merely pensive, studying her as if deciding what further damage she might do.

Mr. Rodriguez glanced down at his watch. "Well, would you look at the time? If I don't get you kids back to class, I'll be answering to your principal."

With that, he stood and led them like a row of ducklings, first to dump the trash, then out and into the beat-up, old Suburban.

Raul held her hand for the car ride back to school and up onto the steps after getting out of the car. Just before they passed through the door, he leaned over and kissed her gently on the cheek.

"You did great," he said. "Gotta run to my class, though. I'll catch up with you later."

Somehow Heather found her way to her locker and then to physics class with the right books, notebook, and pencil. As the class began, Heather stared at her teacher, Mr. Harold, with no more comprehension than a zombie. Unseeing. Unhearing. Beyond emotional exhaustion.

The frequency of Mr. Harold's vocal-cord variations, the amplitude in decibels of each syllable that escaped his mouth, the fluctuations of the classroom air temperature in degrees Kelvin, all formed numbers and equations that cascaded through her mind like water rushing over Niagara Falls. Heather gave up on following the lecture as the beauty and peace of the mathematics washed her brain clean.

CHAPTER 49

Mark sat up in the darkness, a cold sweat drenching his body. For several seconds he had difficulty remembering where he was, the dark room as unfamiliar to his newly awakened senses as some sleazy Juárez hotel room. The clock shone the time at him in luminescent, bloodred numerals, reminding him of a dimly recalled stained-glass window.

2:03 a.m.

His room. He remembered now. He had gone to bed in his own room, so that must be where he now awakened, even if it seemed thoroughly alien in the post-midnight darkness.

Mark listened to the stillness in the house, his enhanced hearing analyzing the smallest of sounds. Down the hall he could hear the breathing of Jennifer in her room. In his parents' room, amid his dad's soft snoring, the sound of his mother's own rhythmic breath softly whispered.

The old house creaked, issuing a small crackling sound as the timbers adjusted to the wind. Outside, that wind moaned through the pines, the sound rising to a wail before dying out completely.

It had been many a year since he had awakened from a dream in terror, but that was apparently what had just happened. The details of the dream were vague, and when he tried to focus his attention upon them, they drifted away as if they didn't want to be remembered.

But that was crazy. He did want to remember. In fact, he had a strong feeling that he needed to remember the dream, that somehow his very survival depended upon pulling its contents from the depths of his mind.

That new kid. What was his name? Raul. Yes, that was right. He had been in the dream, although Mark couldn't think why that would frighten him. All Mark had to do was reach out, grab Raul by the neck, and give a quick squeeze to snap him like a twig. But something in that dream about Raul had scared him.

Mark felt the sweat-soaked bed and received another surprise. Where were the sheets and blankets? Even the bottom sheet was missing.

Mark glanced toward the window. Something was there, blocking his view of the night sky.

An irrational, deep-seated dread consumed him, constricting his chest in bands of iron. The dream. Something in his dream had made its way into his room, had somehow attained physical form in the nondream world.

Mark struggled to gain control of his thoughts. This was stupid. He was one of the quickest, strongest, and most coordinated people on the planet, with neural enhancements that seemed to be continually growing and refining themselves. But here he sat, bathed in sweat, petrified into inactivity by a dream he couldn't even remember. And all because of something draped across his window.

Mark forced himself to move his hand toward the lamp on his nightstand, feeling carefully for the pull chain, while keeping his eyes firmly locked on the window.

With a quick tug on the chain, the lamp illuminated a scene that brought him to his feet, his heart thundering in his chest. One of his red sheets had been tied between the curtain rod and his Olympic weight bar, which now lay directly below the window. The other sheet had been tacked to the window frame.

There, silhouetted against the darkness beyond, was the bloodred image of an inverted cross.

CHAPTER 50

By the time he boarded the bus for school, Mark felt exhausted. It had not taken him long to pull down the bed sheets and remake his bed, but he had been unable to go back to sleep. He had also had no luck in trying to remember the dream.

It was funny, really. He could replay every minute of every day if he so chose. He could read a book he had merely glanced at, even if that glance was a month ago. But the details of his dream whispered at the corners of his mind, only to dissipate like smoke in the wind when he focused on them.

Finally he had given up, pulled out his schoolbooks, and done all the assignments for the coming week. That, in itself, was a frightening thing.

Raul. There was something about that little creep that had his subconscious working overtime. It wasn't that Heather seemed to be infatuated with him. Well, that might have something to do with Mark's dislike of the guy, but it wasn't enough to send him into the land of the walking dead.

No. Something else was going on with that dude, and Mark was determined to find out what it was.

The thought of Heather did little to brighten Mark's mood. He glanced across the bus to the seat where she sat beside Jennifer, smiling and talking to his sister as she always did. She hadn't been that talkative at the dance last night. Every time he had seen her, she had been draped around Raul out on the dance floor.

A vision of his fist smacking Raul hard enough to send him spinning across the dance floor brought a grim smile to Mark's lips. Then he shook his head. What was wrong with him today? He didn't normally take pleasure from imagining beating the crap out of his classmates. With effort he turned his thoughts to other things.

The cold fusion science project was coming along very well. They now had the tank built and were working on the construction of the radiation detection probe, which would also contain what Mark called the subspace tuning fork. In reality it was a doped quartz crystal, carefully mounted in a programmable oscillating circuit.

According to Heather, when in the presence of a small gamma flux, the thing would produce a subspace carrier wave that could be focused wherever they wanted. And that focused subspace signal would induce a real signal at the far end. If Heather's calculations were correct, which they always were, it would let them put signals on any network in the world. But first, they had to get the damned thing finished.

Mark's frustration had been building for weeks. There was so much to discover about the *Second Ship* that he wanted to spend most of his time there. But that wasn't possible. He, Heather, and Jennifer had to be careful, so they rarely visited it.

Then there was their expanding new abilities. As much as Mark loved playing basketball, it practically made him sick to his stomach to have to hold back from what he could really do. Even his aikido practice wasn't as good as it could be, mainly because he couldn't take real classes. He had to rely on what he saw on video and read in books for his training. Frustrating.

In the meantime, the *Rho Ship* sat out there, probed and prodded by people under the domination of Dr. Stephenson, a man illegally experimenting with alien technology on human subjects, experiments that he was keeping from the US government. From what Mark had learned about the *Rho Ship* aliens, that could not be a good thing for this planet.

Flying blind. That was what the three of them had been doing for some time now. They hadn't even checked if there were more QT recordings. And now this new fling Heather had going with Raul was taking more of her time. Christ. There was just too much important stuff happening for her to be getting involved with anyone right now, much less that dweeb.

Mark squeezed his right hand until his knuckles popped.

"It wasn't me," said a voice from across the aisle.

"What?" Mark asked, turning to look at the speaker.

Roger Frederick, a bookish sophomore, stared across the aisle of the bus at Mark, his hands raised in mock defense. "Whoever did something to make you mad, it wasn't me," Roger said.

"What on earth are you talking about?"

"Well, the way you were scowling and popping your knuckles, I figured you were about to start cracking heads."

Mark laughed. "Just thinking about playing the Rockets tonight."

Roger pretended to wipe his brow. "Good. I wouldn't want to be them, then."

"Believe me, they won't want to be themselves either, once we get done with them on the basketball court."

"Aren't the district playoffs starting soon?"

"Two weeks."

"Great. I'm looking forward to watching you play."

"Thanks."

The conversation was interrupted by the bus coming to a stop in front of the school. Jennifer and Heather came up beside Mark as he stepped off the bus.

"What was all that about?" Jennifer asked. "I didn't know you even knew Roger."

"I don't. He just started talking to me for some reason. I actually didn't think the nerd knew what basketball was. Apparently he's a fan, though."

Heather patted him on the shoulder. "Wow. That must be exciting for you."

"Very funny."

"Oops, there's Raul. I'll see you guys in class."

Mark watched her walk across the steps and take Raul's hand. Raul's eyes briefly met his own, and although it was probably only his imagination, it seemed to Mark that Raul had smirked.

"Hey," said Jennifer, "you're getting a little rough on pencils aren't you?"

Mark didn't remember having taken the pencil from the side of his backpack, but apparently he had been carrying it. Now half of it lay on the ground at his feet, the other half having been crushed into small pieces in his hand.

"Must have gotten a defective one," said Mark. "I'll grab another from my locker and meet you at class."

The tension Mark felt failed to abate as the school day progressed, leaving him feeling as if he were strapped to a medieval rack, each turn of the crank stretching him closer and closer to a snapping point. People around him sensed it and gave him a wide berth. Even Jennifer did her best to stay clear.

As the bell announcing the end of the last class rang and Mark headed for the basketball team meeting, Heather came up to him in the hallway.

"Good luck in the game tonight, Mark. Not that you need it." Heather smiled, completely unaware of his foul mood.

"I suppose you'll be watching with Raul tonight?" Mark didn't know why he asked or even why he cared. But he did.

"No, I'll be sitting with Jennifer. Raul runs a private Bible study a couple of nights a week for some of the kids. Tonight is one of those nights."

Mark raised an eyebrow. "A private Bible study group?"

Heather nodded. "Raul's family is very religious, and I guess his miraculous cancer recovery made him even more so. Not surprising considering all he's been through."

"If you say so."

Heather's eyes suddenly narrowed. "Are you angry with me?"

Mark bit his lip. "No. It's not you. I just had a hard time sleeping last night so I've been grumpy today."

Heather's smile returned. "OK."

"Listen, I hate to run, but I can't keep Coach waiting."

"All right. I'll be cheering tonight from our regular spot. See you after the game."

With a wave of her hand, she disappeared into the crowd. For several seconds Mark stared after her, then turned on his heel and headed for the gym, his shoulder grazing Raul as he passed. With no hint of apology, Mark continued down the crowded hall, feeling Raul's gaze bore into his back until he rounded the corner.

CHAPTER 51

Roderick Bogan had gotten the whole story from Raul, but this place was even weirder than he had imagined. Beyond the walls of the casita, an enclosed patio was all that separated the small guest quarters from the main house. The Rodriguez family had added the small apartment-style cottage to their house as a place for the nurse to stay, during that time when Raul had been on heavy-duty chemotherapy.

Once it became clear that neither chemotherapy nor radiation therapy would save her son, Mrs. Rodriguez had removed the bedroom furniture and converted the main room of the casita into a small chapel, complete with a large altar at the far end. Even the windowpanes had been removed and replaced with stained glass.

The walls were adorned with crosses—hundreds of them, in all shapes and sizes, each with a hanging Jesus nailed through the palms and feet, painted blood running from the wounds, head topped with a bloody crown of thorns.

The altar at the back of the room had recently been removed to make room for a full-sized wooden cross. This was a new addition, something Raul had insisted on. It leaned against the back wall at a forty-five degree angle, attached to a track so that it could be cranked up to stand vertically or inclined to a point where someone could lie across it.

Along the walls, candles mounted on small shelves cast flickering shadows that crawled among the crosses like roaches skittering into cracks in the walls.

Sitting on a bench that had been pushed all the way up against the wall sat three young men, all Los Alamos High School students, each of them at least a year older than Raul. Raul, clad in a long, white robe, stood at the head of the chapel, beside the inclined cross that jutted out across the room on its track. He signaled with a slight motion of his right hand, and one of the students rose to throw the deadbolt closed, securing the entrance against interruption.

Raul spoke, his voice resonating with an underlying power and confidence that belied his age.

"Welcome, my brothers. To the three of you who have already entered my service, I extend my blessing." Raul inclined his head slightly toward the three students who sat on the bench to his right. Turning then to the boy who sat by himself on the center bench, Raul stepped forward.

"And to the new aspirant, I say welcome. You have expressed a willingness to be released from the heavy bonds of worldly doubt, so that I may anoint you as one of the chosen. You desire to witness the miracle, so that you may know that I am come and that the end of times is at hand."

Raul paused in front of the young man. "Aspirant Roderick Bogan, rise now."

Rod Bogan stood. He was a senior, his heavy build having earned him years of ridicule from his classmates. That ridicule had taken a toll on his self-confidence, something for which he had tried to compensate by growing his blond hair long and by piercing his nose, eyebrows, tongue, and ears with prominent metal studs. But instead of looking tough, deep in his heart, Rod knew he just looked like a pathetic, fat loser.

Rod also knew what brought him here. It was the changes he had seen in his three friends, who until recently were even bigger losers than he was. Then they had met Raul and been transformed.

Not that they had become popular—far from it. Instead, they had found a heretofore unknown reservoir of inner strength and confidence, as if they knew something nobody else knew, something that made them superior.

Rod wanted that knowledge. He wanted that confidence. Wanted it so badly he could taste it. But now, here in the strange half-light of this chapel of crosses, he felt anything but confident. When his friend Gregg slammed the deadbolt shut, it was all Rod could do to keep from screaming.

"Are you familiar with the book of Revelation?" Raul asked.

Rod cleared his throat. "A little."

Raul smiled. "I am not here tonight to preach you a sermon. I will never preach at you. I will reveal something the book of Revelation promised would come. I will show you the face of God. Mankind is out of time. The end of days is at hand, and I have come to gather the faithful to me, in preparation for Armageddon."

Rod was confused. He glanced at his friends, but the light shining in their eyes matched the intensity of Raul's. With a shock, Rod realized they believed what Raul was saying. Unequivocally. Completely.

Raul turned and lay back on the cross, his arms spread out along the crossbeam, palms out, his knees bent, his bare feet positioned one atop the other. Seeing Raul nod his head, the three others rose, Gregg Carter moving to Raul's right hand, Jacob Harris to his left, and Sherman Wilkes kneeling by Raul's ankles.

Raul's voice rang out clear as a bell in the semidarkness. "Kneel, that you may know that you are in the presence of the Lord."

Before Rod could move, each of his three friends pulled forth a six-inch-long spike. They positioned them over Raul's outstretched hands and feet. In a ritualistic unison that could have been choreographed, three six-pound sledgehammers struck the spikes, driving them through skin and bone, pounding the metal deep into the thick wooden beams of the cross.

Rod was frozen in place, too stunned to move. Again and again, the hammers rose and fell, pinning the hands to the cross, spiking one foot atop the other to the vertical beam. Blood seeped out around the thick spikes, congealing at a rate that was unnatural, and although Raul's jaw clenched in pain, he did not cry out.

Having finished the crucifixion, Jacob moved to the crank and began winding it, slowly pulling the cross along its track until it stood erect against the far wall.

Rod stared in openmouthed wonder at the image of Raul dangling from the cross, the light of the dancing candle flames now jumping as if a sudden breeze had entered the room. Rod's legs lost their strength.

As he fell to his knees on the chapel floor, Rod stared up at the crucified form above him.

"My God."

Raul smiled down at him.

"Yes, Roderick. I am."

CHAPTER 52

"So what is the report?"

Jack spoke into his cell phone as he moved across the parking lot toward the far end of the shopping mall.

"I've been monitoring home lines on all the scientists on the Rho Project." Harold's voice on the far end was delayed and sounded slightly distorted, an annoying side effect of the encryption device. "Other than what is in the report I faxed you, we have nothing of great significance so far."

"What about Dr. Anatole? She was mentioned in the New Year's Day Virus message."

"She's a cold fish. Adheres to security procedures by the book. And forget about Stephenson. His phone calls consist of things like, 'Get over to my office now.' I've never heard someone less talkative on the phone."

"So you're telling me we've got nothing? What about the bugs?"

"If you mean the ones you planted in the McFarland and Smythe houses, there is the barest mention of some of the scientists calling for them to work weekends. They seem more excited by their kids' national science project than anything else."

"What project?"

"Their kids have pooled their money, with help from both fathers, and are trying to build a home-sized cold fusion device."

"Isn't that dangerous?"

"Apparently not very. I did some checking, and several graduate students around the world are doing roughly the same thing. The papers on the subject are flying around the Internet."

"Odd for high school students, though, wouldn't you say?"

"In most places, yes. Not here in Los Alamos, though. Most of the parents have PhDs and work at the lab. Even the teachers are highly qualified. This school is first-rate."

"So we have nothing."

"I didn't say that. We have nothing direct. However, I've been running some cross correlation algorithms against the recorded phone conversations of all of the scientists on the program."

"Yes?"

"It looks like a small subset of them are working on something in a different wing of the Rho Project building."

"Let me guess. Nancy Anatole is one of the ones working in that section."

"Bingo."

"A bit thin. Anything else?"

"One other thing. I ran a voice stress analyzer on every one of the recordings. The voice stress in the Anatole group is higher than the others, in every case."

"Who had the highest measurements?"

"Dr. Anatole and Dr. Rodriguez."

"What about Stephenson?"

"Cool as a cucumber. The man is completely calm and comfortable."

"So you think Rodriguez is in as deep as Dr. Anatole?"

"Maybe. Maybe not. He has some other reasons for stress. His son has been in and out of cancer treatment for the last several years."

"That would do it."

"One final thing, Jack."

"What?"

"I think you can pretty much rule out Gil McFarland and Fred Smythe. No voice stress, and they're not part of the Anatole grouping."

"That's good to hear, although it's what I expected. They seem to be just good, solid folks. Listen, I have to pick up Janet. Get back to me when you have something new."

"Wilco."

Jack flipped the cell phone cover shut and then, glancing quickly around, stepped into the Audi.

CHAPTER 53

It was more than could be hoped for: a sunny, warm February morning after a night of fun with his extended houseguest. Priest Williams stretched his arms wide, letting the bright rays of the sun irradiate his naked body. The thin air of the high country provided little filtration, a fact that sent anyone concerned about cancer or premature aging scurrying for the SPF 45 sunblock, even in the midst of winter.

Priest smiled. That was one of the many things he no longer had to worry about.

Feeling his stomach rumble reminded him of one of the things he did need to attend to, though. Although he imagined that he could survive a very long time without food, it would not be pleasant. And his guest certainly needed to be fed if she was going to last as long as he wanted her to. That meant today was shopping day.

Turning away from the sun, Priest stepped back through the doorway from his deck into the bedroom of his cabin, closing the sliding glass door behind him. As he headed toward the shower, he threw the Navajo rug over the closed trapdoor leading to the soundproof cellar below. Then, whistling the theme song to *The Good, The Bad and The Ugly*, he walked into the bathroom and turned on the shower.

The drive into Los Alamos took a little over forty-five minutes in the truck, most of it a bone-rattling ride along the dirt road that led from his cabin back to the highway. By the time he pulled into the Safeway parking lot, noon was not far away.

Priest's tastes were not fancy. Steaks, burgers, fries, milk, cereal, coffee, beer, chips, and salsa. Throw in a couple of impulse items on the way back to the register, and he was done.

Opening the tailgate, Priest quickly transferred the bags into the bed of the truck. Then, as he was about to slam the tailgate closed, he saw someone who caused him to move out of sight behind the passenger side of the vehicle.

There, on the far side of the parking lot, just getting out of a red Audi Quattro, was Jack Gregory. Priest felt the hair along his neck, back, and arms stand straight up.

"Jack, my boy," Priest breathed. "Now what in the world is a heavy hitter like you doing in town?"

Priest had run into Jack Gregory on three separate occasions. Once in the Horn of Africa, once in Afghanistan, and the last time in Calcutta. Priest had never liked him, and the feeling was mutual. Still, there was one thing to be said for Jack. He was the deadliest man Priest had ever known, perhaps the only one who could handle someone like Abdul Aziz without the special augmentation Priest now enjoyed.

Priest clenched his teeth so hard they threatened to crack. With a deep breath, he forced himself to relax. As much as he owed Jack personally for what he had done to Priest in Calcutta, that would have to be put on hold. Dr. Stephenson would certainly want to know about Jacky boy's presence here.

Priest keyed in the speed-dial number for Stephenson and was reaching for the send button when he saw her. The woman was strikingly beautiful. Tall. Athletic. She moved with all the grace of a dancer right up to Jack Gregory, wrapped her arms around his neck, and gave him a kiss that elevated Priest's heart rate just watching it. She slid into the passenger seat of the Audi, and Jack closed her door behind her.

Suddenly, Jack paused and raised his head, almost like an animal catching a strange scent on the wind. Priest ducked back behind the truck. No doubt about it. That bastard was dangerous.

After several seconds, Jack got into the Audi and drove away. Priest watched the car disappear around the bend and then stepped out from behind his truck once again.

Who was the hot little number with Jack? Without a doubt, she was an operative, and if she was teamed with Jack, that meant she was one of the best.

The last time Priest had met Jack, it had ended badly, with Priest's body broken in so many places he had barely survived. Jack did not like being double-crossed. But now, Priest was not the same man. Now he had a little surprise in store for his old acquaintance.

"I think I'd like to get to know that little gal of yours, Jacky boy," he murmured.

But Dr. Stephenson would not like him playing with the pretty secret agent girl. Priest stared at the cell phone for several seconds before flipping it closed and pocketing it.

What Dr. Donald Stephenson didn't know wouldn't hurt him.

CHAPTER 54

Diving into the stands after a basketball tended to be painful. In this case, thirteen stitches worth of pain.

Mark stared in the bathroom mirror, looking at the swelling just above his left eyebrow. The doctor said he would have a small scar, but that was about it. As Mark stared at it, he thought it might actually come out looking rather cool.

The audience reaction had been great. He grinned as he thought about it. The game was winding down through the last thirty seconds before halftime, and Jerry Clark had thrown him a long breakaway pass that missed. Still, Mark had managed to get a hand on it and deflect it back to his teammates before crashing headlong into the bleachers. He immediately clawed his way back to his feet and was headed for the court when several hands grabbed him. That was when Mark noticed the blood. Even shallow wounds to the forehead tended to bleed like a stuck pig, and this one was no exception. The coach had told him to lie down on the court, and by the time someone rushed over with a towel to put some direct pressure on the cut, his eye sockets had filled with blood.

Jerry, bending over his prostrate form, practically yelled, "Oh my God. It looks like he has twin pools of blood instead of eyes. Hey! Someone get a camera."

His buddies were a little short on sympathy, but the cheerleaders made up for it.

That little stunt had cost the team its first loss of the season. Even though Mark had felt fine to go back in if they would only butterfly bandage the cut, the coach sent him to the hospital to get stitches and to be checked for a concussion. By the time the intern finished sewing his head and shining a little flashlight in his eyes, the game was over.

Roswell Goddard High School 83. Los Alamos High School 78.

So much for the perfect season.

Mark finished dressing, brushed his teeth and hair, and then headed down to breakfast. Unfortunately, the McFarlands had departed early that morning for an appointment in Santa Fe, which meant he and Jennifer would be eating their mom's cooking.

Jennifer caught Mark's eye as he strolled into the kitchen, giving him a small shake of the head, which meant something like, "Abandon all hope, ye who enter this room." The smell of burning toast had not quite reached a thickness that would set off the smoke alarm, but that didn't reassure him.

How a woman as talented as his mother could produce such inedible meals was one of the deep underlying mysteries of the universe. You would expect a bad cook to deliver bland-tasting dishes that left little to look forward to. But Linda Smythe went beyond the normally bad, settling in at spectacularly, amazingly bad. Mark didn't think she could do worse if she tried. Cutting into her eggs either produced hard bits of a yellowish, rubbery substance or, worse yet, slimy little worms of liquid white that crawled toward the edges of your plate.

Oh well. Mark would gut it out and do his best to avoid hurting his mom's feelings. After all, she had made the effort to feed them, so he would make the effort to eat it.

This morning's meal proved to be surprisingly edible, despite the look he had received from Jennifer. A quick scraping of the toast removed most of the charred bits. Adding the firmly cooked eggs, a slice of cheese, and some salt and pepper created an Egg McSmythe that wasn't half bad.

"Thanks, Mom. That was great," he said, rising from the table with his orange juice in hand.

Linda Smythe smiled at him. "You're a terrible liar, but I appreciate the compliment anyway."

Mark laughed and kissed her on the cheek. "Jen and I will be working in the garage for a bit, and then I'm going for a long run."

"Not too fast. Mind those stitches."

"Don't worry, Mom. I promise not to pop a vessel."

Mark led the way to their workshop, Jennifer close on his heels.

"So where are we at?" he asked as they reached the workbench.

Jennifer pulled up the stool in front of her laptop. A new USB cable ran from the back of the computer to an electronic circuit board mounted atop the tank.

"I still have about six hours of work on the program that will manage the subspace tuning algorithm Heather developed. After that, I'll have to write some test-driver software to simulate the responses. With my homework load, I don't think I can finish before next weekend."

“Then you better get to it, Jen. Don’t let me hold you up.”

“So you’re still planning on jogging out to the ship to retrieve the laptop and QT device?”

“Yep. I called Heather last night and told her we needed them here. It’s just not practical to monitor what’s happening with Stephenson otherwise. Besides, you can run your little encryption virus on it and scramble the data.”

“I guess it’s no more dangerous than everything else we’re doing. Kind of a long jog, though. Why not take the bike?”

“I feel like running. It’s only about eighteen miles round-trip. Not even marathon distance.”

“Yes, but coming back you’re going to have that laptop and stuff in your backpack.”

Mark grinned. “I think I can handle it.”

“Well, get going, then. You’ll want to be back for dinner. Mom’s cooking lasagna.”

“Gee, I’d hate to miss that,” Mark said as he headed back inside.

Mark quickly changed into his shorts, sweat suit, and running shoes, threw his backpack over his shoulders, and set off at a steady jog. As he disappeared around the bend onto the trail that led cross-country to the ship, far behind him, staying well out of sight, another jogger mirrored his path.

CHAPTER 55

In the eighteen months he'd been assigned to Jack Gregory's team, Harold had never disappointed his boss, and he had no intention of allowing that to happen now.

In the midst of all the higher-priority wiretaps, Harold had almost missed the most promising lead so far. It was almost midnight, and he'd been about to call it quits for the evening, when old habits forced him to review the recorded calls on the taps labeled "low probability."

15:46:12. The time stamp on the call showed on two recordings, one from the Smythe house and the other at the McFarland house. Nothing unusual there. The families talked to each other so much they should buy an intercom.

Harold jacked up the playback speed, letting the chipmunk voices chatter in his ear, fully expecting to race through another set of best friend chitchat before logging another no-op recording.

Suddenly he hit stop, followed immediately by a tweak of the jog shuttle control, rewinding the last several seconds before letting it play at normal speed.

Mark Smythe's voice spoke clearly on the line. "I think we need to pull the laptop and QT recorder off the ship."

"Do you think that's safe?" Heather McFarland asked.

"Safer than us going out there so often. Without it, we're flying blind."

There was a brief pause before Heather answered. "I guess it'll be OK. I don't have to tell you to be careful not to let anyone see you bike out there."

"I'll just take a backpack and jog. I need the workout, anyway."

"Wow. That's dedication, considering you'll be playing a game tonight. I think I'd take the bike."

Mark laughed. "All in a day's work. Believe me, I'll enjoy the run."

Harold listened carefully until the end of the conversation, but nothing of further interest presented itself. He manipulated the jog control again, replaying the section of interest several times.

The words that had caught his attention were *recorder* and *ship* used in close proximity. Combined with the cautionary tone and references to a laptop, it made Harold feel the need to find out exactly what those kids were talking about.

He considered calling in a report to Jack but decided against it. It was late, and he had relatively thin data to back his suspicions.

So now, clad in his gray sweats, Harold jogged far back behind Mark Smythe on a rough mountain trail that led along the canyon rim country near White Rock. The kid was in great shape, not surprising since he was the finest athlete to ever play ball for Los Alamos High School. No doubt his pace would have left most people holding their knees as they puked their guts out. Harold Stevens was not most people.

By Harold's estimate, they were over eight miles out when he lost Mark's trail. He was in a wood line at the top of a jagged canyon outcropping, another of those fingers of land that stretched out toward the south and west before ending in steep drop-offs into the canyons below. From the lay of the land, Mark must have climbed down off the rim, but on which side of the finger? Left, right, or tip?

Harold ruled out tracking the boy for now. Instead, he moved off the trail, picking out a hide location several hundred feet along the wood line to the north. Then Harold settled in to watch. He did not have to wait long. Within thirty minutes, Mark reappeared, climbing up over the north side of the rim, very near the tip of the plateau's finger. Harold watched him jog back down the trail, the backpack bulging.

Harold waited for an additional two minutes before breaking cover and moving to the spot where he had observed Mark climbing back over the rim. For an experienced tracker like Harold, the boy's path stood out as stark and bright as if he had painted a white line down the slope. A bent twig here, an overturned rock there, a slippage in the loose shale. These and a hundred other signs led the way back down the canyon side.

Reaching a spot about halfway down the steep wall of the canyon, Mark's path turned left and entered a thicket. Harold paused. Odd. The trail, which had been so clear up until this point, disappeared completely three feet in front of the spot where he now stood. From that point on, the brush appeared unbroken, as virgin as if no one had ever passed that way.

Bending closer to the ground, Harold moved forward slowly, touching each broken twig, looking for some sign of deviation from the path. From the jungles of Cambodia and Laos to the deep African bush, he had read trail signs with such unerring accuracy that he had come to the attention of Jack Gregory. Now, he paused, confused. The sign here made no sense.

Feeling his way along the plants, Harold reached forward until his hand disappeared. He pulled back so hard he almost stumbled. What the hell? Examining his hand, Harold caught his breath. Everything was still there. Just a second ago it had not been, almost as if he had dipped his hand into a mirror pool. But there was no water in sight.

Gingerly, he eased forward once again until just a fingertip disappeared inside. Inside what? Harold tested it several times, first with one hand, then the other. Nothing. There was absolutely nothing in his way. Then why the hell couldn't he see through it?

But the kid's tracks led in and out of that place.

Harold reached behind him, extracting his 9mm Beretta from the holster strapped to the small of his back. Then, with the weapon up and at the ready, he stepped inside.

For several seconds, he could see very little as his eyes adjusted from the daylight to the dim light in the cave. There was a light. Sort of a soft, red glow. Glancing back the way he had come, Harold found he could see out into the canyon beyond, but it looked dim, as if he were peering through some sort of polarized sunscreen.

One thing was certain. The technology for this screen was like nothing he had seen in his operations around the world. He considered that for a second. Could it be something new being worked on by a division of the Los Alamos National Laboratory? Unless it was Rho Project stuff, he didn't think so. But this was outside of any secure area, so it couldn't be lab related.

Harold turned back toward the center of the cave, once again catching his breath as a new set of unexpected imagery rocked him. Filling the entire back portion of the cavern was a large saucer-shaped object. The ship. This was the ship that Mark had mentioned to Heather. Not the *Rho Ship* but another ship, a completely different shape from the one the government had at the lab.

Harold moved slowly but steadily around the perimeter of the metallic disk, ducking underneath the rim where it was jammed against the back and side walls. Then he saw the hole. A perfectly round hole, about a meter in diameter, had been punched through the ship, the edges as smooth as a samurai sword's passage through bamboo.

Harold walked underneath and looked up. The hole had punched through several decks and all the way out the topside.

Grabbing his cell phone from its clip on his holster, Harold flipped it open. No signal. Shit. He'd have to call Jack once he got back out of the cave. The ship was probably cutting off all electronic transmissions the way it had erected the cloaking screen at the cave entrance. Well, he'd just have a quick look around inside and then head back out to call in the report. This one was going to blow Jack's skirt up for sure.

Harold spent the next fifteen minutes working his way rapidly through the parts of the ship he could enter, which weren't many. He saw the row of four bands lying on the table, but left them for more careful investigation by a follow-on team.

Having convinced himself there was plenty here to keep the government busy for the next century, Harold dropped the six feet down from the lower deck to the floor of the cavern. As he straightened up, the blow took him by surprise, catching him square in the chest and sending him flying into the cavern wall.

Even though the impact knocked the wind from his body and left him with at least one broken rib, Harold's training took over. As he rebounded from the wall, his gun hand steadied, swinging smoothly toward his assailant. As the trigger finger tightened, sending the jolt of recoil up his wrist and into his arm, the figure before him blurred into motion again, miraculously moving clear of his aim point before the bullet could fire.

Another blow caught him, this one breaking his wrist and sending the weapon spinning outward; it clattered to the stone floor of the cave, sliding to a stop where the metal of the ship touched the floor.

Harold moved in a spinning round kick, which also failed to land. Another punch cracked the ribs on his other side and knocked him to the floor. As he rolled back to his knees, a vicious kick caught him in the stomach, sending him sliding back into the rock wall. Another kick followed, breaking his left arm, although at a spot higher up than the break in his right.

His vision misted over with red, but Harold turned his head to see who his attacker was. The man was skinny, with long, stringy, blond hair, his clothes shabby and dirty. Without a doubt, this had to be the Rag Man Jack had said was stalking Heather McFarland. The man leaned his face close, and the stench of the fellow's breath clogged Harold's nostrils.

"Sin is the transgression of the law."

Harold stared into the deep-set eyes but said nothing.

"You have transgressed. I shall ask our Lord to forgive you of your sins before sending you on your way to face judgment." The Rag Man grabbed Harold's broken right arm and twisted. "But first, you will tell me who you are working for and who, if anyone, is in town with you."

Although he bit nearly all the way through his lip, Harold did not scream.

Harold had been hurt before, although never this badly for this long. Well before three hours of torture had passed, he had no doubt this would be his last day on Earth. Toward the end, although the pain did not ease, in his delirium, it dulled slightly.

And as his senses dulled, the ravings of the Rag Man became more extreme, his anger at the realization he would not break Harold finally sending the Rag Man into a killing frenzy he could no longer control.

The Rag Man's hands tightened in a grip that would shortly break his neck, forcing Harold's thoughts once more to Jack. It was a shame. He would have liked to be around when this dirtbag found out what it was like to get on Jack "The Ripper" Gregory's bad side.

CHAPTER 56

The Rag Man stared up at the body of the unidentified agent, suspended on a meat hook in the cave he called home. Not *the* cave. Not the one with God's Ark. This was his cave, the place he had hidden away from society these last seven and a half years, a place several miles away from the Ark Cave.

Was he not the new Gabriel?

But God must be disappointed in him. He had allowed a longing for fellowship to cloud his vision. When he had seen the three young ones discover the Ark, he had hoped that they, too, would come to understand God's calling, that they would also feel the importance of protecting the Ark against Satan's false ark, which now sat inside the Rho Lab in Los Alamos.

The Rag Man stared up at Harold's broken body, swinging slowly on the hook, and a scowl settled over his thin features. But they had betrayed the trust. They had led a ravager back to the Ark. Now the Rag Man would enforce God's vengeance upon them.

He turned away from Harold's corpse, the long, dirty strands of his blond dreadlocks swinging out behind him, and trotted toward the exit to his cave.

Although the boy had been the one who led the agent to the Ark, the Rag Man thought he would deal with the girl he had been watching first. Certainly God would not begrudge him some pleasure in disposing of her. He was, after all, doing God's bidding. He would do the others in due course.

The Rag Man exited the cave, running through the moonlit night along the trail that led back toward White Rock, his moon shadow stretching away behind him as he ran.

CHAPTER 57

As the car pulled back into their driveway and the old garage door began slowly clawing its way up to let them park the Grunge Buggy inside, Heather watched her mother reach across the front seat to gently stroke the back of her father's head.

It was such a little thing. A gentle petting between her mom and dad that happened so often that it almost went unnoticed. A simple gesture that spoke of affection so profound that few would have believed it possible. But the McFarlands were living proof that true, adoring love was not only possible, it was a fact.

As Heather watched them, her eyes misted.

The car stopped, coughed a couple of times, as if arguing that it did not really want to be put to bed, and then went quietly to sleep.

Her father was the first one out. "Heather and I'll carry in the bags."

"Good," said her mother. "Then I'll start reheating the posole. If you guys are as famished as I am, then I'd better get with it."

"I'm starving," said Heather.

By the time Heather and her dad had carefully put everything away, the wonderful aroma of her mother's special posole wafted out to meet them. That wonderfully spicy New Mexican hominy dish seemed to stretch out an imaginary smoky finger, tapping Heather on the shoulder, then curling itself in a "follow me" signal as it led her to the kitchen.

She arrived at the table just in time to see her mother carrying a large serving dish between two puffy oven mitts, each decorated with images of dancing green chili peppers. Her mother was an excellent cook all around, but it was with New Mexican food that her prowess shone. Heather could not blame the Smythes for all but abandoning their own kitchen in deference to hers.

Dinner passed in pleasant conversation, bedtime arriving almost reluctantly to call her up to her bath. Still, the hour was surprisingly late and church service was early in the morning. By the time she had bathed and pulled on her nightgown, warm robe, and fuzzy slippers, Heather felt so sleepy she could hardly wait to slide between her sheets.

"Good night, babe," her dad called out as she stepped into the hallway and headed toward her room.

"Night, Dad. Night, Mom."

"Good night, sweetheart," her mother called out from her bedroom. "Sleep well."

Heather smiled to herself as she turned the knob on her bedroom door. They might as well be the Waltons.

She was still smiling as she stepped into her room. Before her hand could reach the light switch, a strong arm clamped around her, lifting her off the floor and clamping her mouth shut. Heather screamed, but the sound came out as a tiny, muffled squeak, not loud enough to be heard over the *Tonight Show* now playing in her parents' bedroom at the far end of the hall.

As she tried to claw and kick, she was thrown facedown on the bed, her head tilted to the side in a quick movement as the man jammed a piece of cloth in her mouth and covered it with duct tape. The tape covered part of her nostrils, and Heather struggled to breathe. Jesus, he was strong. Maybe as strong as Mark. Despite her thrashing, she quickly had her hands and feet also bound in loops of duct tape. The man's hands worked so quickly and with such strength that Heather found herself completely immobilized before the shock of the attack subsided.

Then the strong hands grabbed her shoulders and rolled her faceup on the bed. To her horror, she beheld the sunken eyes and insane grin of the Rag Man as he straddled her body. She screamed again, this one producing even less sound than the last. The Rag Man's grin widened.

He moved again, grabbing her like a very small sack of potatoes and tossing her over his shoulder. Moving to the window, he opened it and leaped out, catching a branch with his free hand and swinging himself out and down, landing on the ground from a height of fifteen feet as lightly as if he had just stepped off the porch.

Then, reaching up to pat her gently on the butt, the Rag Man jogged out of Heather's yard, crossed the street, and disappeared along the wooded trail beyond.

CHAPTER 58

Night. The bright headlights of cars passing by as they headed off into the black void, destination unknown. How many times over the years had Jack moved along dark streets, momentarily blinded by that glare as he prowled, a lone hunter in the darkness?

Two hours ago he had found Harold's telephone company van parked along a side street in White Rock, apparently undisturbed since Harold had left it, indicating that Harold had left on foot to go somewhere. The odd thing was that his street clothes were left neatly folded on the passenger-side floorboard.

So Harold had been wearing something that he expected to change out of upon his return—a sweat suit, perhaps. It wasn't like Harold to go jogging from a location where he had parked for surveillance. And his weapon was gone. That meant the jog was strictly business.

Harry, old man, where were you jogging to?

Jack parked his car several blocks away and then returned to Harold's van on foot. This location would have given Harold access to the houses of several of the Rho Project scientists, as well as a couple of the technicians, so it made a good spot to do a little telephone line snooping.

Jack ran through the list in his mind. The closest houses were the least likely to have been of interest: the McFarland and Smythe homes, which were only a couple of blocks from where the truck was parked. Normally he would have ignored this line of inquiry.

But why had Harold gone for a jog? He must have been tailing someone whom he knew would have been jogging. The McFarland and Smythe houses sat very near a spot where several trails led off into the woods.

Of course, Harold could have been jogging along city streets, but that wasn't likely. If he was tailing someone, he would have stood out like a sore thumb in these close-knit neighborhoods as he followed along behind a local. This was no hotel district where a stranger could go unnoticed.

Jack glanced at his watch. Pressing a button on the side sent off a faint indigo light from the digital readout. 23:24. A little over thirty minutes to midnight. He moved off the road, cutting through a gap between houses, and entered the moonlit woods. Jack wasn't quite sure what he hoped to find, but he had stayed alive this far through his instincts, and right now his inner voice said this was the place.

A sudden movement where the trail crossed a meadow, several hundred feet from where Jack stood, caught his eye. His head swiveled like an owl spotting a field mouse. The person moved fast, disappearing into the woods on the far side of the clearing in seconds, but those seconds were long enough to get Jack moving. The running man had been carrying a body over one shoulder.

Jack ran swiftly and silently through the semidarkness, every sense attuned to his surroundings, his nerves so finely monitored that he felt like a tuning fork struck by a rubber mallet. His body hummed.

For over half an hour Jack gradually closed the distance between himself and the man running ahead of him, and in each spot where the moonlight made its way through the trees, Jack could clearly see sign of his quarry's passage, periodically spotting him through the gaps.

At first he thought perhaps it was Harry's body over the man's shoulder, but it soon became obvious it was much too small. The body appeared to be struggling, although with little effect. Anger had bubbled up within Jack at the thought that the man had killed Harry, but the suspicion that now arose within his mind clouded his vision with a red haze. As time passed, his intuition told him the man he chased was the one the McFarlands had called the Rag Man. That left little doubt as to who was draped over his shoulder. Although Jack had already been racing along the rough trail, he pressed himself, jacking up the pace another couple of notches.

Suddenly Jack came to another of the clearings, and he slid to a stop as he gazed out at the broad, open space. There was no sign of the Rag Man. Glancing down, Jack carefully examined the ground all around the spot where the trail exited the woods. There were no tracks, no broken twigs, overturned stones, or twisted blades of grass to indicate that anyone had passed this way within days.

Jack reached into the pouch strapped firmly beneath his left shoulder. From a spot just below where his 9mm Berretta hung, he extracted a set of goggles. Not the bulky night-vision goggles that were standard soldier issue. These were top-of-the-line, barely larger than sunglasses.

He flipped on a switch by his right temple, and the scene around him shifted colors. Another switch shifted the view to black hot as he began walking back down the trail the way he had come. In his left hand he held something that looked like a penlight, although the beam from this one was invisible to the naked eye. With the special lenses, the surrounding ground looked like it had been bathed in a black light search lamp.

It did not take Jack long to find the last spot where the trail showed signs of the runner. Unfortunately, despite his skill, there was no sign at all of where the Rag Man had gone from here.

Jack cursed inwardly. To find the trail again he would have to cut a wide circle through the woods, spiraling outward until he crossed it. If he didn't get very lucky soon, the crazy perp was probably going to kill that sweet girl before Jack could get to her.

Taking a deep breath, Jack began moving outward in a wide spiral around the spot. It would be all right. He would find them. He had always had a knack for this kind of thing, and he wasn't about to start doubting that knack now. And when he found them, Jack was certain of one thing. The Rag Man would never bother anyone ever again.

CHAPTER 59

Mark slept fitfully, his muscles twitching involuntarily in accom paniment to the REM movements of his eyes. Soundless words formed on his lips, the same words over and over and over again.

"Mark! Please help me!"

With a final massive contraction of his muscles, Mark landed on his feet beside the bed, tears streaming down his cheeks.

"Heather."

Mark grabbed for his sweats and running shoes, throwing them on his body as he moved through the door into the hallway. As he stepped out, he saw Jennifer's terrified face looking at him.

She clutched at his arm. "Something terrible is happening to Heather."

"I know. I can feel her in my head."

"We have to help her."

"I'm going to go get her."

"I'm coming with you!"

Mark could see how badly she wanted to accompany him, but she was his sister, and he didn't want her in harm's way.

"I know you want to save her as much as I do, but you'll slow me down. Jen, I have to do this alone."

A sob of frustration escaped his sister's lips.

"But how will you find her?"

"I don't know how exactly, but I can feel her out there. It's like she's pulling me. I'll find her."

As Mark finished sliding on his second shoe and released his hold on the banister, he noticed he had crushed the wood railing beneath his fingers. Discarding the thought, he hugged Jennifer, a wordless assurance that he wouldn't let her down.

"Come back safe," she said.

Then he was down the stairs and out of the house.

Mark's feet moved with a speed he had never imagined humanly possible, propelling him down the dark street and into the woods as if he were slung from a catapult. All conscious thought stopped as his mind focused on the directional pull tugging him. It was getting weaker now as Heather's strength ebbed, or perhaps it was her life force that ebbed. A shudder passed through Mark's body as he pressed himself to the limit.

He no longer followed the trail, moving directly toward the spot from which he felt her call emanate, leaping boulders and deadfalls, crashing directly through the smaller bushes, as tree branches and thorn bushes clutched and tore at him in vain attempts to impede his progress.

As he reached a steep slope and scrambled down, Heather's call faded entirely. Mark stopped, casting his gaze around in a desperate attempt to identify landmarks in the direction he had last felt it. Suddenly, he became aware of a pale, flickering light about a hundred feet down the slope and to the right of where he stood.

Mark resumed his movement, although now he went quietly forward. As he came within view of the spot, he saw the entrance to an unknown cave, the flickering light spilling out of the opening. As Mark prepared to rush across the remaining distance and into the opening, a voice rang out in the darkness.

"Freeze!"

CHAPTER 60

Jack Gregory stepped out of the darkness and into the lighted cave entrance, his weapon locked on a spot in the middle of the Rag Man's head.

"Freeze!" His command rang through the still night air like the tolling of a church bell.

The Rag Man froze, then turned away from Heather's limp body, which hung like a rag doll, suspended by her cuffed wrists, chained to the wall in a way that reminded Jack of cramped Al-Qaeda torture cells in the Middle East. Hanging on a meat hook beside her was Harry's broken body.

"Slowly, now, step away from the girl and drop the knife."

As the Rag Man completed his slow turn, Jack could see that the tip of the knife rested against the jugular vein on the left side of Heather's neck. Insanity shone brightly in the depths of the recessed eyes of the Rag Man, his grin revealing teeth so rotten that Jack expected to see flies swarm from the man's open mouth.

The Rag Man nodded toward Harold's corpse. "So you must be the one that guy called 'Ripper.' You know, I worked long and hard to make that Satan spawn tell me your real name so I could track you down, but he went back to the dark lord's arms with the secret still clenched in his teeth. But the true Lord's power is not to be denied. He has seen fit to deliver you to me anyway."

"Drop the knife."

"Well, no. I don't think I will. You see, even if you manage to shoot me, I will cut this young sinner's throat before your bullet reaches me."

Jack calculated quickly. "Yes, but if you're right and God has seen fit to bring me to you, then you will have failed to do what he desires. You will be dead, and I'll still be alive. Perhaps we can work out a deal."

"I'm listening."

"I'll toss away my gun if you agree to deal with me first, then the girl."

The Rag Man's grin widened. "I agree. Toss the gun."

"Do you swear on the Lord Almighty that you will not hurt that girl again until after you deal with me?"

"I swear it, in the name of the Almighty Father." The Rag Man's carnivorous grin widened.

Jack tossed the gun out of the cave.

CHAPTER 61

Mark froze. A man clad all in black had run into the mouth of the cave, pulled a gun, and given the command in a voice that cracked like a whip.

Mark moved to his left a few yards so he could see inside the cave from the bushes where he crouched. As he looked inside, he barely managed to stifle a horrified cry. Heather hung from chains on the far wall, unconscious or dead. The man they called the Rag Man leaned against her body, having just finished sniffing or licking her neck.

Beside Heather, a dead man's body hung from a meat hook, his limbs twisted like taffy on a stretcher. The corpse's face was a horror. The skin had been sliced open in great slits like bloody gills. The nose had been cut off, and the eyeballs had been carefully pulled from their sockets so they dangled down the cheeks by the optic nerve.

"Slowly, now, step away from the girl and drop the knife."

Mark recognized the voice. With a sudden start, he realized the man in black was their parents' new friend, Jack Johnson. At the moment, he bore little resemblance to the fun-loving man Mark had met at the McFarland house.

Mark's body almost started moving forward of its own accord, something he managed to stop only with a supreme effort of will. As badly as he wanted to help Heather, it was clear Jack was a professional. For now, at least, Mark would let him handle the situation.

As Mark watched, the Rag Man turned toward Jack, the knife in his hand pressed firmly against Heather's throat. Time moved in slow motion as Jack worked to get the man to drop the knife. Mark barely managed to control his breathing as his heart hammered his chest.

Then, Jack calmly tossed his gun out of the cave into the dirt and rocks near the entrance. Mark felt his heart stutter in shock.

The Rag Man closed the gap between himself and Jack in an instant, the hunting knife in his hand sweeping into the spot where Jack's throat had been. But as fast as the Rag Man was, Jack was quicker. That wasn't quite right. Jack didn't move as fast as the Rag Man; he just seemed to anticipate where his opponent's move was going to end up and countered it.

Mark thought he was getting very good at aikido, certainly far better than the local black belt he had watched in town, but Jack made him feel like a novice. As the Rag Man's blade swept through the air, Jack shifted his weight, adding his own force to the maniac's forward momentum. The Rag Man's body arced through the air, flipping head over heels as it slammed into the nearest wall.

Almost simultaneous with the impact, Jack closed with the Rag Man, his hand suddenly filled with a wicked-looking knife of his own. But again, the Rag Man reacted with insane speed, kicking off the wall and propelling himself back at Jack. Metal clattered against metal as the knife blades brushed against each other on their way to their prospective targets. For several seconds, the two fighters whirled around each other, shifting, darting, hammering with knives and feet.

Suddenly, the Rag Man stumbled backward, a look of dismay on his face as he gazed down at the gaping wound in his stomach, a gash from which extruded several feet of entrails. Jack was also bleeding from a long cut down his left arm, but he continued to glide about easily, almost lazily, as he moved toward the dying man.

As the Rag Man's knees buckled, Jack's foot moved like a striking snake, snapping the Rag Man's knife arm and sending the hunting knife spinning out and away.

The Rag Man sagged and then raised his eyes heavenward. "Lord. What is this? Am I not your new Gabriel?"

Jack kicked him in the stomach, reaching in to grab a handful of small intestine as the Rag Man fell. With a couple of quick swirls, which reminded Mark of a calf roper dallying around a saddle horn, he wrapped the intestine around the Rag Man's neck and pulled, his knee driving forward into the small of the man's back.

"Shut the hell up, you crazy son of a bitch."

The Rag Man's body quivered and twitched. Then, with several final spasms, it lay still.

Ignoring his own wound, Jack fished through the Rag Man's pockets until he extracted a key ring. It took him only a couple of seconds to cross the room and unfasten the handcuffs from which Heather hung and then lay her gently on the floor. Jack worked quickly but confidently, checking the pulse at her neck and then wrapping her in his large, black shirt.

Beneath his shirt, Jack had some sort of shoulder pouch fastened along his left side, not quite a shoulder holster. From where he crouched, Mark couldn't tell its purpose. Jack also wore a dark gray T-shirt, which he now ripped off, quickly tearing it into strips with which he bound his wounded arm. With that done, he picked Heather up and carried her from the cave.

As Jack moved out through the entrance and stooped to retrieve his gun, Mark received another shock. The firelight played across Jack's bare chest and back, revealing a crazy quilt of scars, the likes of which Mark had never imagined. Then he was gone.

Suddenly, Mark remembered what he had forgotten to do for some time now. Breathe. As he stared off into the darkness in the direction in which Jack had disappeared, he muttered to himself, "Who the hell are you, Jack?"

CHAPTER 62

Jack hit speed dial on his encrypted cell phone as he jogged through the darkness, Heather's unconscious body cradled in his arms.

"Yes?" Janet's voice in his ear sounded good.

"Alert the rest of our team that we need a cleanup at the location I just uplinked before this call."

"I'll get them moving. Harry?"

"Gone. Anyway, it's a cave and there has been some wet work in it. I want both bodies gone and the place wiped clean ASAP. Let the team know vehicles won't make it out here. They'll need a chopper."

"Got it."

"And they'll need to clean Harry's telephone company van, too."

"I'll take care of that myself. Where is it?"

"No. It's parked too close to the McFarland home. I don't want to risk your being seen. Let the boys do it, but tell them to hurry." Jack rattled off the address where the van was parked.

"It's going to take a couple of hours to get the team out here. They're in Santa Fe, but the chopper will have to come from Albuquerque."

"I want it done tonight, both places."

"Anything else?"

"That's it."

The phone disconnected as Janet terminated the call from her end. Jack knew she would be efficient. She always was.

Jack glanced down at the young girl in his arms. Her pulse was steady, although shock had clearly set in, dropping her blood pressure to a dangerous level. Her head had a bloody welt where she had been struck, probably a slap across the face that bounced her head back against the rock wall. Jack wanted to get her to the emergency room as quickly as possible, so the doctors could get her stabilized. A concussion wasn't usually deadly, but if there were other internal injuries, they could be.

Jack reached his car, which was several blocks closer than the McFarland house, and gently laid Heather in the backseat, belting her prostrate form to the seat. Then, carefully stowing his holster and special equipment deep in some nearby bushes, he slid into the driver's seat and fired the engine, sending the car roaring through the sleeping neighborhoods on its way toward the hospital.

The Audi squealed to a stop in front of the emergency entrance. Within seconds, Jack lifted Heather's limp form and walked into the emergency room. Two alert nurses grabbed a gurney and helped him lay her down, then wheeled her away. Another nurse looked at the blood-soaked rags knotted around his arm, her gaze then passing across his naked upper torso. Suddenly, Jack was very glad that the emergency room was largely empty at this hour of this night.

"Doctor, would you take a look at this man?"

"Take care of the girl first," Jack said.

"She is already being looked at by another physician," said the doctor, a young man who appeared to be an intern. "Since you can obviously walk, please follow me to the examination room."

Jack paused momentarily. "Nurse, the police are going to want to be involved in this incident. Also, please call Mr. and Mrs. Gilbert McFarland in White Rock. That's their little girl in there. Her name is Heather."

"Sir."

"Yes."

"If you'll give me your keys, I'll have someone move your car and park it for you."

Jack reached into his pocket and set the key ring on the counter.

The nurse's face tightened as if she were about to ask more questions, but Jack turned and followed the doctor from the room. Behind him, he could hear the nurse pick up the telephone and dial.

The doctor's office was a typical windowless room, just large enough for a bed-table and chairs. Jack took a seat on the table as the doctor retrieved some scissors from the cabinet and set to work cutting away the blood-encrusted scraps of his shirt.

The doctor frowned at the long wound, which once again began bleeding freely. Grabbing a squirt bottle filled with Betadine, he poured it liberally over the arm and then scrubbed vigorously at the wound with some sterile pads, tossing them into a biohazard bin near his feet. Satisfied with the cleaning, he grabbed a needle, injected a deadening agent along the length of the cut, and set to work stitching.

"That's quite a cut there."

"Yes."

"It looks like you have had a few scrapes in your day."

Jack nodded. "I was an Army Ranger when I was younger. The short version of a long story is that I took a few bullets and managed to get myself captured."

"Most of those look like knife wounds."

"Yeah. Let's just say that the Geneva Convention gets loosely interpreted in some parts of the world."

The intern's eyes widened momentarily, and then he resumed his stitching. "I'm sorry. This is going to leave a scar."

Jack's grin made the young doctor realize how absurd the statement was. He chuckled softly.

The worry that had been growing in Jack's mind found its voice. "How's the girl doing?"

"I'll check on her as soon as I'm done here."

Just as the doctor finished with the last of the sixty stitches, the police arrived, one officer heading off to check on Heather while the other approached Jack, now wearing an airy hospital gown in place of his shirt.

Jack had barely started his statement when Gil and Anna McFarland arrived, panic-stricken looks on both their faces. They walked directly to the nurse's station, oblivious to Jack or the policeman at the side of the room.

"We're the McFarlands. You have our daughter here. How is she?" Mrs. McFarland's voice broke.

Just then, Jack's doctor reappeared, making his way immediately up to Anna and Gil McFarland. "I am Dr. Forsythe. I just left your daughter's room. She is in shock with a mild concussion and some minor scrapes and bruises. Otherwise, she'll be just fine."

"Oh, thank God. Can we see her?"

"In a few minutes, but you won't be able to stay long. She just regained consciousness."

Anna McFarland turned and buried her head in her husband's shoulder as he wrapped his arms around her and held her close, her sobs coming in great shuddering bursts of relief.

Suddenly, Gil McFarland saw Jack and the policeman holding the clipboard. Gil grabbed Anna's hand and led her toward them, his eyes both questioning and accusing. Jack understood the feelings behind that look.

"Jack, what happened to our daughter?"

Jack stood, glancing at the policeman, who nodded an OK.

Jack's story spilled from his lips, his hand shaking in a seemingly involuntary reaction as he spoke. He told how he was returning late from a water sampling survey down in one of the deep canyons near the McFarland house. As he reached his car he saw someone run into the woods carrying a small person's body.

Concerned, Jack had chased the guy, finally catching up to the man in the deep woods, a mile or so along. As Jack got close, he yelled for the man to stop, and the fellow had tossed Heather down, then turned to attack Jack. It was the Rag Man.

Only Jack's old army training had saved him, although he had taken a nasty cut on his arm. In the end, the Rag Man had run off, disappearing into the darkness. Jack had rushed Heather here as fast as he could.

As he finished the tale, Anna McFarland threw her arms around Jack, hugging him hard enough that it threatened to break open his stitches. Despite his training, the years of dealing life and death, Jack felt his eyes mist as he returned her embrace.

"Oh, Jack. Thank you so much for saving our little girl." She kissed him firmly on the cheek, her tears leaving a wet saltiness that dripped into the corner of Jack's mouth.

As she released him, Gil McFarland stepped in and gave him another bear hug.

Then the doctor interrupted. "Mr. and Mrs. McFarland, you can see your daughter now."

With one more grateful glance at Jack, the McFarlands turned and disappeared down the hall after the doctor.

The policeman cleared his throat. "Now, Mr. Johnson. If you don't mind sitting back down, let's go through all this from the beginning, for my report. Then, if you don't mind, I would like to have a look through your car."

"Certainly, officer."

Jack took a deep breath, forcing himself back into character, and began the story from the beginning, pausing to answer questions and to let the officer scribble notes onto the forms on his clipboard. It was going to be a very long night.

CHAPTER 63

Here, well away from the dim light leaking from the cave, the moonlit semidarkness enfolded Mark like the shimmering spectral shroud of a wraith. In the void left by Jack's departure, the silence of the night was complete. No wind, no chittering insects, no bird noises, nothing. It was as if all life in the vicinity sensed the presence of a hunter and remained frozen, hoping that through absolute stillness, a state of safe anonymity could be achieved.

The silence of the night grew so loud it practically screamed at Mark. "Be still. Let that one go on his way. Do not draw his attention."

Thoughts raced through Mark's mind in a torrent. Heather was alive. Jack's actions, the gentle way in which he wrapped her carefully in his shirt and picked her up, reassured Mark. Jack had saved her from the Rag Man. Jack would get her to the hospital.

Mark glanced back toward the cave and shuddered. The violence in Jack had shocked Mark to his core. Not that he cared that Jack had killed the Rag Man. Mark had come here to do that himself. But the way Jack had been able to overcome the incredible speed and strength the Rag Man had displayed. So efficient. So calm. So incredibly deadly. Undoubtedly Jack was a professional killer, but for whom? And why was he interested in the McFarland and Smythe families?

The answers that came into his mind raised the hair on the back of his neck. If Jack was the kind of person the NSA had sent in response to their message, then they were neck-deep in shit.

One thing was for sure: Mark needed to get back home before his parents were notified of Heather's trauma and discovered him missing and Jennifer panicked.

Jennifer. Crap. She was probably near a nervous breakdown by now.

Having made up his mind, Mark turned away from the path taken by Jack, heading directly back toward his house along the way he had come, his powerful stride propelling him forward at a ground-burning run.

He made his way through the front door so silently that Jennifer didn't hear him, although he knew she was listening for his return. Not wanting to scare her to death, he paused outside the door to her bedroom, which remained open a fraction of an inch.

His voice, barely a whisper, called out to her. "Jen, it's me."

The door whisked open, and a small hand grabbed his arm, pulling him into the room and closing the door behind him.

"Tell me!" Jennifer's face was drawn, her eyes red.

"Heather is going to be OK."

"Going to be? Is she hurt badly? What happened? Where is she?"

"It's all right. I think she just passed out. Anyway, Jack Johnson took her to the hospital." Mark was guessing this part, but it seemed a very likely guess.

Jennifer looked confused. "Jack Johnson? From the McFarlands?"

"Right. I ran as fast as I could. When I got close, it turned out to be a cave. Not our cave. Just a cave. The Rag Man had her chained to a wall."

"Oh my God!"

"I was about to rush him when Jack charged in, pointing a gun at the Rag Man."

Mark continued on, working his way through the whole story, pausing many times to answer Jennifer's questions. Although he covered all the important parts, Mark left out the details of exactly how Jack had killed the Rag Man, only telling her that he had killed the maniac with a knife.

"Are you sure he is dead?"

"They don't get any deader. Jack made sure of that."

"But how? Jack against the Rag Man?"

"Believe me, Jack Johnson, or whatever his real name is, is no EPA man. From what I saw, he's a professional killer, an agent for somebody. I'm thinking NSA, although he could be working for Stephenson and therefore the *Rho Ship*."

"But he saved Heather."

Mark paused, reflecting on how gently Jack covered Heather with his own shirt. "Yes, he did."

Jennifer sat back on her bed, piling the pillows high behind her. "So Jack is one of the good guys."

"Listen, I want to think so. It sure looked like he was sincere, and he got cut up bad protecting her. But we still have to assume that if he finds out about us and the *Second Ship*, he'll turn us in. In a heartbeat. And I wouldn't blame him."

Jennifer nodded. "Then we're just going to have to be careful around him and Janet."

Mark raised an eyebrow. "Janet? What has she got to do with anything?"

"Oh, so you just assume that a professional killer agent of the United States government brings his civilian wife along for the ride? Mark, think about it. She has to be an agent too."

Mark frowned. "I don't know about that."

"Let your brain do your thinking instead of your crotch. It makes sense."

Mark shrugged. "I just think we should keep an open mind about Janet, that's all."

"Uh-huh."

"Anyway, the only thing for us to do right now is try to get some sleep. Once Heather is in the hospital, the McFarlands will find out. They'll call Mom and Dad when they get a chance. Then we'll get to see her."

"So, in the meantime, we should just hang tight?"

"You've got it."

Jennifer bit her lower lip. "I guess there's nothing else we can do."

"Nope." Mark opened her door, then paused to look at Jennifer. "It's going to be OK. Get some sleep, and I'll see you in the morning."

Jennifer nodded, then reached over and switched off her lamp.

"Good night."

Despite the stress that had built to a painful tension in his neck, Mark was asleep as his head hit the pillow. He awoke to his father's hand shaking him.

"What?"

"Mark, wake up, Son. We need to go to the hospital. Heather's been hurt."

Mark sat up. “Hurt? How?”

“I don’t know the details. We just got a call from the McFarlands. They spent the night at the hospital. They said that Heather is going to be all right, but they wanted to let us know what was going on.”

Mark slid out of bed and into his robe. “I’ll get through the shower and be right down, Dad.”

“You’ll have to wait a bit. The showers are booked with your mom and sister.”

Mark looked into his father’s eyes. “Did they tell you how she got hurt?”

“No, they just said she had a concussion. It was a little odd. Anyway, they said they’d tell us the whole story once we arrive.”

“What time is it, anyway?”

“It’s almost nine. It’ll be ten before we get Jen and your mom ready and get over there. Come on down and have a cup of coffee with me while you wait for a shower to free up.”

“OK. Give me just a sec, then I’ll be right down.”

“I’ll pour you a cup. See you in a minute.”

“Sure thing, Dad.”

As his father left the room, Mark sat back on his bed. So Heather was truly OK. Despite convincing himself last night that Jack would get her to the hospital, a wave of relief swept over him. All night, in his dreams, he had looked for Heather and had been unable to find her. He felt more tired now than when he had gone to bed.

Arriving at the hospital, the Smythes paraded up to the information station. By the time they had gotten the information on Heather’s room number, Mark’s anticipation level had risen to the point that he could barely contain himself.

He just wanted to see her, to hug her, to tell her how glad he was that she was safe. He was as nervous as a boy before his first date, a thought that both amazed and mortified him. After all, this was Heather, the friend he had known all his life.

As he and his family meandered through the hospital corridors, Mark thought about what he would say to her. Certainly, the tale of how Jack had killed the Rag Man would have to wait. On this visit, he would just be there for her, just let her know how much he cared.

Arriving outside the door to her room slightly ahead of the others, Mark could not contain his grin. As he entered the room, his grin froze. There, sitting in a chair pulled up next to Heather's bed, both hands gently holding Heather's, sat Raul Rodriguez.

CHAPTER 64

Jack stepped out of the Audi into the cold morning air, his breath puffing out in a cloud. Glancing up and down the street, he walked over to the bushes where he had stashed his weapon and goggles. He grabbed the shoulder holster and returned to the car, tossing it onto the floorboard on the passenger side as he slid into the driver's seat.

The morning sky was a brilliant blue, and traffic was light at this early hour, making for what should have been a pleasant morning drive. But Jack was tired, he had a headache, and he had a to-do list in his head that meant he wouldn't get to bed for a good long while yet. Oh well, what else was new? They had never promised him a cushy office job.

Jack pulled into the carport next to Janet's little blue sedan, grabbed his things, and walked into the house. Janet glanced up at him from the kitchen table where she sat cradling a steaming mug of coffee.

"Nice outfit."

Jack glanced down and nodded. They had given him one of those off-white hospital robes to wear as a shirt, and he had tucked it into his black corduroy pants. At least they used to be black. Yesterday had left them torn in several places and stained with a variety of fluids. The ensemble was augmented by the bandages down his left arm.

"Thank you." Jack grabbed a mug from the cabinet, paused at the coffeepot to fill it, and then sat at the table with Janet. "The cleanup?"

She shrugged. "They had a bit of trouble. The cave is spick-and-span, but the police had already towed the van."

"And?"

"Our team didn't have any trouble getting to it in the impound yard. No problem recovering most of the special gear. But Harry's clothes and the laptop had been moved to the evidence room."

"Damn it. Anyone they could get to on the inside?"

"Not in a way you'll like. The night shift at the station had pretty good records. Our guys did manage to bribe one of them, who had some heavy debts he was struggling with."

"So they got it?"

"No. That's the bad news. He balked at taking the laptop out of the cage. Was scared that someone would be on to him. So the team got him to insert a floppy disk, boot the computer, and leave it running."

"Shit. They wiped it?"

"Had to. It was that or storm the station. They figured we didn't need that kind of attention."

Jack rubbed his face with his hands. Now they had no record of what Harry had been working on. Jack had counted on spending the day going through that laptop with a fine-tooth comb. On the plus side, his to-do list had just gotten a whole lot shorter.

"Maybe I could put you to bed," said Janet with a wink. "Unless you're too tired."

Jack raised an eyebrow as he set down the coffee. "If I'm ever that tired, just shoot me. Think I'll grab a quick shower first, though."

"Don't take too long now, Jack."

As he headed for the stairs, Janet's mischievous laughter tickled his ear. The odds of a luxuriant, slow shower dropped precipitously as he listened. Suddenly, the day, among other things, was looking up.

CHAPTER 65

"Mark, Jen! It's so good to see you." Heather's voice snapped Mark out of his sudden foul mood.

He walked rapidly across the room, leaned down, and hugged her. "Good to see you, too. You had us worried."

Jennifer tugged at his arm, and he moved to let her in to hug her friend. When she raised her head, there were tears in her eyes, which she dabbed at ineffectually with the back of her hands.

As Fred and Linda Smythe stepped into the room, followed by the McFarlands, Raul stood, then leaned down to kiss Heather on the forehead. "Feel better."

Mark resisted a powerful urge to reach out, grab Raul by the back of the neck, and toss him out of the room. Instead, Raul said a quick good-bye and departed.

Heather smiled. "Wasn't it nice of Raul to stop by? Dad ran into his father when he went out for coffee this morning."

"It was sweet," said Linda Smythe.

Mark's smile was beginning to feel like the kind you held for a family photo as Aunt Betty fooled around with the digital camera, trying to figure out how to get the flash to work.

The talk in the room quickly turned to questions about how Heather was feeling, to which she responded that she felt fine, except for a residual headache. The doctors were planning to release her later this morning, so they apparently agreed with her own assessment of her condition.

Everyone in the room studiously avoided any reference to her ordeal the night before, the Smythes having already gotten a rundown on events from the McFarlands. Mark felt bad that he couldn't tell Heather that the Rag Man was dead, but that would have to wait for a more private venue.

But something about Heather was not right. Despite her smiles and assurances to the contrary, her normal buoyancy was missing. When Mark looked into her eyes, the spark that had always been there seemed to have gone out.

The ride home inflicted a somber mood on the whole Smythe family. Something about a brutal attack on someone close left everyone feeling vulnerable and angry. Heather had come so close to dying. If it hadn't been for Jack Johnson, Mark doubted that he could have saved her, but he would have tried.

Abilities like the Rag Man's could have only come from the *Second Ship*. The realization hit Mark in the face like a hammer. The Rag Man must have been on the ship, possibly even before they had discovered it. He had tried on one of the headsets. What was it the Rag Man had said in the dream they had shared with Heather?

"I know what you are becoming."

Perhaps the Rag Man had once been as sane as any of them. What if the becoming caused his insanity? Was it possible that they had it all wrong? What if the Rho aliens were the good ones and the *Second Ship* was from an alien race bent upon conquest and destruction? Perhaps Mark, Jennifer, and Heather were being turned into tools of that destruction.

Mark closed his eyes and leaned back so that his head rested against the back of the seat, letting the vibrations of the road pulse against the back of his neck. None of the scenario he had just imagined felt right. For one thing, the *Second Ship* was beautiful, its artistic flowing lines indicative of a race that cared about beauty enough to incorporate it where it wasn't required.

The *Rho Ship*, both in the imagery from the headsets and from what he had seen on TV, was ugly. It was industrial in its stark efficiency. No. If he had to place a bet on which side to back, he would support the side that saw beauty in the universe against that which reminded him of the industrial revolution, with all of its smokestacks and grease-covered gears.

Mark glanced across at Jennifer, sitting beside him, her eyes still shining with wetness, her face taut with the horror of what Heather had been through. It brought a lump to Mark's throat. His sweet sister was so fragile and vulnerable.

The Rag Man was gone, but without a doubt, forces were descending upon their families that threatened to rip their world apart. Well, he'd be damned if he was going to let that happen. Mark was quite sure Jack Johnson was playing the game for keeps, and he intended to do no less.

Jack had saved Heather, and for that, Mark would be eternally grateful. But if a man like Jack was in town, there would be others, many of whom would be up to no good. And even Jack would crush them like bugs if he discovered their secrets.

When the car rolled into their garage, Mark retreated to his room, Jennifer trailing along closely behind him. As Mark reached the top of the stairs, his dad called out.

"Mark."

Mark turned back to see his father right behind them.

"Would you mind telling me what happened to the banister?"

Mark glanced down at the wooden railing where his father was pointing. It had been broken, almost crushed in a section just at the top of the stairs. Suddenly he remembered something that had failed to register at the time it had happened. He had broken it during the adrenaline rush over Heather.

"Dad, I'm sorry. I meant to tell you about it, but forgot in all the news about Heather. I grabbed the railing when I slipped and it just broke. It must have had some weak wood."

His father scowled down at it, scratching his chin. "I'll say. Crap. Maybe we have termites. I'll have to get the inspector out to the house tomorrow and see if they've damaged anything else."

He shook his head and walked back down the stairs, muttering under his breath.

Mark stepped into his room and Jennifer followed, closing the door behind her.

She shook her head. "Weak wood."

"It had to be. Even with my strength, I can't crush wood like that."

"It didn't look like that to me."

"Well, let's forget about it for the moment. We have some pretty important things to get figured out."

"I'll say. Did you see Raul smooch Heather as he left?"

"It's a miracle I didn't blow chunks all over the room."

Jennifer frowned. "Do you think you can be any more melodramatic?"

"I'm working on it."

"Well knock it off. It's going to hurt Heather's feelings. I think she really likes him."

This time it was Mark's turn to scowl. "There's something about that kid I just don't like."

Jennifer's eyebrow rose. "Do I detect a hint of jealousy, perhaps?"

"Don't be ridiculous. This is Heather we're talking about. Our little math wizard, Rain Girl. I just don't want to see her get hurt."

"Uh-huh."

"Whatever." Mark's hand tightened around the back of the chair.

"Please don't go breaking more furniture. I don't think Dad will buy that story again."

Mark's scowl deepened, but he eased his grip. "If you'll quit busting my chops for a second, maybe we can have a serious conversation. This thing with Jack has me thinking. Why is he interested in our families?"

Jennifer's eyes widened. "Do you think he knows?"

"No way. If he knew what we've been up to, he would have no problem throwing us in jail and turning the ship over to the government."

"But he was in our house."

"And Heather's. Then he just happens to show up at the right time and save her?"

"So you think he's watching us?"

"No. I think he's watching Dad and Mr. McFarland."

"That's terrible. Why would he suspect them?"

"I don't know that he does. Maybe he's just being thorough, checking everyone that works on the Rho Project. Anyway, if he was watching our houses, then he must have seen the Rag Man grab Heather. There's something else, though."

"What?"

"The dead man in the cave. I've been playing the whole thing back in my mind. The Rag Man said that he had called Jack a nickname. The Ripper. That means the dead man was an agent, too."

"We don't know for sure that these are NSA people."

"No. We don't. But I think it's likely. After all, we gave them the first heads-up that something strange is going on with Dr. Stephenson and the *Rho Ship*."

"What if they bugged our houses?"

"Crap. I should have thought of that."

"They could have done it at dinner. They got the tour of both houses."

Mark began pacing slowly back and forth across the room. "If they had every room bugged, we would have already been caught. So, either they didn't bug anything or only areas where the adults hang out."

"Like Mom and Dad's room and office."

"That makes sense. It's not likely they're thinking that high schoolers have access to Rho Project info. They probably have the phone line bugged, too. We need to confirm it though."

"They sell those bug sweepers at stores like RadioShack."

"I'd rather build our own. We can pull up the details off the web. The bugs would have to be low-strength transmitters."

"Except on the phone line. They could tap that from somewhere else."

"OK then, I'll get to work on the bug detector. How's your computer interface for controlling the cold fusion tank coming along?"

Suddenly a broad smile lit Jennifer's face. "Come down to the workshop and I'll show you."

Mark followed her back downstairs and into the corner of the garage where they had set up their equipment and the experimental tank. It had been three days since Mark had closely inspected Jennifer's progress with the control panel. His jaw dropped.

A new display filled with row upon row of pulsing multicolored LED lights hung from the lead shielding on the far side of the tank. A thick bunch of labeled wires connected the LED panel to the main circuit board, while a set of ribbon cables ran between the circuit board and the laptop.

A low whistle escaped from Mark's lips. "Wow! You've been busy."

She grinned broadly. "I'm so close I can taste it. You see those readouts?" Jennifer pointed to the panel of flashing colored lights.

"I see a bunch of flashing LEDs."

"Mark, I figured out how to combine a small group of red, green, and blue LEDs so that each little threesome glows in any of sixteen colors."

Mark leaned close to the panel. Sure enough, what he had taken to be individual LEDs were little groups of three. How brightly the red, green, or blue parts of each group glowed determined what color you saw.

"Very pretty."

"Don't you get it? Each color represents a hexadecimal number. I can glance at this panel and see the values change in all of the computer registers. I can see the code playing out. Not just see it, I can read it." She paused. "Mark, I've learned how to think in Hex."

"Very exciting."

Jennifer's smile faded a bit. "OK, let me rephrase. I can glance at that panel and tune this thing exactly. It'll really help with the subspace transmissions."

"Couldn't you have just programmed a GUI display?" "Sure, but this is way cool."

Mark turned to grab the recording equipment he had removed from the *Second Ship*. "I need to go through all the data on this recorder. You keep working on the subspace controls. We need to get those agents focused away from us and onto Stephenson's team. I'm afraid we're going to have to start taking some serious risks."

Jennifer stared at him as if he'd lost his mind. "Start? What, exactly, do you think we've been doing?"

Mark's eyes locked with Jennifer's. "I've got a feeling that it's about to get a lot worse."

CHAPTER 66

If there was anything on the planet more awkward and uncomfortable than a hospital gown, Heather didn't know what it was. If the damn thing wasn't trying to come open at an inopportune moment, it was wadding up uncomfortably when you sat or lay down in it.

The opportunity to slip out of the gown and into her normal attire improved Heather's mood as much as anything that had happened all day. Even though she'd hoped to be released by ten o'clock that morning, the doctors kept her imprisoned at the hospital until well after noon.

Despite her growing appetite, Heather resisted the mandatory offering from the hospital cafeteria, firm in her determination that the next food to pass between her lips be edible. In an act of family solidarity that she found awe-inspiring, her Mom and Dad waited to have their own lunch until they managed to spring her.

By the time they got back home, Heather was so hungry she had begun questioning her decision to wait. As her mother slid the prepared casserole dish from the refrigerator into the oven, Heather headed upstairs to indulge in a hot bath. She glanced at the floral design on the bubble bath bottle, sniffing it before squeezing a couple of dollops into the tub. Herbal Springtime. Perhaps it could help get the lingering scent of hospital disinfectant out of her nose. One could only hope.

All doubts as to the worthiness of the wait came to an end before the first bite of steaming casserole made its cheesy way from Heather's fork into her mouth. Her mother was a sorceress who used a ladle instead of a wand. Of that, there could be no doubt.

Although she had been warned that the casserole was hot, Heather found herself having to shift the first bite around in her mouth as she puffed out air in little whooshes to try to keep her tongue from blistering. Even though a chuckle escaped her father's lips, it didn't matter. It was still worth it.

The meal had barely ended when there was a knock at the door. It was Mark.

"Everybody decent?"

The intensity of the joy Heather felt at seeing his face and hearing his voice surprised her. Joy and something more. But before she could analyze her feelings, Jennifer followed Mark into the kitchen.

Masking her emotions with a grin, Heather looked from twin to twin. "If we aren't, then you're in for a show."

"Can I offer you two some casserole?" her mother asked.

A look of disappointment creased Mark's features. "Unfortunately, no. Mom cooked us lunch a while ago. Thank you, though."

Heather rose from the table, sliding her place setting into the dishwasher before being shooed away by her mother. "I'll get the kitchen. You go talk with Mark and Jen."

"Thanks, Mom."

Heather started to guide her friends to the couch in the living room, but Mark shook his head. "Do you feel up to visiting the workshop for a second?"

"Mom, I'm going over to the Smythes' for a little while."

"All right, but don't push it. No more than half an hour. Then you are going to bed. You don't get over something like that right away."

"OK, Mom."

As she stepped into the Smythe garage, Heather suddenly found herself engulfed in a three-way hug between Mark and Jennifer.

Jennifer started to cry. "Oh my God, it's so good to have you back home. I've never been as scared as I was when Mark and I heard you calling us in our minds."

Heather's mouth dropped open. "You heard me?"

"You bet we did. Mark even broke the railing on our staircase as he was scrambling into his running suit."

"Running suit?"

Mark nodded. "I could feel you out there, tugging me toward you. I ran like I've never run before. Thank God it was a full moon. Anyway, I found the cave where the Rag Man had you."

Heather's knees almost buckled as the memories came crashing back in on her. She sat down on a crate. "I don't remember a cave."

Mark repeated the story, only leaving out the most graphic details of the Rag Man's death.

Heather did not move for several seconds as she tried to absorb what Mark had just said. "But that isn't the story that Jack told Mom and Dad, or to the police."

"Interesting, isn't it?" Mark leaned closer, reminding Heather of someone telling a ghost story around a campfire, just as they were getting to the good part. "One other thing. The Rag Man was fast and strong. Maybe even faster than me. But Jack killed him, anyway. From what I saw, Jack's a professional killer. A damned good one, too."

Jennifer put a hand on Heather's arm. "We think he and Janet are NSA agents."

Heather's mind whirled. Despite the shock at what she had just been told, a huge wave of relief swept through her body. Jack had killed the Rag Man. Despite her brave outer facade, a deep terror had been growing inside her since long before last night. To know that the maniac was dead lifted an invisible weight. She could feel the tension in her shoulders ease.

Jack had killed him.

For the next several minutes, Mark and Jennifer filled her in on everything, including Jennifer's progress on the cold-fusion-powered subspace transmitter controls.

"And check this out," said Mark, pointing her attention to the laptop he had retrieved from the *Second Ship*. "The recording had a bunch of garbage on it and has a lot of gaps, but I saved the interesting parts in an audiovisual file on the laptop."

Mark pressed the play button on the screen. Dr. Stephenson was talking to someone, although neither person appeared in the imagery, most of which was blocked off by some obstruction on the shelf where their small airplane was being kept.

"I am not happy with your progress."

"I'm sorry, sir. The nanites work perfectly, but the suspension fluid is not holding up well at temperatures above about three degrees Celsius."

"That is completely worthless to me. I told you to find a way to keep the suspension valid indefinitely at temperatures up to sixty degrees Celsius. What did you not understand about that?"

"I understand what you want. I'm just telling you that our team has not yet found a solution that doesn't decay at higher temperatures."

"What is the decay rate?"

"As you would expect, it gets worse the greater the temperature. At room temperature it lasts about as long as a nonrefrigerated carton of milk."

"Bullshit. The original fluid had those characteristics. Are you trying to tell me your high-powered team can't do better than my first attempt?"

The other man cleared his throat. "We do have a new formulation that hasn't been tested. The production process should give us a testable sample size within two days."

"I don't care what you have to do or how late your people work. I'm giving you two weeks. I need a solution that can survive shipment to third world countries. And I don't want to hear about refrigeration. You better not disappoint me."

"I will do my best."

"For your sake, I hope you do better than that. Now get out of my office."

Mark stopped the playback. "There are a couple of other short references to nanites and suspension fluid, but this was the only section that makes any sense."

Heather's mind raced. "Could you make out who he was talking to?"

"No names were mentioned in any part of it."

"Nanites are microscopic machines," Jennifer said. "That must be the second technology the Rho Project team is working on."

Heather nodded. "Apparently. But designed to do what? It sounded like the nanites need some sort of solution to survive."

Jennifer shook her head. "They are machines. Technically, it would be more accurate to say they need the solution to keep running."

"You know what I meant."

"Well," said Mark, "whatever they do, I didn't like the sound of Dr. Stephenson's shipping them to third world countries."

"He must think it is something that people are going to want, like cold fusion," said Heather. "I mean, the president will probably have to come out and announce this new thing too, right?"

"Unless Dr. Stephenson thinks he can get this thing out there secretly."

Jennifer shook her head. "That doesn't seem too likely. He's obviously up to something, but the government is funding his research through the lab. I doubt he could hide a project that big."

Mark thought for a bit. "Well, I think we finally have something that our NSA agents are going to be interested in. Maybe we can get them off our backs and onto finding out what's going on at the lab."

"Carefully, though," said Heather. "These people are better at tracing things than we thought. We have to wait to send out our next message until we have the subspace transmitter working. Then we can remotely tap into a secure line that can't be traced back to us."

"Jen said that she would have that working in a couple of days."

"I never said that."

"That's what it sounded like to me."

"What I said is that I have the control system working. We'll need a couple of weeks of testing. And that's if we don't encounter any major gotchas."

Mark frowned. "Crap. I don't know if we have that long. It sounded like Stephenson was really pushing his team hard. What do you think, Heather?"

"I think Jennifer's right. If we push our system before we've fully tested it, we could run into problems that could make us all very dead. Cold fusion is a wonderful thing, but if we cause an unexpected spike in the energy, then this shielding wouldn't be adequate.

"My calculations say these lead panels will shield us fine, so long as the power stays low. We just have to make sure our control station doesn't give us too much of a good thing."

"What?" Mark gasped. "You mean this thing could run away like some sort of Chernobyl meltdown?"

"No. There's no way a chain reaction could become self-sustaining. But that doesn't mean we might not accidentally generate a really big power spike. It wouldn't spread out of control, but it could sure cook our collective geese."

"How come our dads agreed to this experiment if that could happen?" Mark asked.

"Because the published theory doesn't predict that it can with this small an apparatus." Heather pointed toward the computer screen. "I made some slight modifications that Jennifer coded up for us. The embedded algorithms are so subtle I doubt that anyone other than Dr. Stephenson would even notice."

"You tinkered with the equations? What if you made a mistake?"

"That's hardly likely."

Mark laughed. "Really? The world's greatest minds have been spending the last several months analyzing these equations, and you come up with a better variation?"

Heather shrugged, then reached over onto Mr. Smythe's workbench and grabbed a handful of sawdust. With a flick of her wrist, she tossed it out onto the clean concrete floor.

"Three thousand four hundred eighty-seven."

"What?" Mark asked.

"There are three thousand four hundred and eighty-seven individual grains of sawdust in that spread I tossed on the floor.

But if you were to count them, there would be three thousand four hundred and ninety-two."

"That doesn't make sense."

"There is a 93.65894 percent probability that five of the loosely connected granules would break into two parts as they were spread out during the counting process."

Mark just stared.

"Now, if you can show me some scientists that can do what I just did, then I'll withdraw my statement."

"That's if I buy your count."

Heather walked over to the bench where Jennifer had done her fine soldering, grabbed the large magnifying glass, and handed it to Mark, pointing toward the sawdust on the floor. "Be my guest."

Mark grinned. "OK, I believe you. But then what's the point in all the testing delay? I mean, if you're that confident in your equations, why waste the time?"

"The equations are the easy part. Checking the responsiveness of the control circuits and doing the tuning is the really tough work. It looks like Jennifer is making incredible progress, but she needs a chance to conduct her testing. Otherwise, we may not need a tanning bed, ever again."

Mark threw out his hands. "OK, I give up. You girls get with the program, then. We can't let Stephenson complete what he's up to before we get another message to the NSA. And we need to be very worried about Jack in the meantime."

Jennifer nodded. "That's why we need you to finish off that bug detector and run a sweep on both our houses."

"That's just what I was going to do. In the meantime, we have to assume that the only safe places to talk are here and in our rooms or outside somewhere. If those areas were bugged, they would have already nailed our butts to the wall. Oh, and if we do find bugs, we won't be able to remove them. That would be a dead giveaway."

"At least we'll know where they are," said Jennifer.

"I'm going to be reading up on the subject in my room." Mark paused at the door, turning back toward Heather. "Good to have you back in the land of the living."

Heather smiled back at him. "Good to still be with you." As he turned away, Heather called after him. "Mark."

"Yes?"

"Thank you for coming for me. I know Jack was there, but if he hadn't been, I know you would have saved me."

Mark's smile warmed her soul. It also seemed to be elevating her body temperature again, to the point that she thought that sweat would bead on her brow. With a slight nod, he turned and disappeared through the door.

CHAPTER 67

The knock on the door of the McFarland house came just as they had all seated themselves for Sunday dinner, Heather's father at one end of the table, Mr. Smythe at the other, with the other family members congregated around the feast in hungry anticipation. Heather felt a rising sense of dread at the knock. She didn't want anything to go wrong tonight, in what finally seemed like an island of normal in the sea of weird she'd just been through.

"Damn. It's probably one of those magazine salespeople," said Heather's dad, rising.

"Now be nice," her mother called after him.

As he opened the door, Heather's heart leaped into her throat.

"Jack. Janet. We were just sitting down to dinner. Don't just stand out there, come on in and join us."

"Thank you, but we wouldn't want to impose. We just stopped by to check on Heather."

Heather's mother moved across the room toward them with a look that brooked no opposition.

"Nonsense. I won't hear of it. You two are adopted members of our family as surely as if you lived next door. Besides, I'm not going to have room in my refrigerator for all the leftovers if you don't help us. Here now. Jack, you grab that chair, and Gil, you get another and we'll just make room."

Mr. Smythe shook Jack's hand. "You might as well get used to the drop in anytime routine that we've abused over the years. If Anna really minded, she would have run us off a long time ago. You may have noticed that shyness isn't one of her faults."

Janet laughed, leading the way toward the others, who had risen to welcome the new arrivals. "How can we refuse? To tell the truth, we were just headed out to eat, but I would much rather have some good home cooking." Jack's intense gaze locked Heather in a vise that made her feel as though he were wearing X-ray specs, hardly the most pleasant of thoughts.

"It's great to see that you've recovered from your ordeal," Jack said.

"Thanks to you. If you hadn't come along when you did, I doubt I would be here."

"Do you remember much of it? Sorry. I shouldn't ask."

"No, it's all right. Especially since the answer is no. I don't remember much of anything. Just getting hauled out the window, banging my head, and waking up in the hospital."

"I noticed the police outside. I'm glad to see they assigned a watch, even though I doubt the Rag Man will return."

Heather's mother put her hand to her mouth. "The whole thing has me so nervous that I don't think I could stay here if it weren't for the police."

Heather's father put a hand on his wife's shoulder. "It's OK, Anna. I'm having the best alarm system they make installed tomorrow. No one is going to be getting past that. And if someone does try to get in, I'll let Mr. Smith and Wesson talk him out of it."

Janet moved over to put an arm around Heather's shoulders. "Jack, I think we've had quite enough of this conversation tonight. If nobody objects, I propose that we divert our attention to the wonderful meal cooling on the table."

Jack nodded. "Sorry. You're right, babe. I didn't mean to upset everyone."

Heather's mother managed to recover her smile. "Apology accepted. Now if everyone will sit down, I'll get the biscuits out of the oven before they burn."

As good as the meal was, Heather's appetite had departed. While she was grateful to Jack for having saved her life, she found herself wondering what else had brought him here this Sunday evening. It was stupid, really. Jack would naturally want to check in on a person whose life he had saved the night before.

A quick glance at Jennifer revealed she was also having a difficult time eating everything on her plate. Even Mark appeared distracted, but that was most likely because Janet sat beside him, asking about the upcoming basketball tournament.

Heather half expected a couple of buttons on Mark's shirt to come flying across the table as his chest expanded. The smirk on Jack's face indicated that he had also noticed the effect his wife was having on Mark.

As the evening wore on, all signs of the earlier tension in the room evaporated. By the time Jack and Janet said their good-byes, Heather almost regretted seeing them go, and both sets of parents certainly did. They were such a charming couple, you just wanted them around. Something about that scared Heather worse than anything else she knew about them.

Shortly after the departure of the Johnsons, the Smythes also made their way back to their own house. Heather followed Mark and Jennifer out onto the driveway. Catching Mark's eye, she leaned in close.

"You better get that bug detector working, quick."

"Fret not. I'm on it."

As Heather watched them disappear through their doorway, a single thought blocked out all others.

It was definitely time to give Jack and Janet something new to think about.

CHAPTER 68

2:30 a.m.

Donald Stephenson moved through the near darkness of the cavernous room with his head bowed. One of the advantages of not needing sleep was that it gave him more time for thought, and deep thought was something at which he excelled.

Everyone knew that he worked long hours and slept very little, but only he knew how little he slept: never. And judging by the incompetence of the team of scientists that worked for him on the project, it was a very good thing he did not need any rest. Complete morons, the lot of them.

It really irked the deputy director to have to disrupt the truly challenging work that lay before him to have to deal with trivial things, like the formulation of the nanite suspension fluid. But no amount of pressure could drive Dr. Frederick's team to an adequate solution.

So tonight, in a matter of four hours, Dr. Stephenson had interrupted his own work, made his way to Dr. Frederick's section of the lab, and devised his own working formulation. Then, having left a disparaging note with the description of the production process, Dr. Stephenson made his way back to the *Rho Ship*. Idiots.

As he moved up the ramp and through the inner passageways of the ship, Dr. Stephenson glanced up at the arrays of sensors and video monitors that had been installed throughout. Nothing happened on this ship that was not recorded, scrutinized, and analyzed to the nth degree. Not just by himself, but by the assortment of government watchdogs for the program, some of which were under his direct influence while others were not.

Because of this detailed monitoring, Dr. Stephenson had added a few after-hours enhancements to the system's inner workings. A sequence of post-processing algorithms ran the data constantly, usually just passing the input signals, unmodified, to the recording and analysis systems.

But anything that involved Dr. Stephenson's passage into or out of his private third of the *Rho Ship* did not show up. During these times, the video, audio, and other assorted systems showed him moving about other areas of the ship, working on typical, mundane tasks.

The same was true for those rare instances, such as with Dr. Nancy Anatole, when he had taken someone else back with him. The systems within the inner portion of the ship alerted him whenever an unexpected visitor approached, allowing him plenty of time to make his exit and greet them.

Tonight his long, lanky stride carried Dr. Stephenson rapidly to the wall that blocked access to the ship's rear third. He stopped, his hands tracing out the complex fractal pattern required to gain entrance. The door whisked open, snapping shut again behind him, leaving him immersed in a light as colorless as shadow on asphalt.

The apparatus that drew him through the narrow rows of equipment and cables occupied the very center of the large room. It was by far the largest single mechanism on the *Rho Ship*. To develop an understanding of what it did and how it had once worked had taken him thirteen years.

But the onboard power systems had been so badly damaged by the subspace weapon that brought the ship down that they would never again be capable of powering the device. And even if it worked, it simply was not large enough for his needs. Still, it had provided the blueprint.

Running his hands lovingly across its brutish lines, Dr. Stephenson smiled, his face contorting like a Mardi Gras mask.

This coming project was going to take time, but that was something the deputy director had in abundance. In the meantime, global acceptance of cold fusion was going swimmingly.

Very soon now, he would undertake the government release of the second alien technology. It would sweep the planet like wildfire, as the people of nation after nation demanded to be the next to get it. What he was about to accomplish made Hitler's petty attempts at creating a master race truly laughable.

Donald Stephenson didn't care about race; he cared about humanity. He cared about humanity's imperfections, imperfections that led to disease, deformity, death, and the human affinity for violence. There was no longer any reason to accept human imperfection. He was finally ready to prove that all imperfections, genetic or otherwise, could be cured.

After a long procession of petty dictators' misguided attempts, Dr. Stephenson had finally set mankind's evolutionary train in motion. Next stop…Utopia.

CHAPTER 69

The next two weeks passed so quickly it seemed to Heather that they were gone in the blink of an eye. The local news interest in the Rag Man incident was drowned out by rumors that the Rho Project was preparing for release of a second alien technology, this one having nothing to do with energy production. And although neither the president, nor any members of the administration, would comment on the story, speculation in the press continued to rise. For Heather, the rumors only increased her sense of foreboding.

Of course, the buzz around school was all about basketball and how the Hilltoppers had breezed through the district tournament. Now it was on to the state basketball tournament at The Pit in Albuquerque, the traditional home court of the University of New Mexico Lobos.

But what had made the time truly fly was the progress Mark, Heather, and Jennifer made on the cold fusion power supply that would drive their subspace transmitter. The initial tests had gone so well that they had grown cocky, something that had nearly gotten them all killed last Saturday morning.

Deciding that they were ready for a full-up test, the three teens had brought the power supply online. Jennifer had been at the controls while Heather monitored measured power output versus that predicted by the mathematical model. All had gone well until a diode on the primary control circuit board burned out, sending a massive power spike through the system. Only Jennifer's quick reflexes in switching to the backup controller had prevented the power from reaching dangerous, perhaps even deadly, levels.

Although Heather thought the scare probably took two years off her expected life span, the test demonstrated that their backup system worked. It also convinced them they needed more automated fail-safe circuitry.

While Jennifer worked on that, Mark finished building a sophisticated bug detector. A sweep of their houses revealed three bugs in each house, not counting the phone lines, which they just assumed were being monitored. Tiny transmitters were hidden in each kitchen, office, and master bedroom.

After the initial sweep, Mark had become concerned there might also be hidden burst transmitters, which stored data but only sent out quick transmissions at infrequent intervals. Only after he had conducted an extended test did he relax, convinced he had found every bug.

Heather's personal life was improving, too. With the Rag Man gone, her mood lifted, restoring a joy that she had not realized was missing. Also, Raul was rapidly becoming a very good friend, not in the same way that Mark and Jennifer were almost family, but a good friend nonetheless. He didn't press his attentions on her. He was just there when she needed someone to talk to, providing a respite from the drama surrounding her and the twins.

In a wonderful departure from what you would normally expect from a boy his age, Raul listened to her with an easiness that showed he didn't feel he had to prove himself to her. And that allowed him to actually hear what she was saying. Even his strongly held religious beliefs built no wall between them. In fact, when Heather had asked to attend one of Raul's Bible study sessions, he had laughed but demurred, telling her that he just wouldn't feel right pushing his beliefs on her. It gave Heather a warm feeling inside to be around someone who had such a perfect understanding of who he was.

But this was a new Saturday, and there was no time for more than fleeting thoughts of school, basketball tournaments, or even Raul. Heather had barely gotten to sleep last night. After all, today was the day.

Heather had even begged off on the family shopping trip to Santa Fe, saying the science project demanded her full attention today. Although her mother had looked skeptical, her dad had understood. A science project was a science project. Heather had not even had to lie, except by omission.

Today was the day when she, Jennifer, and Mark would become the first humans to tap into the Secret Internet Protocol Router Network, or SIPRNet as it was more commonly known, via an undetectable subspace signal. Actually, that wasn't quite right. The subspace signal could be detected, but only if you had a correctly tuned subspace receiver, something that was pretty unlikely.

Heather was so excited she could barely contain herself. If all went according to plan, they could generate a remote digital signal on any line in the world, assuming they could attain the exact four-dimensional coordinates for that line. And that went for fiber-optic lines as readily as wired networks.

That concept was truly magical: In an optical fiber line, light carried the information instead of an electrical signal, as in a wire line. But in the subspace to normal space interface, there was no difference in the way either signal was generated. It was delicious. The NSA was about to get quite a shock.

It was no great surprise for Heather to discover that Mark and Jennifer were already gathered around the computerized control system for their subspace transmitter by the time she entered the Smythe garage. Her two friends huddled under the tall halogen lamp that provided indirect illumination to the work area.

Heather slid into the folding chair beside Jennifer, a spot she had come to think of as the copilot's seat. As Jennifer's fingers danced across the keyboard of the laptop, gradually bringing the cold fusion tank online, Heather monitored the output indicators. So long as everything stayed within projected norms, she just had to help with the tuning of the subspace wave steering.

Mark was on call with his language skills. Since seeing Jack deal with the Rag Man, Mark had become fascinated with spy agencies. He had read everything he could find on the subject and had also determined to understand the technical side of remotely tapping into the SIPRNet.

"So we're going to tap into one of the lines directly inside the Puzzle Palace?" Mark asked.

"That's the plan," said Heather. "We have the coordinates for the building on Ft. Meade, but picking a line is going to take us a while."

"From what I read, all of the SIPRNet lines will be shielded in TEMPEST-rated facilities."

Jennifer raised her head. "What is TEMPEST?"

Mark turned back toward his sister. "It's a code word used to describe the way secure systems have to be shielded so that the electromagnetic signals they give off can't be monitored remotely."

"Yes," said Heather. "Even typing on a keyboard produces little electronic signals that leak out into the surrounding space. They are weak, but if someone has the right equipment, they can pick up the signal and find out exactly what you were typing. The same thing applies for all electronic equipment."

Mark nodded. "So, TEMPEST-rated facilities have special requirements, like being wrapped with metal or wire mesh that blocks those electromagnetic signals from escaping."

"But that won't cause us any problem," said Heather. "Every signal has a tiny leakage into subspace, and no TEMPEST countermeasures will stop that. We'll be able to pick up the signals from any network once we narrow in on a specific line and pick up the data flowing across it. We only need a tunable subspace receiver for that.

"But putting a signal back on the remote line is what requires all this power and the subspace transmitter. And since we're the only ones with a subspace receiver-transmitter, we're the only ones that can do this."

Jennifer glanced at her readings. "Power levels at seventy-seven percent. Now eighty."

Heather leaned in closer. "OK. Nice and steady."

"Eighty-five."

"Keep it coming."

"Ninety-three."

"OK now, ease off a bit. Steady up at around ninety-eight and let it stabilize."

"Got it. Coming up on ninety-six now. All right. Ninety-seven. Backing down a bit more on the stimulation. There it is, ninety-eight and holding steady."

Heather stared at the displays for several seconds before she was satisfied. “Ever so slowly now, nudge it up that last two percent.”

For almost two minutes Jennifer worked the keyboard, making incremental adjustments to the reaction controlling signal strength. On the side of the tank, the banks of colored LED lights twinkled as data cascaded through the various registers in the central processing unit. As Jennifer watched that, Heather focused on the computer monitor. Perfect.

The sound from the cold fusion apparatus was surprisingly loud. This occurred because the reaction produced heat, and that heat produced steam, which in turn they siphoned off to drive a steam-powered electric generator. The generator itself only produced a whirring sound, but the steam whistled out with a sound reminiscent of a teakettle.

“You know, that is really getting to be annoying,” said Mark.

“I agree,” said Jennifer. “We’re going to have to come up with a better design for the steam recycler or we’ll go deaf.”

“We just have to put up with it a little while,” said Heather. “Just long enough for us to find a SIPRNet line and put the message on it.”

They didn’t actually need the electricity the project generated, just the gamma-ray flux. But since the purpose of the science project was to provide a household energy source driven by cold fusion, they had to have that part of it. Besides, there had to be a means of dumping the excess heat that cold fusion generated, and the state transition of liquid water to steam was a good way of doing that.

Heather read off the latitude and longitude of the Puzzle Palace, allowing a few extra seconds for Jennifer to synchronize the system with Greenwich Mean Time via a remote time server.

Despite having an accurate coordinate for the building, their difficulty was going to lie in the massive amount of electronic systems inside. When they tuned their subspace receiver to that spot, the close proximity of computer systems and network cabling would make it hard to find a particular one, at least the first time.

On the plus side, it didn't really matter which subnet they accessed within the Puzzle Palace, so long as it was a SIPRNet. Since almost everything in the building was classified, that was not going to be hard to find.

"Got one." The excitement in Jennifer's voice crackled like static on a New Mexico AM radio station.

"How's the signal strength?" Mark asked.

"Beautiful. And the power grid is stable, too. Give me just a second to confirm the subnet's SIPRNet status."

Jennifer's fingers danced across the keyboard as a stream of data scrolled through a window on the monitor and lit the LED panel like a Christmas tree at the North Pole.

Jennifer leaned back, beaming. "That's it. We're in."

Heather took a deep breath. Oh, Jesus. They had really done it.

"OK, putting a test sync pattern on the network." Jennifer typed a quick command. "I've got confirmation. The pattern has been successfully uplinked to the SIPRNet."

Mark let out a low whooping sound. "All right. Now uplink the message and then let's power down."

"There's really no rush," said Heather. "We absolutely cannot be traced. To them it will look like the signal just appeared inside their own network, and if they trace it back to its origin, they will find out it originated on a fiber inside their own building."

"Christ, this is great."

Heather frowned. "Still, I guess it would be wise not to spend too long surfing their network, at least for the moment. It might be a little hard to explain what we're up to if your parents come back home unexpectedly."

"Are you kidding? I've got that story down. Our little science project here is cutting their electric bill."

Jennifer shook her head. "Better safe than sorry, though. I'm ready to send."

Heather leaned in closer. "Go for it."

Originally, they had put together a wordy message to the NSA. But after lengthy discussions, they had agreed less was more. With that in mind, they had settled on a very short message, encrypted with the same breakable encryption code as the earlier message their virus had delivered. That should get someone's attention.

"Well, here goes nothing."

Amid the cascading display of colors from the LED panel and the whistling rush of their steam-powered generator, Jennifer's slender fingers flew across the keys like a concert pianist performing the works of Sergey Vasilyevich Rachmaninoff. As Heather watched her friend at work, gooseflesh rose along her arms. Those dancing fingers were about to unleash a firestorm the likes of which the NSA had never seen.

CHAPTER 70

David Kurtz burst into Jonathan Riles's office in such a hurry that the door banged against the doorstop, rippling the surface of Riles's coffee.

Riles looked up from his papers. "Yes, David? What has your panties in a bunch?"

Although the hair on Kurtz's head gave Albert Einstein a run for his money on a normal day, this afternoon it looked like he'd stuck a fork into a 220-volt socket. He tossed a stack of printouts on top of the other papers on Riles's desk.

"We have a situation that requires your immediate involvement."

Riles did not bother to glance at the readouts, focusing his steely gaze on Kurtz. "You have my full attention."

David Kurtz paused, something the most brilliant computer scientist on the planet almost never did. "Since the speculation is so outlandish, I'll stick solely to the facts. We have received another message from the author of the New Year's Day Virus, and this one came in on the SIPRNet."

"Have you traced the source?"

"We have."

"And?"

"It originated right here in the building, on a subnet on the third floor."

"What?"

"I've run a complete trace, including a full message log and router dump. There can be no doubt."

"Have you isolated the subnet?"

"I have taken that subnet and the thirteen connecting subnets off-line, physically disconnecting them from all other systems while we work this."

"Step it out another level."

"Sir, that will take a quarter of the systems in the building off-line."

"I don't care. Do it."

Kurtz pressed a button on his secure cell phone, spoke a couple of words into the mouthpiece, and then flipped it closed. "It is done."

Riles rose from his chair, pacing to the digital display that took the place of the window that would have existed in a non-classified facility. He touched the screen, and the scene changed to a pristine beach in Maui.

"Now, David, tell me about this message."

"Yes, sir. Since the encryption pattern exactly matched the New Year's Day Virus, our IP sniffer picked it up instantly. It decrypted to five words: Rho Project Nanite Suspension Fluid."

"On the SIPRNet in our building?"

"Yes, sir."

"How is that possible?"

"There's no way to do it from outside. The SIPRNet systems do not have a physical connection to any non-SIPRNet line. Also, this message did not propagate to any other systems like the virus did. It just originated on one of our networks."

Riles turned away from Maui. "David, I want every single person with access to that part of the building restricted to site immediately. Place an emergency recall to anyone who is not currently in the building and get their asses in here ASAP. Get the interrogation team briefed and moving. Once we have everyone that could have possibly touched the system here and accounted for, nobody leaves until they are polygraphed. If the message didn't come from outside the building, then I want to know which one of our people is responsible."

Kurtz turned toward the door.

"David."

Kurtz stopped to look back at Riles.

"That means everyone who could have touched any part of those subnets."

"I'll be the first to take the poly," David Kurtz responded, then turned and walked out the door.

The door closed behind David Kurtz with a soft snick as the latch engaged. Jonathan Riles stared at the dark wood of the closed portal. He had just ordered over a hundred people to undergo an emergency polygraph that he did not think for a second would turn up anything. Still, if Jonathan Riles was anything, he was thorough. So he would do his duty. Tomorrow would be soon enough to delve into the other disturbing possibilities that whispered at the edge of his mind.

Walking back to his desk, he glanced down at the words on the topmost of Kurtz's stack of papers.

Rho Project Nanite Suspension Fluid.

The words did nothing to ease his state of mind.

CHAPTER 71

The noise in The Pit was deafening to Heather. It seemed that half the state had turned out to see the basketball state championship game between the Los Alamos Hilltoppers and the Roswell Goddard Rockets. Even people who normally did not follow high school basketball had become enthralled with the story of the junior phenom, Marcus Aurelius Smythe.

Indeed, his entrance into the University of New Mexico basketball stadium generated a welcome that a victorious Caesar would have found thrilling. Heather was stunned by the crowd response, which rose to such a volume that she began to wonder if her ears would start bleeding.

Sitting here in courtside seats with her mom, dad, and the Smythes, the thrill that surged through her enhanced nerve endings was tinged with just a hint of dismay. That Jack and Janet

Johnson stood cheering immediately behind her only heightened her concern.

Janet put two fingers between her lips and sent out a whistle that caused Mark to turn his head toward them and smile. If Heather's ears had not been bleeding before, they certainly were now.

Although the crowd's size was surprising, both Heather and Jennifer had been expecting a response after Friday's article in the sports section of the *Albuquerque Journal*.

"Junior Point Guard Sets the Court on Fire" the sports headline had blared. Immediately below the headline, the picture showed Mark spinning between defenders, the ball passing between his legs in mid-dribble. Jennifer had almost succeeded in making her brother feel guilty about the attention he was drawing when Janet had walked by in the school hallway.

"Mark, congratulations on the wonderful article. Jack and I are so excited for you."

With those few words, the brief hint of guilt had disappeared from Mark's face, vaporized as thoroughly as rainwater on a volcano.

And so, here and now, they all stood together cheering in unison with thousands of others to whom Mark was a total stranger. Surreal.

Jennifer's sharp elbow interrupted Heather's reverie. Her eyes moved across the stadium to the spot at which Jennifer pointed.

"I didn't know George Delome was friends with Raul," Jennifer said.

At the far end of the floor, near the entry hallway from the locker rooms, Raul stood in close conversation with the Hilltoppers' team manager.

"George is a member of Raul's Bible study group."

Just then the horn blared out, sending George scurrying across the floor toward the bench. Although Heather could not hear what was said, it was quite clear that Coach Harmon was less than pleased with George's delay in getting the water bottles distributed.

While he may have been tardy to this point, the alacrity with which the pudgy boy scurried along the bench setting out the individual bottles behind the player positions was impressive. He paused momentarily behind Mark's spot, fumbling through the bag to grab a bottle, but then he was on down the rest of the line in manager record time.

"What a geek," Jennifer said, shaking her head as she watched him trip over some equipment at the far end.

Heather nodded. What Raul saw in the fat kid was beyond her. Maybe he just took pity on him.

The crowd cheered, signaling the tip-off and that the game was underway. Both teams opened up red hot, but the Rockets had no answer for Mark. They quickly abandoned their man-to-man defense, switching to a box-one zone. That let them keep a player man-to-man on Mark while everyone else played zone defense.

Nevertheless, by the end of the first quarter, Mark had already scored fifteen points and had four assists. Hilltoppers, twenty-six. Rockets, twenty.

The Hilltoppers continued building on their lead in the second quarter as Mark worked his magic, his spinning drives bringing the crowd to their feet.

Then he began to falter. Three times in a row, as he brought the ball down the court against the Rocket full-court press, Mark lost the ball to quick double teams. Even his shot deteriorated. Just before halftime, he shot an air ball fifteen feet from the basket. As the buzzer sounded, he walked off the court, shaking his head in disbelief.

The halftime score showed that the Hilltoppers still led, but their twelve-point lead had dwindled to a mere two.

"What's up with your brother?" Heather asked.

"No idea," said Jennifer. "Maybe he's taking my warning about playing too well to heart."

"I don't know. It didn't look like he was trying to mess up."

Jennifer shrugged. "You've got me. Let's go get some popcorn."

By the time they made their way up to the concession stands, conquered the impressive line, and returned back to their seats, the second half had started. If anything, Mark was playing worse than he had at the end of the first half. His movements seemed sluggish, even awkward.

To Heather's surprise, Coach Harmon even yelled at him during a timeout, sitting him on the bench for the last two minutes of the third quarter. Mark just sat there beside the coach on the bench, shaking his head. He even refused the water that George Delome brought to him, despite the portly manager's attempts to get him to drink.

The fourth quarter opened with Mark still sitting on the bench, as his team gradually fell farther behind. Finally, with just over six minutes left in the game and the Hilltoppers trailing sixty-six to seventy-eight, Coach Harmon called a timeout and signaled for Mark to get back in the game.

Whatever the cause of his sloppy play for the last two quarters, the benching seemed to have helped clear Mark's mind. His ballhandling sharpness was back, perhaps not to his normal level, but impressive nonetheless. And as he played, the Hilltoppers clawed their way back into the game.

With thirty seconds left on the clock, the fans in the stadium were on their feet, screaming their lungs out as Mark brought the ball up the court, trailing by one point. Even Jennifer was screaming so loud that Heather thought she might cough out a tonsil.

With the clock ticking down under ten seconds, Heather held her breath as Mark drove into the lane. It seemed that every one of the Goddard Rockets swarmed over him, slapping at the ball as he moved among them.

Mark dived forward, launching a pass between two Rockets to a wide-open Bobby Kline, who caught it cleanly at the top of the key. As the clock ticked to one, Bobby launched a jump shot that seemed to leave his hands in slow motion, arcing up toward the basket as the horn sounded, ending the game. The shot hit the rim, looped around the inside twice, and then rose back up to the balance on the edge before finally dropping through.

If the stadium had been loud before, the sound that filled it now was deafening. People rushed onto the court in a swarm, lifting Bobby on their shoulders and patting Mark and the other players on the back until they disappeared into the throng.

After the hubbub subsided, the rest of the evening passed very slowly. The team stayed to watch the 5A championship game after receiving their own trophy and hitting the showers, and the Smythes and McFarlands stayed to watch that game, too. The question on everyone's lips was asked of Mark again and again throughout the evening.

Finally, Heather got her turn. "What happened in the second and third quarter?"

"I don't know. I was just out of it for a while."

"Yeah. Well, it's a good thing you got it back together. It sure was looking bad for our side."

Mark grinned. "It's a good thing Bobby hit that shot or I don't think I could have lived it down."

"You still played the best game of anyone out there."

"Somehow I don't think the team and the fans would have seen it that way if we had lost that game. I'm just glad Bobby pulled it off."

By the time the last game ended and the McFarlands pulled into their own driveway, Heather was exhausted. At least they had gotten home before the Smythes. Poor Jennifer would have to wait for the team bus to make its way back to the high school before they could pick up Mark and make their way back home. Heather was just glad it wasn't her.

Awakening bright and early Sunday morning, Heather felt more rested than she had in days. Apparently, sleeping the sleep of exhaustion was good for her. By the time she had showered, eaten breakfast, and gotten into the car to head to church, a sense of well-being enveloped her. A quick stop at the convenience store put an end to that.

As she waited for her mother to make her way through the checkout line, Heather's eyes spotted Mark's picture on the front of the *National Inquisitor*. It was a close-up of Mark's glassy stare as Coach Harmon leaned in nose-to-nose yelling at him. But it was the headline that almost made her drop her soda.

High School Prodigy's Pregame Drinking Binge Almost Costs Team Championship

Not good, she thought. Not good at all.

CHAPTER 72

A cold draft swirled across the floor, sweeping dust bunnies from hidden nooks and chilling Jack's feet as he leaned forward, scanning the papers occupying the center of his desk. That was the thing about drafty old attics in wintertime. No matter how many space heaters you strategically positioned, the draft won.

Janet's head emerged through the trapdoor, followed immediately by a very shapely, black-leotard-clad body.

"So what have you got for me?"

She shrugged. "Just as we thought. Mark's water bottle was drugged. It had been emptied, but traces of the Mickey were still present. It's a good thing he didn't drink any more of that stuff or he would have had more pressing problems than an off night on the basketball court."

"And the fat team manager kid?"

"One of the school nerds. The interesting thing is that he's one of a small group of outcasts that have joined a Bible study group headed up by Raul Rodriguez."

"Rodriguez? The son of the Rho Project scientist?"

"Yes. He's an interesting story. Two months ago he was dying of terminal brain cancer. Then, on his deathbed, his cancer suddenly went into complete remission. Looking at him now, you'd never guess he'd been sick."

"So you think Raul got this other kid to drug Mark's water? What's the connection?"

"Heather. Raul has the hots for her, and from what I can tell, she likes him back. Mark doesn't even try to hide his distaste for that friendship. It's obvious that Raul doesn't like Mark either."

Jack nodded. "The name Rodriguez has been popping up a lot this morning. But before I get to that, did you get a chance to read the secure fax from Riles?"

"No."

"The NSA has gotten four new messages from the Rho Project informant. All of them originated on different parts of the SIPRNet inside the Puzzle Palace."

"How is that possible?"

"It isn't. Riles had every one of the associated subnets taken off-line, people polygraphed, the works. Nothing. Even more interesting, they traced each of the messages. All of them seem to have just appeared on the network."

"Has someone managed to physically tap the cables?"

"No. And more than half of the messages seem to have originated on fiber-optic cables."

"So I guess Riles is freaking."

Jack laughed. "Absolutely. He's not the type to tolerate unexplained intrusions on his security systems."

"So they don't have any leads?"

"Not anything they can lay their fingers on. There was one very interesting anomaly. What do you know about the Sudbury Neutrino Observatory?"

"Never heard of it."

"It's a big, two-million-pound bottle of heavy water over a mile below ground in a nickel mine in Sudbury, Ontario. The whole thing is surrounded by a sixty-foot-thick array of photo-multiplier tubes and is suspended in a huge tank of light water."

"Why do they need such a big detector, and why put it so far below ground?"

"Neutrinos are very hard to detect. They can pass through almost anything, including the Earth, and give off almost no sign that they were ever there. They put the detector way below ground to block out other types of cosmic radiation. It lets them focus on the Cerenkov radiation that the neutrino and heavy-water interactions produce."

"So what's the point of measuring them?"

"That's what gets interesting. The neutrinos are a side effect of certain high-energy interactions. The reason Riles got interested was that his team monitored reports of unusual neutrino flux measurements."

"Let me guess. The times corresponded to the times of the SIPRNet hacks."

"Bingo."

"So what technologies would cause that?"

"As far as we know, nothing on the planet could produce that kind of neutrino flux."

"Can its source be traced?"

"No."

"So we're dead-ended."

"Not quite. There's the content of the message itself. It contained exactly the same five words on each transmission. Rho Project Nanite Suspension Fluid."

Janet moved over to look down at the fax. "So we know the message appeared on an unhackable secure network, that at the same time, a fancy detector picked up signals that cannot be produced by anything on Earth, and that the message talks about a Rho Project technology."

"Specifically nanites. Three guesses as to the name of one of the nanotechnology specialists working on the Rho Project science team."

"Dr. Ernesto Rodriguez?"

"Bingo again."

"And his son has just made a miraculous recovery from terminal cancer."

"Too many miracles for my taste."

Janet was pacing now, weaving her way through the sparse furniture, letting her fingertips trace around its edges like a feline. God, she was sexy.

"One thing doesn't make sense. If the next Rho Project technology to be released is some sort of nanotechnology, then why is someone warning us about it? It'll be reviewed when it's released."

"Apparently our mole on the project thinks it's dangerous enough to go to extraordinary lengths to make sure he gets our attention."

"What about the direct approach? Can't Riles just inquire through black-ops channels about the research?"

"It's so compartmentalized that none of the normal channels are working. He's afraid that if he presses, someone will put a stop to his little inquiry before he has anything to back up his suspicions. Despite everything, that is still all we have. Suspicions."

"You want me to focus some extra attention on Raul?"

"While I look into his father. Find out everything you can about his illness, his recovery, any medical history after he got well, his friends. Everything."

As Janet began climbing down the ladder, she paused to look back.

"It's odd, isn't it?"

"What's that?"

"How a sweet young girl like Heather McFarland can be such a weirdo magnet."

Jack only nodded.

CHAPTER 73

Priest knew that in past lifetimes he had been a mighty warrior, a slayer of men, a ravager of women, just as he was now. After all, the old oak tree spread its roots in the soil, growing tall, hard, and strong. And when it died, it sprouted from its own acorn to live again. But it was still an oak. So it was with Priest.

His awareness of his prior existence was more than a belief. Priest often awoke from a dream, and in that moment of awakening, for a brief instant, he could almost recall the men he had been. He could almost hear the screams of the dying as they pleaded with him to spare their lives.

Just as Ms. California begged for her life right now. As he dragged her bound form from the house to the old well out back, she cried and pleaded with him. And Priest almost wavered. Not from any sense of mercy. Hearing her terrified cries aroused him, almost enough to take her back to his basement for a few more days of usage.

But he'd already snipped her fingers for his necklace. It was time for her to join the others.

In the concrete basement beneath a German Gasthaus, a wooden ball makes a unique sound as it rolls down an alley to crash into nine wooden pins. The sound is picked up and amplified by the enclosing concrete walls, sloshing back and forth like Pilsner in the drinking glasses of the red-faced rollers.

Something about the sound of a woman's bound body falling down his well reminded Priest of that. Déjà vu.

As he walked back toward the house, Priest realized he was hungry, although not for food. The source of his hunger was one Janet Johnson, whatever her real name might be.

He didn't know her real name. It was something that had only happened to Priest once before. Usually his sources could deliver a dossier on anybody in the world, a dossier that was thick enough to pop the hinges off a briefcase. But where Janet Johnson was concerned, there was nothing. Nothing real, anyway. There was plenty of stuff about her make-believe life. Birth certificate: Janet Donovan, Gaithersburg, Maryland. High school diploma from Quince Orchard High. BA in history from University of Maryland. Marriage certificate to one Jack Johnson signed in Silver Spring, Maryland.

As he paused at the kitchen table to stare at the papers spread across it, Priest shook his head. Garbage. Every last scrap of it. The only other person he had ever encountered with a similar dearth of information was her pretend husband. But Priest knew some things about Jacky boy that put the lie to the false background. And they put the lie to all the information on Janet that lay spread out before him as well.

Deep cover. Part of Jack Gregory's team. That told him all he really needed to know about that live little minx. And soon enough, he would have all the time in the world to encourage her to tell him the rest.

The sad thing about being a warrior of such high standards was that Priest bored of his conquests so rapidly. He didn't think that would be the case with Janet Johnson. If she was acceptable to Jack, then she would be among the best. She would take a very long time to break. Priest couldn't ask for more than that. That she was drop-dead gorgeous was merely icing on the cake.

Priest turned toward his front door. The day was drifting away from him, and he still had so many things to do. The drive to his hide position alone was going to take an hour and a half by the back roads, and then he had a hard forty-five-minute hike after that. And he wanted to be there well before the high school let out and Janet Johnson made her way home.

Normally he would have selected a hide that was more easily accessible. But this time that would not do. Not when Jack Gregory was involved. The man's nose for trouble was uncanny, almost as if he had a sixth sense that warned him of danger. And Jack was not a man to trifle with. Priest had learned that firsthand.

The vantage point Priest had chosen was a brushy enclave in a crack in the cliff face across the canyon from the house Jack and Janet rented. It allowed entry along a trail hidden from the other side of the canyon. And the way the spot was shaded meant no stray glint from the lenses of his binoculars would betray his position.

He glanced down at his watch: 14:34. Perfect. Just enough time to get settled in before Janet got off work and returned home, provided she kept her routine. Whatever time she arrived didn't really matter. Priest could wait.

As he adjusted his binoculars, Priest smiled. He had all the time in the world.

CHAPTER 74

"You won't believe what that brother of mine is up to now."

Heather glanced up from her book to see Jennifer's spectacled face peering through her bedroom door.

"What?"

"You'll never guess in a million years."

"But you're going to make me try?"

Jennifer walked into the room and plopped down on Heather's bed. "He joined a society."

"You mean like the Moose Lodge or the Masons?" Heather shifted in her desk chair to keep facing her friend.

"Something like that."

"Are you going to tell me or not?"

"Mark is now a card-carrying member of POOTNAS, the Patriotic Order of the Needle and Spool."

Heather found the image that popped into her mind so comical she almost snorted the mouthful of Diet Coke out her nose.

"The sewing circle? The old ladies whose ancestors sewed uniforms for the Civil War? You're kidding, right?"

"That's what I thought when I heard it, but it's true."

"Is it some scheme to meet girls?"

"Not unless he's really desperate. The youngest member of the Los Alamos chapter, except Mark, is sixty-seven."

Heather failed to wrap her mind around it. "So what's his angle?"

"As far as I can tell, he likes sewing."

"Since when?"

"All I know is, a couple of days ago he was watching a program on the invention of various stitches and he got very interested. You could just see his face light up. Since then he has been a fanatic on the whole subject. He even went to the library."

"We are still talking about your brother, Mark, right?"

Jennifer shrugged. "At least it looks like my brother. Currently, he's deeply immersed in articles on slip stitches and the effects of temperature variations on threads."

"Have you asked him why?"

"Of course. He was shocked that I could even ask. The Sisters of Mercy couldn't have looked more innocent."

Heather shook her head. It wasn't the first time Mark had mystified her, but it ranked among the strangest. "Well, there's no making sense out of anything guys do."

"Oh, Mark distracted me so badly I almost forgot what I came over to tell you. I wanted to tell Mark too, but he told me to quit interrupting him and to get lost. Sometimes he makes me so mad I can't see straight."

Heather grinned. "So what did you want to tell me?"

Jennifer propped up two pillows and leaned back against Heather's headboard. "Something's been bothering me for a long time now, something that I'd seen in the data the last time we were on the ship."

The topic of the ship brought Heather to full attention. Though they had thoroughly swept her room for bugs, it still made her nervous to talk about it.

"Bothering you? Why?"

"At first I couldn't put my finger on it. But this morning I was playing the whole thing back in my mind and I found it. Then I went on the Internet to get some data about the Aztec crash back in 1948, and it all started to make sense to me."

Jennifer paused, lacing her fingers behind her head. "The debris they found outside of Aztec wasn't from the ship at the lab. The debris came from our ship."

"You're not making any sense."

"Think about it. Both ships were involved in the Aztec incident. They shot each other down that night, didn't they? But the ship the government found didn't have a hole punched through it. Ours did. I think when the *Rho Ship*'s weapon penetrated the hull of the *Second Ship*, the decompression sucked out some debris. I also wondered about the missing crew. I think they got sucked out through that hole."

Heather nodded. "Like the imagery we saw. Sucked out into the vacuum of space."

"You know what that debris means? The government knows there was a second ship, and Stephenson has probably figured out that both ships shot each other down. Our subspace hack into the NSA's secure networks might put him onto us."

Heather chewed her lower lip, the odds of such a thing working themselves out in her thoughts.

"Possible, but not likely. I still believe the NSA folks think they're getting a warning from someone working on the Rho Project with access to its technology. I don't think they would have tipped off anyone on the Rho Project while they are checking into it."

"Let's hope not. In the meantime, I suggest we be even more careful when communicating with the NSA."

Heather stood up. "OK. Let's go interrupt Mark from sewing a Superman cape or whatever he's up to. It's time to bring that brother of yours back down to this planet."

CHAPTER 75

Jack loved lightning. Sitting on the rock ledge looking at the approaching late spring storm across the high canyon country, the rain hanging from the thunderheads in dark veils, he could almost anticipate when the next bolt would rip the sky.

He had been in many storms, had ridden out a typhoon on a fishing boat in the South China Sea, had been drenched in the monsoon rains of Myanmar—a place the US government continued to call Burma, rest of the world be damned.

But somehow, there was nothing that compared to the high desert storms that rumbled through the mountains of the American Southwest. Thunder crackled through the thin air as if someone had dropped a boulder on a concrete slab, the sound echoing outward between the rock walls, one angry rumble supplanting the next.

It wasn't that Jack needed to be out here at this moment. It was simply that the exertion of the rock climb in the clear mountain air facilitated his thinking. Out here, accompanied by the feel of the approaching storm, the pieces of the puzzle were assembling themselves in his head.

Sometimes luck helped you find the key thread, and as you plucked it, the security that cloaked your opponent's movements unraveled. In this case, the break had come from the incident at the state basketball tournament. The drugging of the water bottle had led Jack and Janet to focus their attention on Raul Rodriguez and, by proxy, on his father, Dr. Ernesto Rodriguez.

The information that Janet had provided this morning added to a growing pool of circumstantial evidence that pointed to the likelihood that Ernesto had taken his work beyond the confines of the lab. Although Jack still didn't have any hard evidence that clarified the exact nature of what Dr. Rodriguez was working on within the Rho Division, he was beginning to develop a fairly good idea.

Not only had the scientist's son made a miraculous recovery from terminal cancer, but he appeared to have remarkable healing powers as well. The school nurse, Harriet Lu, had told Janet that Raul had been rushed to her office a few weeks ago after having suffered a serious cut in shop class. However, by the time she had examined the hand that had slid into the buzz saw, except for a redness where the palm appeared to be mildly skinned, there was no indication of damage.

The shop teacher, Mr. Hendricks, had been certain that he had seen the hand cut open, but when confronted with the evidence of his own eyes, he finally decided that he must have imagined it. Perhaps what he thought he had seen had only been based upon his expectation of injury due to having observed Raul fall forward across the machine. Mrs. Lu would not have even spoken of the incident had Janet not mentioned what a lucky young man Raul was.

Finally, there was the tabloid story of the rat. Jack had come across it in the supermarket; a front-page story in the *Inquisitor* about what a Los Alamos custodian claimed was the Rasputin of rats. It was exactly the sort of tale Jack would normally chuckle at and dismiss, had it not been for the name of the custodian.

Carlos Delgado was on Jack's list of employees with access to the Rho Division, head of a cleaning crew for the building in which Dr. Rodriguez worked. So Jack had purchased the rag and read the story of how Carlos had found a rat that he couldn't seem to kill. Not with poisoned bait. Not with a trap. Upon finding its head caught in the trap, he had stomped down upon it to break the animal's neck. But when he popped the catch open, it had miraculously run off, disappearing down a storm drain.

The story was almost certainly embellished, but had a ring of familiarity about it, considering what he had learned about Raul. Jack would have loved to have a conversation with Mr. Delgado. And he would have, had the custodian not gotten himself killed in an automobile accident the very day that the story appeared in the tabloid.

A late-night trip to the salvage yard had revealed an oddly shaped hole in the brake line, the type of hole that was characteristic of a shaped microcharge. Mr. Delgado had been very unlucky indeed to bring himself to the attention of someone with the rarefied skill set that included the construction and use of shaped microcharges. No doubt the person who had set it off had done so from a promontory overlooking this winding canyon road. Perhaps from the very one on which Jack now sat. The loss of brakes at just that point on the highway below had resulted in the two-hundred-foot plunge that had snuffed out the life of

Carlos Delgado, a family man who left behind a wife and four small children.

As Jack studied the curve in the highway where the guardrail had been insufficient to arrest the flight of the Chevy Malibu, the first drops of rain spattered down onto his face. There was no doubt about it. Someone with a skill set with which Jack was all too familiar was nearby and interested in the same thing that occupied his and Janet's attention. Who was it?

Jack stood up. Almost, it seemed that he sniffed the air. Then, like some great cat, he disappeared into the rocky crevice from which he had emerged.

CHAPTER 76

While school busses weren't her idea of ideal transportation, after eleven years riding the things, Heather had gotten used to them. In fact, Heather often looked forward to the bus rides home from LAHS, since it gave her quality chat time with Jennifer.

As Heather hopped on the bus for the ride home on this early day in May, the school bus was abuzz with discussions of the upcoming junior-senior prom. Normally only juniors and seniors were allowed to go to the prom, but this year was different. This year the senior class had voted to allow all high school classes to attend the event.

The seniors claimed the decision was an example of how they wanted to establish a fresh spirit of inclusion. That it went along with their senior class motto, "Equality, Inclusiveness, Fraternity, and Sorority for all." Mark said that if they had only added "World Peace," they would have achieved the most politically correct motto of all time. Instead, they had to settle for the stupidest.

Heather thought the decision had nothing to do with the senior class motto and everything to do with the utter failure of her junior class's spring fund drive. In the end, since the junior class funded the prom, it came down to a choice of canceling the senior trip and using that money to pay for the prom, canceling the prom, or charging admission to a larger audience.

Whatever the reason behind the decision, Heather knew she'd just have to put up with a bunch of freshmen and sophomores without letting it ruin her evening.

"So, have you been invited yet?" asked Jennifer, plopping down beside Heather.

"No, but I'm pretty sure that Raul plans on inviting me this evening. He asked me to come over to his house for a while after school today."

"Oh, really? You sure he doesn't just want some help with his homework?"

Heather laughed. "I don't think so. He said it was important and that he wanted to talk to me in private."

"What time are you going?"

"Six o'clock; why?"

"Heather! Did you forget that we're getting together to test out Dad's new barbecue grill at seven? The one our dads are so excited about?"

Heather slapped her palm to her forehead. "I completely forgot. I promised my mom I'd help her get ready, too. I guess I could drop by Raul's house a couple of hours early. You don't think he'd mind, do you?"

"Are you kidding me? He's a guy. He'll love it no matter what time you show up."

By the time the bus pulled to a stop near their houses, Heather and Jennifer had pretty much covered every aspect of what Heather planned on wearing to the prom, curfews, and other weighty matters.

As for Jennifer, she hadn't been invited to the prom and didn't plan on attending in any event. First, there were no boys in which she had any current interest. Second, dancing had never been something that she felt any inclination to learn, and no amount of encouragement or cajoling from Heather had been able to put a dent in her resolve on that matter.

"Well, I have to run. If I'm going to bike over to Raul's and get back here by five thirty to help Mom, then I'd better get going."

"OK. See you then."

The bike ride to Raul's house left Heather breathless, although part of it probably had to do with the anticipation of what she was sure was coming. She knew Raul liked her, and as odd as he could be sometimes, she liked him back.

Of course, he might have wanted to talk to her for some other reason than inviting her to her first high school prom. Heather had considered this possibility, but since the odds that she was being invited to the prom were roughly 97.653 percent, her anticipation seemed justified.

Heather pulled her bike up to the steps that led to the overhanging front porch of Raul's house, dropped the kickstand, and walked up to ring the bell. The three gongs of the doorbell reminded her of the rest of the house. It wasn't fancy, but gave ample evidence of the meticulous pride that its owners felt. The Spanish curtains in the windows and the beautiful potted geraniums on the porch were stunning.

After several seconds and no response, Heather thought about ringing the bell again, then decided against it. If someone was in the house, they would have heard it.

Odd. There were several cars in the driveway. As far as she knew, the Rodriguez family only owned two cars, and neither of these currently occupied the carport or the driveway. Who did all these other cars belong to, and where were the owners?

Then Heather remembered. This was the afternoon when Raul hosted his regular after-school Bible study group. She didn't want to interrupt, but how long could it take?

Moving around the house toward the small guest quarters where Raul said he conducted his sessions, Heather decided that she would wait outside for a while. After all, she had nothing else to do until it was time to go meet Jennifer.

Heather had never actually been around to the guest quarters, having only been inside Raul's house on one occasion, an evening when she had been invited over for dinner and a round of dominoes. On that night, Heather had hoped to work her way past the stiff formality, perhaps even suspicion, with which Raul's parents seemed to regard her. And although the atmosphere in the household had been far from what could be considered welcoming, at least she felt tolerated. Progress was nothing to be sneered at.

The guesthouse was not at all what she expected. It looked like a small chapel, the kind you sometimes saw along the road outside of very small towns: a place where people could stop, light a candle, and offer up prayers to the saint of their choosing. At least that's what Heather imagined people did in those chapels.

The door bore the image of a cross, complete with bleeding Jesus, and the windows were stained glass. Heather walked around the building. The back wall was windowless but had a single door, its window blackened out.

For some reason, the site of the plain door with that little blacked-out window filled Heather with irrational dread. She knew that her reaction was stupid, so stupid it made her angry.

What was wrong with her? Just walking around the building made her as frightened as a little girl climbing down a ladder into the darkness of grandma's cellar, her small hand searching for the pull-cord that dangled from the naked bulb in the ceiling.

Fighting off her anxiety, Heather walked right up to the door and tried to peer through the black glass. It didn't work. Whoever had painted the window had done much too thorough a job to allow her any view of what lay beyond.

Driven more by anger at her timidity than by curiosity, Heather put her ear to the pane and listened. Nothing. That, in itself, was odd. On the other side of the building she had been able to hear the rumble of Raul's voice just by standing close to the front door.

But from here, no sound at all reached her ears, at least none from inside the house. It must be some separate room, most likely used for storage. Heather ignored the 16.283 percent probability that popped into her mind, reaching instead for the handle and giving it a slow twist.

The door opened so smoothly and silently Heather almost jumped, yet another thing that added to her growing self-anger. Taking a deep breath and then exhaling slowly, she opened the door all the way and stepped inside.

It took Heather's eyes several seconds to adjust from the bright sunshine outside to the dimly lit room. Hardly bigger than her mother's walk-in closet, the room was empty except for a raised trapdoor in the very center of the floor. Through that opening, she could see a steep set of steps leading down.

"Hello?" Heather's voice sounded oddly muffled in the room. She stepped to the edge of the opening and leaned down. "Hello? Anyone home?"

A lone switch occupied the wall just two steps down, and Heather moved to where she could reach it. At first she thought the lightbulb must be out. Then a gradual flickering, characteristic of fluorescent lamps, gave way to such brightness that she once again found herself momentarily blinded.

As her vision returned, Heather climbed down the remaining stairs into a room so white that the walls seemed to glow as brightly as the fluorescent casings that lined the ceiling.

A solitary bed occupied the center of the room, the type found in hospitals, with stainless-steel railings along both sides and adjustable sections that allowed the operator to raise or lower the back or legs. Beside the bed, a tall, stainless-steel stand held an empty intravenous fluid bag. Just beyond that, the walls were lined with a combination of instruments, a stainless-steel double sink, tables with computers and equipment, and lots of closed metal cabinets. There was also an old refrigerator with rounded corners, reminiscent of one in a fifties sitcom.

This must be the room where Dr. and Mrs. Rodriguez took care of Raul after taking him out of the hospital. But that didn't make any sense. Raul had told her that they had cared for him in his bedroom during all those weeks after everyone else had given up hope. His mother had been determined to keep him comfortable as she placed all her faith in God to heal her only son. No, this place had some other purpose. It seemed more like a laboratory, something straight out of an old B movie.

Heather moved to the row of tables loaded with the computers and instruments. Everything was off, and she had no intention of touching anything electronic for fear of breaking something. She turned to the first set of cabinets. The lower ones held cleaning supplies and chemicals, while the topmost contained beakers, test tubes, glass stirring rods, and gas torches.

The refrigerator door opened with a slight squeal, as if reluctant to reveal its contents. Inside, a set of test tubes stood arrayed in racks, the tops plugged with rubber stoppers. Heather reached in and carefully withdrew one of the test tubes, holding it up so that the light passed through its interior.

It held a gray liquid with the consistency of thin pudding. At first she thought that the goo pulsed of its own accord, but she put this down to her hands shaking from adrenaline overload. What in the world was she thinking snooping around like this?

Returning the test tube to the refrigerator and closing the door, her gaze shifted to the computer sitting atop the small table in the corner, a swivel chair pushed back as if its last occupant had departed in a hurry. The login screen drew her attention, a familiar LANL logo along with a username "RodriguezE" and an empty slot for a password.

Heather glanced back over her shoulder. Nothing. She was completely alone in the room. Despite a growing desire to get the hell out of there, she couldn't shake the feeling that she needed to see what was on that computer, that it held the key to what was going on in this hidden lab.

Ignoring her earlier decision not to touch the electronics, Heather took a seat in the chair and slid it up in front of the computer display. What would Dr. Rodriguez use as a password?

Heather had once browsed through a data security pamphlet her father had brought home from the lab, and it had spelled out the laboratory password requirements—a minimum of ten characters including at least one capital letter, one number, and a special character, such as a period.

Her dad and Mr. Smythe had laughed about the new policy over a game of bridge, something about how the government liked to lower the cone of silence, creating policies that made it impossible for people to remember their own passwords unless they wrote them down or used memory tricks that actually made the systems less secure.

Heather focused, letting her mind play out the possibilities. The likelihood that Dr. Rodriguez had written the password down shrank in comparison to other approaches. From what she had observed, Raul dominated his thoughts.

For a harried scientist, annoyed by the new security rules, the special character would be the first one on the keyboard, "!"—or "bang," as it was commonly known among hackers—most likely appended to the end of the sequence. As her savant mind worked the problem, a sequence of likely answers presented themselves, and the second of these got her in. Raul—birthday—bang.

As hard as her heart pounded in her chest, Heather barely paused to congratulate herself. A rapid scan of the files on the hard drive drew her attention to a folder named "Nano-Test-Subjects" and its two subfolders "Carlton Williams" and "Raul Rodriguez." Each folder contained a large number of spreadsheet data files as well as documents that appeared to contain detailed notes on test procedures and results. Without bothering to read any of the contents, Heather removed her cell phone from her pocket, slid the connector into the USB slot on the front of the computer, and began copying the folders. Exactly eighty-seven seconds later, she disconnected the portable device and reengaged the screen lock on Dr. Rodriguez's computer.

As she started to stand, a large hand closed across her face, covering both her mouth and nose with a soft, moist cloth. Her surprised inhalation sucked a vaguely familiar smell deep into her lungs. A desire to fight back surged through her mind, but never quite made it to her rubbery limbs. Through the rapidly narrowing straw of her vision, she saw Dr. Ernesto Rodriguez staring down at her with sad eyes.

"Young lady, I'm sorry you had to find this."

Indeed, as he strapped her down to the metal bed, the sorrow that shone in his damp eyes looked real. If Heather could have remained conscious, she thought that she probably could have felt pity for the man. Probably. 52.163 percent.

CHAPTER 77

Mark had endured just about enough of the girls' overly cautious thinking. After all, they had worked for almost three weeks to develop a microchip version of the quantum twin device, and it had tested out perfectly. The thing was a masterpiece.

It looked exactly like a wide variety of small multifunction chips common in TV remote controls, cell phones, and computers. Countless numbers of electronics used this chip type. And this one didn't have to be directly inserted into any circuitry. It worked by Faraday's principle of induction, picking up the faint signals from nearby circuitry. Of course, its quantum twin also picked up the same signal with no communications between them.

Even better, a signal could be injected into the quantum twin, and that signal would be propagated to the remote device where the other chip had been placed. It allowed for two-way communications.

There was nothing new about any of this. They had long since modified their own cell phones to have a QT mode, which let Mark, Heather, and Jennifer talk with complete security. What was so exciting about the tiny version was that they could place a bug in someone else's electronics that was completely undetectable unless a person happened to open the electronics and had enough knowledge to spot the extra microchip stuck to the circuit board.

Even though they could now hack into any system through their subspace transmitter, that system was bulky. Worse yet, it required them to specify the exact coordinates of the system where they wanted the subspace tap to occur. If someone was moving the equipment around, like a cell phone, then that just didn't work.

What annoyed Mark most was the two girls refusing to accept his plan to plant one of the new QTs on one of Jack's or Janet's devices. When he had mentioned it, Jennifer's mouth had dropped open wide enough to swallow an orange.

"Mark, are you insane? You're not talking about any Tom, Dick, or Harry here. Those two are intelligence agents."

"Jen's right," said Heather. "There are too many things that could go wrong. We can't risk it."

Mark had argued with them, pointing out that without being able to monitor Jack or Janet, they were flying blind. And hadn't Jack hidden bugs in both the McFarland and Smythe houses?

But the girls refused to cooperate. They had outvoted him, two to one. The subject was closed.

For two weeks, Mark had chaffed under the yoke of the girls' decision, but no more. At least he could stop by the Johnson house after school on the pretense of asking about homework. No doubt Janet would just think he was there because he thought she was hot.

Well, that was true. But it still provided a good excuse to get inside the house. Then he'd just have to see if the opportunity to plant the QT presented itself.

As Mark approached the street with the Johnson house, he saw Janet's car pull out of the driveway and head down the street in the opposite direction. Mark stopped, found a secluded spot to secure his bike, and walked up to the house on foot, a new plan forming in his mind.

Skirting around into the backyard, Mark glanced up to the second-story windows. As he had hoped, one of them remained open, just a crack to let the air in. Apparently, Janet did not plan on being gone for long.

Measuring the distance to the windowsill, Mark jumped, his hand just catching the edge. With a quick pull, he lifted his entire body, holding himself in place with one hand as he lifted the window with the other. Within seconds, he was inside.

His eyes swept the bedroom, but he did not linger. Mark needed to quickly find something they used, plant the bug, and get the hell out. He moved down the hallway, past the stairway leading down to the den, past the bathroom, to the spot where a rope dangled down from the trapdoor to the attic. Mark glanced up, then moved past it to the door at the far end of the hall. The door stood open and led to a room with a desk covered with school papers and a laptop, the screen saver busily constructing a network of multicolored 3D pipes. Bingo.

Moving quickly, Mark flipped the laptop up onto its side, extracted the set of tiny electronic screwdrivers from his pocket, picked a small Phillips head, and began removing a single screw.

Within seconds he had removed the small panel allowing access to the circuit board and memory cards. Picking a spot directly adjacent to the central processing unit, Mark retrieved the QT chip from his pocket, added a tiny drop of superglue, and pressed it into place, holding it just long enough for the adhesive on the back side to take hold.

As he finished replacing the cover and spun the screw tight, he heard the front door open.

Shit.

Mark set the computer back in its spot on the desk, grabbed his tools, and moving as quietly as possible, left the room. As Mark moved down the hallway, he spotted Janet's head in the den. Ducking back from the spot where the stairway opened to the room below, he barely avoided being seen. Making it down the hallway to the bedroom and the window he had entered was impossible without being spotted.

Mark moved back to the spot where the rope dangled down from the attic. Holding his breath, praying that it would open silently, Mark pulled on the cord.

For once his luck was good. The hatch opened, soundlessly lowering the steps leading up into the dark opening above. Mark climbed up and pulled the hatch closed behind him. As he glanced around, he found the small room cluttered with sophisticated-looking electronic gear. Unfortunately, it did not have the one thing he was looking for: another way out.

The sound of footsteps on the stairway ended his perusal of his surroundings. Janet passed through the hall below him heading directly for the office. Through a small crack where the trapdoor closed, Mark could just make out her lithe form.

Suddenly she stopped, staring directly at the laptop computer. As Mark watched, a new horror dawned in his mind.

Damn it. He had forgotten. When he touched the laptop, the screen saver had stopped, leaving the secure login screen in its place. The timeout on that screen had not expired, so the screen saver had not yet restarted. And as she did with everything around her, Janet had noticed.

CHAPTER 78

Hunger gnawed at his guts like a tapeworm so large he could no longer satisfy the primal need that drove him. As he watched Janet walk out of her house and get into her car, Priest was consumed by it. Today it was bearable, though. Today, at last, his hunger would be sated.

Priest started his truck, letting Janet pull out of her driveway and disappear around the bend before he moved out after her. As he slid onto the street, he passed a high school kid walking down the sidewalk. The face looked vaguely familiar. Then he remembered. It was the basketball player in the tabloids, the kid who almost blew the state championship by hitting the bottle before the game.

Priest chuckled softly to himself. The kid reminded him of himself at that age.

But he didn't have long to dwell on stupid high school kids. He wanted to make sure he didn't lose Janet. If he was lucky, her outing might just give him an opportunity to invite her over to his place. Priest licked his lips. His type of invitation never got refused.

Priest stayed well back, only getting close enough to catch an occasional glimpse of her car. He knew the twists and turns of the streets by heart and how to maintain the perfect distance. When she turned into the grocery store parking lot, Priest passed on by, his disappointment palpable. He would get no chance here. Not at this time of day. At least he knew a trip to the grocery store meant she would be returning directly home from the errand.

Priest made his way back to Janet's house by a circuitous route, picking a different spot to park his truck. This time he parked in the woods a full two and a half blocks away from the Johnson house. After all, he wouldn't be needing the truck's secret compartment below the bed for a good while yet.

Priest reached around behind the driver's seat and pulled out a large plastic box. Flipping up the catches, he extracted the tranquilizer gun and put it in the second of his two shoulder holsters. After examining the liquid-filled darts to ensure the little plastic tip-covers were in place, he grabbed a handful and deposited them into the large outer pockets of his fatigue-style pants. He would need only one of them, but Priest liked to be prepared.

Then, closing and locking the door, he slipped into the woods lining the canyon slope behind the winding row of homes. As he approached the back of Janet's house, he noticed the second-floor window had been left wide open. Unfortunately, there was nothing around to climb on, and it was a couple of feet too high for him to jump up and grab the sill.

Instead, he made his way to the back door, inserted a small, oddly shaped tool into the lock, pressed a button, and turned. The lock clicked open. As he stepped inside, he heard a car pull up out front.

Moving quickly to the pantry, Priest ducked inside, leaving the door open, just a crack, behind him. Through that crack he watched as Janet entered the house, two bags of groceries in her hands. She set her purse down and dropped the groceries on the kitchen table. Priest could feel his pulse pounding as he watched her slender body move. Soon now, very soon, she would move to the pantry, open it, and get the biggest surprise of her life.

But Janet did not move directly to the pantry. Instead, she left the kitchen. Priest could hear her light footsteps climbing the stairs to the second floor.

As soon as the sound indicated she was upstairs, Priest moved, his footsteps making no sound as he climbed. At the top of the stairs he paused, but only for an instant.

Janet had stopped in a small room at the end of the hallway, her posture suddenly alert as she stared at the computer on her desk. She must have heard him. Having no time to load a dart into the tranquilizer gun, Priest charged. And as he did, Janet turned to meet him, her spinning side kick only barely missing his groin as he twisted sideways and barreled into her. Still, the blow from her foot disrupted Priest's momentum so that his shoulder only partially caught her side, preventing him from pinning both her arms.

As they hit the floor, Priest scissored his legs in a wrestler's move that would have successfully gathered her into a submission hold had it not been for the quick twist of Janet's flexible torso, a twist that whipped her left arm free. And in the small hand at the end of that arm, a six inch hair-needle glittered briefly as it plunged through Priest's right eye socket and into his skull.

His body twitched and then slid limply to the floor as she kicked him in the throat. Through the red-limned blackness in his head, Priest could hear Janet rise to her feet.

"Good night, sweet prince."

CHAPTER 79

Mark froze. The scene below him unfolded so rapidly he barely had time to assimilate what was happening.

A man, who he only partially saw through the crack, suddenly charged into the room where Janet stood staring at her computer. She twisted, quick as a cat, partially connecting with her foot to his midsection before he hit her and they spun out of view. Before Mark could move to open the trapdoor and jump down to her aid, it was over.

Janet strode back into view looking as unruffled as if nothing had happened.

"Good night, sweet prince."

The casual, flippant response, the way she barely glanced back over her shoulder, said more than her words. The man who had attacked her must be dead.

Janet picked up her cell phone and pressed a single key. After a couple of seconds, she spoke into it.

"Jack, I've had a situation here." She paused for a moment. "No. I handled it, but I'll need you to help me with the cleanup… right. Just get here as quickly as possible."

Snapping the phone shut, she turned, just in time to catch a feathered dart high in her left shoulder. Her look of surprise was quickly replaced with a slackness that spread to her arms and legs. The cell phone clattered to the floor as Janet followed it to the ground.

Instantly, the man was on her, ripping duct tape free from a roll and wrapping it several times around her hands and then her feet, placing another strip across her mouth.

"I guess it's my turn to say good night to you," he said with a low chuckle. "Don't worry, little princess. You'll have plenty of time to think about what went wrong over the coming days."

Mark, who had been too stunned by this new development to move, jerked into motion, kicking open the trapdoor and leaping into the hallway below. As he landed, the man's head snapped toward him, a long, wicked-looking knife appearing in his hand.

Seeing who faced him, a mirthless smile spread across the chiseled features of the man who stood over Janet's prone form, not twenty feet away from Mark.

"Kid, I don't know what you're doing here, but this isn't your lucky day."

CHAPTER 80

"Kid, I don't know what you're doing here, but this isn't your lucky day."

It was the same high school kid Priest had seen on the street when he was following Janet. The lad was tall for his age, about six feet, with a quintessential high school athletic body: muscular and wiry. Too bad for him. That athletic career was about to come to a very abrupt end.

Priest moved forward, and surprisingly the kid moved to meet him, gliding along in a rudimentary aikido style. Priest's smile grew wider. The kid thought he was trained. It was always nice when you didn't have to chase them.

As he approached the optimum range, Priest feinted with his left hand, then darted in low, the SAF survival knife coming in flat to facilitate its passage between the ribs and into the vital organs beyond.

The kid moved to counter the feint, leaving himself wide open for the knife attack. What shocked Priest was the speed with which the kid moved, his motions a blur, even to Priest's trained eye. Unbelievably, the knife missed its target as the kid's fist rocketed into Priest's midsection.

The impact of the blow was extraordinary. It felt more like the kick of a mule than a blow from a human fist. Priest felt himself slammed back into the wall with sufficient force to break three ribs and dislodge the knife from his hand, sending it sliding down the hall toward the stairs.

In full reaction mode now, Priest reached for his shoulder holster, only to have the young whirlwind close with him, the open palm of his left hand slamming into the underside of Priest's chin, sending him sliding down the hallway floor toward his knife.

As Priest reached for it, an athletic shoe caught him full in the midsection, the kick launching him up over the railing to land headfirst on the floor of the den, twelve feet below the top of the stairs. The shock of sensations that accompanied the loud crack from his neck gave ample evidence that it had broken, severing the spinal column high enough to block his lungs. Just before Priest allowed his eyes to slip closed, he had the oddest thought. He had never seen the middle of his own back before.

Priest stilled himself, not that it was difficult, since he was disconnected from control of the vast majority of his body. Still, it was important that the kid, or whatever he was, thought he was dead. Priest had no doubt that the regenerative powers of his own body could heal this set of injuries as thoroughly as they had healed the brain and eye injuries inflicted by Janet. But it wouldn't do to give the kid reason to hang around and watch the process.

Within seconds, he heard the footsteps on the upstairs landing move down the hallway to the room where he had left Janet drugged, bound, and gagged.

Good.

He could already feel the restorative process at work, rebuilding connections in his severed spinal cord and allowing sensations to flood in from his lower body. A red storm of pain clouded his vision as nerves, sinews, and bone were knitted back together. The muscles in his neck pulled his head back into the proper position, allowing the spinal column to be reconnected. Although Priest couldn't be sure, it seemed that his body was healing itself better each time.

As often as Priest had cursed Dr. Stephenson, he had to give the man credit. The gray goo that he and Dr. Rodriguez had pumped into Priest in the basement laboratory below the Rodriguez guesthouse was good stuff. Not that he had appreciated the act at the time.

Stephenson had contacted him through surreptitious channels and had set up a meeting to discuss the acquisition of Priest's special services. But Priest had screwed up, never suspecting that the famous deputy director of the Los Alamos National Laboratory would slip a Mickey into his drink.

The next thing he knew, he was strapped to a hospital bed as Drs. Stephenson and Rodriguez fed the gray goo through an IV into his veins. They had been quite excited about it, their first human trial of the formulation.

The pain flooding through him now was nothing compared to the liquid fire that had coursed through his veins that day. As Priest rose slowly to his feet and loaded a new dart into his tranquilizer gun, he smiled. Indeed, he had been to hell and back, and he had to admit, the trip was worth the price of admission.

Priest had intended to take only Janet back alive to his special place, but this kid moved like no human could move. And Priest wanted to find out where that difference came from. Besides, nobody gave him an ass whipping like that and failed to pay the price, a price extracted in pain. With careful packing, the compartment below the truck bed should be able to hold two.

The dart, fired from a semi-prone position as he peered around the banister at the top of the stairs, struck squarely between the kid's shoulder blades as he bent over Janet, removing the last of the tape from her ankles. But instead of slumping forward as Priest expected, the kid spun to his feet, reaching back over his shoulder to pull the dart free.

Too late. It had deposited its full load into the kid's bloodstream upon impact. The kid staggered, then righted himself, shaking his head as if to clear it. Unbelievably, he began advancing down the hallway toward Priest, and Priest rose to meet him, pulling his other gun from its shoulder holster, just in case.

Once again the kid staggered, this time dropping to his hands and knees, although he continued to crawl forward. Priest moved in rapidly, swinging a beefy right hand that connected with the side of the kid's head, sending him sprawling against the hallway wall. With one last effort to rise, the kid's eyes lost all focus, his limp body slumping to the floor.

Priest moved forward to gaze down at him, the Beretta aimed directly at the young fellow's head.

"Kid, you're one hell of a specimen. I think Dr. Stephenson is going to want to find out just what makes you tick."

Grabbing a foot, Priest dragged the kid down the hall, back to the room where Janet's prone form lay. Within moments he had both bodies bound and gagged with duct tape. Then, moving back downstairs, he took out his Beretta once more and moved to a spot beside the front door to wait.

"Come on, Jacky boy. Time for confession. You wouldn't want to keep the Priest waiting, now would you?"

CHAPTER 81

Priest heard the car pull into the driveway, his senses heightened from anticipation so that the crunch of gravel under the wheels sounded like rock under the treads of an M1 Abrams main battle tank.

A car door opened, then slammed shut again. Footsteps. Coming closer. An even, confident stride. The faint rasp of the doorknob as a hand gave it a twist.

Then a brief pause, so slight that someone without Priest's training probably would not have even noticed it. But Priest did.

The silencer-fitted Beretta was just rising into firing position when the door slammed inward, catching him in the side as he attempted to jump back out of the way. The gun coughed, sending a slug high into the ceiling as the door knocked Priest backward.

Rolling with the impact, Priest came up with the weapon leveled, spitting another three rounds at the doorway. They passed out harmlessly through the empty opening as the door bounced off the wall and swung shut once again.

What the hell? Jack was gone. Priest spun in a tight circle, the weapon following his eyes as he turned. There was nothing—no sign of the man.

He didn't know how Jack had sensed his presence, but some little something, below the awareness of most people, had given him away. And now the one that the covert ops community had nicknamed "The Ripper" was out there, circling.

Priest cursed under his breath. He had lost the element of surprise he had been counting on. Oh well. He still had a surprise or two waiting for his old friend Jacko.

A sound from the kitchen put Priest into motion. Shit. The Ripper must have run around the back of the house to get there that quickly. A lightning-quick glance around the corner revealed the kitchen door open wide but nothing else. An empty kitchen and closed pantry.

Priest leaped into the kitchen, the Beretta ejecting empty shell casings out the side as he pumped rounds into the pantry door. Glancing out through the kitchen door as he passed, Priest moved to follow the slugs, jerking open the pantry door, firing off two additional rounds as it opened. Except for the slow gurgle of a damaged soup can, there was nothing there.

Priest ejected the magazine from the weapon, slapping a new one into place in the same motion. He moved back toward the den, kicking the kitchen door closed as he came, his eyes and his weapon searching for the target along his direction of travel.

That was funny. He thought that the front door had banged closed before he had charged into the kitchen. But perhaps the latch had been damaged. Or maybe The Ripper was already inside the house.

This was stupid. He was playing into The Ripper's hands by hunting for him. Priest needed to get back to the original plan. Make the man come to him. After all, he had the perfect bait.

Having made a decision, Priest did not hesitate, his stride carrying him up the stair steps, two at a time. Not wanting to remain exposed in the hallway for more than an instant, he raced down its length, pausing only briefly outside the open doorway. Just long enough to check that the kid and Janet lay bound, undisturbed, on the floor. Priest stepped through the opening.

Almost, it didn't surprise him when a knife blade thrust through his gun hand, sending the weapon spinning under the desk. Or when The Ripper glided out from his spot behind the office door. It fit with how his luck was running today. Jumping back into the hallway, Priest refilled his injured hand with his own knife.

"Surprised to see me, Jack?"

The Ripper showed no reaction, his dark eyes as unblinking as those of a shark as he moved forward. For the briefest of moments, it seemed to Priest that those eyes glinted red.

Priest feinted with the knife, delivering a low kick at the man's knee. He pulled his foot back with a howl of pain as another thrust of The Ripper's knife punched a hole through his arch.

Priest stumbled backward before the other killer's quick strikes, each one opening a new wound on his extremities. The damned man was playing with Priest, carving him up as calmly as if he was whittling on a stick outside some hick drugstore.

As a growing desperation rose up to overcome his newfound fear, Priest lunged in, absorbing a deep puncture to his abdomen in an attempt to drive his SAF knife into the other man's throat. But once again, The Ripper was just a little quicker, catching Priest's knife hand in an off-hand grip that wrenched it around, snapping the wrist with a loud pop.

The Ripper's knife flashed in an arc, the blade cutting a new mouth into Priest's neck, just below the chin. Priest pitched forward facefirst, the arterial fountain of his blood drenching The Ripper in red as he tumbled to the floor.

For several seconds, Priest lay still at The Ripper's feet before the other man turned away and strode back into the office where Janet and the kid lay bound.

As Priest lay there listening to his enemy cut the bonds of his victims, he could not keep a slow smile from spreading across his face. Yes. The healing was definitely happening faster now. Already the wounds in his throat and abdomen were closing, the bones knitting together in his wrist.

All he needed was a few more seconds and he would introduce Jack to the same sort of unpleasant surprise that the other two had already received. But there would be no tranquilizer dart for Jack. He didn't have a dart loaded, and there would be no time for loading one. If the Beretta had not been flung under the office furniture, Priest would have certainly used that.

His hand flexed around the SAF knife. The knife and massive surprise would have to do the job.

Priest began to count backward in his head, comparing his mental estimate of how long it would take Jack to free Priest's two captives and examine them for wounds to how long the progress of Priest's own healing process was taking. The muscles along his arms, back, and legs tensed. He waited. A lion amid the tall savannah grass. His prey only a few feet from where he coiled for the strike. Almost ready.

The ferocity and speed with which Priest propelled his body forward caught even the dreaded Ripper by surprise. He was, after all, supposed to be dead. Priest thrust the wicked tip of the SAF survival knife down toward the Ripper's back with all the force his two hundred and ten pounds of lean muscle and bone could deliver.

It was the slightest of moves. A bare adjustment in the angle of the back of the Ripper's left arm that caused the blade to glance off the man's elbow and miss the rear of his torso by a fraction of a centimeter.

Priest screamed in frustration as the Ripper's body spun beneath him, using Priest's own momentum to flip him into the side of the oak desk.

Then The Ripper was behind him, his left arm encircling Priest's throat as the right pumped his knife into Priest's right kidney with three staccato thrusts. The Ripper's legs were moving now, driving Priest's body forward, directly back down the hallway, into the bathroom, and then down into the bathtub, facedown.

Priest felt the hard, cold porcelain rise up to meet his face an instant before both of The Ripper's knees landed on his back, hard. A strong hand grabbed a handful of his hair, yanking Priest's head back with a violence that was only surpassed by that of the knife that cut his throat, then continued to saw at his neck.

As his head came free of any connection to the rest of his body, Priest found himself wondering if perhaps he had achieved immortality. His eyes locked for one last time with those of The Ripper, as his glimpse of immortality, along with the last of his life force, drained away.

And as Priest's eyes continued to stare outward, they acquired a look almost as dead and cold as the eyes of the man who held his head.

CHAPTER 82

Jack watched as the head of Carlton "Priest" Williams swung by the hair from his hand, the blue eyes momentarily locking with his own. Then the life in those eyes drained away.

Jack looked down at the bloody mess in the bathtub, a mess that extended in a rapidly coagulating trail out into the hallway. As his eyes shifted back to the headless body beneath his knees, his fascination grew.

Even in death, some vestiges of the unreal healing powers that had manifested themselves in Priest were apparent, trying to seal off wounds, working to repair torn tissue and broken bone. But those attempts at regeneration were now rapidly fading.

Whatever had been done to Priest, he had still retained the basic mortality that made him, at least marginally, human. Jack didn't know what Priest's blood workup was going to show, but he was quite sure Jonathan Riles would find the results more than mildly interesting.

Pulling the shower curtain from its hooks and laying it on the floor, Jack placed the body on it, rolling it into a tight bundle. The head he left in the bathtub.

Jack glanced at his watch, wiping it on his blood-soaked shirt to remove enough blood for the display to be readable. 17:35. He had placed the call to the rest of his team in Santa Fe as soon as he had gotten the message from Janet. That had been almost an hour ago. That meant they should be here to set up the fake federal crime scene lockdown at any time.

Moving to the sink to wash the slathering of Priest's blood from his hands and arms, Jack was surprised to see his left elbow showed no sign of a laceration. He could have sworn that Priest's knife had cut into it as he had spun to deflect the knife attack.

Shaking his head, Jack walked back to the room where Janet and young Mark lay bound. Except for the gentle rise and fall of their chests, they had not moved since he had first seen them, sleeping the untroubled sleep that only true innocence or tranquilizing drugs can bring.

Within seconds, he removed the tape that bound and gagged them. Then, removing his own blood-soaked shoes and socks, Jack carried first Mark and then Janet down to the den, laying Mark on the couch and Janet on the love seat.

Jack's eyes lingered on Mark. What had the lad been doing here, and how much had he seen? Well, time enough to ask those questions once the drug wore off. In the meantime, he would leave the two of them sleeping comfortably while he got to work upstairs. It would certainly help the rest of his team if he got a head start on some of what needed to be done.

The first thing on Jack's to-do list was to get his own blood sample from the thing that had once been Priest Williams.

Getting the kit from his closet, Jack withdrew a needle and an empty plastic syringe. Stripping off the plastic covering, he fitted the needle on the end of the syringe, walked to the bathroom, partially unwrapped the body, and inserted the tip into Priest's left arm. A slow pull filled the syringe with blood.

Jack carried the blood sample downstairs to the kitchen, where he discarded the needle in the garbage, wrapped the syringe in a freezer bag, and placed it at the back of the freezer beneath several packages of hamburger and steak.

Then he moved to the second item on his mental checklist, getting himself cleaned up. By the time he finished his quick shower and gotten dressed in fresh clothes, Jack heard two cars pull up outside.

He met his three team members at the front door.

"Glad to see you, Bronson," said Jack, shaking hands with the barrel-chested man in the lead. He nodded to the other two men wearing FBI windbreakers. "Bobby, George."

"What have we got here, Jack?" Bronson asked.

Jack led the way, his briefing succinct as he showed the team through the house. The tour ended at the upstairs bathroom.

"Well, Jack, it might be possible for you to make a bigger mess of a man, but you'd really have to work at it."

"Let's just say the situation was…unusual. I want the body and head bagged separately and shipped back to the lab in separate containers. Take a couple of blood samples before you bag it and send those via a separate shipment."

Bronson raised an eyebrow. "What was the guy on? Some new kind of drug?"

Jack nodded. "One we are very interested in analyzing. That's why I don't want to take any chances with this shipment."

As Bronson turned to get the rest of the team started, Jack placed a hand on his shoulder.

"Be thorough, but be quick. I want the body out of here and the cleanup finished before the kid wakes up. You've got the cover story ready?"

"All set."

"Good. Then I'll get out of your way."

The speed with which the team cleaned the upstairs, carried several bags out to the waiting unmarked cars, and departed was impressive, even to Jack. By six o'clock, only Bronson remained on site to pretend to conduct interviews with Janet and Mark. But his real purpose was to plant the cover story.

Mark was the first to come out of the drug-induced sleep, although it took several minutes before he was sufficiently coherent to carry on a conversation. Somewhere during that time, Janet joined him in the land of the conscious.

Jack moved over to sit with them. He took Janet's hand.

"Hey, babe. How you feeling?"

Tears welled in the corners of her eyes so convincingly Jack thought she could have had a brilliant career on Broadway had she not had a taste for a more dangerous pastime.

"Oh, Jack. Thank God you're here. I was so frightened."

"It's OK, darling. Can you tell me what happened?"

"I didn't see much. I was dropping off papers in the office. A man was hiding up there, and he shot me with some sort of dart. I don't remember anything else."

Jack turned toward Mark. "Mark, what brought you here?"

The young man's face grew red as he fumbled his words. "Ah, I came by to ask Mrs. Johnson a question about tomorrow's assignment. The front door was open, so I stuck my head in. That's when I heard someone fall. I called out, but when there was no answer, I ran upstairs. The man with the gun was waiting for me. I guess I was lucky it was only a tranquilizer gun."

Agent Bronson strode up as Mark finished.

"Young man, you would not have been lucky if my team hadn't arrived before the man abducted or murdered you."

Mark's eyes locked on the "FBI" stenciled onto the windbreaker.

For the next forty-five minutes, Special Agent Bronson questioned the three of them, taking notes on a small pad. By the time he was done asking questions and responding with information of his own, the story had been planted.

The FBI had been tracking a terrorist cell headed up by a man known as Abdul Aziz. Yes, it was the same man who had reportedly killed the scientist and his family a few months back. One of Abdul Aziz's men had stumbled onto the FBI team this morning and then fled into the surrounding neighborhood.

The FBI team had tracked him to this house, where they discovered Mark and Janet had been taken hostage. Jack had arrived back home as the FBI special team moved into position, but had been forced to wait outside until the situation was resolved.

Luckily, that resolution had come very quickly. A federal agent managed to come in through a second-floor window and incapacitate the terrorist with a Taser stun gun.

Agent Bronson's eyes hardened as he looked at Jack, Janet, and finally Mark.

"We've taken the terrorist suspect into custody, and he has been moved to a more secure location for interrogation. But I want you to understand something. Through no fault of your own, you have become involved in a matter of national security and the ongoing war on terror. Suspects of this importance are not handled through normal channels. We need to extract any information he has before his accomplices discover he's missing. Therefore, I must inform you that everything associated with this incident must receive the highest level of security classification. You are not to speak of this to anyone else. Not to the press. Not to the police. Not to your families. Not even to each other. Any violation of this order will subject the offender to federal espionage charges, the penalty for which is imprisonment for a term of not less than thirty years. Do I make myself clear?"

"Wait just a minute," said Jack. "We have the right to consult with an attorney about all of this."

"No. As a matter of fact, you don't. You are not under any sort of arrest. If, however, you decide to consult with an attorney, or anyone else, about this matter, then you will very much need an attorney. The counterespionage laws tend to paint such breaches of protocol in broad strokes of black and white. Mostly black. Do you each understand me?"

Agent Bronson shifted his gaze to Janet, who swallowed hard, but nodded. The agent turned his attention to Mark.

"Yes, sir," said Mark.

"I understand," said Jack, through clenched teeth.

"Good. Then I won't belabor the point."

Agent Bronson put his notebook into his coat pocket and then paused for a moment.

"Folks, I'm sorry to have to treat you like this. After all, you are the victims here, and you have been through a significant trauma. But there are bigger things at stake."

Agent Bronson walked to the door, then paused and turned back toward them.

"Remember what I said."

With that, he walked outside, got into his black Buick, and drove away.

Jack stood beside Mark and Janet, watching as the car disappeared around the bend. Turning to look at Mark, Jack asked, "Can I give you a ride home?"

Although Mark looked physically drained, he shook his head. "No, but thanks. It would just make my folks wonder why I didn't come back home on my own." Mark glanced at his watch, his eyes widening as he saw the time. "Crap. Oh, sorry. I have to get going. I'm already late to the family barbecue."

Mark's lips moved as if searching for something else to say. He shrugged instead, heading out the door and up the driveway.

Jack watched him go. It seemed odd that Mark hadn't ridden his bike to the house, but it was probably nothing.

"Do you think Bronson sold the story?" Janet asked, sliding her hand under Jack's arm.

"I think so."

"Good, then let me lead you inside and you can fill me in on what really happened."

With one more glance after Mark, Jack turned and followed Janet back into the house, unconsciously rubbing his left elbow as he went.

CHAPTER 83

In her dream, Heather walked along a lofty ledge, barely wide enough for her feet to maintain their purchase. Heavy clouds filled the sky overhead, offering so little light that she could barely see the path. To the left of the trail, the world dropped away into darkness. Ahead of her, the trail continued to narrow as it rounded the cliff face.

She turned so that her back pressed against the hard rock surface that rose up to meet the sky. Taking a deep breath to slow her racing heart, Heather had just decided to turn back when the tip of a sharp spear jabbed her left arm, prodding her forward once again. Looking along the back trail, she could dimly make out a cloaked figure motioning for her to keep moving. Not wanting to be poked again, Heather turned away from him, carefully placing one foot in front of the other.

Who was the man? Where was he taking her?

As if in answer to her question, a soft voice whispered from the darkness. Heather paused to listen. There it was again, that familiar voice.

"Heather? Please answer. I need you."

Jennifer. But where was she? As Heather struggled to see her friend, the sharp point jabbed her arm again.

"What the hell is wrong with you?" she yelled, swinging her arm out to knock the spear away.

Heather's eyes fluttered as a blindingly bright light shone in her face. Her arms felt heavy, but she struck out again, this time connecting with the man's torso.

A surprised cry accompanied a crash of metal and breaking glass. Suddenly memory came flooding back. She was on the metal bed in Dr. Rodriguez's lab. A small trickle of blood leaked from her left arm where a needle had been torn out by the falling IV rack. Heather sat up, although a wave of dizziness threatened to leach away her consciousness.

Six feet away, Dr. Rodriguez regained his feet, his white lab coat splattered with a gray fluid, his face a mask of surprise. "How the hell are you awake already?"

Without waiting for a response, the man lunged toward her. But this time, the anger that bubbled up inside Heather produced an adrenaline surge that coursed through her veins, clearing away the grogginess that had chained her limbs. As the scientist's hand closed on her left ankle, she lashed out with her other foot. A sizzle like an electric shock cascaded through her neurally enhanced musculature, the force of the kick launching the scientist off the floor, sending him spinning into the steel cabinets with another loud crash.

Dr. Rodriguez's body went limp, sliding down onto the floor like a rag doll. Heather slid off the bed, once again assaulted by a wave of dizziness that forced her to clutch onto the railing. Behind her, she heard the sound of the trapdoor being raised.

Heather tensed, turning toward this new threat.

"Heather?" Jennifer's voice called out. "Are you down there?"

A massive wave of relief flooded her body. "I'm here!"

The sound of footsteps on the stairs preceded Jennifer's entrance into the room, but not by much. Her friend's headlong flight came to a sliding stop as her eyes went wide with surprise.

"Jesus! What happened here?"

Heather rushed forward, throwing her arms around Jennifer in a hug that was returned in full measure.

"How did you find me?"

"Listen, you may be the numbers guru, but I'm not exactly stupid. Sometimes things add up to an obvious conclusion."

As Heather released her bear hug, the abridged version of the story bubbled from her lips in a rush of words that left her breathless.

"Did he inject you with that goo in the IV?"

Heather shook her head. "I woke up before he turned it on. See? There's no fluid in the IV tube."

"Is he dead?" Jennifer asked, pointing at the motionless form of Dr. Rodriguez.

Heather's chest constricted. "I don't know. I guess we should check."

Jennifer inhaled deeply, then strode forward to kneel down beside the scientist, her fingers sliding to his neck.

"Careful," Heather warned. "He might be faking."

"For his sake, he better not be. I'd love to kick the crap out of him myself."

"Well?"

Jennifer rose to her feet again. "He's just out cold."

Looking around at the mess in the room, Jennifer turned toward Heather. "So what do we do now?"

Heather let the possible courses of action roll through her mind, each accompanied by its success probability. After several seconds, she turned to the computer desk, retrieving her cell phone from where Dr. Rodriguez had lain it. A quick examination showed that he had not yet deleted the files from its memory stick. The final probability numbers clicked into place in her head.

"Slide on a pair of these latex gloves and help me wipe down every place we touched. I can play it back in my head so we won't miss anything."

Moving quickly, Heather and Jennifer rapidly removed all traces of their presence, including the IV needle that had been inserted in her arm. Then, with one last look around, Heather picked up the telephone that sat beside Dr. Rodriguez's computer and dialed 9-1-1. Covering the receiver with a wadded rag and gravelling her voice, she spoke only two words: "Police emergency."

Leaving the receiver off the hook, Heather turned and led Jennifer from the room and up the stairs.

"Now what?" asked Jennifer as they climbed on their bikes and pedaled away.

"The police will find enough evidence to stop the Rho Project."

"What if they don't? What if Stephenson manages to cover it up? Dr. Rodriguez knows you copied the data."

"Doesn't matter. As soon as we get back to the house, we'll uplink the data on my memory stick to the NSA. Too many people will know about this to cover the thing up."

As they pedaled toward home, the sound of distant sirens echoed through the streets.

CHAPTER 84

The darkness within Dr. Donald Stephenson's windowless office pressed in upon the light of the small desk lamp. The light was so scant it was almost like an old gas street lamp, doused by fog in London, circa 1880. The deep-grained textures of the hardwood furniture that filled the chamber added to the illusion, so that the room's mood took on the nature of the man who had created it.

But the room felt radiant compared to the look on Dr. Stephenson's face as he listened to the frantic voice at the other end of the phone.

Dr. Stephenson hung up and then dialed a single digit. He only had to wait for one ring. When Dr. Stephenson finally spoke, his voice carried an edge as sharp as cracking ice.

"This is Dr. Stephenson. We have a potential national security breach involving a Rho Laboratory employee. I want Dr. Ernesto Rodriguez's house and property secured and sealed off and the good doctor placed under arrest. Get the military response team moving right now. If the civilian authorities are already on site, I want them removed. Any items they may have picked up as evidence must be confiscated. I will be arriving on site within the hour."

"Yes, sir."

Dr. Stephenson hung up, then, picking up his pen, he returned his attention to the differential equations that filled page after page of his notebooks, the solution to which had been so rudely interrupted.

The memory of that moment, so long ago, when he'd first stepped onto the *Rho Ship* suddenly filled his mind. It was funny to recall how he had imagined that his little Cerenkov experiment had somehow opened that ship. All it had done was attract the *Rho Ship*'s attention. After that, it had opened itself to him, had provided him with information he had so desperately desired. If the *Rho Ship* hadn't chosen him, it would have chosen someone else, but he'd been the first to interest it.

That first time inside the ship, he'd learned of the Kasari Collective, the race of beings who had created it. But because the *Rho Ship* had been so badly damaged by its enemy, it had taken Donald all these years to unravel its mysteries. Now, he was rapidly approaching the moment when he would accomplish the Kasari prime objective.

For mankind, that day was coming. Ready or not.

CHAPTER 85

Heather sat on her back porch, looking out across the canyons as the sunset painted the sky orange. Sensing her mood, her parents had wisely left her to her own reflections.

Looking back on the last week's events, it was no wonder she felt like a wrung-out sponge. The press replayed the story until it was impossible to get away from it. The police had arrived at the Rodriguez house to find Dr. Rodriguez dead from a self-inflicted gunshot wound to the head, a suicide note lying near his body.

Unfortunately, the military had taken control of the site shortly after the police had secured the area, confiscating all materials in the name of national security. Only the suicide note had been released to the public, a rambling apology for the unauthorized nanite testing that Dr. Rodriguez had conducted in his private laboratory. Luckily, the note contained no mention of Heather.

If Heather and Jennifer hadn't successfully uplinked the data from Dr. Rodriguez's lab to the NSA site, the military cover-up would have been complete.

Mark was freed of tabloid attention, which now focused squarely upon the secret basement laboratory beneath the Rodriguez house. One lucky thing had happened. In all the commotion, Jack and Janet had failed to discover the QT microchip Mark had placed in Janet's laptop.

And the quantum twin of that device had yielded a wealth of encrypted information since then. While the encryption of the data was first-rate, Heather's unique ability with numbers was better. The decryption of secure message traffic between that computer, the NSA, and some other remote systems had finally given Mark, Jennifer, and Heather an understanding of at least a part of what the NSA knew about the situation.

It had been in one of these communications that Heather had discovered the link between Raul, the water bottle, and Mark's grogginess at the state championship game. More importantly, they had learned that the killer who had attacked Janet and then Mark was a man named Priest Williams, and that Jack had killed him.

As Mark had already told them, the man had displayed incredible healing abilities. The lab tests on Priest's blood had revealed that it was permeated by millions of nanites, microscopic machines that read information from their host's DNA and used that information to repair bodily damage. The data confirmed the information from Dr. Rodriguez's computer that she and Jennifer had uplinked to the NSA.

Heather had read many articles on current nanotechnology research, some of which had speculated that in the future, humans would be able to inject swarms of tiny machines into their bloodstreams to do things like clean arteries and attack infections. But what these nanites did was far beyond any nanotechnology currently envisioned.

There could be no doubt. The technology had come from the Rho Project. Apparently the report on the subject was being kept very classified, with only Jack's team, one individual at the laboratory doing the testing, and two key people at NSA headquarters knowing anything about the report's contents.

Just as it looked like the press furor would abate, today had brought more tragedy to the Rodriguez household. Raul had disappeared, apparently having run away from home. Police had arrived to find Mrs. Rodriguez lost to a hysteria that required hospitalization.

A cool breeze ruffled Heather's hair. Brushing a strand from her face, she watched as the sky changed from red to purple.

Raul. The knowledge that he had tried to drug Mark had destroyed whatever feelings she had held for him. But he didn't deserve this. Shaking her head, Heather rose from the lawn chair, turned her back on the gathering darkness, and stepped back into the light and warmth of her own home.

CHAPTER 86

Griffith Gym, the site of the commencement ceremony for the LAHS graduating class, was packed to near capacity. Heather didn't particularly like graduation ceremonies of any type. Why Mark had been so keen on having their families attend this one was another of the mysteries that came together in the person of Marcus Aurelius Smythe.

As far as she knew, the only seniors Mark knew were the ones who had tormented him during the year. But when she and Jennifer had quizzed him, he had merely laughed and shrugged off those antics as an age-old high school rite of passage. Perhaps he was growing up after all.

As the graduation speaker droned on endlessly, Heather smiled to herself. Considering all she had been through, all they had all been through, she was glad this year was coming to a close. Even the fact that she had missed the junior-senior prom could not dampen her mood.

Mark's elbow brought her focus back to the stage. The top scholastic leaders of the senior class had just been recognized, and the senior athletes and cheerleaders were next. Heather recognized Colleen "All Cars" Johnson along with the obnoxious quarterback, Doug Brindal, and his buddies.

The group on stage raised their awards above their heads. As they did, Heather noticed Mark fiddling with something in his hand, a devilish grin on his face.

A sudden gasp from the crowd snapped Heather's head back toward the stage.

"Oh my God!" Jennifer gasped.

The graduation gowns of Colleen Johnson, Doug Brindal, and two of the other athletes came apart at the seams, the separate pieces fluttering to the ground beside them, revealing that none of the four were wearing pants or underwear.

As they recovered from their stunned silence, the students in the crowd erupted into a wild fit of laughter. The objects of that laughter scrambled to cover themselves with the pieces of their robes before fleeing from the stage. Bedlam descended upon the graduation ceremony, lasting several minutes as the principal and teachers struggled to restore order.

In an effort to get things over with, the remaining seniors were called across stage in near record time, although they received their rolled diplomas without further incident.

As the ceremony concluded and the crowd made its way out of the gymnasium, there were some expressions of outrage, but the bulk of the audience thought it was the most entertaining graduation ceremony ever.

Once in the parking lot, Heather turned to stare at Mark. Jennifer joined her.

"How in the world did that just happen?"

"Well, let's just say that a few weeks ago I happened to overhear those four planning to moon the crowd after graduation ceremony. Anyway, I thought to myself, why should they go half-ass when I can help them achieve the full Monty?"

"Happened to overhear? You planted a bug, didn't you?"

" 'Planted' is such an unpleasant word. I think I'll stick with my original description."

"But how did you get their gowns to come apart like that?"

"You know, it's amazing how a remotely directed heat source can affect certain thread types. Combine that with just the right stitching modifications, and the sky's the limit."

It was Heather's turn to gasp.

"The old ladies' sewing club! So that's what you were learning."

Mark's grin spread to epic proportions.

"Viva POOTNAS!"

CHAPTER 87

When Jonathan Riles passed through security and pulled his car into the White House parking lot, one of the junior White House aides, a prematurely graying man in his early forties, met him and offered to carry his briefcase. When Jonathan declined the offer, the aide nodded and led the way into the White House.

That briefcase was not going to be leaving the NSA director's hands until he opened it in the office to which he was headed. Riles had no doubt that he now had enough information to bring high-level scrutiny to the top secret, compartmentalized activities that Dr. Stephenson was conducting under the umbrella of Rho Project research. He could certainly put the clamps on the overly aggressive research into alien nanotechnology.

Riles smiled to himself as he walked. Normally, it would have taken even a man in his position considerably longer to line up the appointment at the White House. After all, the White House schedule was done up well in advance, and any changes to that schedule affected travel plans, appearance schedules, even the schedules of meetings with foreign leaders. You just didn't get an off-the-cuff meeting, no matter how important the topic.

It's not what you know, it's who you know. The old saying held a power that went beyond what it implied. They had been best friends since they had been roommates at Annapolis, since they had been stars on the Navy football team. It was funny how he had made vice admiral while his oldest friend had just made it to navy captain, only to have his buddy bypass him in rank once he transitioned to civilian life.

The door opened to admit him, and Riles extended his hand, a grip that his old friend met heartily.

Riles smiled as his old roommate ushered him into the office, dismissing the aide in the process.

"Good of you to see me on such short notice."

"Jon Boy, you know I'd see you anytime, even if you hadn't said it was so important. Now show me what you've got."

Jonathan Riles flipped open his briefcase, spreading the pages of the report out along the small table in a fashion that made it easy to illustrate the report's content. For the next hour, Riles ran through what he had hard proof of and what, at this point, he could only speculate on. The only thing intentionally omitted was any mention of Jack Gregory's team. After all, it was just as important as ever to provide the president and his key staff deniability in that area.

At the end of the briefing, he paused for comment.

"Jon, I've never seen anything like it. I'm glad you brought this directly to me. I'd like you to keep it that way, just between the two of us, until I get a chance to brief the president when he gets back from Europe tomorrow. Then I'll bring you in to see him."

"George, you know you can always count on my natural proclivity for silence."

"Good. Just leave all this stuff here. I look forward to getting you in to brief the president tomorrow."

Vice President Gordon rose from his seat, walked Riles to the door, and shook his hand once again. As the door closed behind his old friend, the vice president turned back to the table, walked to the Secure Telephone Unit, and dialed a rapid sequence of numbers into the STU.

"Yes?" The familiar voice on the phone was as cold as a January morning.

Vice President Gordon ran his fingers over the thick folder. "Riles knows too much."

A slight hesitation at the far end of the line preceded the response. "You want me to activate the Columbian?"

"He's left us no choice."

The soft intake of breath barely rose above the encrypted circuit noise. "You're the boss."

As Vice President Gordon broke the secure connection, he stared down at the report on his desk.

"Damn it, Jonny. You always were too smart for your own good."

ACKNOWLEDGMENTS

I want to thank Alan Werner for brainstorming this story with me, putting in many long hours as we explored the twists and turns that brought it to this conclusion. I also want to express my thanks to my agent, Paul Lucas, who worked hard to help me bring this work to a broader audience. My fabulous editor, the talented Jeff VanderMeer, helped me put the finishing touches on all three of the Rho Agenda novels, and his expert touch is evident throughout. Finally, I want to thank my wife, Carol, whose love, support, and encouragement makes life worth living.

ABOUT THE AUTHOR

Photograph © 2008

Richard Phillips was born in Roswell, New Mexico, in 1956. He graduated from the United States Military Academy at West Point in 1979 and qualified as an Army Ranger, going on to serve as an officer in the US Army. He earned a master's degree in physics from Naval Postgraduate School, completing his thesis work at Los Alamos National Laboratory. After working for three years as a research associate at Lawrence Livermore National Laboratory, he returned to the army to complete his tour of duty. Today he lives in Phoenix, Arizona, with his wife, Carol, dividing his time between developing simulation software for the US military and writing science fiction.